Stories from the Diary of a Doctor

Also from Westphalia Press
westphaliapress.org

Stories from the Diary of a Doctor

Snippets of Early Medicine and Life in England

by L.T. Meade &
Clifford Halifax, M.D.

WESTPHALIA PRESS
An imprint of Policy Studies Organization

Westphalia Press
An imprint of Policy Studies Organization
1527 New Hampshire Ave., NW
Washington, D.C. 20036
info@ipsonet.org

ISBN-13: 978-1-63391-236-6
ISBN-10: 1633912361

Cover design by Taillefer Long at Illuminated Stories:
www.illuminatedstories.com

Daniel Gutierrez-Sandoval, Executive Director
PSO and Westphalia Press

Updated material and comments on this edition
can be found at the Westphalia Press website:
www.westphaliapress.org

Stories from the Diary of a Doctor

BY

L. T. MEADE

AND

CLIFFORD HALIFAX, M.D.

CONTENTS

CREATING A MIND

CREATING A MIND

THE extraordinary story which I am about to tell happened a few years ago. I was staying for a short time in a small village in Warwickshire, and was called up suddenly one evening to see the Squire of the place, who had met with a bad accident, and was lying in an almost unconscious condition at his own house. The local doctor happened to be away, and my services were eagerly demanded. Under the circumstances, there was nothing for it but to comply. I stepped into the brougham sent for me to the village inn, and, after a very short drive, found myself at Hartley Castle. It was an ancient, castellated pile, and village gossip had already informed me that it had been the property of the Norreys family for hundreds of years. The night was a bright and moonlight one in July, and as I drove down the straight avenue, and passed under a deep archway into a large courtyard, I caught my first distinct view of the house.

As soon as ever the carriage drew up at the front door an old servant in livery flung it open, and I saw in the background a lady waiting with some nervousness to receive me. She came forward at once, and held out her hand.

"Dr. Halifax, I presume?"

I bowed.

"I have heard of you," she said. "It is a lucky chance for us that brings you to Hartley just now. I am Miss Norreys. My father was thrown from his horse two hours ago. He seems to be very ill, and is unable to move. When he was first discovered lying in the avenue he was unconscious, but he is able to speak now, and knows what is going on—he seems, however, to be in great discomfort, in short——" she broke off abruptly, and her thin, colourless face turned paler.

"Can I see the patient?" I interrupted.

9

"Oh, yes," she replied; "I will take you to him immediately—come this way, please."

I followed Miss Norreys up some shallow stairs, which led into the Squire's bedroom.

I found my patient stretched flat in the centre of the bed. A manservant and an elderly woman, whom Miss Norreys addressed as Connor, were standing at a little distance. One of the windows was thrown open for air, and the bed-curtains were flung back.

When I approached him, Squire Norreys fixed two rather fierce and strained black eyes upon my face—he was breathing with extreme difficulty, and it required but a brief glance to show me that he was suffering from injury to the spinal cord.

I bent over my patient and asked him a few questions. He replied to them in a perfectly rational manner, although his words came out slowly and with effort. He gave me a brief account of the accident, and said that his last conscious impression was falling somewhat heavily near the nape of the neck. When he recovered consciousness, he found himself lying in bed.

"What is the matter with me?" he asked, when he had finished making his brief statement.

"You are suffering from injury to the spinal cord," I answered. "I cannot tell yet what the extent of your injuries may be, but I hope they are not very serious, and that after a time your most uncomfortable symptoms will abate."

"I find it hard—to breathe," he said, with a gasp. Then he closed his eyes, being evidently too exhausted for further conversation.

Miss Norreys asked me to come with her into another room. I did so, and when there briefly described the case to her.

"My opinion is, that the paralysis will pass off before long," I said. "I do not think that any serious effusion of blood into the spinal cord has taken place. The brain, too, is absolutely clear, which is an excellent symptom. Of course, if the Squire is not better to-morrow, I should like to consult a specialist—now there is nothing to be done but to apply the simple remedies which I have ordered, and to watch him."

"I will sit up," said Miss Norreys.

"You must do as you please, of course," I replied; "but as I am here, it is scarcely necessary."

"I should prefer it," she answered.

I did not argue the point with her, and half an hour later took my place by my patient's bedside. Miss Norreys occupied an easy chair in a distant part of the room, and the old servant, Connor, sat within call in the dressing-room. The night passed without any special incident—the patient was restless and suffered much from thirst and want of breath. Towards morning he dropped off into an uneasy sleep—from this he awoke with a sudden sharp cry.

"Where am I?" he asked, in a husky whisper.

I bent over him instantly.

"In bed," I answered. "You have had a fall and have hurt yourself—I am sitting with you."

"I remember now," he said: "you are a doctor, are you not?"

"Yes—my name is Halifax—I am taking care of you for the present; Dr. Richards, your family doctor, being away. Drink this, please, and lie still. You will soon, I trust, be much better."

I held a glass to the Squire's thirsty lips. He drained it off eagerly, then looked past me into the dark recesses of the room.

"Is Orian in that chair?" he asked, a queer, startled quiver coming into his voice.

"No, father, it's me," replied Miss Norreys, alarm in her tone.

"I made a mistake," he answered. He closed his eyes, giving vent as he did so to a heavy sigh. A moment or two later he fell into a natural sleep.

In the morning I thought him better, and told Miss Norreys so.

"I am convinced," I said, "that the injury is only slight, and that the symptoms of paralysis will diminish instead of increasing. There is no present necessity for calling in a specialist, but I should like your family physician, Dr. Richards, to be telegraphed for. He knows your father's constitution and, in any case, ought to be here to take charge of his patient."

"I will telegraph for him," said Miss Norreys; "but I hope,

Dr. Halifax," she continued, after a pause, "that you will not resign the care of my father for the present."

"I will remain with pleasure," I replied; "but it is only just to Dr. Richards to consult him, and I should like him to be telegraphed for."

Miss Norreys promised to see to this immediately: the telegram was sent off, and a reply reached us within an hour or two. The family doctor was laid up with a severe chill in a distant part of the country, and could not return to Hartley for another day at least.

"That settles the matter, then," said Miss Norreys, with a sigh of relief. She was a wiry-looking woman, with a nervous expression of face. Her age might have been forty: her hair was thin, her brow deeply furrowed. It was easy to guess that trouble had visited this poor lady, and that even now she lived under its shadow.

The special nature of that trouble I was quickly to learn.

As the day advanced Squire Norreys grew distinctly better. His upper limbs were still completely paralyzed, but his breathing was less laboured, and the expression of anxiety and apprehension on his face less marked. When the evening arrived I was able to give a good report of my patient to his daughter.

"I have every hope that your father will completely recover," I said. "The effusion of blood into the cord, which is the symptom most to be dreaded in such an accident, is slight, and is being quickly absorbed. Of course, it will be necessary for a long time to keep the patient free from the slightest care or worry."

I paused here. Squire Norreys face was not a placid one. There were fretful lines round the mouth, and many furrows surrounded the deeply set and piercing eyes. I remembered, too, the name he had spoken suddenly in the night, and the tone of consternation in which his daughter had assured him of his mistake.

"Undue excitement, worry, indiscretion of any sort, would be bad for him now," I said, "and might easily lead to dangerous symptoms."

Miss Norreys, who had been looking at me fixedly while I was speaking, turned very pale. She was silent for a moment, then she said, with passion :—

"It is so easy for doctors to order a sort of paradise for

their patients—it is so difficult on this earth to secure it for them. How can I guarantee that my father will not be worried? Nay——" she stopped—a flood of crimson swept over her face—"I know he will be worried. Worry, care, sorrow, are the lot of all. If worry, care, and sorrow are to cause dangerous symptoms, then he is a doomed man."

"I am sorry to hear you speak so," I replied. "Your words seem to point to some special trouble—can nothing be done to remove it?"

"Nothing," she answered, shutting up her lips tightly. She moved away as she spoke, and I returned to my patient.

The following night I again sat by the Squire's bedside. He was restless, and there was a certain amount of fever. Soon after midnight, however, he quieted down and sank into heavy slumber. About three in the morning, I was half dozing, when something made me start up wide awake. I saw that the Squire's eyes were open—a second glance showed me, however, that though the eyes were open, the man himself was still in the shadowy land of dreams—he looked past me without seeing me—his eyes smiled, his strong under-lip shook.

"Is that you, Orian?" he said. "Come and kiss me, child —ah, that's right. You have been a long time away—kiss me again—I have missed you—yes, a good bit—yes, yes——" He closed his eyes, continuing his dream with satisfaction reflected all over his face.

Who was Orian? It was not difficult to guess that, whoever she was, she had something to do with the Squire's too evident distress of mind. In the morning, as my custom was, I resolved to take the bull by the horns. I should be in a better position to help my patient if I knew exactly what ailed him—I determined to speak openly to Miss Norreys.

"Your father is going on well," I said, "but his improvement would be even more marked if his mind were at rest."

"What do you mean?" she stammered.

"You gave me a hint yesterday," I said—"you hinted at something being wrong. In the night the Squire had a dream —he spoke in his dream with great passion and feeling to someone whom he called Orian—he seemed to find great relief in her presence. Is that your name?"

Miss Norreys was standing when I spoke to her—she now clutched hold of the back of the nearest chair to support herself.

"My name is Agnes," she replied. "I knew, I guessed," she continued—"I guessed, I hoped, that the old love was not dead. Did he speak to her, to Orian, as if he still loved her, Dr. Halifax?"

"Yes," I replied. "Who is she?"

"I will tell you—come into my boudoir."

She led me down a corridor and into a quaint little room furnished in old-fashioned style. Her movements were quick, her manner full of agitation. She hastily opened a davenport which stood against one of the walls, and took out a photograph in a velvet case.

"That is Orian's picture," she said, placing the photograph in my hand. "You will see for yourself that there is not much likeness between that young girl and me."

I looked at the photograph with interest. It represented a tall, finely-made girl. Her face was dark, her eyes brilliant —the expression of her face was full of fire and spirit— her lips were beautifully curved, and were just touched with the dawn of a radiant smile. A glance was sufficient to show me that her beauty was of a remarkable and distinguished order.

"I will tell you Orian's story in as few words as I possibly can," said Miss Norreys. She sank down into a low chair as she spoke, and clasped her hands on her knees. I laid the photograph back on the table.

"We are step-sisters," she began. "Orian's mother died at her birth—she asked me to be a mother to her. I loved my step-mother, and the baby became like my own child. She grew up in this house as gay and bright and fresh as girl could be. From her earliest days, she was my father's special darling and idol. It would have been impossible anywhere to meet a more winsome, daring, fascinating creature. The Squire is kind at heart—yes, I will always maintain that; but he has a somewhat fierce and overbearing manner—at times also his temper is irritable. Most people show a little fear of the Squire. Orian never feared anybody, and her father least of all. She would go about the place hanging on his arm. She would sit on his knee in the evening; she would ride with him all over the property—those two were scarcely ever apart, and a look, a glance from Orian would soothe the old man in his most irritable moods.   Her entrance into the room was like a ray of sunshine to my father.

"We all felt her influence," continued Miss Norreys, with a heavy sigh; "her brightness made the old place gay; she was liked by young and old, rich and poor alike.   Never was there a more warm-hearted, spirited, and brilliant girl. She could sing like a lark, and had also a considerable talent for art.   My father would not allow her to go to school, but the best masters from Leamington used to come here to instruct her.

"Amongst them was a young man of the name of Seymour: he was an artist, and seemed to have talent above the average.   He came here once a week to give Orian lessons, and he and she, in my company, used to go out to sketch.   I liked him and was interested in his future; he expected to do great things with his art by-and-bye. Orian and I were both interested in his day-dreams.   Although poor, he was quite a gentleman, and was good-looking, and refined in appearance.

"When my sister was nearly eighteen, my father came to me one day in order to make a confidence.   There was no male heir to inherit the estates, but the property was not entailed, and the Squire could leave it to whom he pleased. He knew that I inherited a considerable fortune from my mother, also that I had no wish for matrimony.   My father told me on this occasion that he wished Orian to marry well and young, and that he intended her eldest son to take the name of Norreys and be his heir.   He further said that he had fixed upon the man who was to be the child's husband —a Sir Hugo Price, whose property adjoins ours.   Sir Hugo had fallen in love with Orian, and a day or two before this conversation had asked my father's permission to woo her and win her if he could.

"I was startled, and begged for longer time—my father, who never could brook the slightest opposition, became indignant and firmly declared that the marriage should take place before the year was out.   I thought Orian would settle matters by refusing to have anything to do with Sir Hugo Price, who was considerably her senior, and whom she never had shown the least partiality for.   To my surprise, she made little or no opposition. She consented to be engaged to Sir Hugo, and the wedding was to take place immediately after her eighteenth birthday. The whole county was invited to Orian's wedding—no preparations were too great to do honour to such a bridal.

"The night before, however, quite late, the bride stole into my room; she flung her arms round my neck, kissed me, and burst into violent weeping. I guessed at once that she was in trouble, but she would not confide in me. I could do nothing but soothe and pet her, and after a time she wiped away her tears, kissed me again, and went away.

"The next morning, you can imagine our consternation—the house was full of wedding guests, the bridegroom arrived in good time, but there was no bride for him to marry. My sister could not be found—she had left Hartley Castle, how and when no one seemed to know. I learned long afterwards that our old servant Connor was in the secret, but nothing would induce her to breathe a word which might injure her darling. I can never tell you what that terrible day was like. The next morning a letter in Orian's handwriting arrived by post—it bore a London postmark, and was addressed to my father. He read it standing by the hearth in this room. When he had finished it, he placed it in my hands, and said, abruptly:—

"'She has made her bed and she shall lie on it. I forbid you to mention your sister's name again to me, Agnes.'

"He left the room as he spoke; when he had gone I read the poor child's brief words. She was now, she said, the wife of Charles Seymour, the young artist who had given her drawing lessons the previous summer, and to whom she had long been secretly and passionately attached. Nothing, she said, could bring her to marry Sir Hugo Price, but as she knew that her father would never consent to her engagement to Mr. Seymour, she was forced to take this cowardly way of securing her own happiness.

"'Yes,' she said, in conclusion, 'I know what I have done is cowardly, and I fear it will be a long time before you forgive me; still, I do not repent.'

"There was no address on poor Orian's letter. I offered to return it to my father—he took it from my hands with a great oath, and, tearing it into shreds, flung the pieces on the fire.

"'I forbid you to mention your sister's name to me,' he said, 'and, what is more, I lay my commands on you never to write to her or to have any further dealings with her of any sort whatsoever—if you do, you can also go.'

"Of course I could not leave my father; he wanted me during those fearful days of suffering more than he had any idea of.

"A year after the marriage the birth of Orian's son was announced in the *Times*. My father was the first to see the announcement. He pointed it out to me with a trembling finger. He had aged greatly during the year, and his temper, always irritable, was sometimes almost unbearable. He showed me the announcement of the child's birth now, and abruptly left the breakfast-table.

"That evening, however, to my great surprise, he came and spoke to me.

"'I never go back on my word,' he said. 'Orian is exactly to me as if she were dead. She gave me up, and I give her up, but there is no reason why her son should not inherit the property.'

"My heart gave a leap at the words.

"'What do you mean, father?' I asked.

"'What I say,' he replied. 'Orian has a son: he can take our name, he can be educated here—I can make him my heir, and he can inherit Hartley Castle after me—that is, if he is in all respects presentable—strong in limb and sound in intellect. Write to your sister, Agnes, and tell her to send the child here for me to see when he is a year old—write to-night, do you hear me?'

"I promised gladly—that evening my letter was posted. I begged of my poor sister to consider the splendid prospect for her child, and to think well before she refused the Squire's offer. Her answer came back within a fortnight.

"'I was glad to hear from you again,' she said; 'your letter satisfied some of my heart hunger, but not all. Only a letter from my father himself could do that. I have called the boy Cyril, after my father—he is in every respect a noble child. I should like him to inherit the old place. If my father will allow me to bring him myself to Hartley Castle, when he is a year old, and if at the same time he will forgive me for having married the man whom I really love, my baby Cyril shall be his heir—if not, my husband and I would prefer to keep our boy to ourselves.'

B

"I showed this letter to the Squire, whose face turned crimson as he read it.

"'I never go back on my word,' he said, 'tell her that from me. If the boy is presentable I'll have him, but I'll have nothing to do with her, or the miserable pauper whom she has married.'

"I was obliged to write to Orian to tell her that there was no chance of a reconciliation for her or her husband. She never answered my letter. Months went by; the boy's first birthday passed without my sister making any sign. Then, one day, I had a short letter from Orian. It ran as follows:—

"'My husband is ill; I am in great anxiety. If my father still wishes to see little Cyril, I will send him to Hartley Castle when he is two years old.'

"I showed the letter to the Squire.

"'Aye, tell her to send him,' he responded.

"'Won't you give her a kind word, father? She is in dreadful trouble,' I pleaded.

"'I have nothing to do with her,' he answered; 'she is dead to me.' He turned on his heel as he spoke, slamming the door after him.

"I wrote to my sister, telling her to send the child as soon as she could. My father never mentioned him again, but I saw by the expression in his eyes and by the eager way in which he watched when the post arrived each morning, that in reality he was always thinking of the child. One day I saw the announcement of Charles Seymour's death in the *Times.* I rushed into my father's study, holding the open paper in my hands.

"'I know what you are going to tell me,' he exclaimed when he saw me. 'I looked at the *Times* before breakfast— the fellow's death is nothing to me.'

"'But Orian,' I interrupted.

"'How often am I to tell you that she is dead to me?' he replied.

"I turned away. As I was leaving the room he called after me.

"'When do you expect that child to be sent here, Agnes?'

"'He was to have come after his second birthday,' I answered, 'but it is scarcely likely that poor Orian will find herself able to part with him now.'

"My father stared at me when I said this; then, whistling

to one of his dogs, he walked out of the room. On the child's birthday a letter arrived from his mother. It contained a photograph of the boy and a few words.

"'I am sending baby's photograph,' she wrote. 'Perhaps my father will be able to judge by it whether the child is sufficiently presentable to inherit the property. At any rate, I cannot spare the boy himself for the present.'

"She made no allusion whatever to her husband's death. I took the photograph and letter to my father. He read the letter through and then scanned the photograph eagerly.

"'As far as I can see there is nothing amiss with the little chap,' he said; 'but you don't suppose, Agnes, I am such a fool as to choose my heir from a photograph. Tell your sister to send the boy here with his nurse—I will defray the expense. After I have seen him, his mother can have him back again if she fancies it, until he is five or six years of age. If I adopt him as my heir, I will give a suitable allowance for his maintenance. You can mention that when you write.'

"I took the photograph and letter away with me, and wrote as I was bidden. A reply came within a week.

"'I cannot fix any date for sending the child to Hartley Castle,' wrote my sister. 'As I said in my last letter, I do not wish to part with him at present. It is possible that I may send him in a few months for my father to see, but I do not make any definite promise.'

"That letter arrived about six months ago—the boy is now two and a half years of age, and we have not yet seen him. My father, I can see, lives in a constant state of fret and irritation. He often threatens to make his will, leaving the property to a distant relation, but for some unaccountable reason he never takes any active steps in the matter. You speak of this anxiety being bad for him—what can I possibly do to remove it?"

"I should recommend you to see Mrs. Seymour," I replied, "and to find out for yourself what is her real objection to sending the boy here. I am firmly convinced that at bottom your father still retains a real and deep affection for her. I have known characters like his before. Such men will rather die than allow their indomitable pride to be conquered. The presence of the child might work wonders, and for every reason he ought to be sent for immediately."

Miss Norreys stood up in great anxiety and indecision.

"If I only dared to do it," I heard her murmur under her breath.

She had scarcely said these words when a rustling noise in the passage caused her to turn her head quickly—a look of eager and startled expectation suddenly filled her eyes. The next instant the room door was flung hastily open, and the disturbed face of the old servant, Connor, appeared—she rushed into the room, exclaiming, in an agitated way :—

"Oh, Miss Norreys, I hope you'll forgive me—I never, never thought she'd be so mad and wilful. What is to be done, miss? Oh, suppose the Squire finds out !"

Before Miss Norreys had time to utter a word a tall, gracefully-made young woman, in deep widow's mourning, followed the maid into the room ; behind the young widow came a nurse carrying a child. One glance told me who the widow and child were.

"Oh, Miss Orian, you shouldn't have come back like this," called out the old servant.

"Nonsense, Connor," she replied, in an imperious but sweet voice ; "could I stay away, when you telegraphed that my father was so ill? Give me baby, nurse, and go away, please. Aggie, this is baby—this is little Cyril—I have brought him at last, and I have come myself. Connor telegraphed to me yesterday about my father's accident— she said his life was in danger. Aggie, kiss me. Oh, I have been so hungry for you, and for the old house, and for my dear father most of all. I was too proud to come to him until yesterday—but now—now—yes, he *shall* forgive me—I'll go on my knees to him—I'll—— Oh, Aggie, don't look at me with such startled eyes—I have suffered—I do suffer horribly. Aggie, I am desolate—and—and—*here is baby.*"

There was a wild sort of entreaty in her words and in the way she held the child out as she spoke. He was a heavy boy, but her young arms seemed made of iron. As to poor Miss Norreys, she was too stunned to reply. She stood with clasped hands gazing up pitiably at her sister.

"Take baby, Connor," said the younger woman. "Oh, Aggie, how old and worn you are. There, come to me, come into my arms." In a moment her strong young arms were swept round Miss Norreys' slight figure. She took the little lady into her embrace as though she were a child. Her long black widow's dress swept round her sister as she held her head on her breast.

Presently I went upstairs to sit with my patient. The improvement which I have already spoken of was more marked each time I saw him. The Squire's eyes were bright, and I saw by their expression that his mind was actively at work.

"I fancied I heard carriage wheels," he said; "has anyone come?"

I was about to make a soothing reply, which should lead his thoughts from dangerous ground, when, to my extreme consternation and amazement, Miss Norreys entered the room, carrying her sister's little boy in her arms. I would have motioned her back if I could, but I was too late—the Squire had seen the boy—I saw him start violently—all the upper part of his body was still completely paralyzed, but the features of his face were worked with agitation, and a wave of crimson mounted to his brow.

"Keep yourself calm," I said to him in a firm voice. "I cannot answer for the consequences if you allow yourself to get excited. Miss Norreys, you ought not to have brought that child into the room without my permission."

The poor lady gave me a piteous glance; her eyes were red and swollen with weeping.

"Let me see the youngster," exclaimed the Squire. "Bring him over to the bed, Agnes. I know who he is—he is Orian's boy—she has sent him here at last. Heavens! what a look of the family the little chap has—he is a Norreys, not a doubt of that."

Miss Norreys stood with her back to the light.

"Bring him round to the other side of the bed," said the Squire, "and let me have a good look at him."

Miss Norreys obeyed with some unwillingness.

The full light now streamed on the child's face—it was beautiful enough to please anyone—the features were perfect, the contour aristocratic—the full eyes were lovely in colouring and shape; and yet—and yet it needed but one glance to tell me that no soul looked from the little fellow's tranquil gaze, that, in short, the mind in that poor little casket was a sealed book. The beautiful boy was looking at no one;

he was gazing straight out of the window up at the sky. Presently the faintest of smiles trembled round his lips, but did not reach his serene eyes.

"He's a fine little chap," said the Squire, "but——" there was a fearful pause. "How old is he, Agnes?"

"Quite a baby, as you can see," said Miss Norreys.

"Folly," said the Squire; "he's over two—put him on the bed."

Miss Norreys obeyed.

The boy sat upright where he was placed; he never glanced at his grandfather, but his eyes followed the light.

"He's a fine little chap," repeated the old man; "very like us, but—when did you say he came, Agnes?"

"About half an hour ago," she replied, with firmness. "He's a lovely boy," she repeated; "he is as beautiful as an angel."

The Squire knit his brows—his face was getting flushed, his keen, sharp eyes looked from the crown of the child's head to his daintily clothed feet.

"Take him away," he said, suddenly. His voice was harsh, there was a tremble in it.

I motioned to Miss Norreys to obey. She lifted the little fellow into her arms again, and carried him out of the room.

The moment the door closed behind them, Squire Norreys turned to me.

"You are a doctor," he said, "and you know what's up."

I made no reply.

"That boy's an idiot," said the Squire—"he's a beautiful idiot—he's no heir for me—don't mention him again."

"There is something the matter with the child," I said; "what, I cannot exactly tell you without giving him an examination. As he is in the house, I should like to go carefully into his case, and will let you know my true opinion as soon as possible."

"Aye, do," said the Squire; "but you know just as well as I do, Halifax, that the unfortunate child has got no mind—that accounts—that accounts——" he paused—the pink spots grew brighter on his cheeks.

"I must send for my man of business," he said, speaking with great excitement. "I cannot rest until I have made a suitable disposal of my property—the dream about that child inheriting it is at an end."

"Now listen to me," I said, in a firm voice; "unless you wish your heir, whoever he may be, to step into possession at once, you are to attend to no business at present. You have met with a serious accident—a very little more, and your life would have been the forfeit—as it is, you are making a splendid recovery, but excitement and worry will throw you back. In short, if you do not remain quiet, I cannot be answerable for the consequences. With care and prudence, you may live to manage your own property for many years. I am very sorry that you saw the little fellow to-day—the thing was done without my permission. I am going downstairs, however, to examine him thoroughly, and will give you my verdict on his case when next I see you. Now you are to take your medicine and go to sleep. Nurse, come into the room, please."

The professional nurse whom I had engaged to help me entered from the dressing-room. I gave her some directions, desired her to admit no one, and went downstairs.

Miss Norreys was anxiously waiting for me—she came out of her boudoir to meet me.

"Is my father worse?" she asked.

"I hope not," I replied; "but why did you bring that child into his room without my permission, Miss Norreys?"

"Oh, it was Orian," she replied; "she would not be reasonable—she seemed carried out of herself by excitement and distress. It was as much as I could do to keep her from bringing the boy to my father herself. Of course, I know *now* why she kept him away all these months; but she thought—she hoped—that my father might not notice how things were with the child while he was so ill himself."

"You both did very wrong," I answered. "Of course, Mr. Norreys could not fail to observe the child's strange condition. By the way, I should like to see the boy again."

"Orian is only too anxious to consult you about him," replied Miss Norreys. "Will you come in here?"

She led me again into her boudoir, said, in a husky voice, "I have brought Dr. Halifax to see you, Orian," and closed the door behind us.

Mrs. Seymour was standing near one of the windows—the boy sat on a sofa facing the light. He was looking as usual up at the sky. The mother started when she heard my name, and gave me a quick glance.

"Come here," she said; "you can see him well from here.

He won't mind—he never notices, never—he loves the light, he hates the dark—he has no other loves nor hatreds. It's easy to satisfy him, isn't it?"

She glanced at me again as she said the last words, tears brimming over in her eyes.

"My sister tells me that you know something of my story, Dr. Halifax," she continued. "I have heard of you, and am glad to make your acquaintance. Agnes wishes me to consult you about the boy, but I do not think there is anything to consult about. Anyone can see what is wrong—he has no mind. He is just beautiful, and he is alive. Even the cleverest doctors cannot give baby a mind, can they?"

"I should like to ask you a few questions about him," I said in reply.

I sat down as I spoke and took the boy on my knee. He did not make the slightest objection to my handling him, but when I turned his face away for a moment from the bright light which streamed in from the window, a spasm of unrest seemed to pass over it. I felt the little head carefully; there was no doubt whatever that the child's intellect was terribly impaired: one arm and one foot also turned inwards—a common accompaniment.

While I examined the child the mother stood perfectly still. Her hands were locked tightly together; her attitude was almost as impassive as that of the baby himself.

She had expressed no hope a moment before, but when I looked up at her now, her "Well?" came in a hoarse and eager whisper.

"I can tell you exactly what is the matter," I said; "the state of the child's head makes the case abundantly clear. He is a very finely made child—see his shoulders, and the size of his limbs generally—but observe, also, how small his head is in proportion to the rest of his frame. That smallness is at the root of the mischief. The little fellow is suffering from premature ossification of the cranial bones. In short, his brain is imprisoned behind those hard bones and cannot grow. The bones I refer to should, at his tender age, be *open*, to allow proper expansion of the growing brain."

"He was born like that," said Mrs. Seymour. "The nurse told me so when he was a few days old. She said that most babies have a soft spot on the top of the head, but my boy had none."

"When he was quite an infant, did you notice anything peculiar about him?"

"He was very bright and intelligent until he was three or four months old."

"Yes," I continued: "and after that?"

"One day he was taken with a violent attack of screaming, which ended in a sort of fit—we sent for a doctor, who attributed the convulsions to teething, but after that the child's mind seemed to make no progress. He still knew me, however, and used to smile faintly when I approached him. This continued for some time, but of late he has ceased to notice anyone—in fact, as I said just now, the only pleasure he has is in turning to the light. Oh, his case is hopeless, and," she added, with passion, "he is all I have got."

Tears gathered in her eyes, but none fell—she turned her head away to hide her emotion. When she looked at me again her manner was quite quiet.

"My father has offered to make the little fellow his heir," she said; "but, of course, after to-day, he will put such an idea out of his head. I do not think I care very much now whether Cyril is his heir or not, but I should be glad, if in any way possible, to have a reconciliation with my father."

"I am afraid you must not see him to-day," I answered; "it would never do for him to know that you are in the house. He is going on well, so you need not be anxious about him, but you must have patience with regard to seeing him. As to the child," I continued, "most people would consider his case hopeless, but I am not at all sure that I do."

"What can you mean?" she exclaimed. "Cyril's case not hopeless! Surely I don't hear you aright—not hopeless! Speak, Dr. Halifax—your words excite me—speak, tell me what you mean?"

"I will tell you after I have considered matters a little," I said. "An idea has occurred to me—it is a daring one; when you hear of the thought which has visited me, you may recoil from it in horror, but I cannot divulge it, even to you, until I have thought it over carefully. I will see you again on the subject in an hour or two."

A brilliant rose-colour had come into Mrs. Seymour's cheeks, her beautiful eyes grew full of light.

"You think that I won't consent," she said, "to *anything*

that offers a gleam of hope! Oh, think out your plan as quickly as possible and let me know."

I said I would do so—my heart ached with profound pity for her. I went out of the house and took a long walk. During the walk my idea took shape and form. The child's case was so hopeless that, surely, strong measures were justifiable which had even the most remote possibility of giving him relief. I felt inclined to do what had not to my knowledge been yet attempted, namely, to try to give release to the imprisoned brain.

When I entered the house the Squire was awake, and was asking to see me. I went up to him at once. He was no worse, and the eagerness which filled his eyes to learn my news with regard to the boy made me resolve to speak to him quite openly on the subject. I gave him a brief account of what I considered the state of the case—then I told him what I wished my line of treatment to be.

"I propose," I said, standing up as I spoke, for the thought of what I was about to do filled my mind with profound interest—"I propose to open the casket where the child's mind is now tightly bound up, and so to give the brain a chance of expansion."

"I don't understand you," said the Squire.

"It is difficult for me to explain to you the exact nature of the operation which I hope his mother may permit me to perform," I continued. "I admit that it is an experiment, and a tremendous one; but I know a clever surgeon who can give me invaluable assistance, and, in short, I am prepared to undertake it."

"Suppose you don't succeed," said the Squire, "then the child—— "

"The child may die under the operation," I said, "or he may live as he now is."

"And if successful?" continued Squire Norreys.

"Then he will be as other children."

The Squire was silent. After a long pause he said, "And you think the mother will consent to such a risk?"

"I can but ask her," I responded; "I am inclined to believe that she will consent."

"You are a queer fellow, Halifax; your enthusiasm excites even my admiration; but pray, why do you tell *me* all this?"

"Because I want you to abide the result of the operation."

"How long, supposing everything goes well, shall I have to wait?"

"Between three and six months."

"I may be in my grave before then."

"Not likely—you are already better. Nothing will be so good for you as hope. Live on hope for the next six months, and give your heir a chance."

"You're a queer man," repeated the Squire. He said nothing further, but I knew by his manner that he was prepared to abide by the issue of the operation.

I saw Mrs. Seymour soon afterwards, and explained to her as fully as I could the idea which had taken possession of me.

My few words of the morning had already given her hope. She listened to me now with an enthusiasm which gave me as much pain as pleasure—her longings, her passionate desires, had already swept fear out of sight—she was eager, excited, restless, longing for me to try my skill upon the child. I told her that my idea was to divide certain portions of bone in the skull, so as to allow the closed-in brain to expand properly.

"It seems to me," I said, "the common-sense view of the matter to take some steps to give the cramped brain room for expansion. The child is healthy. With extreme care, and with all that surgical skill can devise, I cannot see why such an operation should not succeed. At the same time I must not mince the matter; if it fails, there is danger, great danger, to life."

The boy was seated in a perfectly impassive attitude on his mother's knee. She squeezed him close to her when I said this, and gave me a quick glance from an eye of fire.

"The operation will not fail," she said.

"I believe it will succeed," I answered her. "In any case, I should advise it. The child's present case is so hopeless and deplorable that, in my opinion, very great risk is justifiable in any surgical interference which offers even a hope of cure."

"I consent," she exclaimed—she sprang up as she spoke, and still holding the boy to her breast, pulled one of his little arms round her neck—"I consent," she repeated. "If his father were alive, he would wish it. When can the operation be performed, Dr. Halifax?"

"As soon as possible," I answered. "Your father is now

out of danger. Granted nothing unforeseen arises, he will completely recover from his accident—there is nothing to prevent my leaving him, more particularly as a telegram has arrived from Dr. Richards, who hopes to reach here this evening. I propose, therefore, that you and your boy return to London with me to-night. I can see Terrel, the surgeon whose assistance I wish to secure, to-morrow morning, and all arrangements for the operation can be quickly made."

"Very well," she replied, "I will be ready."

That night Mrs. Seymour, her nurse, and the boy accompanied me to London. We arrived there soon after midnight. Mrs. Seymour had rooms in Baker Street; and, when I saw her into a cab at Euston, I promised to call there at an early hour on the following morning.

I went to my own house to spend an almost sleepless night. Soon after eight o'clock on the following day I went off to see Terrel. He was one of the cleverest surgeons of my acquaintance, and I was anxious to talk the matter over with him in all its bearings. He was startled and amazed at what I proposed to do, but after much argument and consultation, admitted that my plan was feasible. The obvious common-sense view of opening the skull to give the imprisoned brain room for expansion appealed to him forcibly. He offered to give me all the help in his power, and we decided to perform the operation the following day.

I went straight from Terrel's house to Mrs. Seymour's lodgings, and told her of the arrangements we had made. She came to greet me with extended hands of welcome. The brightness of renewed hope still filled her eyes, but something in the expression of her face showed me that she had also passed a sleepless night.

Having described to her what preparations she ought to make, and further telling her that I would send in a good professional nurse to take charge of the case that evening, I went away.

The next morning Terrel and I, accompanied by the anæsthetist, arrived at the house. All was in readiness for the operation, and when we entered the bedroom where it was to take place, Mrs. Seymour appeared almost immediately, carrying the little boy in her arms.

"Kiss me," she said to him, eagerly—there was such passion in those words, that any spirit less firmly imprisoned must have responded to them. But light—light, was all that baby needed just then; as usual, his eyes turned to it. The mother pressed him to her heart, printed two kisses on his brow, and put him into my arms. Her look of eloquent pain and hope almost unmanned me. As she was leaving the room I had to turn my head aside.

Doctors are a race of men who have little time to give way to mere sentiment. I soon turned with eagerness to the delicate task which lay before me. The baby was put immediately under an anæsthetic, and when he was unconscious I proceeded quickly with the operation. Briefly, what I did was somewhat as follows: Having laid back the coverings of the skull over those parts where I proposed to divide the bone, the long openings and the shorter transverses were successfully accomplished without injury to the delicate membranes underneath them, and I had the satisfaction of seeing the trenches which I had formed widening under my manipulation. Every detail of antiseptic dressing was carried out with scrupulous care, and the operation was finished without any untoward event. It took altogether an hour and a half. When I laid the little fellow back in his cot, and called the mother into the room, I felt sure that she knew by my face how hopeful I felt with regard to the result. She was white to the lips, however, and quite incapable of speech.

I left the house with the most extraordinarily mingled sensations of relief, triumph, and anxiety which I have ever experienced.

The suspense of the next few days can better be imagined than described. The gradual but sure dawning of hope, the fact that no bad symptoms appeared, the joy with which we noticed that the child rallied well! In three days my fears had nearly vanished. There was already an improvement in the child's intelligence—in a week's time this improvement was decisive. He no longer sat absolutely still—he began to take notice like other children—he ate and slept fairly well.

On the tenth day I dressed the wound, which was healing fast.

One month after the operation I heard the boy laugh— he turned his head away, too, when I entered the room, and hid his face shyly against his mother's breast. His behaviour, in short, was that of an ordinary infant of from six to eight months of age. Mrs. Seymour looked up at me on this occasion—my thoughts must have been plainly written on my face—for the first time during all these trying days she burst into tears.

"I cry because I am happy," she said, with a gasp in her voice. "He knows me, Dr. Halifax—baby knows his mother—you have seen for yourself how he has just distinguished between me and a comparative stranger."

"I congratulate you from my heart," I replied. "So far the success of the operation has been magnificent, but I should like to wait a little longer before I say anything to the Squire."

The months went by—the improvement in the child continued—the imprisoned brain developed with rapidity—the intellect seemed to expand with leaps and bounds. I saw the boy on his third birthday, and in every respect he was almost up to the average child of his age. I had made up my mind that the time had come to see Squire Norreys, when one day, a foggy one in late November, his card was put into my hand. I had just seen the last of my morning's patients, and was preparing to go out. I desired the servant to show the Squire into my consulting-room immediately. I could not help starting when he entered the room. He was a splendid-looking man of a type fast dying out. His olive complexion, his black eyes, and sweeping black moustache were in strong contrast to his abundant white hair, which was cut close to his head. There was no trace of weakness or illness about him now—he walked into the room with a firm step, carrying his great height well. He gave me one of his keen glances and held out his hand.

"How do you do?" he said. "I happened to be in town, so I thought I'd call. I am, as you see, quite myself again."

"I am delighted to see that you are," I answered. "It needs but a glance to tell me that you have made a splendid recovery. Won't you sit down?"

"I am rather in a hurry," he replied. He took a seat nevertheless and looked at me. I saw the question in his eyes which his lips refused to ask.

"I am particularly glad to see you," I said. "The fact is, I was just about to write to you."

"It occurred to me that I might hear from you about now," he answered, in a would-be careless tone.

"Yes," I said, "I was going to propose to come to see you."

"Then," said the Squire, his voice getting a little rough, "you have news about—about my grandson?"

"Yes," I said; "I should like you to see him."

"Look here, Halifax," he exclaimed, eagerly, "is there any use in it? With all your cleverness, you know, you can't give a child like that a mind. I came here to-day because I gave you a sort of tacit promise that I would take no steps with regard to my property for a few months' time, but this kind of thing can't go on. I don't wish to lay up anxieties for a future death-bed: all must be settled now."

"All shall be settled now," I said. "Will you stay here, or will you come back again within an hour?"

"What do you mean? What folly is this?"

"Will you come back here within an hour and see your grandson? After seeing him you can then decide at once and for ever the question which worries you."

"You think him better, then?"

"I do."

"Remember, no half-witted person shall inherit Hartley Castle."

"The matter will lie in your own hands," I replied. "I should like you to see your grandson. I can bring him here within an hour; will you wait to see him?"

"All right," he replied.

My carriage was at the door—I jumped into it and drove straight to Baker Street. Mrs. Seymour was in. The boy was playing vigorously with a wooden cart and horse. He was using manly and emphatic action with his wooden steed —he was, in fact, quite noisy and obstreperous. No trace of any wound disfigured his face—his wealth of beautiful curls was flung back from a white brow.

"Capital," I said, as I entered. "Now, Mrs. Seymour, I want to borrow this boy for an hour."

"Why?" she asked.

"His grandfather is waiting to see him at my house."

"Oh, then, I'm coming too," she said at once. "My father shan't have Cyril without me—I am resolved."

I stared at her for a moment—then I said: "Very well; get ready as fast as you can."

In three minutes' time we were driving back to Harley Street. The boy could not speak much yet, but he called his mother "Mummie," and constantly turned to look at her with eyes brim full of love. We entered the house, and I took the two straight into my consulting-room. The Squire started up when he saw them; a look which I can scarcely find words to describe filled his eyes—a sort of starved look, of sudden rapture; he scarcely glanced at the child, who walked as upright as a little soldier by his mother's side, he made an effort to frown and to be severe, but it was a poor pretence, after all.

"Cyril, this is your grandfather," said Mrs. Seymour. "Come and speak to him at once."

The Squire sank down again in his chair—he was almost weak from emotion—not a single word, good or bad, had yet passed his lips. Mrs. Seymour took the child and placed him on his grandfather's knee.

The little fellow turned and looked full up into the stern old face; the mother knelt on the floor at his side. The boy's brow puckered—his lips pouted for a moment as if he would cry, then something bright attracted his eyes— he made a violent tug at his grandfather's chain, and pulled his watch out of his pocket. With a laugh he turned to his mother, and held the watch to her ear.

"Tick, tick, mummie," he said.

"Pon my word, I'm blest," exclaimed the Squire.

When he said these words I left the room.

It goes without saying that all went right after that. When last I heard of Squire Norreys, I was given to understand that he was much bullied by his grandson, who, in short, rules everyone at Hartley Castle. Mrs. Seymour, who, of course, is completely reconciled to her father, told me this in her last letter.

THE SEVENTH STEP

THE SEVENTH STEP

A PLEASURE yacht, of the name of *Ariadne*, was about to start upon a six-weeks' cruise. The time of the year was September—a golden, typical September—in the year of grace 1893. The *Ariadne* was to touch at several of the great northern ports: Christiania, St. Petersburg, and others. I had just gone through a period of hard and anxious work. I found it necessary to take a brief holiday, and resolved to secure a berth on board the *Ariadne*, and so give myself a time of absolute rest. We commenced our voyage on the second of the month; the day was a lovely one, and every berth on board had secured an occupant.

We were all in high spirits, and the weather was so fine that scarcely anyone suffered from sea-sickness. In consequence, the young ship's doctor, Maurice Curwen, had scarcely anything to do.

The passengers on board the *Ariadne* were, with one exception, of the most ordinary and conventional type, but a girl who was carried on board just before the yacht commenced her voyage aroused my professional sympathies from the first. She was a tall, dark-eyed girl, of about eighteen or nineteen years of age—her lower limbs were evidently paralyzed, and she was accompanied by a nurse who wore the picturesque uniform of the Charing Cross Hospital.

The young girl was taken almost immediately to a deck cabin which had been specially arranged for her, and during the first two or three days of our voyage I had not an opportunity of seeing her again. When we reached the smooth waters of the Norwegian fiords, however, she was carried almost every day on deck. Here she lay under an awning, speaking to no one, and apparently taking little interest either in her fellow-passengers or in the marvellous beauties of Nature which surrounded her.

Her nurse usually sat by her side—she was a reserved-looking, middle-aged woman, with a freckly face and thin, sandy hair. Her lips were perfectly straight in outline and very thin, her eyebrows were high and faintly marked—altogether, she had a disagreeable and thoroughly unsympathetic appearance.

I was not long on board the *Ariadne* before I was informed that the sick girl's name was Dagmar Sorensen—that she was the daughter of a rich city merchant, and was going to St. Petersburg to see her father's brother, who was a celebrated physician there.

One morning, on passing Miss Sorensen's cabin, my footsteps were arrested by hearing the noise of something falling within the room. There came to my ears the crash of broken glass. This was immediately followed by the sound of rapid footsteps which as suddenly stopped, as though the inmate of the room was listening intently. Miss Sorensen's nurse, who went by the name of Sister Hagar, was probably doing something for her patient, and was annoyed at any-one pausing near the door. I passed on quickly, but the next moment, to my astonishment, came face to face with Sister Hagar on the stairs. I could not help looking at her in surprise. I was even about to speak, but she hurried past me, wearing her most disagreeable and repellent expression.

What could the noise have been? Who could have moved in the cabin? Miss Sorensen's lower limbs were, Curwen, our ship's doctor, had assured me, hopelessly paralyzed. She was intimate with no one on board the *Ariadne*. What footsteps had I listened to?

I thought the matter over for a short time, then made up my mind that the stewardess must have been in Miss Sorensen's cabin, and having come to this conclusion, I forgot all about the circumstance·

That afternoon I happened to be standing in the neighbourhood of the young lady's deck-chair; to my surprise, for she had not hitherto taken the least notice of me, she suddenly raised her full, brilliant dark eyes, and fixed them on my face.

"May I speak to you?" she said.

I went up to her side immediately.

"Certainly," I answered. "Can I do anything for you?"

"You can do a great deal if you will," she answered. "I have heard your name: you are a well-known London physician."

"I have a large practice in London," I replied to her.

"Yes," she continued, "I have often heard of you—you have doubtless come on board the *Ariadne* to take a holiday?"

"That is true," I answered.

"Then it is unfair——" She turned her head aside, breaking off her speech abruptly.

"What is unfair?" I asked.

"I have a wish to consult you professionally, but if you are taking a holiday, it is unfair to expect you to give up your time to me."

"Not at all," I replied. "If I can be of the slightest use to you, pray command me; but are you not under Curwen's care?"

"Yes, oh, yes; but that doesn't matter." She stopped speaking abruptly; her manner, which had been anxious and excited, became suddenly guarded—I looked up and saw the nurse approaching us. She carried a book and shawl in her hands.

"Thank you, Sister Hagar," said Miss Sorensen. "I shall not require your services any more for the present."

The nurse laid the shawl over the young lady's feet, placed the book within reach, and, bestowing an inquisitive glance on me, walked slowly away.

When she was quite out of sight, Miss Sorensen resumed her conversation.

"You see that I am paralysed," she said.

I bowed an acknowledgment of this all-patent fact.

"I suffer a good deal," she continued. "I am on my way to St. Petersburg to see my uncle, who is a very great physician. My father is most anxious that I should consult him. Perhaps you know my uncle's name—Professor Sorensen? He is one of the doctors of the Court."

"I cannot recall the name just now," I said; "but that is of no consequence. I have no doubt he is all that you say."

"Yes, he is wonderfully clever, and holds a high position. But it will be some days before we get to Russia, and—I am ill. I did not know when I came on board the *Ariadne* that a doctor of your professional eminence would be one of the passengers. Perhaps Mr. Curwen will not object——" She paused.

"I am sure he will not object to having a consultation with me over your case," I answered. "If you wish it, I can arrange the matter with him."

"Thank you—but—I don't want a consultation. My wish is to see you—alone."

I looked at her in surprise.

"Don't refuse me," she said, in a voice of entreaty.

"I will see you with pleasure with Curwen," I said.

"But I want to consult you independently."

"I am sorry," I answered; "under the circumstances, that is impossible."

She coloured vividly.

"Why so?" she asked.

"Because professional etiquette makes it necessary for the doctor whom you have already consulted to be present."

Her eyes flashed angrily.

"How unkind and queer you doctors are," she said. "I cordially hate that sentence for ever on your lips, 'Professional etiquette.' Why should a girl suffer and be ill, because of anything so unreasonable?"

"You must forgive me," I said. "I would gladly do anything for you; I will see you with pleasure with Curwen."

"Must he be present?"

"Yes."

"I cannot stand this. If he consents to your seeing me alone, have you any objection to make?"

At that moment Curwen appeared. He was talking to one of the ship's crew, and they were both slowly advancing in Miss Sorensen's direction.

"Mr. Curwen, can I speak to you?" called out Miss Sorensen.

He went to her at once.

I withdrew in some annoyance, feeling pretty well convinced that the young lady was highly hysterical and required to be carefully looked after.

By-and-bye, as I was standing by the deck-rail, Curwen came up to me.

"I have talked to Miss Sorensen," he said. "She is most anxious to consult you, Dr. Halifax, but says that you will not see her except in consultation with me. I beg of you not to consider me for a moment. I take an interest in her, poor girl, and will be only too glad to get your opinion of her case. Pray humour her in this matter."

"Of course, if you have no objection, I have none," I answered. "I can talk to you about her afterwards. She is evidently highly nervous."

"I fear that is the case," replied Curwen. "But," he added, "there is little doubt as to her ailment. The lower limbs are paralyzed; she is quite incapable of using them."

"Did you examine her carefully when she came on board?" I asked.

"I went into the case, certainly," replied Curwen; "but if you mean that I took every step to complete the diagnosis of the patient's condition, I did not consider it necessary. The usual symptoms were present. In short, Miss Sorensen's case was, to my mind, very clearly defined to be that of spastic paralysis, and I did not want to worry her by useless experiments."

"Well, I will see her, as she wishes for my opinion," I replied, slowly.

"I am very glad that you will do so," said Curwen.

"Do you happen to have an electric battery on board?" I asked.

"Yes, a small one, but doubtless sufficient for your purpose. Will you arrange to see Miss Sorensen to-morrow morning?"

"Yes," I answered. "If I am to do her any good, there is no use in delay."

Curwen and I talked the matter over a little further, then he was obliged to leave me to attend to some of his multifarious duties.

The nightly dance had begun—awnings had been pulled down all round the deck, and the electric light made the place as bright as day. The ship's band were playing a merry air, and several couples were already revolving in the mazes of the waltz.

I looked to see if Miss Sorensen had come on deck. Yes, she was there; she was lying as usual on her own special couch. The captain's wife, Mrs. Ross, was seated near her, and Captain Ross stood at the foot of her couch. She was dressed in dark, rose-coloured silk, worn high to the throat, and with long sleeves. The whiteness of her complexion and the gloomy depths of her big, dark eyes, were thus thrown into strong relief. She looked strikingly handsome.

On seeing me, Captain Ross called me up, and introduced me to Miss Sorensen. She smiled at me in quite a bright way.

"Dr. Halifax and I have already made each other's acquaintance," she said. She motioned me to sit by her side. The conversation, which had been animated before I joined the little party, was now continued with *verve*. Miss Sorensen, quite contrary to her wont, was the most lively of the group. I observed that she had considerable powers of repartee, and that her conversational talent was much above the average. Her words were extremely well chosen, and her grammar was invariably correct. She had, in short, the bearing of a very accomplished woman. I further judged that she was a remarkably clever one, for I was not five minutes in her society before I observed that she was watching me with as close attention as I was giving to her.

After a time Captain and Mrs. Ross withdrew, and I found myself alone with the young lady.

"Don't go," she said, eagerly, as I was preparing to rise from my chair. "I spoke to Mr. Curwen," she continued, dropping her voice; "he has not the slightest objection to your seeing me alone. Have you arranged the matter with him?"

"I have seen him," I replied, gravely. "He kindly consents to waive all ceremony. I can make an appointment to see you at any hour you wish."

"Pray let it be to-morrow morning—I am anxious to have relief as soon as possible."

"I am sorry that you suffer," I replied, giving her a sudden, keen glance—"you don't look ill, at least not now."

"I am excited now," she answered. "I am pleased at the thought——"

She broke off abruptly.

"Is Sister Hagar on deck?" she asked.

"I do not see her," I replied.

"But look, pray, look. Dr. Halifax—I *fear* Sister Hagar."

There was unquestionable and most genuine terror in the words. Miss Sorensen laid her hand on mine—it trembled.

I was about to reply, when a thin voice, almost in our ears, startled us both.

"Miss Sorensen, I must take you to bed now," said Nurse Hagar.

"Allow me to help you, nurse," I said, starting up.

"No, thank you, sir," she answered, in her most disagreeable way; "I can manage my young lady quite well alone."

She went behind the deck chair, and propelled it forward. When she got close to the little deck cabin, she lifted Miss Sorensen up bodily in her strong arms, and conveyed her within the cabin.

During the night I could not help giving several thoughts to my new patient—she repelled me quite as much as she attracted me. She was without doubt a very handsome girl. There was something pathetic, too, in her dark eyes and in the lines round her beautifully curved mouth; but now and then I detected a ring of insincerity in her voice, and there were moments when her eyes, in spite of themselves, took a shifty glance. Was she feigning paralysis? What was her motive in so anxiously desiring an interview with me alone?

Immediately after breakfast, on the following morning, Sister Hagar approached my side.

"Miss Sorensen would be glad to know when it will be convenient for you to see her, Dr. Halifax," she said.

"Pray tell her that I can be with her in about ten minutes," I replied.

The nurse withdrew and I went to find Curwen.

"Is your electric battery in order?" I asked.

"Come with me to my cabin," he replied.

I went with him at once. We examined the battery together, put it into order, and then tested it. I took it with me to Miss Sorensen's cabin. Sister Hagar stood near the door. She came up to me at once, took the battery from my hands, and laid it on a small table near the patient. She then, to my astonishment, withdrew, closing the door noiselessly behind her.

I turned to look at Miss Sorensen, and saw at a glance that she was intensely nervous. There was not a trace of colour on her face; even her lips were white as death.

"Pray get your examination over as quickly as you can,' she said, speaking in an almost fretful voice.

"I am waiting for the nurse to return," I replied. "I have several questions to ask her."

"Oh, she is not coming back. I have asked her to leave us together."

" I cannot apply the electric battery without her assistance,"
I replied.   " If you will permit me, I will call her."

" No, no, don't go—don't go ! "

I looked fixedly at my patient.   Suddenly an idea occurred
to me.

I pushed the table aside on which the battery had been
placed, and stood at the foot of Miss Sorensen's bed.

" The usual examination need not take place," I said,
" because——"

" Why ? " she asked.   She half started up on her couch ;
her colour changed from white to red.

" Because you are not paralyzed ! " I said, giving her a
sudden, quick glance, and speaking with firmness.

" My God, how do you know ? " she exclaimed.   Her face
grew so colourless that I thought she would faint.   She
covered her eyes with one trembling hand.   " Sister Hagar
was right," she continued, after a moment.   " I did not
believe her—I assured her it was nothing more than her
fancy."

" I have guessed the truth ? " I said, in a stern voice.

" Alas, yes, you have guessed the truth."   As she spoke,
she sprang with a light movement from her couch and stood
before me.

" I am no more paralyzed than you are," she said ; " but
how, *how* do you know ? "

" Sit down and I will tell you," I replied.

She did not sit—she was far too much excited.   She stood
near the door of her little cabin.   " Did you really hear the
bottle fall and break, yesterday morning ? "

" I heard a noise which might be accounted for in that
way," I answered.

" And did you hear my footsteps ? "

" I heard footsteps."

" Sister Hagar said that you knew—I hoped, I hoped—
I earnestly trusted that she was wrong."

" How could she possibly tell ? " I replied.   " I met
her on the stairs coming towards the cabin.   I certainly
said nothing—how was it possible for her to read my secret
thoughts ? "

" It was quite possible.   She saw the knowledge in your
eyes ; she gave you one glance—that was sufficient.   Oh !
I hoped she was mistaken."

"Mine is not a tell-tale face," I said.

"Not to most people, but it is to her. You don't know her. She is the most wonderful, extraordinary woman that ever breathed. She can read people through and through. She can stand behind you and know when your eyes flash and your lips smile. Her knowledge is terrible. She can almost see through stone walls. I told you last night that I dreaded her—I do more than that—I fear her horribly—she makes my life a daily purgatory!"

"Sit down," I said, in a voice which I made on purpose both cold and stern: "it is very bad for you to excite yourself in this way. If you dislike Sister Hagar, why is she your nurse? In short, what can be your possible motive for going through this extraordinary act of deception? Are you not aware that you are acting in a most reprehensible manner. Why do you wish the passengers of the *Ariadne* to suppose you to be paralyzed, when you are in reality in perfect health?"

"In perfect health?" she repeated, with a shudder. "Yes, I am doubtless in perfect bodily health, but I am in—oh, in such bitter misery of mind."

"What do you mean?"

"I can no more tell you that, than I can tell you why I am in Sister Hagar's power. Pray forget my wild words. I know you think badly of me, but your feelings would be changed to profound pity if you could guess the truth. Now listen to me—I have only a moment or two left, for Sister Hagar will be back almost directly. She found out yesterday that you had guessed my secret. I hoped that this was not the case, but, as usual, she was right and I was wrong. The moment my eyes met yours, when I first came on deck, I thought it likely you might see through my deception. Sister Hagar also feared that such would be the case. It was on that account I avoided speaking to you, and also remained so silent and apparently uninterested in everyone when I went on deck. I asked for this interview for the express purpose of finding out whether you really knew about the deception which I was practising on everyone on board. If I discovered that you had pierced through my disguise, there was nothing for it but for me to throw myself on your mercy. Now you know why I was so desirous of seeing you without Mr. Curwen."

"I understand," I answered. "The whole matter is most strange, wrong, and incomprehensible. Before I leave you, may I ask what motive influences you? There must be some secret reason for such deception as you practise."

Miss Sorensen coloured, and for the first time since she began to make her confession, her voice grew weak and faltering—her eyes took a shifty glance, and refused to meet mine.

"The motive may seem slight enough to you," she said; "but to me it is, and was, sufficiently powerful to make me go through with this sham. My home is not a happy one; I have a step-mother, who treats me cruelly. I longed to get away from home and to see something of life. My father's brother, Professor Sorensen, of St. Petersburg, is a very celebrated Court physician—my father is proud of him, and has often mentioned his name and the luxurious palace in which he lives. I have never met him, but I took a curious longing to pay him a visit, and thought of this way of obtaining my desires. Professor Sorensen has made a special study of nervous diseases such as paralysis. Sister Hagar and I talked the matter over, and I resolved to feign this disease in order to get away from home and pay my uncle a visit. All went well without hitch of any sort until yesterday morning."

"But it is impossible for you to suppose," I said, "that you can take in a specialist like Professor Sorensen."

"I don't mean to try—he'll forgive me when I tell him the truth, and throw myself on his mercy."

"And is Sister Hagar a real nurse?" I asked, after a pause.

"No, but she has studied the part a little, and is far too clever to commit herself."

Miss Sorensen's face was no longer pale—a rich colour flamed in her cheeks, her eyes blazed—she looked wonderfully handsome.

"Now that you have confided in me," I said, "what do you expect me to do with my knowledge?"

"To respect my secret, and to keep it absolutely and strictly to yourself."

"That is impossible—I cannot deceive Curwen."

"You must. Why should two—two be sacrificed? He is so young, and he knows nothing now—nothing. Pray have mercy on him! Oh, my God, what wild words am I saying? What must you think of me?"

She paused abruptly, her blazing eyes were fixed on my face.

"What must you think of me?" she repeated.

"That you are in a very excitable and over-strained condition, and perhaps not quite answerable for your actions," I replied.

"Yes," she continued; "I am over-strained—over-anxious —not quite accountable—yes—that is it—but you will not tell Mr. Curwen—Oh, be merciful to me, I beg of you. We shall soon reach St. Petersburg. Wait, at least, until we get there before you tell him—promise me that. Tell him then if you like—tell all the world, then, if you choose to do so, but respect my secret until we reach Russia."

As Miss Sorensen spoke, she laid her hand on my arm— she looked at me with a passion which seemed absolutely inadequate to her very poor reason for going through this extraordinary deception.

"Promise me," she said—"there's Sister Hagar's knock at the door—let her in—but promise me first."

"I will think the whole case over carefully before I speak to anyone about it," I replied. I threw the door open as I spoke, and went out of the little cabin as Sister Hagar came in.

That afternoon Curwen asked me about Miss Sorensen.

"I will tell you all about the case in a short time," I said. "There is a mystery which the young lady has divulged, and which she has earnestly implored of me to respect until we reach St. Petersburg."

"Then you believe she can be cured?"

"Unquestionably—but it is a strange story, and it is impossible for me to discuss it until I can give you my full confidence. In the meantime, there is nothing to be done in the medical way for Miss Sorensen—I should recommend her to keep on deck as much as possible—she is in a highly hysterical state, and the more fresh air she gets, the better."

Curwen was obliged to be satisfied with this very lame summary of the case, and the next time I saw Miss Sorensen, I bent over her and told her that I intended to respect her secret until after we had arrived at St. Petersburg.

"I don't know how to thank you enough," she said—her eyes flashed with joy, and she became instantly one of the most animated and fascinating women on board.

At last we reached the great northern port, and first amongst those to come on board the *Ariadne* was the tall and aristocratic form of Professor Sorensen. I happened to witness the meeting between him and his beautiful niece. He stooped down and kissed her on her white brow. A flush of scarlet spread all over her face as he did so. They spoke a few words together—then Sister Hagar came up and touched Miss Sorensen on her arm. The next moment I was requested to come and speak to the young lady.

" May I introduce you to my uncle, Dr. Halifax ? " she said. " Professor Sorensen—Dr. Halifax. I can scarcely tell you, Uncle Oscar," continued the young lady, looking full in his face, "how good Dr. Halifax has been to me during my voyage."

Professor Sorensen made a polite rejoinder to this, and immediately invited me to come to see him at his palace in the Nevski Prospect.

I was about to refuse with all the politeness I could muster, when Miss Sorensen gave me a glance of such terrible entreaty that it staggered me, and almost threw me off my balance.

"You will come ; you must come," she said.

"I can take no refusal," exclaimed the Professor. "I am delighted to welcome you as a brother in the great world of medical science. I have no doubt that we shall have much of interest to talk over together. My laboratory has the good fortune to be somewhat celebrated, and I have made experiments in the cultivation of microbes which I should like to talk over with you. You will do me the felicity of dining with me this evening, Dr. Halifax ? "

I considered the situation briefly—I glanced again at Miss Sorensen.

" I will come," I said—she gave a sigh of relief, and lowered her eyes.

Professor Sorensen moved away, and Sister Hagar went into the young lady's cabin to fetch something. For a moment Miss Sorensen and I were alone. She gave me an imperious gesture to come close to her.

" Sit on that chair—stoop down, I don't want others to know," she said.

I obeyed her in some surprise.

" You have been good, more than good," she said, " and I

respect you. I thank you from my heart. Do one last thing for me."

"What is that?"

"Don't tell our secret to Maurice Curwen until you have returned from dining with my uncle. Promise me this; I have a very grave reason for asking it of you."

"I shall probably not have time to tell him between now and this evening," I said, "as I mean immediately to land and occupy myself looking over the place."

At this moment Sister Hagar appeared, carrying all kinds of rugs and parcels—amongst them was a small, brass-bound box, which seemed to be of considerable weight. As she approached us, the nurse knocked her foot against a partition in the deck, stumbled, and would have fallen had I not gone to her assistance. At the same time the heavy, brass-bound box fell with some force to the ground. The shock must have touched some secret spring, for the cover immediately bounced open and several packets of papers were strewn on the deck. I stooped to pick them up, but Nurse Hagar wrenched them from my hands with such force that I could not help glancing at her in astonishment. One packet had been thrown to a greater distance than the others. I reached back my hand to pick it up, and, as I did so, my eyes lighted on a name in small black characters on the cover. The name was Olga Krestofski. Below it was something which looked like hieroglyphics, but I knew enough of the Russian tongue to ascertain that it was the same name in Russ— with the figure 7 below it.

I returned the packet to the nurse—she gave me a glance which I was destined to remember afterwards—and Miss Sorensen uttered a faint cry and turned suddenly white to her lips.

Professor Sorensen came hastily up—he administered a restorative to his niece, and said that the excitement of seeing him had evidently been too much for her in her weak state. A moment later the entire party had left the yacht.

It was night when I got to the magnificent palace in the Nevski Prospect where Professor Sorensen resided.

I was received with ceremony by several servants in handsome livery, and conducted immediately to a bedroom on the first floor of the building. The room was of colossal size and height, and, warm as the weather still was, was artificially heated by pipes which ran along the walls. The hangings and all the other appointments of the apartment were of the costliest, and as I looked around me, I could not help coming to the conclusion that a Court physician at St. Petersburg must hold a very lucrative position.

Having already made my toilet, I was about to leave the room to find my way as best I could to the reception-rooms on the ground floor, when, to my unbounded amazement, I saw the massive oak door of the chamber quickly and silently open and Miss Sorensen, magnificently dressed, with diamonds in her black hair and flashing round her slim white throat, came in. She had not made the slightest sound in opening the door, and now she put her finger to her lips to enjoin silence on my part. She closed the door gently behind her, and, coming up to my side, pressed a note into my hand. She then turned to go.

"What is the meaning of this?" I began.

"The note will tell you," she replied. "Oh, yes, I am well, quite well—I have told my uncle all about my deception on board the *Ariadne*. For God's sake don't keep me now. If I am discovered, all is lost."

She reached the door as she spoke, opened it with a deft, swift, absolutely silent movement, and disappeared.

I could not tell why, but when I was left once more alone, I felt a chill running through me. I went deliberately to the oak door and turned the key in the heavy lock. The splendid bedroom was bright as day with electric light. Standing by the door, I opened Miss Sorensen's note. My horrified eyes fell on the following words :—

"We receive no mercy, and we give none. Your doom was nearly fixed when you found out the secret of my false paralysis on board the *Ariadne*. It was absolutely and irrevocably sealed when you saw my real name on the packet of letters which fell out of the brass-bound box to-day. The secret of my return to Russia is death to those who discover it unbidden.

"It is decreed by those who never alter or change, that you do not leave this palace alive. It is utterly hopeless for you to try to escape, for on all hands the doors are guarded ; and even if you did succeed in reaching the streets, we have plenty of emissaries there to do our work for us. You know enough of our secrets to make your death desirable—it is therefore arranged that *you are to die.* I like you and pity you. I have a heart, and you have touched it. If I can, I will save you. I do this at the risk of my life, but that does not matter—we hold our lives cheap—we always carry them in our hands, and are ready to lay them down at any instant. I may not succeed in saving you, but I will try. I am not quite certain how your death is to be accomplished, but I have a very shrewd suspicion of the manner in which the final attack on your life will be made. Your only chance—remember, your only chance—of escape, is to appear to know absolutely nothing—to show not the ghost of a suspicion of any underhand practices; to put forth all your powers to fascinate and please Professor Sorensen and the guests who will dine with us to-night. Show no surprise at anything you see—ask no impertinent questions. I have watched you, and I believe you are clever enough and have sufficient nerve to act as I suggest. Pay me all the attention in your power—make love to me even a little, if you like—that will not matter, for we shall never meet again after to-night. After dinner you will be invited to accompany Professor Sorensen to his laboratory—he will ask no other guest to do this. On no account refuse—go with him and I will go with you. Where he goes and where I go, follow without flinching. If you feel astonishment, do not show it. And now, all that I have said, leads up to this final remark. *Avoid the seventh step.* Bear this in your mind—it is your last chance.—DAGMAR."

I read this note over twice. The terrible feeling of horror left me after the second reading. I felt braced and resolute. I suspected, what was indeed the case, that I had fallen unwittingly into a hornet's nest of Nihilists. How mad I had been to come to Professor Sorensen's palace! I had fully made up my mind that Miss Sorensen had told me lies, when she gave me her feeble reasons for acting as she had done on board the *Ariadne.* No matter that now, however. She spoke the truth at last. The letter I crushed in my hand was not a lie. I resolved to be wary, guarded—and when the final moment came, to sell my life dearly.

I had a box of matches in my pocket. I burnt the note to white ash, and then crushed the ashes to powder under my foot. I then went downstairs.

Servants were standing about, who quickly directed me to the reception-rooms. A powdered footman flung the door of the great drawing-room open and called my name in a ringing voice. Professor Sorensen came forward to meet me. A lady also came up at the same moment and held out her hand. She was dressed in black velvet, with rich lace and many magnificent diamonds. They shone in her sandy hair, and glistened round her thin throat. I started back in amazement. Here was Sister Hagar metamorphosed.

"Allow me to introduce my wife, Madame Sorensen," said the Professor.

Madame Sorensen raised a playful finger and smiled into my face.

"You look astonished, and no wonder, Dr. Halifax," she said. "But, ah, how naughty you have been to read our secrets." She turned away to speak to another guest. The next moment dinner was announced.

As we sat round the dinner table, we made a large party. Men and women of many nationalities were present, but I quickly perceived, to my own surprise, that I was the guest of the evening. To me was given the terribly doubtful honour of escorting Madame Sorensen to the head of her table, and in honour of me also, English—by common consent—was the language spoken at dinner.

Miss Sorensen sat a little to my left—she spoke gaily to her neighbour, and her ringing, silvery laugh floated often to my ears. There had been some little excitement caused by the bursting of a large bomb in one of the principal streets that evening. Inadvertently I alluded to it to my hostess. She bent towards me and said, in a low voice :—

"Excuse me, Dr. Halifax, but we never talk politics in Petersburg."

She had scarcely said this before she began to rattle off some brilliant opinions with regard to a novel which was just then attracting public attention in England. Her remarks were terse, cynical, and intensely to the point. From one subject of interest to another she leaped, showing discernment, discrimination, and a wide and exhaustive knowledge of everything she touched upon.

I listened to her and replied as pertinently as possible. A sudden idea came to me which brought considerable comfort with it. I began to feel more and more assured that Miss Sorensen's letter was but the ugly result of a mind thrown slightly off its balance. The brilliant company in which I found myself, the splendid room, the gracefully appointed table, the viands and the wines of the best and the choicest, my cultivated and gracious hostess—Professor Sorensen's worn, noble, strictly intellectual face—surely all these things had nothing whatever to do with treachery and assassination! Miss Sorensen's mind was off its balance. This fact accounted for everything—for the malingering which had taken place on board the *Ariadne*—for the queer letter which she had given to me before dinner. " *When you saw my real name to-day, your doom was irrevocably sealed*," she said. " *Avoid the seventh step*," she had continued. Could anything be more utterly absurd? Miss Sorensen was the acknowledged niece of my courtly host—what did she mean by attributing another name to herself?—what did she mean by asking me to avoid the seventh step? In short, her words were exactly like the ravings of a lunatic.

My heart, which had been beating uncomfortably high and strong, calmed down under these reflections, but presently a queer, cold, uncomfortable recollection touched it into fresh action as if with the edge of bare steel.

It was all very well to dispose of Miss Sorensen by treating her wild words as the emanations of a diseased brain; but what about Madame Sorensen? How was I possibly to account for her queer change of identity? I recalled her attitude on board the *Ariadne*. The malevolent glances she had often cast at me. The look on her face that very morning when I had saved her from falling, and picked up the papers which had fallen out of the brass-bound box. She had seen my eyes rest upon the name " Olga Krestofski." I could not soon forget the expression in her cold eyes when I returned her that packet. A thrill ran through me even now, as I recalled the vengeance of that glance.

The ladies withdrew, and the men of the party did not stay long over wine. We went to the drawing-rooms, where music and light conversation were indulged in.

As soon as we came in, Miss Sorensen, who was standing alone in a distant part of the inner drawing-room, gave me a look which brought me to her side. There was an imperious sort of command in her full, dark eyes. She held herself very erect. Her carriage was queenly—the lovely carnation of excitement bloomed on her cheeks and gave the finishing touch to her remarkable beauty. She made way for me to sit on the sofa beside her, and bending her head slightly in my direction, seemed to invite me to make love to her.

There was something in her eyes which revived me like a tonic.

I felt suddenly capable of rising to my terrible position, and resolved to play the game out to the bitter end.

I began to talk to Miss Sorensen in a gay tone of light badinage, to which she responded with spirit.

Suddenly, as the conversation arose full and animated around us, she dropped her voice, gave me a look which thrilled me, and said, with slow distinctness :—

"You Englishmen have pluck—I—I admire you !"

I answered, with a laugh, "We like to think of ourselves as a plucky race."

"You are! you are! I felt sure you would be capable of doing what you are now doing. Let us continue our conversation—nothing could be better for my purpose—don't you observe that Hagar is watching us ?"

"Is not Madame Sorensen your aunt ?" I asked.

"In reality she is no relation ; but, hush, you are treading on dangerous ground."

"It is time for me to say farewell," I said, rising suddenly to my feet—I held out my hand to her as I spoke.

"No, you must not go yet," she said—she rose also—a certain nervous hesitation was observable for a moment in her manner, but she quickly steadied herself.

"Uncle Oscar, come here," she called out.   Professor Sorensen happened to be approaching us across the drawing-room—he came up hastily at her summons.   She stood in such a position that he could not see her face, and then gave me a look of intense warning.

When she did this, I knew that the gleam of hope which had given me false courage for a moment during dinner was at an end.   There was no insanity in those lovely eyes.   Her look braced me, however.   I determined to take example by her marvellous coolness.   In short, I resolved to do what she asked me, and to place my life in her hands.

"Uncle Oscar," said the young lady, "Dr. Halifax insists upon leaving us early ; that is scarcely fair, is it ?"

"It must not be permitted, Dr. Halifax," said the Professor, in his most courteous tone.   "I am looking forward with great interest to getting your opinion on several points

of scientific moment." Here he drew me a little aside.
I glanced at Miss Sorensen : she came a step or two
nearer.

"You will permit me to say that your name is already
known to me," continued my host, "and I esteem it an
honour to have the privilege of your acquaintance. I should
like to get your opinion with regard to the bacterial theory
of research. As I told you on board the *Ariadne* to-day, I
have made many experiments in the isolation of microbes."

"In short, the isolation of those little horrors is my uncle's
favourite occupation," interrupted Miss Sorensen, with a light
laugh. "Suppose, Uncle Oscar," she continued, laying a
lovely white hand on the Professor's arm—"suppose we take
Dr. Halifax to the laboratory? He can then see some of
your experiments."

"The cultivation of the cancer microbe, for instance," said
Sorensen. "Ah, that we could discover something to destroy
it in the human body, without also destroying life ! Well,
doubtless, the time will come." He sighed as he spoke.
His thoughtful face assumed an expression of keen intellectu-
ality. It would be difficult to see anyone whose expression
showed more noble interest in science.

" I observe that all my guests are happily engaged," he
continued. "Shall we follow Dagmar's suggestion, then, and
come to the laboratory, Dr. Halifax ? "

" I shall be interested to see what you have done," I said.

We left the drawing-rooms. As we passed Madame
Sorensen, she called out to me to know if I were leaving.

"No," I replied ; "I am going with your husband to his
laboratory. He has kindly promised to show me some of
his experiments."

"Ah, then, I will say good-night, and—farewell. When
Oscar goes to the laboratory he forgets the existence of time.
Farewell, Dr. Halifax." She touched my hand with her thin
fingers ; her light eyes gave a queer vindictive flash. Fare-
well, or, *au revoir*, if you prefer it," she said, with a laugh.
She turned abruptly to speak to another guest.

To reach the laboratory we had to walk down more than
one long corridor—it was in a wing at some little distance from
the rest of the house. Professor Sorensen explained the reason
briefly.

"I make experiments," he said ; "it is more convenient,

therefore, to have the laboratory as distant from the dwelling-house as possible."

We finally passed through a narrow covered passage.

"Beneath here flows the Neva," said the Professor; "but here," he continued, "did you ever see a more spacious and serviceable room for real hard work than this?"

He flung open the door of the laboratory as he spoke, and touching a button in the wall, flooded the place on the instant with a blaze of electric light. The laboratory was warmed with hot pipes, and contained, in addition to the usual appliances, a couple of easy chairs and one or two small tables; also a long and particularly inviting-looking couch.

"I spend the night here occasionally," said Dr. Sorensen. "When I am engaged in an important experiment, I often do not care to leave the place until the early hours of the morning,"

We wandered about the laboratory, which was truly a splendid room and full of many objects which would, on another occasion, have aroused all my scientific enthusiasm, but I was too intensely on my guard just now to pay much attention to the Professor's carefully worded and elaborate descriptions. My quick eyes had taken in the whole situation as far as it was at present revealed to me: the iron bands of the strong door by which we had entered; the isolation of the laboratory. I was young and strong, however, and Professor Sorenson was old. If it came to a hand-to-hand fight, he would have no chance against me. Miss Sorensen, too, was my friend.

We spent some time examining various objects of interest, then finding the torture of suspense unendurable, I said, abruptly: "I should greatly like to see your process of culti-vation of the cancer microbes before I take my leave."

"I will show it to you," said Dr. Sorensen. "Dagmar, my love, light the lantern."

"Is it not here?" I asked.

"No; I keep it in an oven in a small laboratory, which we will now visit."

Miss Sorensen took up a silver-mounted lantern, applied a match to the candle within, and taking it in her hand, preceded us up the whole length of the laboratory to a door which I had not before noticed, and which was situated just

behind Dr. Sorensen's couch. She opened it and waited for
us to come up to her.

"Take the lantern and go first, Uncle Oscar," said the
young lady. She spoke in an imperious voice, and I saw the
Professor give her a glance of slight surprise.

"Won't you go first, Dagmar?" he said. "Dr. Halifax
can follow you, and I will come up in the rear."

She put the lantern into his hand.

"No, go first," she said, with a laugh which was a little
unsteady. "No one knows your private haunts as well as you
do yourself. Dr. Halifax will follow me."

The Professor took the lantern without another word. He
began to descend some narrow and steep stairs. They were
carpeted, and appeared, as far as I could see through the
gloom, to lead into another passage farther down. Miss
Sorensen followed her uncle immediately. As he did so, she
threw her head back and gave me a warning glance.

"Take care, the stairs are steep," she said. "Count them;
I will count them for you. I wish, Uncle Oscar, you would
have this passage properly lighted."

"Come on, Dagmar: what are you lingering for?" called
the Professor.

"Follow me, Dr. Halifax," she said. Her hand just
touched mine—it burnt like coal. "These horrid stairs,"
she said. "I really must count them, or I'll fall." She
began to count immediately in a sing-song, monotonous voice,
throwing her words back at me, so that I doubt if the
Professor heard them.

"One," she began, "two—three—four—five—six." When
she had counted to six, she made an abrupt pause. We stood
side by side on the sixth step.

"Seven is the perfect number," she said, in my ear—as she
spoke, she pushed back her arm and thrust me forcibly back
as I was about to advance. At the same instant, the dim
light of the lantern went out, and I distinctly heard the door
by which we had entered this narrow passage close behind us.
We were in the dark. I was about to call out: "Miss
Sorensen—Professor Sorensen," when a horrid noise fell upon
my ears. It was the heavy sound as of a falling body. It
went down, down, making fearful echoes as it banged against
the sides of what must have been a deep well. Presently
there was a splash, as if it had dropped into water.

The splash was a revelation. The body, whatever it was, had doubtless dropped into the Neva. At the same instant Miss Sorensen's mysterious words returned to my memory: "Avoid the seventh step." I remembered that we had gone down six steps, and that as we descended, she had counted them one by one. On the edge of the sixth step she had pushed me back, and then had disappeared. The Professor had also vanished. What body was that which had fallen through space into a deep and watery grave? Miss Sorensen's mysterious remark was at last abundantly plain. *There was no seventh step*—by this trap, therefore, but for her interference, I was to be hurled into eternity.

I sank back, trembling in every limb. The horror of my situation can scarcely be described. At any moment the Professor might return, and by a push from above, send me into my watery grave. In my present position, I had no chance of fighting for my life. I retraced my steps to the door of the upper laboratory and felt vainly all along its smooth, hard surface. No chance of escape came from there. I sat down presently on the edge of the first step, and waited for the end with what patience I could. I still believed in Miss Sorensen, but would it be possible for her to come to my rescue? The silence and darkness of the grave surrounded me. Was I never to see daylight again? I recalled Madame Sorensen's face when she said "farewell"— I recalled the passion of despair in Miss Sorensen's young voice. I had touched secrets inadvertently with which I had no right to meddle. My death was desired by the Invincible and the Merciless—of course, I must die. As I grew accustomed to the darkness and stillness—the stillness itself was broken by the gurgling, distant sound of running water— I could hear the flow of the Neva as it rushed past my dark grave.

At the same moment the sound of voices fell on my ear. They were just below me—I felt my heart beating almost to suffocation. I clenched my hands tightly together—surely the crucial moment had come—could I fight for my life?

The Professor's thin, polished tones fell like ice on my heart.

"We had better go back and see that all is safe," he said. "Of course, he must have fallen over, but it is best to be certain."

"No, no, Uncle Oscar, it is not necessary," I heard Miss Sorensen reply. "Did you not hear the sound—the awful sound—of his falling body? I did. I heard a splash as it fell into the Neva."

"Yes, I fancy I did hear it," answered the Professor, in a reflective voice.

"Then don't go back—why should we? It is all so horrible—let us return to the drawing-rooms as quickly as possible."

"You are excited, my dear—your voice trembles—what is the matter with you?"

"Only joy," she replied, "at having got rid of a dangerous enemy—now let us go."

Their voices died away—I could even hear the faint echo of their footsteps as they departed. I wondered how much longer I was to remain in my fearful grave. Had I the faintest chance of escaping the doom for which I was intended? Would Miss Sorensen be true to the end? She, doubtless, was a Nihilist, and as she said herself, they received no mercy and gave none. My head began to whirl—queer and desperate thoughts visited me. I felt my nerves tottering, and trembled, for a brief moment, for my reason. Suddenly a hand touched my arm, and a voice, clear, distinct, but intensely low, spoke to me.

"Thank God, you are here—come with me at once—don't ask a question—come noiselessly, and at once. I rose to my feet—Miss Sorensen's hot fingers clasped mine—she did not speak — she drew me forward. Once again I felt myself descending the steps. We came to the bottom of the sixth step. "This way," she said, in a muffled tone. She felt with her hands against the wall—a panel immediately gave way, and we found ourselves in a narrow passage, with a very faint light at the farther end. Miss Sorensen hurried me along. We went round a sort of semi-circular building, until at last we reached a small postern door in the wall. When we came to it she opened it a few inches, and pushed me out.

"Farewell," she said then. "I have saved your life. Farewell, brave Englishman."

She was about to shut the door in my face, but I pushed it back forcibly.

"I will not go until you tell me the meaning of this," I said.

"You are mad to linger," she replied, "but I will tell you in

a few words.   Professor Sorensen and his wife are no relations
of mine.   I am Olga Krestofski, suspected by the police, the
owner of important secrets : in short, the head of a branch of
the Nihilists.   I shammed illness, and assumed the name
under which I travelled, in order to convey papers of vast importance to our cause, to St. Petersburg.   Professor Sorensen,
as Court physician, has not yet incurred the faintest breath of
suspicion—nevertheless, he is one of the leaders of our party,
and every individual with whom you dined to-night belongs to
us.   It was decreed that you were to die.   I decided otherwise.
There was, as you doubtless have discovered, *no* seventh step.
I warned you, and you had presence of mind sufficient not to
continue your perilous downward course beyond the edge of
the sixth step."

"But I heard a body fall," I said.

"Precisely," she replied ; "I placed a bag of sand on the
edge of the sixth step shortly after my arrival this morning,
and just as I was following Professor Sorensen through the
secret panel in the wall into the passage beyond, I pushed the
bag over.   This was necessary in order to deceive the Professor.
He heard it splash into the water, and I was able to assure
him that it was your body.   Otherwise he would inevitably have
returned to complete his deadly work.   Now, good-bye—
forgive me, if you can."

"Why did you bring me here at all ? " I asked.

"It was your only chance.   Madame Sorensen had resolved
that you were to die.   You would have been followed to the
ends of the earth—now you are safe, because Professor and
Madame Sorensen think you are dead."

"And you ? " I said suddenly.   " If by any chance this is
discovered, what will become of you ? "

There was a passing gleam of light from a watery moon—it
fell on Miss Sorensen's white face.

"I hold my life cheap," she said.   "Farewell.   Don't stay
long in St. Petersburg."

She closed the postern door as she spoke.

THE SILENT TONGUE

THE SILENT TONGUE

IT was a day in late October when I found myself in a train which was to convey me from Waterloo to Salisbury. I was on my way to pay a week's visit to my old friend and patient, General Romney. After retiring from active service he had bought a place in Wiltshire, and had repeatedly begged of me to come to see him there.

My multifarious duties, however, had hitherto made it impossible for me to visit High Court; but the present occasion was of such special moment that I determined to make a great effort to gratify my old friend, and do myself a pleasure at the same time.

I was to arrive at High Court on Thursday afternoon, and on the following Tuesday, Iris Romney, the General's beautiful and only daughter, was to be married to a young man of the name of Vane, a captain in the —th Lancers. I had known Iris from her childhood, and was prepared to congratulate her now on a most suitable match. From the letters which I had received from General Romney, Captain Vane was all that was desirable: an upright, good, honourable fellow. His position in society was well assured, and he had ample means.

"It is not only that Vane is all that her mother and I could desire," continued the General, in his last letter to me, "but there is another reason which makes this marriage a relief to our minds. Our poor Iris, whose beauty, as you know, is much above the average, has been persecuted for many months past by the unwelcome and, I may almost add, the unscrupulous attentions of our next-door neighbour, the squire of this place, an ungentlemanly boor of the name of Ransome. The fellow won't take 'No' for an answer, and things have come to such a pass that Iris is quite afraid to go out alone, as Ransome is sure to waylay her, and renew his unwelcome protestations and demands. Indeed, were it not for this happy marriage, we should have been obliged, for our child's sake, to leave High Court."

I paid little heed to this part of my friend's letter when reading it, but it was destined to be brought very vividly before my mind later on.

I arrived at High Court about three o'clock in the after. noon, and found Iris standing in the square entrance-hall. She was surrounded by dogs, and was pulling on a pair of gauntlet gloves ; she wore a hat, and was, evidently, in the act of going out. On hearing my steps, she turned quickly and came eagerly to meet me.

"Here you are," she exclaimed, holding out both her hands. "How nice! how delightful! Am I much altered, Dr. Halifax —would you recognise me ?"

"Yes, I should recognise you," I answered, looking with admiration at the lovely girl. "You have changed, of course. How tall you are! You were only a child when I saw you last."

"I was fifteen," answered Iris; "the most troublesome monkey in existence. Now I am eighteen—quite grown up. Well, it is a real pleasure to see you again. Let me take you to father : he has been talking of nothing but your arrival all day."

I accompanied Miss Romney to her father's study. To her surprise it was empty.

"Where can father be ?" she exclaimed. "He knew you would arrive about now. Perhaps he has gone to lie down— he has not been quite well. We won't disturb him, unless you particularly wish it, Dr. Halifax ?"

"Certainly not," I replied.

"Mother is out—she had to go to Salisbury on business. May I have the pleasure of your society all to myself for a little ? I am just going out to meet Captain Vane—will you come with me? I should much like to introduce him to you."

"And I should like to know him," I replied. "Let us go for a walk, by all means—there is nothing I should enjoy more."

We went out together. Miss Romney's step was full of the light spring of youth. She entertained me with many animated remarks, and took me to several points of interest in the beautiful grounds. From a place called "The Mound" we could see the long, evening shadows falling across Salisbury

Plain; turning to our right we got a peep, in the dim distance, of the far-famed Cathedral.

"Yes, it is all lovely," she cried, "and I am in the mood to enjoy it to-day—I am very happy. I do not mind telling you how happy I am, for you are such an old friend."

"You may be sure I rejoice to hear of your happiness," I replied. I looked at her as I spoke. She was standing at a little distance from me, very upright. The dogs had followed us, and a great mastiff stood near her. She rested her white hand on his head. Some rays from the evening sun sparkled in her hair, which was very bright in hue, and looked now like burnished gold. Her eyes, full of happiness, looked frankly into mine. They were lovely eyes, with a tender, womanly expression in them. I thought what a happy fellow Vane would be.

As we were standing together the silence was suddenly broken by the sharp report of a gun.

"Who can possibly be shooting in our grounds?" exclaimed Miss Romney.

"The report came from that copse," I answered her— "down there to our left. Perhaps Captain Vane is amusing himself having a shot or two."

"He did not take his gun with him," she answered; "I saw it in the hall as we passed through just now. No, I am afraid I guess who did fire the shot"; she paused suddenly, and a hot flush of annoyance swept over her face. It passed almost as quickly as it came.

"There is David," she said, in a glad voice. "Do you see him? He is just coming up that path through the trees. Let us go to meet him."

We soon reached the bottom of the mound, and Captain Vane came quickly up to us. He was a tall, well-made man, of about twenty-eight years of age. His face was moulded in strong lines. He was somewhat dark in complexion, and had resolute eyes.

"David, this is our old friend, Doctor Halifax," said Miss Romney.

"I am glad to meet you," said Vane to me. He made one or two further remarks of an indifferent character.

We turned presently to go back to the house. We had only gone about half the distance when Iris uttered a horrified exclamation.

"What is that on your handkerchief?" she cried to her lover.

He had pulled his handkerchief out of his pocket. He looked at it when she spoke, started, and turned pale.

"I must apologise to you both," he exclaimed. "How stupid of me; I forgot all about it."

"Your handkerchief is all over blood. Have you hurt yourself?" asked Iris.

"No, not a bit of it!" He thrust the handkerchief out of sight. "The fact is simply this. That brute of a Ransome has been shooting round the premises this morning, and, like the cur he is, has only half done his work. This handkerchief is stained because I have been putting a pheasant out of his misery. It was a horrid sight. Don't let us talk about it any more."

"I had a premonition that Mr. Ransome was somewhere near," said Iris. "The mere thought of that man affects me disagreeably."

She shivered as she spoke. Vane looked at her, but did not reply. Their eyes met—he gave her a quick smile, but I could not help noticing that he looked pale and worried.

We reached the house; Mrs. Romney came out to meet us. She gave me a hearty welcome, and asked me to go with her at once to her husband.

"The General is lying down in his study, Dr. Halifax, or he would come to you," she explained. "The fact is, he has not been well for some days, and just now I found him trembling violently, and scarcely able to stand. Oh, I do not think there is much the matter—he will be all right by-and-by, and nothing will do him more good than a quiet chat with you."

I followed Mrs. Romney to the study. The General was lying on a sofa, but when we approached, he rose quickly, and came to meet us. He was a tall, largely-made man, somewhat full in habit, and with a fresh-coloured face. That face now was flushed, and his eyes looked suspiciously bright.

"Welcome," he exclaimed, holding out both his hands to me. "Here I am, and nothing whatever the matter with me. I had an attack of giddiness, but it has passed off. Has my wife been making out that I am an invalid, eh? Well, I never felt better in my life. It would be a shabby trick to play on you, Halifax, to bring you down here, and then give you doctoring work to do."

"I am always prepared for doctoring work," I answered, "but I am delighted to see you so fit, General."

"You can leave us now, Mary," said the General, turning to his wife, and giving her an affectionate glance. "The giddiness has quite passed, my love, and a chat with Halifax will do me more good than anything else."

Mrs. Romney went immediately away. The moment she did so, the General sank into an arm-chair, and covered his eyes with one of his hands. I noticed that his big hand shook.

"The fact is," he said, in an altered tone, "I am *not* quite the thing. I did not want the wife to know, nor Iris, bless her. You are aware, or perhaps you are not, that there is to be a dance here to-night, Halifax—it would never do for an old chap like me to spoil sport. You have just come in the nick of time. Give me something to steady my nerves."

I prescribed a simple dose, the ingredients for which were fortunately close at hand. I mixed it, and General Romney took the glass from my hand and quickly drained off the contents.

"It takes a good bit out of a man to part with his only child," he said. "I consider myself, however, the luckiest father in existence. There never was a better fellow than Vane. You have seen him. What do you make of him, eh?"

"I have scarcely spoken two dozen words to Captain Vane," I said.

"What does that signify? You are a keen observer of character. What do you make of the lad?"

"I like what I have seen of him," I replied.

"I am delighted to hear you say that," exclaimed the General. "When I tell you that I consider Vane worthy of Iris, you will understand that I cannot give him higher praise. They are devoted to one another, and as happy as children. We shall have a gay time until the wedding is over. To-night there is to be a dance; to-morrow we go to the Sinclairs', for a farewell dinner; the next day—but I need not recount all our gaieties to you, Halifax. Your dose has done me good—I feel as well as ever I did in my life at the present moment."

The General certainly looked more like himself. The violent colour on his face had subsided; his eyes were still too excited, though, to please me, and I purposely led the conversation to every-day subjects.

There was a large dinner-party at High Court that evening. This was to be followed by a dance, to which a number of guests had been invited.

Iris sat near me at dinner—she wore white, which suited her well. Her face was so vivacious, her hair so bright, the sparkle in her flashing eyes gave so much light and movement to her expression, that no vivid colour was needed to set off her remarkable beauty. Vane sat opposite to his bride-elect, and I found myself looking at him several times during dinner with much interest. He was on the whole the most silent of the party, and I guessed him to be a man of few words, but I felt certain by the thoughtful gleam in his eyes and the firm cut of his lips that he was one to be relied on and rested upon in the battle of life.

Immediately after dinner, the ladies went upstairs to re-arrange their dresses for the coming ball, and General Romney motioned me up to his end of the table. He resumed the conversation we had had before dinner, and assured me several times in a low voice that the medicine I had given him had completely removed the nervous attack from which he had been suffering when I first saw him.

"Not that I have been at all the thing for some time," he added; "but we'll talk of my ailments when the ball is over. Nothing must interfere with Iris's bridal ball, bless her."

We did not stay long over wine, and I presently found myself standing in the great central hall. A footman came up to place some fresh logs on the glowing fire. As he did so he glanced at me once or twice in a queer, nervous sort of manner. Suddenly he looked behind him, found that we were alone, and said, in a hurried, eager voice:—

"You are the doctor from London, ain't you, sir?"

"Yes," I answered, in some surprise.

"Might I speak to you for a moment, sir? I have something to say—something that must be told. Might I see you by yourself, doctor—I won't keep you a minute?"

"Certainly," I replied; "say what you have got to say at once."

The man's manner alarmed me, he was shaking all over.

"On this night, of all nights," he said. "'T will upset the General, for certain. Oh, sir, what is to be done?"

"If you will tell me what the news is, I can, perhaps, answer your question," I replied. "Now, pull yourself together, and tell me what is the matter."

The man stood up.

"It's a tragedy," he began, "and has happened, so to speak, at our gates. It's this: Squire Ransome was found dead in the copse at the back of the house, not an hour ago. He was lying on his face and hands with his skull smashed in, and his gun lying by his side. They have took him home, and they say there's to be a warrant took out immediately for the arrest of the murderer. Who could have done it? I wouldn't have the General know this for £500."

Some people came into the hall; I turned quickly to the man.

"Hush," I said, in a peremptory voice; "keep your information to yourself for the present. If this thing is kept from the family until after the ball, so much the better. You were right to tell me, and we must trust that nothing will be known here until to-morrow."

The man nodded and walked away. Vane approached me at that moment, and taking my arm led me to the ball-room.

"The band has just struck up," he said. "Iris and I are going to open the ball, as a matter of course, but no doubt she will want you to be her partner in one or two dances later on."

"I hope she will," I replied.

"There she is; let us go to her," said Vane.

We walked up a long and splendidly decorated ball-room. Iris was standing beside her father and mother, near the principal entrance. They were busily engaged receiving guest after guest, who arrived continuously. In a few moments the great room was full of animated couples whirling round to the music of a splendid string band, which had been brought from London for the occasion. Vane and Iris opened the dance together. All eyes followed the graceful pair as they flew around in the giddy mazes of the waltz. Iris's face looked so animated, and there was such a flashing brilliancy about her eyes, that I began to compare her to her quaint name, and to think that she had some of the many lights of the rainbow, in its shifting, changing colours, about her.

One dance was quickly followed by another. General Romney and his wife still stood near the entrance. I noticed to my dismay that the deep, crimson flush which had some-what alarmed me in the General's appearance before dinner had again returned. He was a man of full habit, and I did not like the glittering light in his eyes. I sincerely hoped for every reason, that the terrible tragedy which had taken place in the copse before dinner would not reach his ears until the evening's amusement was over. For a time I stood rather apart from the gay and brilliant throng. Iris had promised to give me one or two dances, but our turn had not come yet.

As I stood and waited, I recalled the sound I had heard when I stood with Miss Romney on the mound. "At that moment, in all probability, the murder was being committed," I said to myself. "But, no, that could not have been the case, for the unfortunate Squire was found with his skull broken in; he could not have come by his death from a gunshot wound."

At that moment Miss Romney made her way to my side.

"Ours is the next dance," she said, looking into my face, "but——" she hesitated.

"What is it?" I asked, smiling at her.

"I am tired, I do not want to dance," she said. "Shall we sit this waltz out? Will you come with me to the conservatory, it is so hot here?"

"With pleasure," I replied.

She put her slim hand on my arm, and we left the ball-room. We had to cross the great hall to reach a large conservatory at the further end.

"I am anxious to have a talk with you," said the young girl, almost in a whisper, as we pushed our way through the throngs of guests. "I have known you since I was a child, and I am anxious——"

We had almost reached the conservatory now, but before we entered, Iris Romney turned and faced me.

"Dr. Halifax," she said, "is my father well?"

I was about to answer her, when a commotion behind caused us both to turn our heads. A man who was neither a a guest nor a servant had pushed his way into the hall. He was a dark man, plainly dressed. Two of the powdered foot-men had come up and were speaking to him. They seemed to be expostulating with him, and he appeared to be resisting them. One of the servants put his hand on the man's arm;

he pushed him impatiently aside, and came farther into the hall.

The guests were everywhere—in the hall, on the stairs, trooping in and out of the ball-room. They all stood still now as if moved by a common impulse. Every eye was fixed on the stranger. I suddenly felt that the moment had come for me to interfere. I cannot say what premonition seized me, but I knew beyond the possibility of doubt that that strange, queer-looking man had pushed his way into this festive scene on some terrible errand.

"Pardon me," I said to Iris, "I will just go and speak to that fellow, and be back with you in a minute."

"What can the man want?" exclaimed Iris.

"I will tell you in a moment," I said; "pray stay where you are."

To my annoyance, I found that she was following me.

The servant, Henry by name, who had given me the news of Ransome's death, came eagerly up when he saw me approaching.

"I am glad you are here, Dr. Halifax," he said. "Perhaps you can get Constable Morris to go away. I keep on telling him that he can come back later on."

The footman spoke in a hoarse whisper; agitation had paled his face; he clutched hold of my coat in a sort of nervous frenzy.

"Keep quiet," I said to him, sharply—then I turned to the policeman: "If you have any business here, you had better come into this room," I said.

The room in question was a small smoking-room, the door of which happened to stand open.

"Yes, sir, it would be best," said the man, in a perfectly civil tone. He stepped across the hall immediately—I followed him—Miss Romney did the same.

"Had you not better go away?" I said to her.

"No," she answered, "I prefer to stay and hear the matter out. Why, this is Constable Morris. I know him perfectly well. What do you want here to-night, Morris? You see we are all busy; if you have anything important to say, we can see you at any hour you like to arrange in the morning."

"I must do my work to-night, miss," he answered. "I'd rayther cut off my right hand than give you pain, miss," he continued—"but, there, business is business. A constable's life ain't none too pleasant at times—no, that it ain't."

Here he drew himself up and taking a red pocket handkerchief out of his pocket, wiped the moisture from his brow. His eyes travelled quickly from Iris, in her white dress, to me and then back again to Iris.

"Sir," he said, addressing himself to me, "can't you get Miss Romney to leave the room?"

"I'm afraid I can't," I replied.

"Well, I suppose I must go on with the whole black business afore the young lady. If the thing is done quickly, there's no call for anyone to know, except the family. I beg a thousand pardons for coming into the hall as I've done, but I could not get a servant to hear me in the back premises. My colleague is outside with a trap, and we can take the young gent away as quiet as possible, and no one need know. Lor'! it's sure to turn out a big mistake, but duty is duty."

"What gentleman do you want to take away?" asked Iris, going up and standing opposite to the man. "Is it one of our guests?—which?"

"God Almighty knows, miss, that I don't want to trouble you."

"Speak out, man," I said. "Tell us your business, good or bad, immediately. Can't you see that this suspense is very bad for Miss Romney?"

The man glanced at Iris, but immediately looked down again.

"Well, sir," he said, addressing himself to me, "it's an ugly job, but here is the long and short of it. There has been a murder committed in these grounds. Squire Ransome, of Ransome Heights, was found dead in the copse not three hundred yards from the house. The gamekeeper here and a labourer from the village found him and gave the alarm. He was took home, and I hold a warrant now for the arrest of Captain David Vane on a charge of having murdered him."

"On a charge of what?" said Iris. She had been very pale—as white as death, until the man had finally delivered himself of his cruel errand—then a great wave of brilliant colour flooded her face, and restored the dancing light to her eyes.

"This is such utter folly, that I am not even afraid about it," she said. "Oblige me, Dr. Halifax, by remaining with this man for a few minutes while I go to fetch David. It needs but a word or two to clear him of this monstrous charge."

She drew herself up to her full stately height, and left the room with the air of a queen.

Morris looked after her with a red face and troubled eyes

"·Ef you 'll believe me, sir," he said, "I 'd rayther than five hun dred pounds that I was out of this job—it's a bad business altogether "—here he shook his head ominously.

The constab e had scarcely said the words before Iris returned, accomlpanied by Vane.

"What is all this about?" said Vane. He looked full at the man, then at me.

Iris must have prepared him. He came into the room holding her hand. As he stood and faced the police-constable, he still kept it in a tight grip.

"Is it true," he said, "that I am charged with murder; and that you have a warrant to arrest me?"

"Are you Captain Vane, sir?"

"Yes."

"Then that is what I' ve got to do, I am sorry to say, sir. I 've a trap outside, and my colleague is there, and the best thing we can do is to go off quietly at once. If you 'll give me your word as you 'll not try to escape, Captain Vane, I won't use the handcuffs. It's only to look at you, sir, to know that you're a gent of your word."

"Had you not better leave us, Iris?" said Vane, looking down for the first time at the girl's white face.

"No, I 'll see it out to the end," she answered. "But can't you say something, David? Can't you clear yourself? Can't you put this dreadful thing straight?"

"I can and will, dearest," he replied, in a low tone; "but I 'm afraid I must go with this man to-night."

"There 's no help for it, sir. The warrant must be carried out. The inquest is to be held at the poor gentle-man's own place to-morrow, and, as sure as sure, you 'll be cleared; but now it 's my duty to take you with me, Captain Vane."

"Cheer up, Iris," said Vane. "It is sure to be all right,'

He gave her a smile with his eyes. It was a queer, strong sort of smile, but it never reached his lips.

For the first time poor Iris broke down—she gave a low, heart-broken sob, and covered her face with her trembling hands.

"Take care of her," said Vane to me. "Keep it up if you can until the dance is over, and, above all things, try to conceal this horrid business from General Romney until after the guests have gone."

Here he turned to the policeman.

"I am ready to accompany you," he said. "Will you allow me to fetch my overcoat?"

"I'm afraid, sir, it's my duty not to let you out of my sight; perhaps the other gentleman would bring the coat."

"No, I'll fetch it," said Iris, recovering herself like a flash. "Yes, I wish to fetch it—I know where it is."

She ran out of the room, but had scarcely done so when the door was suddenly flung open and General Romney, holding one hand to his head and stretching the other out before him, as though he were groping blindly in the dark, tottered into our midst.

"What in the name of Heaven is all this about?" he exclaimed. "Vane, what are you doing here? Is not that man Constable Morris? Morris, what is your business in my house at this hour?"

Iris had now returned with the coat. She gave it to Vane, who began to put it on, and then went up to her father.

"Come away, father, do," she said.

"Folly, Iris," he replied; "keep your hand off me. I am not a baby to be coerced in this style. Ah, Halifax, so you are here, too! Now, what's the mischief? Vane, can't you speak? Are you all struck dumb?"

"It's a bad business, sir," said the policeman. "I've a warrant here to arrest this young gentleman, Captain David Vane, on a charge of murder."

"A charge of *murder?*" shouted the General.

"Yes, sir. Squire Ransome has been found in the copse close to this house with his skull knocked in, and there's circumstantial evidence of a grave nature which points to Captain Vane as his murderer. It is my business to arrest him, and——"

"And I will come with you," said Vane. He turned to the
General as he spoke. "I beg of you, General," he said, "to
take Iris away from here. This matter is very horrible, but it
can have only one termination. I am innocent, and my
innocence can be easily proved. In all probability I shall be
back here to-morrow, none the worse for this experience.
Think of Iris, General, and for Heaven's sake take her out
of this."

Iris tried again to lay her hand on her father's arm.

He shook her off as if she had struck him. His red face
was no longer red—it was purple. The veins stood out in
great knots on his neck and temples.

"You are charged with murder?" he said, turning to his
future son-in-law. "And you have come here to arrest him,"
he continued, facing about and staring at the policeman—
"then let me——" he broke off abruptly. A groan came
from his lips, he stretched out both hands wildly as though to
clutch at something.

"My God, I am blind and deaf!" he panted. "There is a
roaring of water in my ears, I——" He stumbled forward,
and fell in an unconscious heap on the floor.

The confusion which followed can scarcely be described.
It was my duty to attend to General Romney. I knelt by
him, raised his head, loosened his collar and necktie, and
desired someone to fetch Mrs. Romney. Figures kept passing
to and fro. I knelt on by the side of the unconscious man.
Presently Mrs. Romney came hurrying in. Two or three
footmen also appeared. We raised General Romney with
great care, and carried him through the hall full of guests, up
the broad staircase, and into his own spacious bedroom on the
first floor. There he was undressed and laid in his bed.
There was no doubt with regard to the nature of his illness.
General Romney had been smitten down with a severe attack
of paralysis. I asked Mrs. Romney to send for the family
physician, Dr. Haynes. He arrived on the scene in an
incredibly short space of time. We had a hurried consultation
over the case. Dr. Haynes arranged to sit up for the night
with the unconscious man, and then for the first time I had a
moment to think of others. What had become of Vane?
Where was Iris?

Absorbed in anxiety about them, I ran hastily downstairs.
The lights were still burning all over the house, but every

guest had vanished : the place wore a neglected aspect. Some flowers were scattered about on the marble floor of the great hall. The fire on the hearth was reduced to ashes. All the doors leading into the hall stood open.

A girl in a white dress stood motionless by the empty hearth. Two or three dogs crouched at her feet. On hearing my steps she raised her head with a start. Her face, which had been dull and almost vacant in expression, lit up into full light. She sprang to meet me and stretched out her hands.

"I'm so glad you have come," she exclaimed. "How is father?"

"I am sorry to say he is very ill," I replied. "He is suffering from a severe stroke of paralysis."

Iris put her hand to her forehead.

"Is he in danger, Dr. Halifax?" she asked.

"I would rather not give any opinion about him to-night," I replied.

"I ought to be with him," she said. "I will go to him in a moment—after—after I have spoken to you."

"You cannot possibly do him any good by going to him now," I replied. "He is quite unconscious, and would not know you. He knows no one. Your mother is with him, and also Dr. Haynes. He wants for nothing at the present moment—nothing, I mean, that man can do. His life is in Higher hands. All we have to do is patiently to await results. Now, do you know that it is past two o'clock? You ought to be in bed."

Iris shuddered.

"I could not sleep if I went," she said. "Dr. Halifax, I want to tell you something."

"What is that?" I asked.

She looked full up at me—her eyes were bright again.

"Do you know why I fetched David's overcoat?"

"I cannot say—you probably knew where it was to be found."

"I did—but I had another reason. I wanted to take the handkerchief away."

"What handkerchief?" I asked, in some astonishment.

"Have you such a short memory?" she cried, looking at me with a puzzled expression. "Don't you remember the handkerchief which David pulled out of his pocket this afternoon as we were coming up the avenue ? It was blood-stained. Don't you recall the circumstances ? "

"Yes," I replied, gravely, "I do—I had forgotten it when you first spoke of a handkerchief."

"Well, I remembered it," she replied ; "it flashed suddenly across my memory when David asked for his coat. I knew that the handkerchief would be found there, and that they would use the blood-stains against him. That was why I was in such a hurry to fetch it. I removed the handkerchief and——"

"Yes," I said, when she paused, "and what did you do with it ? "

"I burnt it—here on this hearth. *That* horrible witness is, at least, reduced to ashes. Why, what is the matter, Dr. Halifax ? How grave you look."

I felt grave. I knew that Iris had done wrong in burning the handkerchief. It might have been an important witness in *favour* of the accused. There was no use, however, in adding to her misery now.

"I wish you would go to bed," I said. "You are looking very ill."

She did not reply at once ; she kept staring at me—her quick intuition read disapproval on my face.

"Have I done wrong ? " she exclaimed, in a voice of terror.

"I sincerely hope not," I answered, as soothingly as I could speak. "Perhaps nothing will be said about the handkerchief."

"But why are you so grave ? Are you not glad that it is gone ? "

I gave her a quick glance—she was the sort of girl who could bear the truth.

"You acted with natural, but mistaken, impulse," I said. "It would have been possible to prove that the stains on the handkerchief were caused by pheasant's blood, which differs in essential particulars from man's—but doubtless," I continued, raising my voice to a cheerful key, "the monstrous charge against Captain Vane will be shattered without the least difficulty at the examination before the magistrates to-morrow morning."

"David is the noblest fellow in the world," said Iris, with a shining light in her eyes. " But," she added, suddenly, and as if the words were wrung from her, "he *did* hate Mr. Ransome, and he had good cause."

The next day Vane was brought before the magistrates at Salisbury. General Romney was lying in a prostrate condition, and Haynes decided to remain with him until the nurse from London arrived. I was, therefore, free to accompany Mrs. Romney and Iris to the police-station at Salisbury. I have no space here to go into full particulars of the examination. The case against Vane was as follows :—

His dislike to Ransome was well known. On the day of the murder Vane had gone out early—during the time of his absence Ransome undoubtedly met his death. This fact alone could not have incriminated the young man, but, unfortunately, he had been seen by two labourers, returning from their work, having high words with Ransome. Ransome was seated on the gate by the fence which divided General Romney's grounds from those of Ransome Heights. When the labourers passed, Ransome was using excited words, and Vane was replying to them with a degree of heat and intemperance quite foreign to his usual character. The men lingered near as long as they decently could, but seeing that Ransome noticed them they slunk off. They reached the road and were walking rapidly towards their homes, when they heard a shot fired. They remarked on the circumstance to each other, and wondered, as they expressed it, "if the young gents were up to mischief." That evening, on repairing to the village tap-room, the first news that reached them was that of the murder of Squire Ransome. On their evidence a warrant was taken out for the arrest of Vane.

The magistrates listened gravely to all that was said, and then stated that there was no course open to them but to remand Captain Vane until the result of the coroner's inquest was known.

As Mrs. Romney, poor Iris, and I were leaving the police-court, the lawyer who was employed in Vane's defence, one of the leading men in his profession at Salisbury, came up and asked to speak to me alone. I conducted the ladies to their carriage, and then went into a small room with him.

"What is the matter?" I asked.

"This is a grave business," he replied. "Of course, I hope to get my client off, but I must own that circumstantial evidence points strongly against him. His own story is as follows : He frankly admits that he quarrelled with Ransome yesterday. He was walking across a field in General Romney's grounds when he came across a wounded pheasant lying on the path. He took his handkerchief out and strangled the bird. While doing so he heard a loud, mocking laugh, and looking up he saw Ransome astride of the gate in the fence. Vane called out to him with, as he acknowledged, considerable temper in his tones. His words were as follows :—

" 'I should think, if you are cad enough to shoot another man's game, you would at least have the decency to kill it, and not leave it maimed.'

"He says that he finished this speech by flinging the pheasant at Ransome's feet.

"The Squire got into a towering passion, and broke immediately into a volley of oaths. Vane says that Ransome took good care to drag in Miss Romney's name in the most offensive manner.

"He acknowledged that he had some difficulty in keeping himself in control, and presently thought the most prudent course was to turn on his heel and walk away. He had only gone a little distance when he heard the report of a gun. He says he thought nothing of the circumstance beyond concluding that Ransome was continuing his sport. This is his tale," concluded the lawyer, "and a very lame one it will appear if there is no testimony to support it. Vane speaks of having stained his handkerchief with the pheasant's blood. He says he left it in his overcoat. Now, I cannot find it there. Would it be possible, Dr. Halifax, for you to get it for me?"

" I am afraid not," I replied, gravely.

I then told Mr. Selwyn of poor Iris's rash act of the previous night.

The lawyer looked very grave.

"What mad creatures women are," he said after a pause. "The mere fact of the handkerchief being destroyed will incriminate the unfortunate young man."

We spoke together for a little longer, and then I was obliged to leave Selwyn to accompany Mrs. Romney and Iris to High Court.

I made a strong effort for their sakes to overcome the gloomy forebodings which seized me, and resolved that Iris should hear nothing more of her own rash act, unless circumstances made it impossible to keep it from her.

In the course of the afternoon, a messenger from Ransome Heights brought me a brief note to say that the coroner's jury had returned a verdict of wilful murder against Captain David Vane. I can scarcely explain the emotion which overcame me when I read this brief note. I crushed it in my hand, pushed it into my pocket, and went out for a long walk.

That evening I was sitting alone in General Romney's study, when my thoughts were interrupted by a message from Mrs. Romney, desiring my presence in the sick room.

I went upstairs at once. The General was lying on his back, breathing stertorously; the flush on his face was not so marked as it had been when first the seizure had taken him; his lips were slightly open, and occasionally he moved his eyelids very faintly.

"He has looked at me once or twice," said Mrs. Romney, who was standing by the bedside; "and," she added, "his eyes have had a question in them."

"He doubtless has much he wants to tell you," I said, in a soothing voice. "This is a good sign of his returning intelligence."

"But I fear you do not think well of him, Dr. Halifax."

"The case is a very grave one," I replied.

Mrs. Romney was silent for a moment—then she laid her hand on my arm and drew me to a distant part of the room.

"Do you think," she said, looking full up at me as she spoke—"do you think that my husband knows anything of the murder?"

Her words startled me.

"How could he?" I answered. "General Romney has not been out for some days——"

"That is true," she replied, "he has not been well—not quite himself. Still, what does the strange, anguished look in his eyes mean? Oh, I know he wants to tell me something very badly. See, doctor, his eyes are open now. Come to him: he would beckon us if he could."

I approached the bed where the stricken man lay. He gazed at me fixedly—his eyes were bloodshot and dull; nevertheless, beneath the dulness, beneath the ebbing powers of life, I thought I caught a glimpse of a tortured soul. The look in the General's eyes startled me. I laid my hand gently over them to close them.

"Do not think—sleep," I said to him.

Perhaps he did not understand me—perhaps he did.

Soon afterwards I left the room. I returned once more to the study. My mind was now filled by a very anxious thought. Suppose Mrs. Romsey was right? Suppose the dying man did know some fact which might clear David Vane? The feeling that this might possibly be so, and the knowledge also that the dull brain would in all probability never have the power of expressing its thoughts again—that the man who was so soon to leave the world would most likely carry his secret in darkness and silence to his long home— gave me a feeling of intense pain. I felt absolutely powerless to do anything in the matter, and in order to wile away the wretched moments, I looked around me to see if I could find something to read.

The General was not a reading man, and, with the exception of a few sporting journals, there were no books to be found in his study. I was about to leave the room to seek some literature further a-field, when a cabinet of old-fashioned make, which occupied a niche in one corner, attracted my attention. The cabinet was of oak, old, and beautifully carved; it had doors which could be shut or opened by the turning of brass handles. It was possible that I might find something to read in this cabinet. I went to it and opened the doors. I saw at a glance that it did not contain what I had come to seek. Some guns, one or two rusty pistols, a few old files and bottles, were scattered about on the different shelves; but what particularly attracted my attention was a battered-looking hat, which seemed from the way it had been pushed in on the top of bottles and various other débris, to have found a hasty hiding-place in the cabinet. I took it into my hands and looked at it — at first without any special interest. Then the faint smell of singeing attracted my attention. I held the hat between me and the light, and noticed that it had been considerably injured. On close examination I saw that it had been shot through. There were holes apparent in the crown; one round hole about the size of a shilling, and three or four smaller ones. These holes must have been caused by a charge of shot. For what possible reason had anyone made a shooting target of the old hat?

I put it back again in its place, shut the cabinet doors, and returned to my place by the fireside. I felt excited, and no longer cared to divert my thoughts by reading. Why was the hat in the cabinet, and why had it been riddled with shot?

"Suppose," I said to myself, "General Romney really knows all about this affair—and suppose Vane is hanged for it."

I began to think hard. I had scarcely time, however, to arrange my thoughts before the study door was opened, and Iris came in. There were red rims round her eyes as if she had been crying—otherwise she was quite calm. I looked at her attentively, and it occurred to me that she might help me to throw light on the mystery which was now occupying all my thoughts.

"Sit down," I said to her; "I want to talk to you about your father."

"How is he?" she asked.

"Very ill indeed," I replied.

Her face grew a shade paler.

"Is he dying?" she asked of me.

"I have grave fears for him," I answered; "but you know the old saying, that 'while there is life there is hope.' It is important that I should know the symptoms which preceded this sudden attack, and it has occurred to me that you can possibly help me. What did your father do, for instance, yesterday?"

Iris's brow contracted with a certain impatience.

"My father has not been well for some days," she said. "He spent yesterday as he has spent most days lately, in his study."

"He did not go out, then?"

"Go out!—no, he has not been out for a fortnight."

"Are you certain on that point?" I asked.

"Yes—what do you mean? Even if he did go out, it does not greatly matter, does it? But I know that he did not."

"In the state he was in," I said, "exercise would have been extremely injurious to him, and if he took it, it might have hastened the attack."

"He was not out, Dr. Halifax," said Iris, "and," she continued eagerly, "it so happens that I can prove it. Father would never stir a yard without a certain old hat which he had a fancy for. That hat has been hanging in the hall for the last fortnight. I will fetch it for you."

"Do," I said; "I am sorry to trouble you, but it is important that I should know if the attack was in any way caused by unwonted exercise."

Iris quickly left the room; she came back in a moment with empty hands.

"The hat is not there," she exclaimed. "It was on the stand yesterday morning. I saw it; perhaps one of the servants has removed it."

"Is this it?" I asked, going suddenly to the cabinet, flinging it open, and producing the hat. I held it high, for I did not wish Iris to notice the holes made by the shot.

She came eagerly to my side.

"That is certainly the hat," she replied. "I wonder why father hid it in the cabinet?"

"Finding the hat here points to the conclusion that he went out yesterday," I said. "He perhaps put it in this cabinet to avoid the trouble of returning it to its place in the hall."

"Perhaps so," replied Iris. "And you think he injured himself by going out?"

"He certainly did," I said, in a grave voice.

I did not add any more. My suspicions were confirmed.

"You are looking tired," I said to Iris. "You had better go to bed. Rest assured that I mean to take this matter up, but you mustn't question me. If I fail I fail, but I may succeed. Go to bed and sleep. Rest in the knowledge that I will do my best."

Iris suddenly seized my hand.

"You are good, you comfort me," she said; "you strengthen me."

She ran out of the room.

I sat down again by the fire. I was now concentrating my thoughts on one object, and one only. Having clearly made up my mind that General Romney possessed a secret, it was my mission to restore to him the power of divulging it. How could I do that?

The General was suffering from embolism—there was little doubt, also, that there was progressive paralysis of the brain. The case was a bad one, and under ordinary circumstances the doomed man would go down into his grave in unbroken silence. In this case the silence must be broken. How?

Suddenly, an idea came to me—the shadow of a hope possessed me. Thin and poor as this hope was, I determined to act upon it. I went up to General Romney's bedroom. Haynes was there, seated by the bedside; a trained nurse, who had arrived from town, was also present, and Mrs. Romney was lying on a sofa in a distant part of the room. The General lay as motionless as of old. I went over and sat by the bedside—the pallor was deepening over the sick man's face, the shadow of death was on it; his eyes, however, were wide open: they looked at me now, full of speech, but of speech which I had no power to interpret. I took his hand in mine, and felt his pulse, it was weak and fluttering; I bent down and listened to his breathing, then I asked Haynes to come into the next room for a moment.

"What do you think of the case?" I said to him.

"Quite hopeless," he answered. "I do not think our patient will be alive in the morning."

"He is certainly very ill," I replied. "His respiratory centres are affected, out of proportion to the severity of the attack of paralysis; in short, even if the hemorrhage on the brain does not proceed, he is likely to die of asphyxia."

"I have noticed the affection of the lungs," said Haynes. "Can nothing be done to relieve the breathing?"

"I am inclined to try the inhalation of oxygen gas," I answered. "I propose that we send immediately to Salisbury for some bags of the gas, and give it to the patient to inhale."

Haynes looked at me in doubtful surprise.

"Where so much is wrong," he said, "what is the use of trying what may only prolong life to cause further suffering? The patient is almost unconscious."

"He is not unconsious," I replied. "He knows us. Have you not noticed the expression in his eyes?"

"I have," said Haynes. "To tell the truth, I do not like their look. They give me a sense of being haunted."

"The inhalation of the gas can do no harm," I said, almost cheerfully. "I am quite aware that it is not usually tried in such cases, but I have a special reason for wishing not to leave a stone unturned to give the General a chance of even partial revival. Now, can we get a messenger to go to Salisbury at once?"

Haynes looked dubious and disturbed.

"I will go, if anybody must," he answered; "but in addition to not feeling sanguine as to the success of your remedy, I am quite certain that we cannot get the oxygen gas in Salisbury."

" We 'll make it, then," I replied. " Such a trivial obstacle must not baffle us at a crucial moment like the present. Will you go for me immediately to Salisbury, Haynes, and get two nitrous oxide bags from any dentist you happen to know? Then get from the chemist a retort and a spirit-lamp, some chlorate of potash, some peroxide of manganese, some caustic potash, some rubber tubing, and two big glass jars. Bring these back with you as fast as ever you can. I believe in the remedy, but there is not a moment to lose in preparing the oxygen gas."

Haynes left me, and I returned to the sick room. I shall not soon forget those weary hours of watching. I knew that with all possible speed Haynes would not be back with the necessary materials for preparing the gas under a couple of hours. Meanwhile, the patient's strength was ebbing fast. Any moment that fluttering pulse might cease. I administered restoratives at intervals, and held the limp hand in mine. Shortly before Haynes returned, Mrs. Romney stirred on her sofa, rose, and motioned to me to follow her into the next room. When I did so, she spoke, eagerly.

" How is my husband?" she asked.

I looked at her.

" You must know the truth," I said. " You are brave—you will bear up—General Romney is dying—nothing can be done to save his life, but I have sent to Salisbury for a special remedy, which will, in all probability, relieve the breathing, and it is quite possible give him the opportunity of communicating to us that thought which haunts his dying bed."

" Yes, yes, he wants to tell us something," said Mrs. Romney. She turned white, and trembled so excessively that I made her sit down on the nearest chair.

At this moment I heard steps on the stairs, and Haynes arrived with all the necessary materials for making the gas.

There was not a moment to waste. I got the apparatus quickly into order, mixed the chemicals, and soon had the satisfaction of seeing the bag slowly fill with pure oxygen gas. Haynes and I then hurried into the sick room. I directed the nurse to place a lamp in such a position that the light should fall on the patient. My object now was to revive him —in short, to untie, if possible, that silent tongue. Mrs. Romney followed me into the room. The gas was quickly applied, and the effect of even the first few whiffs was marvellous. The death-like pallor on the sick man's face left it. The returning colour first stole into the tips of the ears, then to the lips, then the eyes grew bright. The General heaved a deep sigh, as though an awful weight had been lifted from him. I removed the rubber tubing which I had introduced into one of his nostrils, and noticed the quick, strong respirations which now proceeded from the relieved lungs. This relief did not last long; but when I administered the gas again, the effect was in every way satisfactory. At the third application General Romney sat up in bed. His mouth twitched, he tried to speak, but no intelligent words would come to him. He was now, however, fully conscious, and I knew that the moment had arrived for me to speak to him.

"I want to tell you something, General," I said. "Captain David Vane——"

"Oh, don't, I beg of you," interrupted Mrs. Romney.

I motioned her to step aside.

"Do not interrupt me," I said; "look at his face."

That face was, indeed, eloquent with suppressed speech. The General moved his arms impatiently. I turned to him and began to speak again in a low, distinct voice.

"Captain David Vane," I said, "has been arrested for the murder of Mr. Ransome, of Ransome Heights. It is very probable that a verdict of wilful murder may be returned against him, unless you, General Romney, you who are a dying man, can throw light on the mystery."

His face worked; a hopeless jumble of unintelligible sounds proceeded from his lips.

I held the gas again to his nostrils and he revived. Making an effort, he suddenly threw out his right arm and hand and pointed with his fore finger to some writing materials which lay on a table not far distant. I went to the table, secured blotting-pad and paper and a sharply pointed pencil. I brought them back with me, placed the pencil in the dying hand, and supported the old man in such a way that he was able to write without much difficulty.

"Quick," I whispered to him, "a life depends on what you want to say."

His fingers immediately began to move across the paper. I looked over his shoulders as he wrote.

These were the words which I read :—

"David Vane is innocent. I am the person who killed

Thomas Ransome. This is how the deed was done. On the day you arrived I went out, contrary to my doctor's advice, for a short walk. I went into the copse. I saw Ransome sitting on the fence which divides his property from ours. He was in the act of aiming at a pheasant in my copse when I saw him. I called to him in a loud voice to abstain. I called him what he was—a scoundrel. He raised his eyes—looked at me and burst out laughing. I saw that he was the worse for drink. I came close up to him.

"'It isn't pheasants alone I have come to knock down,' he said, with a jeer. 'I'm looking for bigger game.'

"The next instant I heard a noise and felt some heat. The fellow had presented his gun at me at near quarters. I closed with him, and we had a terrible tussle. I seized the gun, and gave him one blow on the head—only one. I thought I had stunned him—he rolled into the ditch and lay quiet. I went back to the house and saw that the full charge of the gun had entered my hat. I regarded my life as a miracle, and put the hat away—not to alarm my family. I felt ill and shaken—I had been unwell for some time. I had no idea that I had killed Ransome. You came in and gave me a restorative, and I felt better. I was in the ball-room receiving my visitors when someone rushed up and told me that Ransome was dead, and that a police-officer had arrived for the purpose of arresting Vane. I ran, as if the devil were behind me, to find Vane, and tell the truth. Before I could do so, I was stricken down."

Having written so far, the General paused. The pencil fluttered out of his feeble fingers. I applied the gas once again—his respiration grew easier, but I saw that the last flicker of strength was leaving him, and that soon even the revivifying gas would fail in its effects.

"For God's sake, rouse yourself, General," I cried to him. "Sign the statement you have just made. Sign it quickly."

Haynes, Mrs. Romney, and the nurse were all standing round—the General took the pencil in his hand.

"Sign, sign," I said.

I held him up, and he managed with the last flicker of strength to put his name in full at the bottom of the paper. I gave the paper to Mrs. Romney, with an expressive look. She took it and laid it on the table. I put General Romney back on his pillows.

"You have done bravely," I said to him. "This paper will completely clear Vane. Your girl will be happy yet—you may die in peace."

He looked up at me, and I saw that the question and the agony had left his dying eyes for ever. Iris was hurriedly sent for, but before she arrived the old man was unconscious. She sat by his side, and took his hand in hers. As she sat so, I read over to her the words which her father had just put on paper. She burst into tears, and fell forward on his breast.

Perhaps he knew she was there, for the eyelids seemed to flutter, but gradually and surely the laboured breath quieted down, and before the morning dawned General Romney died.

THE HOODED DEATH

THE HOODED DEATH

H ER friends always expected that Edith Keen would marry her old lover, Donal O'Brien. Their astonishment, therefore, was great when it was announced that she was engaged to a retired West Indian of the name of Talbot. Maximilian Talbot was over fifty years of age, and Edith was twenty. He had been born in the West Indies, but his father was an Englishman by birth. He had amassed a great fortune before he came to settle in England, and as he was a good-looking man, with an aristocratic, old-world sort of flavour about him, those who met him in society expected that he would make a good match. His choice, however, fell upon Edith, who was no one in particular, her father being a man who had come to grief through his speculations. Edith was poor, and went very little into society, but Talbot happened to meet her at a country house, and from the moment he saw her, it was all too evident that his mind was made up. He proposed and, to the astonishment of lookers on, was accepted. Worldly people said that Edith had done well for herself, but all the same, those who really knew her were amazed. Donal O'Brien had been her lover for years—it was even hinted, although no one was quite certain of the fact, that there had been an engagement between them; of course, he was poor—too poor to think of matrimony, but Edith was the last girl in the world, so her friends said, who would be likely to sacrifice love to money.

That she did so, however, was an all too patent fact. She married Mr. Talbot on a certain morning towards the end of May. She made a very interesting and beautiful bride, and notwithstanding the disparity in their years, her handsome bridegroom seemed quite worthy of her. I happened to be present in the church when the knot was tied, and I can truly say that I seldom saw a more lovely face than that of the sweet, slender, white-robed bride.

The couple went away amidst the usual scene of rejoicing, and, busy with my ever-increasing work, I soon forgot all the circumstances of the wedding.

Three months afterwards I was in my consulting-room looking over one of my case-books, when my servant flung open the door and admitted a visitor. I looked up, and was surprised to see Donal O'Brien enter. He was a bony, red-haired fellow, with a mixture of Scotch and Irish in his composition. He was very tall, broad-shouldered, and gaunt; his eyes had a red gleam in them; he had a broad, firm forehead; his lips were closely set, and his square chin, which was cleft in the middle, had the determination of a bulldog about it.

I bade him welcome, drew forward a chair, and asked what I could do for him.

He stared fixedly at me for a moment without making any reply. I noticed then that there was a dumb sort of misery in his eyes. I recalled the old story about his love affair with Edith Keen, and roused myself to take an interest in him.

"The fact is," he began, "I have come here to consult you."

"Pray tell me what your symptoms are," I answered.

O'Brien laughed harshly.

"Bless you, I'm all right," he said. "I'm not here as a patient. You have always taken an interest in Miss Keen, have you not?"

"I have known Mrs. Talbot since she was a child," I answered.

"Yes, yes," he replied, impatiently, "but I never think of her as the wife of that man if I can help it. You know she was engaged to me, do you not?"

"I did not know that there was an actual engagement," I replied.

"Well, there was: it lasted for some months. I don't blame her a bit. She asked my leave to break it off. She told me, poor girl, that she had by no means ceased to love me, but her father, who has been, as perhaps you know, more or less mixed up in shady speculations, had got into trouble. Talbot found out that Keen was hard up and likely to be publicly disgraced. He played upon Edith's affections, and told her that he would set her father straight if she married him. On this fact being known, all her family brought great influence to bear upon the poor girl. Keen himself came to see me, and begged of me not to stand in her way. She joined her entreaties to her father's. I was mad to yield, for I saw all through that she was only sacrificing herself. She never really loved the fellow, but like many another girl, she did not realize what marriage with a man of Talbot's temperament would mean."

"You speak as if you knew something about Talbot," I said."

"So I do; I 'm coming to that part immediately. I made a fatal mistake in releasing Edith. I love her still to distraction. Poor girl, she has put her father straight, and tied herself for life to a cold-blooded, inhuman monster. So much for self-sacrifice."

O'Brien jumped up as he spoke, and began to pace the room. He was in a state of great excitement. He clenched his hands, and now and then violent words burst from his lips.

"Quiet yourself, and sit down," I said, after a pause. "You have doubtless come to tell me all this for some specific reason. You had better do so at once, for my time is valuable."

I pitied the poor fellow from my heart, but I knew that it was necessary to bring him up to the point in the most matter-of-fact way I could manage.

He looked at me fixedly—shook himself as if he were a great mastiff, and then sank into the nearest chair, bending slightly forward, and pressing his hands upon his knees.

"God knows I've come for a specific reason," he said. "It is this: Edith came to see me a week ago."

"Have they returned from their honeymoon?" I interrupted.

"Yes, they are staying in Surrey, near Dorking—Talbot has a bungalow there. She managed to elude his vigilance for a day, and came up to see me."

"That was the act of a mad woman, if you like," I said.

"I acknowledge that it was indiscreet; but, God help her! how could she think of proprieties in her terrible position? She wanted to ask me a question. She wanted me to do something for her. Can you guess what it was?"

"No, I'm sure I can't.'

"Well, I'll tell you. You know my profession. I'm an experimental scientist. In especial I have devoted myself to zoology—and to that branch of the subject known as ophiology. I have made several valuable experiments with regard to the most interesting snake poisons under the guidance of the well-known Sir John Hart; our object is to discover antidotes for these terrible venoms. The most poisonous snakes of all are to be found in India, and amongst these the cobra undoubtedly takes the lead. My most exhaustive experiments, therefore, have been made in connection with cobra poisoning. I have been given special opportunities for studying the cobra and its mode of attack at Antwerp, and have discovered a method by which I can distil the poison, over the description of which I need not now waste your time. I should like, on a future occasion, to talk over the antidotes which I consider most efficacious."

"Then you have really found out an antidote for cobra poisoning?" I asked, so much interested that I could not help interrupting the speaker.

"No; I wish I had. To a certain extent, antidotes have been discovered, but nothing up to the present has been proved to be of the slightest avail where *much* poison has been allowed to enter the system. Now, however, to return to Mrs. Talbot. I had just come back from Antwerp on the day she called, and had gone to report myself to Sir John Hart. On hearing that I was out, she asked my servant to admit her into my laboratory, and when I rushed in presently in a violent hurry, there she was standing by the window.

"She turned round when she heard my step, and came to meet me, with her face as white as death, and her hands tightly locked together. You know the peculiar fascination of her big, dark eyes. I never saw eyes with so much power of speech except in the case of a dog. They looked full at me as she came swiftly up to my side, but for a brief moment neither she nor I uttered a single word.

"'For God's sake, what have you come for, Edith?' I burst forth, at last. 'You know this is madness,' I continued, for I felt so wild at the sight of her, and at the thought of the barrier which now lay between us, that I could scarcely control myself. 'You must be mad to come here,' I said. 'I wonder you do it—and why don't you speak? Why are you dumb except with your eyes? What's up, Edith, what's up? For Heaven's sake, don't tell me that your marriage has turned out a failure!'

"She raised her hand with a mute gesture for me to forbear.

"'I have not come here to talk of my husband,' she said, in a broken, faltering voice. 'I have not come here in any sense to complain of my terrible position.'

"'Your terrible position,' I interrupted. 'Then the whole thing has been a mistake. God knows, I ought never to have released you, Edith.'

"'We must not talk of this,' she answered. 'I have come to see you to-day to ask your advice, and I can only do that if you will put sufficient control on yourself to listen to me quietly. My husband has a terrible dual nature. There are two distinct phases to his character. For days, perhaps a fortnight at a time, he is gentle, courteous, affectionate—a perfect gentleman in word and deed—but at any moment, without the slightest provocation, from no reason that anyone can account for, I see another completely different side to his character. When this phase overtakes him, he becomes not a man but a demon. He tortures me, he insults me; he is cruel, very cruel. At such times, such misery is mine that I often fear I cannot retain my senses.'

"'Is the man insane?' I asked.

"'No,' she answered, 'there is not a trace of insanity about him; at least, if one understands the word in its ordinary sense. He is cool, calculating—he seldom rouses himself to be really excited. He seems to have the cunning and the cleverness of the devil. When he enters upon this strange mood, I can scarcely endure my life. There is no possibility of escaping from him. Oh, I can't talk further on the matter. I have come here, Donal, to ask you to help me. You know how fond you are of collecting snake poisons. You have even described to me the symptoms, and the certain effect of cobra venom. Donal, will you give me a bottle of this poison?'

"'In the name of Heaven, what for?' I asked.

"'Need you ask after what I have just told you? I want to have the poison by me, in order that I may take it if I find that there is no other door of escape from my terrible husband when he enters on his dark moods.'

"'Folly,' I answered. 'Sorrow has driven you mad.'

"She broke down when I said this, Dr. Halifax, and burst into the most bitter, terrible weeping I have ever listened to. I stood and stared at her as speechless as if I were a dog instead of a man. I was enduring the worst torture which could possibly be laid upon me. I loved her to distraction, and yet I could do nothing for her—I dared not even attempt to comfort her. When she got over her fit of crying, she began to appeal to me again.

"'Do grant my request,' she said. 'I faithfully promise not to use the poison unless the most dire necessity arises; but to feel that I have it in my power to put an end to my misery will strengthen my nerves. For the sake of the old love we felt for one another, be generous enough to grant my request, Donal.'

"'No, no,' I replied. 'I must save you from yourself, at any cost.'

"I had to say this many times. She went on her knees to me at last—still I refused her. When she found that all her entreaties were hopeless she ceased to argue, but sat perfectly motionless, staring out of the window. My servant came to tell me that I was wanted for a moment to speak to a messenger from Sir John Hart. I was absent about three minutes. When I came back, Edith rose and gave me her hand.

"'Good-bye,' she said.

"Her manner had completely altered. Her tears were all dried. Her beautiful eyes wore a veiled expression, and no longer gave me a glimpse of her tortured heart. I saw her to the door. It was a relief to see her calm, even though I knew how forced was her apparent serenity.

"Half an hour afterwards I went back to my laboratory. What was my horror to see that the small cabinet in which I keep my specimens of snake poison had the key in it. As a rule I keep it securely locked, but I remembered now, when too late, that I had, on my return from Antwerp, placed some new bottles of very valuable specimens of snake poison in the cupboard, and had, alas, forgotten to remove the key.

"Had Edith discovered the fatal mistake I had made? I rushed to the cupboard, opened it, and found that amongst the neat rows of carefully labelled bottles one was missing. There was not the least doubt what had occurred. Edith had helped herself to a bottle of snake poison. This accounted for the self-control with which she had parted from me. It is impossible for me to describe my sensations when I made this discovery. After thinking for a few moments I resolved to seek your advice. Here I am: what is to be done?"

"You are in a very awkward position," I answered.

"I should think I am. Is that all you can say?"

"Is the bottle of poison which Mrs. Talbot has taken very deadly?" I asked.

"Yes; she has helped herself to cobra poison; it would have a fatal effect immediately. She has taken a bottle of what we call 'Venom Peptone,' the most deadly part of the venom of the cobra. Don't let's waste time talking of it. What is to be done to get the bottle from her?"

Here O'Brien fixed his red-rimmed, anxious eyes on my face.

"You are a man of many resources. Have you nothing to suggest?" he asked, impatiently.

"Something must be done, certainly," I answered.

"Yes, what? Ought I under the circumstances to go and see her?"

"Certainly not," I replied. "A man like Talbot is certain to be consumed by jealously. He may or may not have heard of your old engagement to his wife. A visit from you at this crisis could only precipitate the mischief we dread."

"Then you will go, Halifax?" said O'Brien.

"I don't well know how I can without arousing suspicion."

"You must devise some subterfuge—you must invent something to account for your presence."

I thought hard.

"I have it," I said, after a moment. "Where do you say the Talbots live?"

"In Surrey, close to Dorking."

"And this is Saturday afternoon," I said, half under my breath.

"What in the world has that to do with it?"

"A good deal, as far as I am concerned. I have more leisure on Saturday afternoon than on any other day of the week. The case is an extreme one. Edith is an old friend. All right, O'Brien, I will take the matter up."

"God bless you, but won't you tell me what you mean to do?"

"I can't do that, for I don't quite know myself. I will go

down to Dorking to-night—put up at the White Horse, and go over to the Talbots' house early to-morrow morning to pay a visit to my old friend."

"How can I ever thank you?" exclaimed O'Brien. He sprang forward and took my hand, which he wrung violently as if it were a pump-handle.

"I'll get that bottle of poison from Mrs. Talbot before I return to town," I answered. "How, I cannot say, but in some manner the deed will be done. Now leave me, like a good fellow, for I must see one or two patients before I start."

Two hours later I found myself in a train on my way to Dorking. I put up for the night at the White Horse, and the next morning, shortly after breakfast, set off to walk to the Talbots' place, which was beautifully situated on a rising ground, no quite two miles out of Dorking. The house was a long, low bungalow. It was picturesquely made, and was surrounded by beautifully kept gardens. The name of the place was The Elms. As I walked up the avenue under the shelter of a long double row of these stately trees I saw Mrs. Talbot standing on one of the lawns, talking to her husband. They were a tall couple, and made a striking effect as they stood together with their figures silhouetted with great distinctness against the summer sky. They were evidently engaged in amicable conversation, and Edith's silvery laughter floated down to me as I approached them.

There was nothing in the attitude of this pair to suggest even the most remote suspicion of unhappiness. Remembering O'Brien's words, however, I concluded that Talbot was in his amiable phase, and almost regretted that I had not an opportunity of seeing him at his worst. Edith heard my footsteps, and turned to see who was coming to intrude on their Sunday peace. We had always been good friends, and she coloured with pleasure when she saw me. Talbot also gave me a most courteous welcome. He was a remarkably good-looking man. His voice was low and somewhat languid. He had a slight drawl, which at times almost produced a sense of irritation; but his words were exceedingly well chosen, and when he addressed his wife his manner was the perfection of gentle and affectionate courtesy. I noticed, however, as I watched him carefully, an uneasy gleam flit now and then through his cold, grey eyes. It vanished almost as soon as it came, but I further observed that Mrs. Talbot seemed to watch for this expression with ill-concealed anxiety. At the present moment, all was undoubtedly sunshine.

"I am delighted to see you, Dr. Halifax," she said. "I know my husband joins with me in bidding you welcome. Are you not glad to see Dr. Halifax, Max?"

"I am pleased to welcome any friend of yours to The Elms, my love," answered Talbot.

"But where are you staying, and why have you come?" asked Edith.

"I am staying at the White Horse," I answered. "I was rather hipped with work, and thought a day in the country would set me up. It enhanced the pleasure of my intended holiday to know that Dorking was within a short distance of your place."

"You shan't stay another hour at the White Horse," said Mrs. Talbot—"you must come here. Am I not right in asking Dr. Halifax to be our guest, Max?" she continued, glancing at her husband.

"Certainly," he replied. "We shall be pleased if you will come to us, Dr. Halifax, and remain as long as you can be spared from London. A servant can go to the White Horse and fetch your traps up presently."

After a moment's reflection, I replied, with a smile, "I shall be very glad to spend the day with you, but as I must return to town at a very early hour to-morrow morning, it is not worth while sending for my belongings. It will be more convenient for me to sleep at the White Horse, but I can stay here until the evening with pleasure."

"That is better than nothing," replied Edith. "Now won't you come and let us show you our gardens—we are so proud of them—at least I am."

"My wife has quite a passion for the cultivation of orchids," said Talbot. "Are you fond of orchids?"

I replied in a light spirit, and we spent the next couple of hours in the conservatories and out of doors wandering about on the beautifully kept lawns.

By-and-by we went into the house to lunch.

During lunch, I could not help noticing that Talbot drank a good deal of wine of a rare quality and flavour. It had little apparent effect upon him—it brought no added colour to his face, nor any additional light to his cold, dull eyes. I saw at a glance that he was accustomed to imbibing great quantities of the poison, for, notwithstanding his outward calm, I was quite certain that wine had a poisonous effect upon a man like him.

Instead of taking the head of her table, Mrs. Talbot sat close to her husband, and to my surprise, took care to fill his glass whenever it was empty. This she did in a very quiet and unobtrusive manner—he never seemed to notice the action, but he invariably drained off the full glass when it was presented to him.

After lunch he came for a moment to my side.

"I am the victim of a very intolerable form of neuralgia," he said, "and am forced to keep it at bay by various sedatives, also by the aid of wine, which acts on me as a narcotic—you will excuse me if I go to lie down for an hour—I shall hope to join you and my wife later on in the garden."

"We'll have tea in the garden about four o'clock," said Mrs. Talbot; "you will find us there whenever you have finished your nap, Max."

He tapped her lightly on the shoulder, and gave her an affectionate smile, which she returned with pleased and heightened colour. Then she asked me to accompany her into the garden.

The moment had now arrived when I must make the real object of my visit known. I found it a little difficult to break the ice, and in consequence kept silent for a time, scarcely replying to the light and happy talk of the pretty girl by my side. She looked so fresh and animated—so young and peaceful—that I could not help sincerely hoping that O'Brien had exaggerated matters, and that Mrs. Talbot could never have contemplated the terrible sin of self-destruction. Still, there was no doubt that the bottle of venom peptone had disappeared from O'Brien's laboratory, and no one else could have taken it.

"Forgive me for interrupting you," I said, suddenly. "We are alone, and I must not lose so good an opportunity. I wish to tell you why I have really come to see you to-day."

The moment I said this she turned pale. Her pretty lips trembled, and she fixed her eyes on my face with a glance which gave me distinct pain. I avoided looking at her again, and began to speak slowly and calmly.

"Yesterday Donal O'Brien came to see me."

"Ah," she answered; "he discovered it, then?"

"Yes," I continued, "he discovered what you had done. You took a bottle of very deadly poison from his laboratory, having first begged of him in vain to give it to you. In his brief absence from the room, you stole the bottle—forgive me if I use very plain words."

"What does that matter?" she answered. She pressed her hand against her heaving chest. "Yes, it is true," she interrupted. "I took the bottle without his knowledge, and I know—I am glad to know—that it contains deadly poison."

"You must not keep it," I answered, in a firm voice. "I have come to fetch it. Will you run and get it for me now?"

She gazed at me with a mixture of terror and astonishment on her face.

"Do you really mean what you say?" she asked.

"I undoubtedly do," I replied.

"Then I defy you—I will not give it back to you."

"In that case——" I began.

She interrupted me hastily.

"No, don't say what you are going to say," she exclaimed. "I will tell you the truth. I have got the poison, but I don't mean to use it. It comforts me to know it is in my possession, but except under the last and most terrible extremity, I should never dream of taking my·life. Assure Donal on this point. Tell him, by the love I used to have for him, to believe that I am speaking the truth."

I laid my hand for a moment on Mrs. Talbot's arm.

"Before we go into the subject of your keeping that bottle of poison or not," I said, "I want to say a few words to you on another matter. When I arrived here this morning, no young wife could look happier or more united to her husband than you did to yours. You made O'Brien acquainted with some strange facts. Do you mind repeating them to me?"

"They are true," she answered, in a low voice. "My husband's nature has two distinct sides. In one phase he is an angel, in the other he is a demon. More and more, as time goes on, the demon dominates over the angel. Oh, my God, my God! I can't endure the agony much longer. When he is in his torturing mood, he is cruel to me in the most refined, the most awful, ways. His one pleasure is to devise means of putting me on the rack. I see his eyes fill with a terrible sort of joy when he sees me shrink and suffer. To know that I have at hand a weapon which can deprive him at any moment of the one interest of his life, will enable me to bear up against the torture. Believe me, I value my life, and will not throw it away except under the most fearful pressure."

"You are very much to be pitied," I answered; "I need not say that I wish beyond words that it were in my power to relieve you. Your husband must be a very strange character, for even the most acute observer could detect nothing the matter with him in the mood which he is in to-day."

"I wish you could see him in his other mood," she replied.

"I will endeavour to do so. I may be able to assign causes for it, and trace so fearful a change to a physical reason."

"Oh, he is not mad," she answered. "We can't get out of the difficulty by that door."

"Well," I said, "I must devise some means for seeing him when his mood changes to the one you describe."

"He would be careful and gracious before you."

"I should manage to see him when he is not on his guard," I answered. "But now to return to yourself, Mrs. Talbot. You must let me have that bottle of poison back. Whatever your circumstances, you have no right to attempt self-destruction. Your life has been given you by God; it is wicked to throw away His gift. If you patiently wait the Divine will and pleasure, I make not the least doubt that your misery will be removed in time. You were a good girl once: I have known you since you were a child. No life need be unendurable to those who seek for assistance from above. I am not a man to cant, but I believe in Divine power. Fetch me the bottle of poison—we will throw it away together. Don't keep this terrible temptation in your possession another moment."

While I was speaking, Mrs. Talbot stood with clasped hands; her face was deadly pale, and her eyes wore a fearful look of dumb misery.

"Think of the agony you are causing to the man you used to love," I said, after a pause.

She flushed crimson at these words.

"Wait for me here," she said, in a hoarse whisper; "I will fetch the bottle."

She ran into the house. I could not help thinking with great anxiety of her strange case.

Mrs. Talbot came back sooner than I expected; she looked excited and almost wild.

"I cannot find the bottle of venom peptone," she exclaimed. "I have searched everywhere—it has vanished."

For a moment I thought she was deceiving me, but a glance into her eyes told me that she spoke the truth.

"Are you sure?" I said.

"Certain," she replied. She leant against a neighbouring elm tree as she spoke—she was trembling from head to foot. "I don't understand it," she said. "I can't imagine how anyone could have got to it. There is a cabinet in my room with a secret drawer. No one knows the secret of the drawer but myself. I brought the cabinet from my own home, and have used it since we came to The Elms to hold the treasures which used to belong to me when I was a happy girl. When I stole the bottle of poison from Mr. O'Brien, I put it immediately in the secret drawer of my cabinet. It was there yesterday, I know. When I opened the drawer to-day it was empty. Oh, what is to be done?"

"The bottle may have fallen to the back of the drawer," I said. "Are you certain you looked everywhere?"

"Certain—positive. I looked in every corner. The poison has vanished."

She had scarcely said these last words before Talbot appeared walking slowly across the lawn. Edith recovered her serenity as if by magic. She ran to her husband, and asked him in quite a tender tone how he felt now.

"Better, my dear," he replied, giving her face a keen but very brief glance.

"I am so glad you were able to do without the morphia," she cried.

"Oh," said Talbot, smiling, "you must not tell tales out of school, little girl; but after all, I don't mind a medical man like Halifax knowing. The fact is," he added, turning to me, "my neuralgia becomes so unendurable at times, that I am forced to resort to morphia as a mode of relief, and have taught these delicate little fingers"—here he took his wife's hand in his—"to manipulate the hypodermic syringe."

"As a medical man I must protest," I replied. "The use of morphia is extremely bad for you."

"In large doses, I grant, but not as I take it," replied Talbot.

A servant now appeared carrying a tea-tray, and our conversation drifted to indifferent matters.

I had not yet by any means accomplished the object of my visit. The strange disappearance of the venom peptone gave me a very queer sense of uneasiness. I had no opportunity, however, of again referring to the matter to Mrs. Talbot, and presently the hour arrived when I must bid my host and hostess "Good-bye," and return to the White Horse.

Just before I left, as I was standing on the veranda with Talbot, he dropped his voice to a low tone.

"I have often heard of your medical skill," he said. "I have a great mind to call on you some day and put my case into your hands."

"You suffer from neuralgia, do you not?" I asked.

"Yes, and other matters. Can you appoint a day and hour to see me in Harley Street?"

"Certainly," I replied. "Can you be with me to-morrow at twelve o'clock?"

"As well to-morrow as any day," he answered.

I made a note of the engagement, and soon afterwards took my leave. Talbot walked a little way up the avenue with me.

"To-morrow at twelve," he said, as we parted. He half turned to go, hesitated, and came back to my side. "By the way," he said, "I should like to ask you as a medical man a question. Did you ever hear of a person who was bitten by a cobra recovering?"

Knowing what I did of Mrs. Talbot and the bottle of poison, this remark startled me. There was a moon in the heavens, and I saw a gleam, unsteady and uneasy, glittering in Talbot's eyes.

"Did you?" he asked, seeing that I hesitated.

"I know very little of serpent poisoning," I said. "A man bitten by a cobra would, I make no doubt, have a poor chance of life."

"You see a man before you who escaped death," he answered. "Years ago, in India, a cobra fastened its fangs into my leg. I was bitten severely; I was at death's door, but I recovered. I have never been the same man since. I recovered from the worst effects of the poison, but my nerves were destroyed. Good-night."

He held out his hand. I took it. It was limp and fibreless —cold as a fish.

"God help that poor girl," I could not help muttering, as I wended my way back to the White Horse.

I went to bed, and the thought of this ill-assorted couple mingled with my dreams.

I was awakened from sleep quite early in the night by hearing someone knocking loudly at my door. I sprang up and opened it—the landlord of the White Horse stood without.

"If you please, sir," he said, "you are sent for immediately to go to The Elms—Mr. Talbot is alarmingly ill. There's a brougham at the door, and Mrs. Talbot begs that you will go without a moment's delay."

"Tell the messenger that I will be down immediately," I answered.

I hurried into my clothes, slipped a small medicine case, without which I never travelled, into my pocket, and stepped into the brougham. It bore me quickly to the bungalow. As we drove up the avenue I saw that the house was full of light —figures were flitting here and there. When we reached the front door, a servant ran out to open the door of the carriage.

"My mistress wishes to see you immediately in the morning-room," he said.

I was shown into a pretty little room, where Edith was waiting for me. She was in a long white dressing-gown, and her masses of hair lay in confusion on her neck and back. Her eyes looked wild—her face was ghastly pale. She came up to me and clasped my hand.

"Oh, what am I to do?" she cried.

"Try to keep calm, and tell me what is the matter," I answered.

"I can't bear it," she exclaimed, wringing her hands frantically. "How can I tell you what has happened?"

"You must try, my dear young lady, if you wish me to help you. You have sent for me because your husband is very ill. Had I not better see him?"

"Yes, he is ill—dying," she answered. "I will tell you what has occurred as briefly as I can. When my husband suffers much I generally sleep in a room near—I heard him groaning, and went to him. I had injected morphia into his arm as usual before I went to bed. I thought he wanted a larger dose. As soon as ever I appeared I knew by his voice that he had entered into one of his fiendish moods—he called out to me in harsh and terrible tones—he said that he had discovered the bottle in my cabinet, and knew that I concealed it there for the express purpose of taking his life. He accused me of having injected him, not with morphia, but with the awful cobra poison."

"The man must be off his head," I replied.

"No, no, he has only got into the phase of his terrible dual nature when he resembles a demon, not a man. He says that he is certain to die, and that I shall be arrested for his murder. Oh, can it be true, Dr. Halifax? Will anyone believe such a monstrous story? Tell me that you, at least, don't believe it!"

"Of course I don't, I replied. "But now you must let me go to him. If he is really poisoned in the way you describe, he must have done it himself. The poison is a fearful one, and almost momentary in its effects—he must be nearly dead by now. The important thing is to try and save his life—this is necessary both for your sake and his."

"One of the servants was by when he accused me of having injected him with the contents of that dreadful bottle," said Edith. "Oh, why did I ever steal it from Donal? I am justly punished now. How am I to endure this fearful position?"

I saw that the poor girl was frantic with fright and agony of mind. I also perceived that her presence would be of no use whatever in the sick room.

"Stay here until I come back," he said. "Believe me that I am your friend and will do my utmost to save you."

I went upstairs, and a servant showed me into the room where the sick man lay. He was lying on his back—his hands and arms were thrown outside the counterpane—he was breathing quickly—his eyes were wide open. Now and then he clenched his hands, and a slight convulsive motion ran through his frame; he was conscious, however. The moment he saw me he opened his lips and began to speak with a quick, nervous energy.

"She has had her desire," he said. "Is that you, Halifax? I am glad you have come. She concealed a bottle of cobra poison in her private cabinet for the purpose of injecting it into me. She accomplished her fiendish act an hour ago. I am dying—so much for the loving young wife—I gave her everything that man could give, and she has tried to take my life in return. Well, I vow that she shan't escape."

"You gravely accuse your wife of having poisoned you?" I said.

"It is a fact," he replied.

"How did she do it?"

"She injected cobra poison instead of morphia into my arm."

"Where did she get the poison?"

"I told you just now that I found a small bottle of it in her private cabinet."

"Where is the bottle?"

When I asked this last question, a cunning, secretive sort of look became immediately apparent in Talbot's eyes.

"You had better ask her that question," he said, in a sulky tone.

"Well, keep still and let me examine you," I said.

I had never come across a case of snake poisoning, and did not therefore feel as competent to judge symptoms as I did on most occasions; but, looking now fixedly at Talbot, it darted through my mind that the state in which I found him was unlike that which I should expect such deadly poison to produce. I opened his eyes and looked into the pupils—they were contracted; the eyes were full of a strange excitement. Beads of perspiration stood on the man's forehead; he was evidently not only in violent pain, but was also suffering from excitement almost maniacal in its intensity.

"Can you administer an antidote?" he asked, in a rapid but quivering voice.

"I will give you something to quiet you," I answered. "Now keep still."

I took his wrist between my finger and thumb—there was no depression of the heart's action. The pulses were beating fast and full. The man's heart was going like a sledge-hammer. Even as I stood by him, he began to talk rapidly and in a sort of semi-delirium.

"I'll be even with her yet. Ha, Ha, my *widow*—the inheritor of all my wealth—*I'll* put a spoke in your wheel." Then he recovered himself and looked at me cautiously. "I don't want any blundering, stupid servants about the room," he said. "Can you stay with me alone, Halifax? I wish to make a full and clear statement of what has occurred. Can a magistrate be summoned?"

I replied in soothing tones, and desired the servant to wait in the ante-room.

Snake poison or not, the man was not dying at present. I knew of antidotes to many poisons, but it suddenly flashed through my mind that the only person who could really cure Talbot was O'Brien. He had spent many years of his life in studying this special subject. I made up my mind to go immediately to see him.

Desiring the servant to remain in the ante-room, I went downstairs to where poor Edith sat, with her elbows on a table, her face covered by her hands—she started up when I entered—her eyes looked quite wild.

"Now listen to me," I said. "You must on no account lose your self-control. I am convinced that I can get you out of this, but it is necessary for you to be calm, and to show no fear. Of course, you are innocent. I know you well enough to be certain that you could no more take a man's life than you could fly—but this is a delicate matter, and it is necessary for your own sake that you should not be too much broken down in the presence of the servants. You must get one or two of the men-servants to remain in the ante-room in case the patient should become violent, but if you have strength of mind sufficient to go back to your husband, I should like you to do so and to remain with him until I return."

"Are you going to leave me?" she said with a terrified cry.

"I must for a short time. I must go to London."

"Why?" she asked, with parted lips.

"I must see O'Brien. It is my private opinion that your husband has not taken the poison."

She started up with a joyful cry.

"But I am not certain," I repeated, "and I must see O'Brien. Cobra poison is fatal almost immediately, and your husband's symptoms, although dangerous, are not those of a dying man. It is impossible for me, however, to be quite certain what the final result will be, and I wish to consult O'Brien. Talbot has imbibed alcohol in large quantities for a long time, and that fact may possibly arrest the quick action of the poison. If there's an antidote, O'Brien knows it—I must go and see him by the next train."

We looked in a time-table and found that an early train left Dorking between three and four in the morning. If I drove off immediately I should just catch it. The bell was rung, the carriage ordered, and three minutes later I found myself driving to Dorking station.

Mrs. Talbot had recovered her nerve in the most wonderful manner, and when I again begged of her to take her place in her husband's room she promised to obey me.

I reached the station in time to catch the train, and early on this summer's morning I found myself back again at Victoria. I hailed a cab and drove straight to O'Brien's lodgings. It was too early for any of the servants to be up, but I fancied I saw a light burning in the laboratory. I rang the house bell loudly, and to my relief O'Brien himself opened the door for me.

"In the name of all that's wonderful, what have you come about, Halifax?" he asked.

"I want to speak to you immediately," I replied.

He was an excitable fellow, and my presence evidently disturbed him very much. He led me with speed to his laboratory, shut the door, and faced me.

"Now, out with it," he said; "for Heaven's sake, don't keep me in suspense. Is anything wrong with Edith? Has she—oh, my God, if she has lost self-control and taken that poison, I shall administer a dose to myself. Speak, Halifax, speak."

"Keep quiet," I said. "The blow you fear has not fallen. Things are in a terrible position, though, at the bungalow. I spent yesterday there. I was alone for a time with Mrs. Talbot, and spoke to her quite frankly on the subject of the venom peptone. She confessed that she had it—and did not mean to part with it. After a little very plain speaking, I induced her to promise to give it to me. She went to fetch it, but returned in a few moments to say that it had vanished. She was much disturbed, and could in no way account for its disappearance. We hadn't any opportunity of discussing the subject, for Talbot appeared on the scene.

"I left The Elms late last evening, and returned to the White Horse. I was called up in the middle of the night to see Talbot, who, the servant said, was alarmingly ill. On returning to the bungalow, Mrs. Talbot took me into her morning-room, and told me that her husband had accused her of injecting cobra poison into his arm instead of morphia."

"The brute. Impossible!" exclaimed O'Brien.

"Try to keep calm, O'Brien. This is not a moment for any outsider to give way. Of course, the unhappy wife is innocent—that fact goes without saying—but I greatly fear that matters may look very ugly for her if Talbot dies. The first thing to be done is to try to save him. If he dies there will be a very black case against the poor, innocent wife."

I never saw anyone look paler than O'Brien when I told my story.

"Is there an antidote to the poison?" I asked, speaking quickly.

He leant up against an old oak bureau before he replied.

"The case is hopeless, Halifax," he said then. "The bottle which Edith stole from my cabinet contained a preparation of cobra poison which we call Venom Peptone. This is in truth the very essence of the cobra venom. If the man has got the contents of that bottle in his blood, nothing can save him. He is a doomed man—nay, he is dead by now."

"You have studied this poison very carefully?" I said.

"Carefully? I should think so."

I looked at my watch.

"I have a moment or two to spare before I must catch my return train to Dorking," I said. "It might help the case if you were to give me a few particulars with regard to the symptoms."

"I will do so. Perhaps I'd better tell you, first, how the poison is obtained. I collect with the aid of the snake loop. This I fasten round the neck of the cobra. The lip of a saucer is then slipped into its mouth. It grows angry, lifts its fangs, which catch on the inner edge of the saucer, against which it bites furiously again and again. Very soon a thin yellow fluid squirts out. This is the venom. It is innocent-looking enough. It has no smell and no taste. Injected, however, beneath the skin, the victim becomes immediately dull and languid. In some cases death takes place within a minute—but this would not be the case unless the dose given were especially large, or by chance entered a vein. The heart is immediately enfeebled, but after a time recovers partially; the respiration becomes slower and weaker, and still more weak; paralysis seizes the legs; the chest becomes motionless, and death quickly follows, as a rule without convulsions. If by any chance the victim survives the injection for half an hour, the part affected swells and the tissues soften as if they were melted—a horrible putrefaction occurs, and the tissues swarm with bacteria, which, as you know, are the cause of putrefaction. Meanwhile the breath-sustaining centres become weak and cease to stimulate the muscles so as to cause them to move the chest. The victim finally dies from failure to breathe. With the dose which I had collected in that small bottle death would be a certainty. I mention this to show you that there is no antidote, and Talbot has probably breathed his last long before now."

"Well, then," I said, springing up and speaking with animation, "my hopes have become certainties—none of the symptoms which you describe have taken place. There was no depression of the heart's action when I saw the patient—on the contrary, he was in a highly excitable and even maniacal state. What I believe is this, that the man is not quite accountable for his actions. I noticed a peculiar look in his eyes the moment I saw him. I think on one or two points he is insane. He told me last evening that, some years ago in India, he was bitten by a cobra. I presume the bite was a very slight one, for his life was saved. He said that ever since that day his nerves have been in a high state of irritation. Since his marriage he has been without question very jealous of his wife. A person once bitten by a snake of any sort has a horror of the reptile to his dying day. Talbot is not, I should say, a very scrupulous person. There is no doubt whatever that he discovered the bottle of cobra poison, and that the mere sight of it excited his strongest animosity. His nerves, already terribly affected in this direction, gave way—he lost all self-control, and thought of a fiendish plot by which to ruin his unhappy wife. Thank you, O'Brien; I must now return to the bungalow. I believe I see my way out of this mystery. As I said, I had a hope when I came to you, which you have made a certainty."

"Can I not go with you?" said O'Brien. "It's awful to think of the state that poor girl must be in."

"No, you had better stay away," I replied, "Your presence, under the circumstances, would do far more harm than good."

I left him, jumped again into my hansom, and returned to Victoria. I caught a train after a brief delay, and found myself, still quite early in the morning, back again at Dorking.

I had desired the Talbots' carriage to be in waiting for me, and drove out to the bungalow.

A servant came to open the carriage door.

"Is your master alive?" I asked of the man.

"Yes, sir," he replied.

I could not help breathing a sigh of relief and thankfulness. Even granted that the action of the poison was rendered slow by presence of alcohol in the system, if Talbot had really been injected with the cobra poison, he must long ago have succumbed to such a large dose. I went upstairs prepared for immediate action, and entered the room without knocking. Talbot was sitting up in bed—his whole face was deeply red; his eyes slight protruded. He was using violent and excited words. Edith was standing close to him holding his hand. I never felt a greater admiration for Mrs. Talbot than I did at that moment. She had just been accused of the most awful crime that can be laid at anyone's door. She had gone through months of racking nerve torture, and yet she stood now close to the side of the man who had accused her, absolutely forgetting herself. When he spoke wildly, when he flung himself about madly, she tried to soothe him. I noticed that he clutched her hand in a firm grip. Although he hated her, he dreaded to let her go.

"Now, Mrs. Talbot," I said, "will you have the goodness to leave the room? I should like to see your husband by himself."

My presence and the sound of my voice evidently gave her such relief that she was on the verge of breaking down. She looked at me with a pathos which I have never seen equalled, and went softly out of the room, closing the door behind her.

"Why have you sent her away?" cried Talbot, his voice harsh and penetrating. "I order her back again. What is a wife for if she can't stand by her husband's dying bed? She has poisoned me—she can at least see me out of the world. It will be a pleasure to her to see the effect of her deadly work."

"Now, look here, Talbot," I said, "there is no use wasting breath over a man in your condition, but you have still got sufficient sense to understand what I am saying to you. You are no more the victim of cobra poisoning than I am. Why, man, if the dose you accuse that innocent girl of injecting into you were really in your veins, you would have been dead two or three hours ago. You are guilty of a devilish plot to destroy the life and reputation of a helpless and innocent girl. In the presence of a physician you cannot for a moment maintain your position, and I advise you to confess the truth without delay."

The man looked at me while I was speaking, with lack-lustre eyes—he was quite dazed and puzzled for a moment, then his jaws slightly fell, and he lay back half fainting on his pillows.

I saw that my words had told, but the patient was in no physical condition for me to say anything further to him just then. I administered restoratives, felt his pulse, listened to his heart, and came to the conclusion that he was undoubtedly poisoned, but not by the deadly weapon which he had accused his wife of using.

I left him after a time, and went downstairs to speak to Mrs. Talbot.

"You may take comfort," I said to her. "Your husband is in a very dangerous state at the present moment, but, in the first place, he is not dying; in the second, he has never been injected with the deadly poison which he accuses you of having administered to him. Now you must keep up your courage—I am anxious to have a talk with you. Talbot is very ill, but I think it probable that he will recover from his present state. You told me yesterday that you were in the habit of injecting him with morphia. Are you quite certain that you only used morphia for this injection?"

"He sometimes used morphia alone, and sometimes with another preparation," she replied. "When he was in a terribly depressed state he used to mix the morphia with another drug—I have got the bottle upstairs. Shall I run and fetch it?"

"Yes," I replied.

She left the room and returned in a few minutes with a small bottle, which she placed in my hand. The mixture had been made up by a chemist, and the label on the bottle only contained some of the usual directions. I removed the cork, and smelled and tasted the contents. Like a flash the solution of Talbot's queer attack was made plain to me.

"Why, this is *cannabis indica*," I exclaimed.

"What does that mean?" asked Edith, looking at me with wildly dilated eyes.

"It means this," I answered, rising to my feet: "all your husband's symptoms point to poisoning with *cannabis indica.* Venom peptone would depress the heart's action, would stop respiration, and cause death from failure to breathe. None of these symptoms are present in your husband's case. The heart is much excited instead of being depressed—there is no difficulty of breathing. Now, my dear Mrs. Talbot, the case against you is completely broken down. If venom peptone had been injected into your husband's arm he would have been a dead man hours ago. He is a living man now, but very ill—his symptoms all point to poisoning by *cannabis indica,* which, taken in large doses, produces maniacal excitement of brain and heart. He has doubtless injected himself with this deadly drug."

"He often did, I know," answered Mrs. Talbot. "Whenever he mixed the drug he used to inject from the hypodermic syringe himself into his arm—when he only used morphia he liked me to do it for him—but oh," she added, "what is to be done? What does it all mean?"

"I should like to see your father," I said, after a short pause, during which I had been thinking hard. "He probably knows something of Talbot's past."

"What can he know? My husband returned from the West Indies eighteen months ago, he settled here, and we met him quite by accident."

"Exactly; still, I am anxious to become possessed of some of his past history, and it is possible that it may have reached your father's ears. Can you send for him?"

"Of course I can: my father only lives five miles from here. I will send the carriage with a note and ask him to come over immediately."

"Do so," I replied; "meanwhile I will go up to the patient."

"Dr. Halifax," said Mrs. Talbot, "you will not leave us to-day?"

"I will certainly not leave until your husband is better," I answered.

A faint smile was perceptible for a moment around her sad lips. She sat down to write a note to her father, and I went upstairs to Talbot. I administered soothing remedies, and after a time some of the violent symptoms abated. As I sat by the man's bedside, and watched him as he sank into a heavy sleep, I became more and more fully persuaded that this was an undoubted, although strange, case of insanity. I could not be certain, however, on this point until I could learn some particulars with regard to Talbot's previous life.

In a little over two hours Edith came to inform me that her father was downstairs.

I knew Keen slightly, but not so well as I knew his daughter. He was a thin, cadaverous-looking man, with a drawn, anxious expression of face. Edith had evidently been confiding in him, for he looked very much excited and disturbed.

"I am so glad you are here, Halifax," he said, grasping my hand. "What an awful tragedy has occurred—my poor, poor child; what is to be done for her?"

I asked Mr. Keen to accompany me into Talbot's private study; there I shut the door, and, turning round, began to speak abruptly.

"I have sent for you, Mr. Keen," I said, "to ask you a very straightforward question. When you gave your daughter to Mr. Talbot, did you know anything of his past life?"

Keen coloured painfully.

"God forgive me," he exclaimed. "Why do you ask me that question, Halifax?"

"It is necessary that I should do so," I replied, "in order to enable me to throw light on a mystery which now exists. I will tell you frankly, that it has never been my lot to listen to a more diabolical scheme to injure an innocent and good woman than that which Talbot has perpetrated. I can only account for it by believing him to be out of his mind. Can you help me to find someone who knew Talbot in the past?"

"It is quite unnecessary, Dr. Halifax," said Keen, "I, alas, am terribly to blame. When I gave Edith to Talbot, I knew his past history. He had been insane for some years, and spent that period in an asylum in the West Indies. At the time of his marriage he was supposed to have completely recovered, or, although pressed as I was, I would not have given my child to him."

"Did Edith know of this?" I asked of Keen.

"No, I was careful to keep the knowledge from her."

"I need not say that you behaved in a very unjustifiable manner," I replied; "but it is not my place to call you to account. Please help me at the present juncture with all the explanations in your power. Was there anything peculiar with regard to the nature of Talbot's insanity?"

"I was given some particulars at the time," continued Keen. "It so happened that Talbot, when a young man, was severely, but not fatally, bitten by a cobra in India. He was never very strong mentally, and the shock had a strange effect on his nerves, producing, at intervals, violent fits of insanity. On such occasions it was one of his most constant illusions to imagine that someone had injected him with cobra poison."

"You knew this when you gave your daughter to him?"

"I regret to say that I did. I was almost off my own head with misery at the moment. Much depended on the money relief which Talbot was prepared to offer. He had been in his right mind for many years, and my firm conviction was that he would never again become insane. I was wrong— may God forgive me."

"I hope He will," I answered. "I must return now to my patient. You have thrown light on the whole mystery. The thing now to be done is to get hold of the bottle of poison, for it will not be safe for Talbot and his wife to live together while he has it in his possession."

"How do you know he has it?" asked Keen.

"There is no doubt on that point—he evidently stole it from a cabinet in Mrs. Talbot's room. I must not leave a stone unturned to get it from him."

"Then he never injected himself with it?"

"Never. Had he done so, he would have been a dead man hours ago."

I went back to my patient, who was sleeping heavily. The effects of the *cannabis indica* were subsiding, and I thought it likely that when Talbot awoke from his sleep, he would more or less be restored to his right mind.

This proved to be the case. He opened his eyes late in the afternoon, and looked at me in some surprise.

"What is the matter?" he asked. "Why are you here, Dr. Halifax?"

"I am glad to see you so much better," I replied. "You have been very ill."

"Have I? I have no recollection of it."

I looked at him steadily. He moved restlessly on his pillow and asked for his wife.

"Do you really want to see her?" I asked.

"I certainly do. No one can make tea like Edith—I want her to give me a cup."

"I wonder you can bear to look at her, after the cruel and shameful way in which you have treated her," I answered.

When I said these words, Talbot's face blazed with angry colour.

"Sir," he said, "you forget yourself."

"I do not, Mr. Talbot," I answered. "It is my painful duty to recall something to your memory. Last night you were very ill—at death's door. You accused your wife of having attempted to poison you with a bottle of cobra venom."

When I said the word "cobra," the man started, and an uneasy, troubled light filled his eyes.

"You accused your wife of having poisoned you," I continued, "when you knew perfectly well that she had done nothing of the kind. The cause of your illness was due to your own mad act—you had injected yourself with a strong dose of *cannabis indica*. This drug, when recklessly administered, produces maniacal excitement."

Talbot was quite silent for a moment after I had spoken. Then he said, in a subdued voice:

"Then you think I was a maniac last night?"

"I not only think it, I know it," I answered.

"You say I injected *cannabis indica* into my body?"

"You did, Talbot—you know it; I have proof of it, so it is useless for you to attempt to deny it."

"In my fit of mania," continued Talbot, "you say I accused my wife, my young wife, of having poisoned me?"

"That is so."

"If I did such a thing I must have been insane."

"The drug you injected made you insane for the time," I answered.

"Do you think I am insane now?"

"No, the effects of the *cannabis indica* are lessening, and you are in your right mind."

"Will you believe me if I tell you, as a man of honour, that I have not the faintest remembrance of all that you describe as occurring last night? My wife is the gentlest and sweetest of women; I love her better every day."

"I believe you," I answered suddenly; "and yet, Talbot, since your marriage you have been cruel to her. You have given her moments of intense agony—such fearful moments of torture that the idea of self-destruction has occurred to her."

"Heavens! You don't say so. Why, I have always loved her to distraction. What sort of brute do you take me for?"

"I take you for a man who at times does not quite know what he is about," I replied.

"Yes, yes, I recall things now," said Talbot. "I was in an asylum once—it was years ago. My madness was caused by shock after cobra bite."

"By the way," I said, as soothingly as I could speak, "you have a bottle of cobra poison in your possession. I should like you to give it to me."

He looked at me watchfully. Up to that moment he had been sane and calm—now an uneasy glitter returned to his eyes.

"Ha, ha! I want that bottle," he said; "it may be useful."

"Will you give it to me to take care of?" I asked.

He looked at me again, and with a violent effort managed to curb the strong excitement which was rising within him.

"Halifax," he said, bending forward and grasping my arm with one of his hands, "I dread the thought of cobra poison more than anything else in all the world. I found the poison a week ago in my wife's cabinet; since then the thought of it has haunted me day and night. I have seen pictures in my dreams. I have seen the cobra, with its hooded head—I have watched its eyes with their wicked and unchanging expression. When I have dropped off to sleep I have felt its sudden stroke, and have awakened bathed in perspiration and sick with terror. Many times a day I have tried to throw away the poison, but I have never gained sufficient courage to do it. For God's sake, take it and destroy it."

"Where is it?" I asked. "You will be much calmer when it is no longer in existence."

"No," he interrupted, his whole tone changing. "I had better keep it. Any moment it will free me from my haunting agonies—the death would be painless. After the first horror of the injection the agony would be past."

"Don't be a fool, Talbot," I said. "You are exciting your nerves in the most unjustifiable manner. You have been perfectly sane for years, and if you take my advice you may remain so for all the remainder of your days."

"My days are numbered, Halifax. I have an incurable disease, which I meant to consult you about when I called at your house as we arranged."

"Be that as it may," I replied, "have the courage to end your days as a temperate and good man should—don't yield to this horror. Give me the poison."

He hesitated. A mighty struggle seemed to convulse him. Suddenly he thrust his hand under his pillow, and pulled into view a tiny bottle with a glass stopper. When he looked at it he laughed as only a madman could. I sprang upon him and wrested it from his hand. My movement was so sudden as to be unexpected. I had just time to glance at the name printed in firm characters on the label, "Venom Peptone," then I dashed the bottle with its fatal contents into the midst of a small fire which was burning in the grate. I expected Talbot to spring upon me as I did so, but when I looked round I saw that he had fainted.

The rest of this strange story is told in a few words. When Talbot recovered from his fainting fit, he was quite gentle and sane. I sent for his wife to come to him. He received her with a smile of the deepest affection, and seemed restless and uneasy when he did not hold her hand in his. I made a careful medical examination of the man that evening, and found that his own conjectures about himself were correct, and that his days on earth were numbered. He lived for about a fortnight, when he died. During his brief remaining days he had no return of insanity. His last words and looks of affection were for the young wife who in his insane moments he had so basely and cruelly maligned.

THE RED BRACELET

THE RED BRACELET

ONE morning, just at the close of my hours of consultation, my servant introduced into my consulting-room a tall, good-looking, middle-aged man. His name was Stafford. I had never seen him before. His face was slightly bronzed, and looked as if it had been much exposed to wind and weather. He had keen blue eyes, a frank expression of mouth, and a hearty manner which impressed me favourably. I motioned him to a chair, and enquired what I could do for him. He looked at me for a moment or two without replying. I saw that he was taking my measure; I also noticed that there was considerable anxiety in his eyes. After a time he spoke abruptly.

"I fear I have come here on a wild-goose chase."

"Perhaps you will allow me to decide that," I answered, with a smile.

"Yes," he continued; "of course, you are the one to decide. I had better tell you what I want at once—I am not here on my own account—I have a daughter——" Here he broke off abruptly, and taking his handkerchief from his pocket, wiped the moisture from his brow. As he did so he sighed.

"Your daughter is ill, and you want me to see her," I interrogated.

"I want you to see her, certainly, but she is not ill," he answered, springing suddenly to his feet—"that is, not ill in the ordinary sense of the word. I don't suppose anything can be done—still, I have heard a great deal of you. You have a facility for helping people out of difficulties. The facts of the case are briefly these: My girl—she is my only child— is blind, she is affected with congenital blindness. I have taken her to the best oculists in Europe, and they all alike regard her case as hopeless."

"I am sorry to say that I agree with them," I interrupted. "Congenital blindness is, as a rule, hopeless. It arises, in all probability, from some defect in the construction of the eye. The optic nerve, or some other important part of the wonderful mechanism of sight, is omitted. I shall be glad to help you, but in the first place I am not a specialist, and——"

"I have not come to ask you to help me in the matter of the blindness," said Mr. Stafford. My daughter is so accustomed to this that she scarcely feels her defect. She has been splendidly trained, and can do almost every single thing that a person with full sight can attempt—she rides, she walks, she rows, like any other girl; as to her music, it is wonderful. But, there, I must come to the point."

"Is your daughter in town?" I interrupted.

"No, she is in the country. We live in Yorkshire. Molly hates town. The atmosphere of a town has a particularly irritating effect upon her nerves. Her mother and I can seldom get her to visit London with us."

"What are her special symptoms?" I asked.

"In the ordinary sense she is not ill at all. She sleeps well, eats well, and enjoys life to the full."

"What are you uneasy about, then?" I asked.

"I'll tell you. You must know that our child is the heiress of great wealth. I am a rich man, and she inherits all I possess. About two months ago a man, who went by the name of Winchester took up his abode in our village. He stayed at the *White Hart*, and spent the greater part of his time fishing. No one knew anything about him. He was tall, good-looking, and about fifty years of age. On a near view his eyes repelled you—they were too close together, and had an ugly expression in them. In an evil moment my little girl made his acquaintance. He had the luck to save her life. You may think I ought to be grateful for this; but upon my honour, whatever he did in the first instance, I don't think I could feel a sense of gratitude towards that man. Well, I'll tell you how they came to know each other. I mentioned that the girl could ride—she can, as if she had the keenest sight under Heaven. She was fond of having a gallop across the moors on her mare, of course accompanied by someone.

"One afternoon, a little more than a month ago, the mare

took fright and ran off with her. The brute made straight for the line of rail. I don't know what might have happened had not Winchester suddenly appeared and caught the mare by her bridle just as the groom came galloping up. Yes, I acknowledge that it was a brave act, and of course I had to thank the fellow, and to make his acquaintance. He called at our place, and from the very first I noticed that he had an extraordinary influence over my child. My belief is that he hypnotized her almost directly. To make a long story short, this fellow, old enough to be her father, has had the presumption to propose for my girl, and she is so desperately in love with him, that if I don't give my consent to the marriage, her health, reason, or even perhaps her life itself, may be endangered."

"You use strong expressions," I answered. "May I ask what you expect me to do in the case?"

"I want you to open my child's mental eyes, in some way or other, in order that she may see this man as he really is. It is a craze—a regular craze—with the girl. Winchester hasn't a penny; he only wants the child for her money. Do you think he would saddle himself with a blind wife if he didn't want her gold?"

"Perhaps not," I answered; "and yet I have known blind girls very attractive."

The father gave an impatient sigh.

"My child would be a lovely creature if her eyes were right. The sightless balls are well formed, the eyelashes black and long, and the eyelids well open; but the eyes are covered with a thick film, and this film gives to her face a peculiarly strange, and even startling, appearance. I know Winchester doesn't care a bit for her except for her gold, and I'm determined he sha'n't have her."

"I am truly sorry for you," I answered, "but I must frankly say I am puzzled to know how to help you. How is it possible for me to influence your daughter, when I don't even know her?"

Stafford gave me a hopeless stare.

"I thought you might suggest something," he said. "I have heard of you from several friends. I tell you the man has hypnotized my girl, and what I want you to do is to hypnotize her in another direction. Now, can you, and will you?"

"I am afraid you ask for an impossibility," I replied. "You will forgive me for saying that I think the matter simple enough. It is plainly your duty to remove your daughter from the immediate vicinity of this man. You don't like him, you think his object in paying his addresses unworthy, you have but to be firm, to refuse your consent to the marriage, to take your child away, and the influence which Winchester exercises over her will be weakened, and will gradually die out."

When I said this, Stafford shook his head—he walked across the room, turned his back on me, and gazed out of the window.

His manner annoyed me, and I spoke with some slight irritation.

"Surely you, as Miss Stafford's father, can forbid the union?" I said. "Surely you have trained your child to obey you?"

"I have, Dr. Halifax; a sweeter and more obedient child never lived until she met this fellow. I must tell you frankly, however, that now I have lost all power over her. Molly has told both her mother and me that she will marry Basil Winchester whether we wish it or not. Our wishes, our distress, have not the slightest power over her. We consider her, in short, scarcely responsible for her actions. The man's influence is the strangest thing I have ever seen. I believe he can hypnotize her even from a distance, and he is so clever that if we take her to the other end of the world, he will contrive to follow us."

"Well," I said, "as you cannot influence Miss Stafford to yield to your wishes, had you not better try the other way round? You think that Winchester wants your daughter for her gold. Can you not inform him that if he marries her without your permission, you will cut her off with the proverbial shilling?"

Stafford shrugged his shoulders, and gave a grim smile.

"I might say so twenty times," he replied, "but Winchester would not believe me. He would know, what is a fact, that whatever the child did, I could not be unkind to her. He is well aware that she is the apple of her mother's eye and mine. At the present moment she is simply lost to us: she is deaf to our entreaties. She thinks of nothing morning, noon, or night, but this man, who has contrived to get an appalling power over her. I tell you what it is, Dr. Halifax, I have such a dislike to the fellow, that I would rather see my only child in her grave than his wife, and yet I feel that if something is not done at once, he will contrive to accomplish the marriage."

"The case is a strange one," I said; "still——"

"You will do something for us, won't you? I have come up to London on purpose to consult you."

"You are very good, but you place more faith in me than I deserve."

"You do acknowledge that there is a power in hypnotism?" asked Stafford.

"Undoubtedly."

"Well, can't one hypnotist counterbalance the will of another, if he happens to have a stronger power?"

"Perhaps so," I replied. "To tell the truth, I have never gone thoroughly into this subject."

"Well, at least, will you do this? Will you come down to Yorkshire, and see my girl?"

"Certainly, if you wish it."

"I do. When can you come?"

"Towards the end of the present week, if that will suit you."

"Admirably. Come on Saturday, and stay till Monday. We will speak of you to Molly as a friend, and not address you by your name of doctor."

"As you like," I replied.

"Very well, then—that is happily arranged. Our place is called Mount Stafford, and is situated about five miles out of York. If you will send a telegram to state the hour when you will leave town, I will meet you at York station. I am heartily obliged to you for giving me so much of your time."

On the appointed day I went down to Yorkshire. Stafford met me at the railway station. It only needed one glance at his face to see that something fresh had occurred.

"Thank God, you have arrived," he said, taking my hand in his great grip. "Now come along to the carriage."

"Is anything the matter?" I asked, as we hurried across the platform.

"Yes, yes; but I won't wait to tell you here. What a relief it is to see your face. Here we are. Step in, doctor. Home, Jenkins, as fast as you can."

The carriage door was shut by a footman. Immediately afterwards a pair of spirited horses started forward at a quick pace. We soon left the picturesque city of York behind us.

"What has happened?" I asked, turning to my host.

He took off his hat, and, pulling a handkerchief out of his pocket, wiped his overheated face.

"What do you think?" he exclaimed. "That scoundrel made an appointment, no later than yesterday morning, to run off with my child. To this last act of wicked folly had he brought the gentlest and most obedient creature that ever breathed. She waited for him in the pine wood, at the back of our house, for one hour—two hours. It rained—she was wet to the skin. By the merest accident I found her there— she looked like one in a trance. I touched her, and called her name. She turned round quickly, and told me what she meant to do, just as though it were the most natural thing in the world. I expressed some of my horror to her—I expostulated —I appealed to her old affectionate feelings—I might as well have spoken to a stone.

"'I am going with him—I shall die without him,' she reiterated over and over again.

"There was no shame in her—no sense of guilt. I had finally to bring her back to the house by force. I left her with her mother, and went off to the *White Hart*. You can imagine my feelings. When I inquired for Winchester, I was told that he had left—gone off, bag and baggage, at an early hour that morning—left no address, and owed some debts in the neighbourhood. He has not since been heard of."

"He is a good riddance," I could not help exclaiming.

"Yes, yes; but, Halifax, the child is dying."

"Oh, come; it can't be so bad as that!" I exclaimed.

"But it is—I tell you it is. You don't know the power that man had over her. She was the brightest creature you can possibly imagine; but, after all, she was not like other girls, and this love affair was not of the ordinary kind. I told you, of course, that it was, in my opinion, a case of hypnotism from first to last.

"Even in the short month of their intercourse she has changed from a hardy, healthy-looking girl, to a mere shadow. Sleep and appetite have failed. The scoundrel won her heart by the most underhand means, and then deliberately forsook her."

"I sympathize with all your feelings with regard to that man," I answered; "but, under the circumstances, he did the best thing he could when he left your daughter."

"You say so, because you have not seen her," replied Stafford. "She has touched no food since yesterday morning —her sleep is more like torpor than natural slumber. Her low moans would ring anyone's heart. In short, she only takes consolation in one thing."

"What is that?" I asked.

"The fellow gave her a bracelet, which he told her he had hypnotised—it is made of red coral. He had the face to inform the child that when she wore it round her arm she would be able to ascertain his wishes—he said it was a link between her and him. Badly as he has treated her, her over-powering passion for him is beyond all reason—she clings to the bracelet as if it were her life. It is piteous to see her sitting apart from everyone worshipping this silly trinket, and imagining that the scoundrel is communicating with her through it."

"There is no doubt that Winchester's influence has affected Miss Stafford's mind for the time being," I replied. "We must see what can be done to get it into a healthy channel as quickly as possible. As to the bracelet, it is bad for her to have it, and, if possible, it ought to be taken from her."

"There is no use in thinking of that, Halifax. She would find it wherever we put it. Her mother managed to slip it from her arm last night while she slept. Mrs. Stafford took it from the room, and locked it in her own wardrobe. What do you think happened? Molly awoke, felt her arm, found that the bracelet was missing, and walked straight from her own room into ours, approached the wardrobe, placed her hand on the drawer which contained the bracelet, and asked her mother for the key.

"'I want to get my bracelet out of that drawer, mother,' she said.

"'How can you possibly know it is there?' asked my wife, quite startled, and thrown off her balance, by the child's words.

"'I see a light pointing to the red bracelet,' she answered. 'I shall go mad if I don't have it. Give it to me at once,'

" There was nothing for it but to humour the child — her mother gave her back the bracelet, she pressed it to her lips, sighed with pleasure, and carried it off at once. Well, here we are. You shall see my daughter in a moment or two. She knows you are coming. I have told her you are a friend of mine — I have not mentioned the fact of your being a physician. Try and get her confidence, if you can."

The carriage drew up before a tall portico. A footman ran down a flight of steps to open the door. The next moment we were in my friend's entrance-hall.

" Tell your mistress we have arrived," said Stafford, turning to the servant.

The man immediately left the hall, and in a moment Mrs. Stafford came hurrying out of one of the reception-rooms to meet us. She was a tall, dignified-looking woman, with a pale face, and large, dark grey eyes. These eyes showed traces now of recent tears.

" How is Molly ? " asked Stafford, when he had introduced me to his wife.

" Just the same," answered Mrs. Stafford, with a sigh.

" Have you tried to get her to eat anything ? "

" I have, but it is useless," replied the mother. " She pushes all food aside with the extraordinary remark that her throat is closed. She is lying down at present, and when I left her room she had the red bracelet tightly pressed against her cheek. I think she sleeps just now. As I was leaving her room I heard her murmur that terrible man's name."

" Suppose I go up and see her while she sleeps ? " I said. " I will be very careful not to arouse her."

Mrs. Stafford gazed at me fixedly.

" Perhaps you forget," she said, " that our poor darling is blind. All you have to do is not to speak. Molly has never seen anything in the whole course of her life. She will not know you are in the room if she does not hear your voice."

" Well, that is all the better," I answered, cheerfully. " I can watch her without her noticing me."

" She is very weak," answered the mother, as she took me upstairs and led me down a corridor to Miss Stafford's room. "Her failure of strength is most remarkable. It is now nearly thirty hours since that man disappeared. Each moment seems to take something from her vitality. I could never have believed that hypnotism was such an awful power if I did not witness its effects upon my child."

"It is a fearful and dangerous power," I replied. "The sooner your daughter is released from its spell, the better."

"Sometimes I fear that it may be necessary for us to find Basil Winchester," said Mrs. Stafford. "He has exercised this spell over the child: he alone may be able to remove it."

"I hope we may relieve Miss Stafford by some other means," I answered. "The less she sees of Winchester in the future the better—but now take me to her. Is this her room?"

"Yes; let us tread softly—I should like the child to have her sleep out."

We entered a very dainty and prettily-furnished girl's room. The last rays of the evening sun were streaming into the chamber, and one of them now fell right across the foot of the bed on which the recumbent figure of a very young and remarkably pretty girl lay. Thick, dark lashes shaded the cheeks — the brows were delicate, finely pencilled, and perfectly black. The hair, which was thrown back over the pillows, was abundant, and of the luxurious and curly order. Its shade was of a rich tone of brown, with a slight admixture of red in it—the complexion was delicate—the features regular. As I looked for the first time at Molly Stafford, I could not help feeling a distinct pang at my heart. She was an only child—she was the one treasure of this rich and prosperous couple. Without her, of what avail to them would be their house, their lands, their gold? If ever a girl appeared ill unto death, this one did. There was a transparency about her complexion—a waxlike hue was spread all over her face, which showed me how serious was the drain on her system made by a mysterious and little understood power. I took one of her limp hands in mine, and felt her feeble, fluttering pulse. The other hand was pressed against her cheek. On the wrist of this small, right hand I saw the bracelet—the red beads pressed the sleeper's soft cheek, making faint marks there. The mother came up and stood by my side as I gazed. Suddenly she bent forward and touched my arm.

"What do you think of her?" she asked, in a whisper of uncontrollable anxiety.

"I will talk to you presently," I answered.

As I spoke I bent down over the child, and pushing back the hair from her brow, listened to her hurried breathing. When I did this she suddenly, and without the least warning, opened her eyes wide. The effect was so startling that I stepped back. While she slept I had forgotten the fact of her blindness—now it was abundantly manifest. The opened eyes made such a complete change in her whole appearance that her beauty vanished, giving place to positive ugliness—ugliness of an almost repellent order. The sightless eyes themselves were well-formed, and of a good size. They were turned now full upon me, and the brows became slightly knit. I had never seen such eyes before. I can only describe them as all white. There was no cornea, no iris, no pupil. The entire eyeball was white, as is the outside margin of the ordinary eye.

"Who touched me?" said the girl, starting up in bed, and covering the wrist on which she wore the bracelet with her other hand. "There is an adverse influence in the room. I won't have anything to do with it. Mother, are you there?"

"I am close to you, Molly."

"But there is someone else in the room—someone who is against me. Who is it?"

"Tell her at once," I said to the mother; "there is no use in deceiving her."

"You can't deceive me, even if you try," said Miss Stafford. As she spoke she flung the bed-clothes aside and sprang out of bed—she had lain down in her dress—she came quickly up to where I was standing.

"Who are you? Tell me at once," she repeated.

"I am a friend of your father's," I answered, "and I hope also to be a friend of yours. Your father and mother have told me that you are in trouble."

"Yes, I am—I am in great trouble."

"Well, as I am a doctor, I may be able to do something for you."

She laughed wildly.

"Of all people in the world, I wish least to see a doctor," she answered. "I am not ill—at least, in the ordinary sense. I am in trouble because—because my heart bleeds—but this comforts me. It is warm—it has life in it—some of his life."

Here she pressed the coral beads passionately to her lips.

"Listen to me," I said, in a firm voice. "You are at present under the influence——"

"Oh, you need not tell me," she interrupted. "I glory in being under Basil Winchester's influence."

"You are at present under the dangerous influence of hypnotism," I continued.

She started violently when I said these words; then, with a swift movement, infinitely touching, went straight up to her mother, and put her arms round her neck.

"Mother, darling, don't let that man say anything more to me," she whispered—"he is a stranger—his influence is adverse—I don't want to get under it—take him away from me, mother."

"You are mistaken, Molly," answered Mrs. Stafford; "this gentleman would not hurt you for the world: he is a friend of ours, Dr. Halifax."

"I don't wish to have anything to do with him. I know what he has come for—he wants to take my bracelet away."

"You are altogether mistaken," I said, coming near her as I spoke. "If you will do something for me, I faithfully promise not to touch your bracelet."

A look of great relief came over her face.

"I will do anything, if I may keep my bracelet."

"On one condition you may keep it."

"What is that?"

"That you eat something which I am going to order for you."

"I can't eat, my throat is closed."

"That is folly," I replied. "You are giving way to a feeling of hysteria. This is causing your father and mother great unhappiness. Your throat is not closed, you only imagine it. Mrs. Stafford, will you get your daughter to wash her face and hands, and then bring her downstairs to one of the sitting-rooms? You will eat something, Miss Stafford, when I tell you to?" I finally added.

She made no reply, but detaching her arms from her mother's neck, she let them fall to her sides, and followed me with her queer sightless eyes as I left the room. The terrible eyes seemed to watch me as if they could see. I went immediately downstairs, and in about ten minutes Mrs. Stafford appeared in one of the drawing-rooms, leading her daughter by the hand.

To my astonishment, the girl loosened her grasp of her mother's hand and came straight up to me, exactly as a person with sight would do.

"Here I am," she said. "I promise to obey you if I may keep my bracelet. Now, what am I to do?"

"Take this glass of port wine, and drink it off," I said.

I had asked Stafford to have wine and biscuits in readiness, and I now filled a glass with good old port, and put it into Miss Stafford's hand.

"Drink," I said; "you can do so if you wish."

She didn't even attempt to struggle against my stronger will. Taking the glass, she raised it to her lips and drained off the contents at one draught.

"That is capital," I answered; "now eat this biscuit."

She did so with a sort of queer, desperate haste. When she had finished the first, I gave her another, which was also devoured quickly.

"That will do," I said, when she had finished the second biscuit. "Now sit here—I want to have a talk with you."

"I may keep my bracelet?" she inquired.

"I have said so," I answered. "I hope, before long, that you will give it to me of your own free will, but until that time comes I, for one, will certainly not deprive you of it."

"I believe that you are speaking the truth—I believe that I can trust you," she answered, with a profound sigh of relief.

She sat down on a low seat. The coral bracelet was on her left wrist; she stroked the red beads tenderly with the fingers of her right hand. As she did so, pleased smiles began to flit across her worn, little face.

"I am better for my food," she said, after a pause.

"Of course you are," I answered. "It was very silly of you to refuse to eat. You must have another meal presently, but not just yet."

She raised her head and gave me one of her sightless gazes; alarm became manifest in her face.

"I don't believe I shall be able to eat any more," she said; "my throat is getting that dreadful closed feeling again."

"You won't feel your throat troubling you when I wish you to eat," I said.

"But, surely, doctor, you are not going to hypnotize me?"

"I am not," I answered.

"Then why do you suppose that I shall obey you?"

"Because I intend to exercise my strong will over yours—yours is just now weakened by sorrow."

"Oh, yes," she interrupted, "by terrible, maddening grief."

"You have parted for the time being with common-sense," I continued, taking no apparent notice of her anguish. "I mean to bring that precious possession back to you."

I spoke so far in the driest way, but then, seeing how weak she was, I allowed some of the sympathy which I really felt to get into my voice.

"I pity you sincerely," I said. "It is possible that I may be able to help you, if we can have a little talk alone. May I see Miss Stafford for a few moments by herself?" I continued, turning to the parents.

"Certainly," said Stafford. He and his wife had been watching us with the most intense anxiety. They now left the room. Molly took no notice of their departure. She sat huddled up near a fire, which was not unpleasant on this late autumn day. Her sightless eyes seemed to watch the flames as they flickered.

"Do you know that there is a fire in the grate?" I asked, suddenly.

"Yes," she replied.

"You doubtless feel the warmth," I continued.

"I feel the warmth," she answered; "but that is not all. I have a sensation when my eyes are fixed on a fire, or on the sun, as if at any moment I were going to understand the full meaning of light. I have had that strange sensation all my life. I daresay most blind people know it."

"Possibly," I replied; "you were born blind, were you not?"

"Yes, but pray don't talk about my blindness now, it is incurable; my eyes are not made the same way as other people's. That which gives sight has been denied them."

"So I have heard," I answered, briefly.

"Don't let us talk of it now. I don't miss what I never had; but oh, my God, my God, I miss one thing *inexpressibly*."

Here she clasped her hands so tightly together, that the delicate blue veins started into view. She stood up and gave utterance to a low and bitter cry.

"You know what has happened?" she said, turning swiftly round to me. "The man I love has left me."

"I know," I answered—"your father has told me. You see, he is not a good man."

"What does that matter? He is necessary to me."

"Do you really love him?" I asked. My words evidently surprised her; she paused in thought.

"I can't tell you whether I love him or not," she said at last. "I can only repeat that he is necessary to me. I have only known him for a little over a month, and during that short time he has become an essential part of my life. All the rest of the world may go; but if he remains, I shall be happy. He has gone, and the world is dark—dark as my sightless eyes. Oh, this agony will kill me. I feel as if my heart were bleeding inside—it will soon bleed itself to death."

The poor girl gave utterance to a groan as she spoke—she sank back into a chair, her face looked ghastly.

"If this man were back with you, you would be happy?" I asked.

"My heart would stop bleeding."

"But, answer me, would you be happy?"

"I don't—quite—know." She brought out these words with distinctness.

"When people love, and are together, they are generally happy," I said.

"I have heard so," she replied. "I never thought that love of that sort could come into the life of a blind girl. It came, but I don't think my sensations were ever those of happiness. I can't tell you what I really felt. An irresistible and great force surrounded me. I knew that I had no will apart from that of Basil Winchester's. Anything he told me, I did—even if he asked me to do wrong I did it. My father and mother were opposed to our marriage, but I cared nothing for their opposition. I lived—I live—only for him. He has gone now, and—I am dying—it is as if the sun had set."

"You ought not to speak in that way—think of your parents."

She shook her head.

"It is useless," she murmured.

"They love you dearly."

"I know that, but the knowledge of their love doesn't affect me in any way."

"Don't you love them in return?"

"No, I don't think I love anyone. The only emotion my heart

is capable of is of a great, passionate, starved yearning to be with Basil."

"Suppose you found out that Winchester was not a good man—that he was, in short, a scoundrel?"

"I should not care—he would still be Basil Winchester to me."

Beads of perspiration were standing out on her forehead. As she spoke she panted. I saw that I must not question her further.

"Well," I said, in a soothing tone, "you have my promise not to take your bracelet from you—that is, if you will continue to eat when I think it necessary to give you food."

"I will do anything if you will leave me the bracelet. I am certain that, without it, I shall lose my senses."

She began again to stroke the beads with her thin fingers. As she did so, a look of calm returned to her face.

"This bracelet is part of the man I love," she said. "When I press it to my cheek, I experience a very strange sensation. I feel as if cords were drawing me to where my lover is. I feel as if I must arise, and go to him—then I seem to hear his voice telling me to stay where I am—I try to be patient— I endure—but the drops of blood come from my heart all the time. My starved heart is dying. Dr. Halifax, can anything be done for me?"

"Certainly," I answered; "what you need more than anything else just at present is quiet sleep—you have talked quite enough. I am going to ask your mother to put you to bed, and then I will give you something to make you sleep."

"But my bracelet?"

"You have my promise that it shall not be touched. Now, I am going to speak to your mother."

I left the room—Mrs. Stafford was waiting for me in the ante-room.

"The strain and excitement are considerable," I said. "I can't conceal from you that the case is one of great anxiety. The hypnotist has exercised his wicked power to the full. I by no means despair, however, and the first thing necessary to be done is to get your daughter to have a long, refreshing sleep. Will you see that she goes to bed at once, Mrs. Stafford? When she is comfortably in bed, I will give her a composing draught."

Mrs. Stafford hurried off to obey my orders. In half an

hour the exhausted girl was lying between the sheets. I took a draught which I had specially prepared to her bedside.

" Drink this at once," I said.

I was glad to find that my voice had already considerable power over her. The moment I spoke, she raised herself obediently on her elbow. I put the glass containing the medicine in her hand—she drained off the dose.

" Now you are certain to have a pleasant sleep," I said. "I am going to sit with you until I find you are in refreshing slumber."

I took my seat by the bedside. Miss Stafford closed her eyes immediately. In less than ten minutes she was in the land of dreams.

The rest of the evening passed quietly Soon after dinner Mrs. Stafford went up to her daughters room. She was absent for nearly an hour ; when she returned there was an excited, triumphant expression on her face.

" What has happened, Mary ? " asked her husband.

" I think I have done a good thing," she replied. " I have got rid of the coral bracelet at last."

I started up in annoyance. " Have you really taken the bracelet from Miss Stafford's arm ? " I asked. " If so, I must beg of you to put it back at once."

Mrs. Stafford gazed at me in astonishment.

" I don't understand you," she said. " The influence of that bracelet has been most pernicious—I removed it just now when the child was in such a heavy sleep that she did not in the least notice what I was doing."

" I promised Miss Stafford that she might keep the bracelet," I repeated. " Will you kindly give it to me, and I will slip it back again."

Mrs. Stafford looked startled and distressed.

" But I can't," she replied. " I was wondering where to hide it, for Molly's instinct about recovering it has been marvellous. As I was hurrying downstairs, one of the servants came to tell me that a gipsy woman, whom I knew very well, was waiting in the lower hall to speak to me. It occurred to me that I would give her the bracelet. I did so ; she slipped it on her baby's arm, and left Mount Stafford some minutes ago."

Mrs. Stafford had scarcely said these words, and I had no time to reply, when a slight noise near the door caused us all to turn our heads. To our astonishment and dismay, Molly Stafford, in her long white night-gown, entered the room. She was staring straight before her with her queer, sightless eyes. She walked across the room in the direction of an open window. One glance into her face showed me that she was walking in her sleep.

" Hush," I whispered to her parents, " we must not awaken her--let us follow her."

She stepped over the window-sill and went out into the starlit night. Straight up the avenue she went—her rich hair fell over her neck and shoulders—her feet were bare, and I wondered that the pain of walking on the gravel did not awaken her. We all followed her at a little distance. Presently she paused at a wicket gate which led up to one of the lodges ; she opened the gate quickly, and with a decided push ; walked up the narrow path, and lifting the latch of the door entered. There was a bright light inside ; the lodge-keeper and his wife were sitting over their supper, and in one corner I saw to my astonishment the dark face of a woman who evidently must have been a gipsy. A baby sat on her knee. On the baby's arm dangled the coral bracelet.

With a warning gesture Mr. and Mrs. Stafford enjoined silence on the amazed group. Miss Stafford walked quickly to the child, snatched the bracelet from its arm, slipped it on her own, and left the cottage as abruptly and noiselessly as she had entered. As quickly as she had left the house, she now returned to it, entered the drawing-room by the open window, crossed the room, and went straight upstairs to her own bedroom. She lay down in bed with a sigh of relief, folded the bed-clothes around her, and clasped her recovered treasure to her cheek.

The whole occurrence must have been a dream to her, and she would not in all probability know anything about it when she awoke.

" I should like to watch by her for the present," I said to the mother.

" I will share your watch," she replied.

The sick girl slept far into the night. As the hours went by her condition satisfied me less and less. The sleeping draught I had given her produced heavy slumber, but there was no doubt, from her restless movements and her heavy groans, that her mind was awake and active. Few doctors believe in the well-known phrase, "a broken heart," but if anyone were likely to die of this malady, the girl over whom I was now watching would be the one. Her blindness and her peculiarly nervous and highly strung temperament would all conduce to this effect. Amongst the many victims of hypnotism, there would be no sadder case than that of Molly Stafford, unless I could devise some means for her relief. Up to that moment no light dawned upon me, but I waited in hope.

About three in the morning, the sick girl awoke. She opened her sightless eyes, and in her own peculiar fashion turned them immediately upon the person nearest to her. I happened to be that person. She appeared to look at me; presently she put out the hand on which she wore the bracelet, and touched my coat-sleeve.

"You are there?" she said, in a whisper.

"Yes," I answered.

"Why do you watch me?"

"Because you are ill," I replied. "Now, I am going to give you something to eat."

"My throat is closed," she began.

"I am not going to listen to that sort of nonsense," I answered. As I spoke I motioned to Mrs. Stafford—she approached the bedside with a cup of strong beef-tea. I took the cup in one hand, and putting my other hand under the girl's shoulder, raised her to a semi-sitting position.

"Drink this at once," I said.

For a moment she seemed to shrink into herself, but then, making an effort, she held up her lips obediently. I held the cup to them—she emptied the contents, lying back again on her pillow with a sigh.

"Now you are going to sleep again," I said. "Give me your hand."

"No," she answered, "you will hypnotize me; Basil used to hold my hand when he wanted me to do what he wished— I don't wish anyone else to hold my hand."

"I promise not to hypnotize you," I answered, "but I should like to hold your hand for a few moments, for I think it will help you to sleep."

"I want to rest," she answered, in a low voice—"I am tired—tired to death!"—as she spoke, she slipped her little hand into mine.

For the first few moments she was restless, then she quieted down; she had nearly dropped off to sleep, when she raised herself to say a few words.

"I don't feel the dreadful, drawing sensation so badly now," she whispered. Then her eyes closed in slumber.

When she was quite sound asleep, I motioned to Mrs. Stafford to take my place by the bedside, and softly left the room.

I had thought hard while the sick girl slept—an idea had come to me at last.

Stafford was waiting for me downstairs; he was far too anxious to go to bed.

"Well," he said, when he saw me, "what do you make of the case?"

"It is serious," I answered. "It would be wrong for me to tell you anything else, but I don't consider it hopeless."

"What do you mean? Can you do anything to counteract the terrible influence under which our child is lying?"

"At present I am not quite certain," I answered. "The right thing—the only thing to do will be, by some means or other, to divert your daughter's thoughts into a completely new channel. Her illness is due to a strange and overstrained condition of the imagination. All her thoughts are turned inwards. Her blindness adds much to this condition. If I could only give her back her sight?"

Stafford laughed, hoarsely.

"My dear fellow," he exclaimed, "even doctors can't do impossibilities—remember, the child was born blind."

"I know," I answered. I did not add any more.

"Her mother and I have taken Molly to nearly every oculist in Europe," continued Stafford. "One and all pronounce the case hopeless. A glance ought to show you, Halifax, that the eyes are not properly formed—there is no coloured part—the entire eye is white."

"Yes," I answered again. I was silent for a few minutes, thinking deeply; then I spoke.

"With your permission, Mr. Stafford, I should like to examine your daughter's eyes very carefully by full daylight. I have doubtless no right to differ from my brother doctors, but I have noticed a strange peculiarity about your child, which I have never seen before in a blind person. She is stone blind, but she turns her eyes fully upon the person she is speaking to. She confessed to me also that in strong light, such as bright fire-light or the full rays of the sun, she has a sensation which she thinks must resemble the feelings of those who see light. I own that I have very little to go upon, but I shall not be satisfied with regard to the condition of your daughter's eyes until I have examined them for myself."

My words could scarcely fail to excite Stafford—his eyes sparkled, his voice shook.

"You speak in a strange way," he said, "and I am the last to put an obstacle in your path, but for God's sake don't arouse a hope in that poor child which can never be realized."

"In her present condition, even the presence of such a hope for a few hours can be nothing but beneficial," I answered. "When I examine her eyes it will be necessary for me to ask her a few questions. If I am right—if there are really perfect eyes behind the curtains which now shroud them—I am firmly convinced that your girl will be completely cured from the strange infatuation under which she labours. The effect of hypnotism is overpowering to some natures. Your daughter was an easy victim. I can scarcely think of that scoundrel with patience, but if Miss Molly can get back her sight, I am convinced that all will be well with her."

"I believe you," exclaimed Stafford. "To think of Molly with eyes like other girls is too great a hope to be realized quickly."

"Don't build on it," I answered, "but allow me to examine the eyes as soon and as thoroughly as possible."

The day which was now about to dawn was Sunday.

Soon after eleven o'clock Miss Stafford softly entered the room where I was sitting. I did not know that she was awake, and could not help starting when I saw her. She was dressed in white, and looked very young, beautiful, and child-like. A glance, however, at her sightless eyes changed the beauty into ugliness. Oh, that I could but remove the hideous veil which covered them. She came into the room with a gliding, graceful motion peculiarly her own, and as was her wont, came straight up to me as though she saw me. She put out her hand and spoke in a low, musical voice.

"I feel a little better," she said. "That last sleep refreshed me. You soothed me when you held my hand. I don't think any the less of Basil—the links between us are still complete, but I am less restless when you are by."

"That is right," I answered, in a cheerful tone. "Please remember what I told you yesterday—the man whom you call Basil Winchester has hypnotized you. I am not going to hypnotize you, but I am going to exercise my will over yours."

"You have done so already," she answered. "I eat when you tell me; I sleep when you wish me to; I don't feel wicked when I am with you. I even begin, just a little, a very little, to take an interest in my father and mother again. Basil used to make all the rest of the world a blank. He always stood himself in a wonderful light, but beyond him was darkness."

"You talk of light," I said, suddenly; "what do you know about it?"

A wave of colour rushed up to her pale cheeks.

"Nothing really," she replied, "and yet a great deal. I am always imagining what light is like. On a sunshiny day nothing gives me such pleasure as to go out and gaze directly up to where the great heat comes from. I seem to see light then. I know well it is only seeming, for I shall never see light, but I picture what it is like."

"I wish you would try to describe your picture," I said.

"It is difficult," she answered, "for, of course, you know I have no knowledge of colour. I can best describe what I fancy light to be by telling you what noises are to me. Do you know the clashing sound of a full string band? Bright light seems somewhat to resemble that. Twilight is like the slow movement in one of Mendelssohn's 'Songs Without Words,' and darkness resembles the 'Dead March.' Oh, I know I am talking nonsense!"

"Not at all," I replied; "you describe your sensations well. Now come and stand in this sunshine, and tell me what you feel."

To my surprise, she went immediately and stood by the window. The noonday sun was pouring a great flood of light into the room.

"How did you guess that the sunshine was here?" I asked.

"I heard the noise of the string band," she answered; "now I feel the heat on my face. Oh, I have a rapturous moment—it is almost as if I must burst some veil at any instant, and really see."

"Stay still for an instant," I said; "I should like to look into your eyes."

"Don't, they are terrible to look at."

"They are peculiar; now stand perfectly still while I examine them."

She stood as motionless as a statue. The sightless balls were turned full upon me; I examined them carefully. The white sclerotic membrane completely covered the entire ball, but where the cornea ought to be in the ordinary eye, I noticed a very slight bulging. That was enough.

"Thank you, Miss Stafford," I said to her; "that will do for the present."

She replied, in a fretful tone:

"I wish you hadn't looked at my eyes. Many doctors have done so already. I have had many brief moments of hope, but they have always been extinguished in despair. You are not an oculist. Why did you raise hopes that can never be realized?"

"How do you know they can never be realized?" I asked.

"How do I know?" she answered. "I have got no eyes in the ordinary sense."

"It would make you very happy to see like other people?" I continued, after a pause.

"Happy," she answered; "it is unkind of you even to speak of it."

She stood perfectly still, while large tears gathered in her sightless eyes and rolled down her cheeks.

"I can't bear it," she said, after a pause; "no one knows what the longing for light has been to me. There have been moments, but that was before I knew Basil, when I even wished to die, because I believed that afterwards I should see."

"Come over here," I said, taking her hand. "Sit down, I have something to say. I have just looked at your eyes, and an idea which occurred to me last night has been very much strengthened. Now you must stay quite calm while I speak to you. Your blindness is of a very peculiar and uncommon type. I don't *know* that it can be cured."

"Cured!" she exclaimed. "You speak as if it were a possibility. Oh, Dr. Halifax, do you dare to give me hope?"

"Yes," I answered, slowly, "I do. You are blind—you are afflicted with congenital blindness, but, nevertheless, I believe there is a chance of your sight being restored. Now, I will tell you frankly what my idea is. I think—remember, it is only conjecture after all ; but I am strongly inclined to believe that you possess perfect eyes under the thick membrane which covers them. My reasons for this idea are twofold. First, you have a conception of light, which a totally blind person who has never seen does not, as a rule, possess. Second, your sensations are intensified when you look full up at the sun, or when you gaze at a very bright fire. This would be scarcely likely to be the case if the organs of vision were altogether absent. I have a third reason for my hope. Where the cornea ought to exist in the normal eye, you have a very slight bulging. In short, my hope with regard to your recovery of sight is sufficiently strong to induce me to ask you to consent to a slight operation. If, after all, my hopes are false, you will be no worse off than you are at present. If, on the other hand, I am right —— "

" Yes, if you are right ? " exclaimed Molly—she grasped my hand, holding it with the strength of iron. " If you are right ? " she repeated.

" If I am right," I said, quietly, " you will see as well as any other person."

" Oh, merciful and kind God," she exclaimed—she covered her face with her trembling hands—"then I shall see Basil ! I can scarcely dare to think of this rapture ! "

" I am going to speak to your parents now," I said ; " stay quietly here until I return to you."

I left her and went to seek Stafford, who was wandering restlessly about, evidently waiting for me.

" Well," he said, when he saw me—" well, did you examine her eyes ? "

" I did—let us come into this room, I want to talk to you."

Stafford drew me into his smoking-room. Mrs. Stafford was there—she looked even more excited than her husband.

" My husband has told me all about your extraordinary thought, Dr. Halifax," she said. " Have you looked at our child's eyes ? Is there a vestige of hope ? "

" There is," I replied. " I have examined your daughter's eyes very carefully. Their condition is peculiar—the sclerotic membrane covers the entire eyeball. The present condition of the eyes points to hopeless congenital blindness ; neverthe-less, I am not without hope. In examination I noticed a bulging where the cornea ought to be. My hope is that there is a perfect eye behind the membrane, which now completely covers the whole ball. I have told my hope to your daughter."

"You have told Molly? How cruel of you!" exclaimed Mrs. Stafford.

"No," I answered, "if you saw Miss Stafford now, you would not think what I have done cruel. She is so excited—so lifted out of herself—that, for the time, at least, she has almost forgotten the strange craze which is over her. She will willingly submit to an operation."

"An operation? We ought not to risk it," said the mother.

"There is no risk," I answered. "At the worst the slight scar which I shall make will quickly heal, and the eye will be no worse than it is now. At the best—remember all that that includes—sight!"

"Oh, dare we think of anything so joyous?" said Mrs. Stafford.

"Allow me to perform the operation," I said, going up to her. "I am not a rash man; believe me, I would not advise this if I did not think there was a fair hope of success."

"Suppose you are wrong, the child will then be in a worse condition than ever."

"Even if I am wrong, that will not be the case," I replied. "The thread of her present thoughts will have been broken, if only for a few hours. That fact alone will be greatly to her benefit. If I am the means of giving her sight, I am fully convinced that the spell under which she now labours will vanish."

"You are right," said Stafford, who had not spoken a word up to this point. "Mary, my dear, we will allow our good friend to have his way. If the operation is successful, we shall have our child as we never had her yet. Remember, too, that if by any chance she is permitted to see Winchester's face, her love for him must vanish on the spot—those sinister eyes of his would repel anyone."

"She does not love him now," I interrupted. "What she feels is not love. She is hypnotized. The restoration of sight will make such a complete revolution in her whole being, that I doubt if the man could hypnotize her again, even if he tried. She will soon forget this strange and terrible episode in her life. In short, I believe in the acquisition of sight as a complete cure."

"We will make up our minds to the operation," said Stafford. "Am I not right?" he added, turning to his wife.

"Yes, we will consent," she answered.

I looked at her when she spoke—her face was as white as a sheet, but her eyes blazed with light and colour. I noticed for the first time the strong likeness between mother and daughter. In the case of the mother, however, the eyes were of the deepest, clearest grey—scintillating eyes, full of light and expression. I thought of the blind girl's charming face, and wondered what it would look like if it could ever be lit up with eyes like her mother's. The thought cheered me, and strengthened my resolve to do my utmost for Miss Stafford.

"Very well," I said; "I have your consent to perform the operation. In order to get the necessary instruments, I will take the next train to London. I can return here at an early hour to-morrow, and will operate on one eye immediately."

"Will the operation be painful?" asked Mrs. Stafford. "Will it be necessary for you to use chloroform?"

"No; I shall put cocaine into the eye—don't be alarmed, Miss Stafford will feel no pain. I shall only operate on one eye at a time. A very slight incision will enable me to confirm my theory, or to see that it is hopeless. While I am absent, please talk frankly about the operation. Induce your daughter to eat and drink plenty; get her to bed early to-night; do everything to keep up her strength. I will go back to say a word to her now."

I re-entered the drawing-room. Miss Stafford was sitting just where I had left her; her hands were crossed on her lap, the right hand clasped the red bracelet, which encircled the left-hand wrist. She knew my footstep, and looked up with a face of expectation.

"Well?" she said, in a hoarse whisper.

"Good news," I replied, cheerfully. "Your father and mother consent to the operation. I am going to town by the next train, and will return with my instruments to-morrow. Keep up your courage—by this time to-morrow we shall know whether the precious gift of sight is to be yours or not."

"If you fail, I shall die," she answered, speaking in a low and intense voice.

"No," I replied, "even if I fail, you will be too brave, too good, deliberately to throw away your life. Try to think now of success, not failure—try to think of what life may be to you if you can see like other girls."

She sighed; there was hope, even joy, in that sigh. I hurriedly left her. The next day, at an early hour, I was back again at Mount Stafford. The operation which I meant to perform was quite simple in character, and I did not require any help. I suggested to Mr. and Mrs. Stafford that it would be best for me to be alone with my patient.

"She feels the presence of anyone so intensely," I said, "that she will be less nervous, and will keep more quiet, if I am alone with her."

The father and mother agreed to this suggestion, and decided to wait in the outer drawing-room. I placed Miss Stafford in a chair facing the window.

"Now, you must keep up your courage," I said. "I shall operate to-day on your right eye. You must keep perfectly quiet. This will be easy—for you won't feel the slightest pain."

"I could even bear pain with the great hope of sight before me," she answered.

I saw that she was in a state of tense and rapt excitement. She had strung herself up to bear anything.

"You will feel no pain," I said, taking her hand as I spoke. Her pulse was fluttering, but not weak and fitful like yesterday. I supported her head with props, and then dropped the cocaine into the eye. After waiting until complete insensibility was produced, I quickly began to operate. I carefully divided the sclerotic at the upper part of the eyeball, just where I had seen a bulging, such as there is at the edge of the cornea in the normal eye. After dividing the sclerotic, I made a small flap, which I raised. It did not need my patient's sudden exclamation to tell me that I was right in my conjecture, and that there was, under the thick membrane, a cornea intact and transparent. To dissect off the whole of the fibrous curtain which covered this cornea was but the work of a few minutes.

After her first cry, Miss Stafford did not utter a sound. But when I had finished she started up and looked wildly around her.

"I see," she exclaimed—"I see! How queer everything is—how confusing—I would almost rather be in the dark again. I feel as if mountains were surrounding me. I don't know where I am—all is hopeless confusion. I see—oh, I am glad, I am glad ; but I can't *use* my sight. Now that I have it, I don't know what to do with it."

As she uttered these last words she fell back in her chair in a semi-conscious state.

I applied restoratives, and then carefully bound up the wounded eye.

The shock and joy were almost too much for her in her weak state. I had her taken straight to bed. I gave her a composing draught, and she fell quickly asleep. Having seen her in a satisfactory slumber, I hurried downstairs to speak to her father.

"Your girl will have as beautiful and perfect eyes as anyone need care to possess," I said. "I will operate on the left eye in a week's time. For the present, the right eye must be kept bandaged, but the bandage may be removed in a day or two. She will then have to learn to see just as if she were an infant."

"What do you mean ?" asked Stafford.

"What I say," I replied ; "your daughter cannot focus at present. She has no idea of distance—she must learn to use her sight just as a baby does."

"But she possesses eyes," said the mother, who had followed me into the room. "Oh, Dr. Halifax, how can we thank you ?"

The second operation was performed as successfully as the first, and in a month's time from the date of the last operation, Molly Stafford could use her new possession with tolerable freedom. The eyes were beautiful—clear grey, like the mother's, with black rims. They transformed her face, making it a specially lovely one.

A few weeks later, as I was about to leave my consulting-room, after my morning's work, Stafford was announced. He came into the room in a hurry, and with signs of agitation on his face. He held in his hand a little box, which he laid on the table.

"How are you, Halifax ?" he said, grasping my hand in his great grip. "I won't take up more than a moment or two of your valuable time. I have come with news."

"What is it ?" I asked. "I hope nothing bad has happened. How is my patient ?"

"In perfect and blooming health."

"Something has disturbed you," I continued, giving him him a keen glance; "what is it?"

"Yes," continued Stafford, "I am both disturbed and relieved. I hurried up to town on purpose to tell you. What do you think happened yesterday?"

"How can I tell?" I said.

"Molly sees as perfectly as I do," said Stafford. "Her joy in her new possession is beyond all words. Since the date of the first operation she never once mentioned Winchester's name. Her mother and I hoped she had completely forgotten him, but we did not fail to remark that she still wore the coral bracelet."

"I should take no notice of that," I interrupted.

"Well, let me proceed. She wore the coral bracelet day and night, but she never spoke of the man. Yesterday she went out accompanied by a girl, who is a great friend of hers. This girl, Miss Henderson, is the daughter of our next-door neighbour. She told us exactly what occurred. The were walking in the pine wood, chatting, as girls will, when who should appear directly in their path but that scoundrel, Winchester! He came up to Molly and tried to take her hands.

"She started back in amazement.

"'Pray, don't touch me,' she said. 'I don't know who you are.'

"He laughed, and spoke in that confoundedly seductive voice of his—

"'I am the man whom you love—Basil Winchester,' he said. 'I have come to explain why I could not meet you six weeks ago. Can I see you alone?'

"'You, Basil Winchester?' exclaimed Molly. She looked full at him with an expression of puzzled incredulity. Then her voice took a half frightened, half scornful tone. 'You must be mistaken,' she said. 'I could never, never at any moment have loved a man like you.'

"Before he could utter a word, she turned from him and fled back to the house. She rushed into her mother's presence, flung her arms round her neck, and burst into tears.

"'Mother,' she exclaimed, 'I met a dreadful man in the wood just now. He told me his name was Basil Winchester. He said that I—I loved him once.'

"'But you don't love him now, my darling,' said her mother, soothing and kissing her.

"'I could never have loved that man, mother,' said Molly. 'I have a dim remembrance of an awful time, when someone of the name had a terrible power over me; but it could not have been that man, mother. I looked in his face, and I saw his ugly soul.'

"Miss Henderson came in just then and gave us a full account of the interview. The moment Molly fled from him, Winchester left the pine wood. Perhaps you think that is the end, but there is more to follow. Two hours afterwards the news reached us that the fellow had been arrested. The fact is, the police had been wanting him for a couple of months. His reason for deserting Molly on that first occasion was fear of arrest. He ventured back, hoping to secure his prize, the spell was broken, and he saw he could do nothing with the child. He was arrested on a grave charge of forgery, and is now in York Gaol awaiting his trial."

As Stafford said these last words, he sank back in a chair in manifest agitation.

"When I think of my child's narrow escape, I can't help shuddering, even now," he said.

"She has escaped, and all is well," I answered.

"Yes, all is well. We have our child as we never thought to have her—beautiful, perfect, with eyes as lovely as her mother's. By the way, she told me to give you this."

When Stafford left me, I opened the little parcel. It contained—the red coral bracelet.

LITTLE SIR NOEL

LITTLE SIR NOEL

" I F you please, sir," said my servant, Harris, "there's a young gentleman waiting to see you in your consulting-room."

I paused—I was coming home in a hurry to lunch.

"But this is not my hour for seeing patients," I said.

"He is a very young gentleman, sir; he came with a lot of luggage—here it is, all piled up in the hall."

I looked around my neat, well-appointed hall in astonishment. In one corner of it were a couple of large trunks. A strap with rugs, a hat-box, and other belongings of the traveller accompanied the boxes.

"Who in the world can have arrived?" I thought to myself.

I hurried off to my consulting-room as I spoke. I was not feeling too well pleased. I was in a great hurry, and had a specially hard afternoon's work before me. When I opened the door, however, my momentary irritation vanished. It was impossible for it to survive the expression of the little face which started suddenly into view when I appeared. A boy of about eight years old, in a brown velveteen jockey suit, jumped up from his seat by one of the windows and came forward to meet me with one small hand outstretched.

"You are Dr. Halifax, are you not?" he asked.

"Right, my little fellow, and who are you?" I answered.

"I'm Noel Temple. Mother sent you this note: she said you'd look after me. I hope I sha'n't be very troublesome."

He sighed a little as he spoke, poised himself on one leg, and looked up into my face with the alert glance of an expectant robin.

"Noel Temple," I repeated—" Temple!—forgive me, I don't know the name."

"You used to know mother very well—she said so—she said you were playfellows long ago, and you used to quarrel—don't you remember?"

"What was your mother's name before she was married, Noel?" I inquired, suddenly.

"Forester—Emily Forester."

"Then, of course, I know all about her, and you are most heartily welcome," I said, in a cordial tone. "Find yourself a seat while I read this letter."

I threw myself into a chair and opened my old playfellow's letter. It ran as follows:—

"MY DEAR DR. HALIFAX,—I hope you don't forget the Grange, where we once spent a long and happy summer when we were children? I am in a desperate difficulty, and have resolved to throw myself on your mercy. You can't have forgotten the name of your old playfellow, Emily Forester. I married when I was eighteen, and have been in India ever since. My husband, Sir Francis Temple, died six months ago. Noel is our only child. I have just seen a doctor about him—he says his heart is affected, and that there is irritability of the left lung. He has ordered him to leave India immediately; I have no time to explain why it is impossible for me to accompany him home. I am sending him, therefore, at the eleventh hour, in charge of the ship's captain, who, on landing, will put him into a cab and send him straight to you. For the sake of old times—be his guardian to a certain extent. Please take care of the child's health, and place him in a suitable family who will look after him and attend to his interests in every way. His solicitors are Messrs. Biggs and Flint, of Chancery Lane. They will supply you with all necessary funds. I am certain you will be good to the boy.

"Your sincere friend,
"EMILY TEMPLE."

When I raised my eyes after perusing this epistle, little Noel was standing in front of me; he was evidently making a minute study of my character. I looked up at him without speaking. He gave a sigh of relief.

"What's the matter?" I said then.

"You'll do," he replied. "I wasn't certain. I was dreadfully anxious, but I see it's all right." He held out his hand.

I clasped the little brown paw and, rising abruptly, said :—

"Come along, Noel. If you're as hungry as I am, you'll be glad of lunch."

"I should rather think I am hungry," said Noel. "I've had nothing to eat since eight o'clock this morning, when Captain Reeves bought me two sponge cakes. Do you like sponge cakes, Dr. Halifax?"

"I can't say I do," I replied. "Now, here we are—place yourself opposite to me at that end of the table. Harris, lay a place immediately for Sir Noel Temple."

Harris left the room. Noel burst out laughing.

"It's so funny of you to call me Sir Noel," he said. "Don't you think it's rather stiff? Aren't you going to say Noel? We can't be really friends if you don't."

"All right," I replied, "you are Noel to me—but I must give you your title to the servants."

"I hate my title," said the child.

"Why so! Some people think it very fortunate to have a handle to their names."

"You wouldn't think so if you had got it because you had lost your father," said Noel, fixing his big eyes steadily on my face.

His lips quivered—I saw that he could have cried if he hadn't been too brave to allow the tears to come.

"I quite understand what you mean, little man," I said. "Come, I can see we'll be capital friends. Now, here's a cutlet—fall to. If you're not in a hurry to eat, I am."

When lunch was over I took Noel back to my consulting-room, and made a careful examination of his lungs and heart.

I saw that he was free from organic disease as yet, but was a fragile, delicate boy, and one who was likely to develop serious mischief at any moment.

I saw that it would be impossible for me to keep him in my bachelor establishment; besides, London was no place for him.

The next two or three days passed without anything special occuring. I found it impossible to take Noel out with me, but I desired Harris to walk with him in the parks, and concluded that he was having a fairly good time. On the evening of the fourth day, however, I observed that the child's face was slightly paler than usual—that he ate little or nothing as he sat perched up opposite to me at late dinner, and that he sighed heavily once or twice.

The weather was autumnal, and the winter would soon be on us. I thought that Bournemouth would be a suitable place for the little fellow, and that evening before I went to bed I wrote a long letter to his mother, telling her what I thought of the boy's health, and also saying that I was about to advertise for a suitable home for him.

My advertisement appeared in due course, and, as a necessary consequence, answers arrived in shoals. A friend of mine, a Mrs. Wilkinson, who only lived a few doors away, promised to attend to the matter for me. She would look over the answers, and reply to those she thought at all suitable. She did so, but nothing satisfactory seemed likely to be the result.

One evening, on returning home, Harris met me with the information that a lady had called, who wanted to see me on the subject of the advertisement.

"Where is she?" I asked.

"In your study, sir."

I went there at once, and found myself face to face with a tall, sweet-looking woman of between forty and fifty years of age. She wore a neat-fitting bonnet, a jacket of old-fashioned cut, and a pair of shabby gloves. She looked like what she was—a lady in poor circumstances. Her face wore an anxious and troubled expression. The moment I appeared she started up to meet me.

"You are Dr. Halifax, are you not?" she said.

"That is my name," I replied.

"I am Mrs. Marsden. I saw your advertisement by chance this morning. I hurried up to town at once. I went to see Mrs. Wilkinson—she asked me to lose no time in having an interview with you. While talking to her, I made a remarkable discovery. Under the circumstances, it is strange that such an advertisement should have been inserted. I am unwilling to take offence, however. Poor Emily has always been peculiar. I wish to say now that I am desirous to have the boy. I will promise to take every care of him."

"Do you know Lady Temple?" I asked, in astonishment.

Mrs. Marsden smiled faintly.

"Lady Temple is my sister," she replied. "She is my sister, and I am married to her late husband's cousin. My husband, Mr. Marsden, is first cousin to the late Sir Francis Temple. The dear little boy is, therefore, a near relation on both sides."

"How is it that Lady Temple never thought of sending the boy to you?" I enquired.

"It is impossible for me to tell you. I am naturally the person who ought to have received the child on his arrival in England. My husband and I are not well off. We have a house at Bournemouth, and have long wished to have the care of a child in order to add to our income. Your advertisement attracted us both. I came up to town to answer it. You may imagine my surprise when I learned who the child really was, from Mrs. Wilkinson."

. "It is strange that Lady Temple never mentioned your name," I replied.

"She must have forgotten it—this seems an unaccountable reason, but I can give no other. She is erratic, however—she has been erratic all her life. I am much older than my sister. I was married when she was a child. Still, of course, I love her, and would do all a mother could for her boy."

I thought for a moment—then I said : "The child has been absolutely committed to my care by his mother. He is very delicate, and is the heir to a large fortune."

When I said these words Mrs. Marsden turned very pale, then a brilliant colour flooded her face.

"I wish to say something," she remarked, after a pause. "What I am going to say may prejudice you against me. I am desirous to have the child for every reason—I am his near relation, and can naturally do more for him than a mere stranger. I also sorely need the money which his advent into our family will bring ; nevertheless, I won't take charge of the boy, in case you are good enough to entrust him to me, without your knowing the simple truth. It is this—in the event of Little Noel dying, my husband inherits the Temple property. In short, that delicate child is the only person who stands between my husband and considerable fortune."

"Thank you for telling me the truth," I replied.

"I hope this will not prejudice you against me, Dr. Halifax. The fact of my telling you what I have done ought to assure you of the honesty of my purpose."

"It would be impossible for me to doubt you," I said, glancing at her face.

"I am glad you say that." She clasped her thin hands together. She had removed her gloves during our interview. "I have had much trouble, and I am not a happy woman. I have suffered the sorest straits of poverty; the money which we will receive with the child will be of great value to us. My husband will be astonished when I tell him what the result of my inquiries has been."

"Well," I replied, hastily, "I can do nothing without consulting the mother. I am anxious to have the boy comfortably settled, and to get him out of town. I will send a cablegram to Lady Temple to-morrow, asking her to reply at once, and to tell me what she wishes."

"Thank you. Are you likely to get her answer to-morrow?"

"I may do so in the evening. Are you staying in town, Mrs. Marsden?"

"I shall remain until you hear from my sister."

"Kindly write your address on that slate. I will let you know as soon as ever I receive Lady Temple's reply."

At the first possible moment in the morning I sent a cablegram to Lady Temple. It was worded as follows:

"*Can't keep boy in London—his aunt, Mrs. Marsden, wishes to take charge of him. Shall he go to her? Wire reply.*"

I received the following answer at a late hour that night:

"*Yes—arrange with Helen.—Emily Temple.*"

This reply ought to have filled me with satisfaction, but it did not. I could not doubt Mrs. Marsden, but what about her husband? The boy was delicate—the man would gain immensely by his death. I resolved, notwithstanding Lady Temple's cablegram, to do nothing definite until I had seen Marsden. I wrote to ask Mrs. Marsden to call early in the morning. She came. The sweet expression of her face, and a certain honesty of eye, made me ashamed of my suspicion.

"Here is Lady Temple's reply," I said, putting the cablegram into her hand when she entered the room.

She glanced at it.

"Thank God!" she exclaimed. "You scarcely know what a relief this will be to us."

I broke in abruptly.

"I have something to say," I continued. "Notwithstanding Lady Temple's permission, I don't intend to part with little Noel without stringent inquiries. The mother is in India— the boy has been committed by letter to my care. Please don't suppose that I mistrust you personally, but the case is peculiar. I must have an interview with your husband. I will come down to Bournemouth on Saturday, and will bring Noel with me. I may or may not take him back with me to town again. When I see you on Saturday we can discuss the matter further."

"Thank you—thank you," she replied. "I respect you all the more for being particular. At what hour may I expect you on Saturday?"

I glanced over a time-table.

"Noel and I will run down in the afternoon," I said. "Expect us between four and five o'clock."

She rose instantly. I bade her good-bye, and she left me.

I said nothing to Noel about the proposed change until the Saturday morning. Then I asked him if he would like to accompany me to the seaside.

His eyes danced with pleasure.

"I love the sea," he replied. "I mean to be a sailor when I'm a man."

"Well," I said, "you will chose a very good life. I intend to take you with me to Bournemouth to-day. Ask Harris to pack some things for you, and be ready when I come home to lunch."

The child nodded his head brightly. I left him and went out to see my patients.

When I returned to the house I was met by Harris, who wore a very anxious expression of face.

"I'm so glad you've come back, sir," he said. "Little Sir Noel is ill."

"Ill!" I cried. "Where is he?"

"He is lying on a sofa in your consulting-room, sir; he particularly wished me to take him there. He says he would rather be in the consulting-room than any other part of the house. He seemed so ill that I thought you wouldn't mind."

"Quite right—I will go and see him," I replied.

I entered my consulting-room quickly. Little Noel was lying on a sofa. I had left him in the morning in apparently fair health. I was startled now with the change in his appearance. He could scarcely speak—his breath came quickly—there was a suspicious blue tint round the lower part of his face.

I brought my stethoscope and applied it to the heart,

There was considerable anæmia, but I could trace no sign of absolute heart disease. The child, however, was very weak. I saw that he must not travel that day.

I telegraphed to Mrs. Marsden to tell her that Noel was ill, and that she could not expect us that day.

The child remained feverish and poorly during the greater part of that Saturday, but on Sunday he was nearly himself again. I saw with a pang that he was extremely delicate. There was not only heart weakness to contend against, but considerable irritability of the left lung. I began to consider whether he ought not to winter abroad — it was certainly necessary to send him out of London as quickly as possible. Nevertheless, as the hours went on, all my prejudices against placing him with the Marsdens increased rather than diminished.

I was just going to leave the house on that Sunday morning, and was standing on my door-steps preparatory to entering my carriage, when a hansom drew up and stopped abruptly. A tall, good-looking man stepped out of it. He favoured me with a somewhat insolent stare, then ran up the steps and spoke abruptly.

"Am I addressing Dr. Halifax?"

"That is my name," I replied.

"And this is mine," he said, pulling a card out of his pocket.

I glanced at the name—"Mr. Paul Marsden."

"Indeed," I said, with some annoyance. "You have come up to town doubtless on receipt of my telegram?"

"Precisely—my wife has a cold, or she would have accompanied me. We were sorry to hear of the boy's illness. I want to speak to you about him. Can you give me a few moments of your time?"

"Yes—come this way, please."

I ushered Mr. Marsden into my consulting-room. Little Noel hadn't yet come downstairs. Marsden had a bold manner and a certain swagger about him. His eyes were dark; he wore a sweeping moustache; his head was closely cropped. There was the unmistakable air of the bully in his manner. I saw at a glance that he meant to carry things with a high hand. I disliked the man from the first.

"Now, look here, Dr. Halifax," he said, "I know everything; my wife has told me exactly what transpired between you and her. By the merest accident, she and I are both acquainted with the fact that her nephew and my cousin has been sent to England. My wife is willing to take care of the boy, if the terms are satisfactory. She will give him a mother's care, and will devote herself to his health and to his training generally. She does this because I wish it, and because, to be quite honest with you, we both need the money. We should expect the boy's guardians to pay us a sum which could be discussed later on."

I interrupted.

"Money is not the consideration," I said. "I want a thoroughly comfortable home for the child, where his interests are certain to be made the first consideration."

"I understand you—that's your point of view. If we are well paid, it will be to our interest to keep the boy in health. I have never seen the child, and have, naturally, not a spark of affection for him. The late Sir Francis was my first cousin. Failing this child, the estates and title come to me. The boy's death, should it occur, would therefore be to my benefit. I state this fact quite frankly. The fact of my having done so ought to assure you of the integrity of my purpose. I feel it, under the circumstances, to be absolutely to my credit not to leave a stone unturned to keep the child's fragile life in existence. I understand, however, the sort of feeling which makes you hesitate to commit him to my care. Your telegram of yesterday I regarded as humbug — I felt sure that the reluctance which my wife perceived in your manner would be likely to increase, not diminish, as time went on. I took the liberty, therefore, of sending a cablegram myself to Lady Temple. I have her reply in my pocket. Here it is."

As he spoke, Marsden unfolded a sheet of thin paper. He put it into my hands. I read the following words:—

"*Ask Dr. Halifax to deliver Noel to your care and Helen's without delay.—Emily Temple.*"

"You see," continued Marsden, "that I have come with authority. I shall be glad to take my wife's nephew back to Bournemouth this afternoon, if he is fit to travel."

I didn't speak for a moment.

"In the face of that cablegram you can't detain the boy," continued Marsden.

"If his mother really wishes him to go to you, I have not another word to say," I replied, after a pause. "I regret, that she did not know her own mind when she first sent the child to England. It is still, however, my duty to care for his health, and I must see that your house is in all respects the most suitable for him to live in."

"You can do as you please with regard to that," said Marsden. "I have no doubt you will not like the house; but if money is no object, we can soon move into one more suitable."

He rose as he spoke, and walked towards the window, putting his hands into his trousers' pockets as he did so. The more I looked at the man, the more cordially did I dislike him. Could I have invented the smallest excuse, I would have kept Noel from his tender mercies at any risk. While I stood and thought, Marsden turned quickly and faced -me. He pulled his watch out of his pocket.

"I am anxious to return to Bournemouth at once," he said. "If the child is well enough to travel, can you not bring him down to-day? I should like to have this matter settled as quickly as possible."

"I believe the child can travel to-day," I said. "Will you have the kindness to take a chair? I will go and give directions about his clothes being packed."

Shortly afterwards we were on our way to Waterloo Station. We caught our train, and in due time found ourselves at Bournemouth. Noel was nearly quite silent all the way down. I observed him without appearing to do so. His sensitive eyes, with their distended pupils, a sure sign of delicacy, often travelled to the hard, flippant face of Marsden. Marsden whistled, joked, and was as vulgarly disagreeable as man could be.

We reached Bournemouth, a cab was secured, and we drove straight to the Marsdens' house. Mrs. Marsden came to the door to receive us. The moment I glanced at her, I was struck with the nervous expression of her face. She gave her husband a glance of almost terror, then, with a forced smile, turned to the boy, stretched out her arms, and clasped him to her heart. Her manner to the child was full of affection.

"What fools women are," said Marsden, roughly. "To see my wife, anyone would suppose that she was the mother of that little brat. Come along in, Dr. Halifax. I hope Mrs. Marsden's manner satisfies you. You can see for yourself into what a snug corner your fledgling has dropped. Mrs. Marsden, when you've done hugging that boy, will you see about tea? Here, doctor, make yourself at home."

As he spoke he ushered me into a stuffy little parlour with a smell of stale tobacco about it. Mrs. Marsden followed us into the room—she held Noel's hand in hers.

"Can I see you alone for a few moments?" I said to her.

"Certainly," she answered.

She led me into a small drawing-room, shutting the door carefully behind her.

"I see," she said, the moment we were alone, "that my husband has had his way. He went up to town determined to have it."

"I will be frank with you, Mrs. Marsden," I replied. "Your husband would not have had his way but for Lady Temple's cablegram. In the face of that I could not detain the boy. Until I hear to the contrary, however, the care of his health is still in my hands, and while this is the case, it is my duty to arrange matters so that he may have a chance of recovery."

"Is his life in danger?" inquired Mrs. Marsden.

"It is in no danger at present."

"He looks sadly delicate."

"He is delicate. He suffers from weakness of the heart and a general delicacy, probably due to his early years being spent in a tropical climate. At the present moment the boy has no actual disease. He simply requires the greatest care. Can you give it to him?"

"I think so."

"I believe you will do your best," I answered, gazing at her earnestly. "The child needs happiness—plenty of fresh air, and the most nourishing food. If his mind is satisfied and at rest, and if his body is kept from exposure, he will probably become quite strong in time. Are you prepared to undertake the care of the child, Mrs. Marsden? Remember that he will require the closest care and watching."

"He shall have the best that I can give him," she answered. "Before God, I promise to be true to the child—he shall want for nothing—I will be a mother to him."

"I believe you will be good to him," I said; "but please understand, I am not so certain about your husband. I don't suppose for a moment that he would do the boy a grave injury.

If I seriously thought that, notwithstanding Lady Temple's cablegram, I would not leave him here; but without meaning to injure the child, he would probably be rough to him. In short, it is necessary that the little boy should be placed in your hands altogether."

"I will manage it, you needn't fear," she answered.

Pink spots burnt on each of her cheeks — her hands trembled.

"Very well," I said, "I am willing to trust you. I will see the child's solicitors to-morrow. Terms can be made which will abundantly satisfy your husband's expectations. I will leave Noel with you until I have had time to write to Lady Temple and to receive a reply from her. If the boy improves in health, the arrangement can be permanent. The first thing necessary to be done on your part is to leave this house. Please see an agent to-morrow, and select a house in a dry and sunny part of the pine wood."

"I will do so," replied Mrs. Marsden, "and now I think tea is ready. Will you come into the dining-room with me?"

I accompanied Mrs. Marsden into the shabby room where Marsden had first led me—the close smell again affected me disagreeably.

"May I ask you to open that window at the top?" I said to Marsden; "my patient must not be exposed to draughts, but it is necessary that he should have a certain amount of fresh air."

"What do you mean?" said my host, with a scowl.

"What I say, sir," I replied. "The boy must not have his meals in such a close room as this."

Marsden went up to one of the windows, opened it about an inch, and then took his seat at the table. Mrs. Marsden sat opposite the tea equipage; she had helped Noel to a cup of tea, and was just handing one to me, when the room door was opened and a cadaverous-looking young man of about one or two and twenty entered.

"Oh, is that you, Sharp?" said Marsden. "Dr. Halifax, let me introduce my young friend, Joseph Sharp. Sharp, you have the privilege of making the acquaintance of a Harley Street doctor, of some reputation. Take a good look at him, my boy; if you are prudent and clever, you may follow in his footsteps some day. Sharp is studying medicine," continued Marsden, by way of explanation to me—"he looks like one of the fraternity, doesn't he? Sharp has just the right hand for an operator—so I always say. He prefers medicine, but I tell him he's lost to surgery."

While Marsden was speaking, Sharp wiped the perspiration from his face—his appearance was by no means prepossessing. He sat down near me, and once or twice raised his eyes to glance inquisitively at Noel. Noel was studying him with the frank stare of a child.

"Are you preparing yourself for the medical profession here?" I asked, after a pause.

"Yes," he replied, "I am filling in my vacation by studying *materia medica* and dispensing at Dr. Biggs's—I work there all day."

"And sleep here," interrupted Marsden. "Sharp is a good fellow, Dr. Halifax. I often say he has the making of a fortune in him if he only knows how to apply himself. By the way, in case that boy is ill, I suppose you will like Biggs to see him?—we can't telegraph for you whenever he has a cold in his head or anything of that sort."

"I will arrange that," I answered. "My friend, Dr. Hart, will look after the child—I am going to see him before I return to town. I am afraid I must now say 'Good-bye.'"

I rose as I spoke; at the same moment little Noel sprang to his feet and ran to my side.

"I want to go back to town with you," he said; "I don't wish to stay here."

"Come, my little man, no folly of that sort," said Marsden, roughly. He stepped forward and laid his hand on the child's shoulder.

"Leave him to me," I said. "Come, Noel, I will speak to you in the drawing-room."

I took the child's hand and led him out of the room.

"You must be a brave boy," I said, steeling my heart against his tearful face. "Your mother wishes you to stay here for a little, and your aunt has promised to be very kind to you. I'll come and see you this day fortnight. Now, you know, you are not going to cry—manly boys don't cry."

"No, I won't cry," said Noel. He made a valiant effort to swallow a lump in his throat. "I'll stay if you wish me to," he added, "but you'll promise faithfully to be back in a fortnight?"

"You have my promise," I replied.

"Thank you," said Noel; "I trust you—you are a perfect gentleman—gentlemen can always be trusted."

He put his hand into mine and we returned to the parlour. I was shaking hands with Mrs. Marsden, when I was attracted by an unusual sound. I looked around me, thinking that a bird had come into the room. To my astonishment, I noticed that Sharp was imitating the dulcet strains of the nightingale with wonderful accuracy. After producing some exquisite notes, he stopped abruptly, and beckoned Noel to his side.

"Are you fond of music?" he asked.

"Yes," replied Noel.

"Would you like to whistle like that?"

"Yes—oh, yes."

"Let me look at your throat—if you have the right sort of throat, I can teach you to imitate any bird that ever sang."

The boy opened his mouth eagerly—his sorrows were completely forgotten—he didn't even notice when I left the room.

At the end of ten days, I had a letter from Mrs. Marsden. She had not only found a house, but had moved into it— Noel was well and happy, and was looking forward with interest to my visit.

I kept my word, and the following Sunday went to Bournemouth. Mrs. Marsden had given me the new address, and I soon found the house. She received me in the hall.

I scarely knew her for the same woman who had interviewed me a fortnight ago. Her face was bright—the anxiety had left her manner. She was neatly and properly dressed, and looked like what she was, the mistress of a charming and well-appointed house.

"You will like to see Noel," she said; "he is in the garden with Joe, as we always call Mr. Sharp. He is devoted to Joe, and will never stay with anyone else when he is in the house. Oh, there they both are. How delighted Noel will be to see you again."

Mrs. Marsden opened the French windows of the pretty drawing-room as she spoke, and called the boy's name.

"Here is Dr. Halifax, Noel," she cried.

"Hullo! I'm coming," answered little Noel, in his clear tones; "you must come, too, Joe—yes, I insist." Then he called out again, "Tell Dr. Halifax that I'll be with him in a minute with Joe, Aunt Helen; now then, Joe, come on."

The two approached the window together. They made a strong contrast. The boy looked lovely and blooming—there was colour in his cheeks, animation and hope in his eyes. Sharp's cadaverous face, his undersized, undeveloped person, his large mouth and small eyes with their red lids, gave him altogether a repulsive *tout ensemble*. Nevertheless, the child adored him. By what possible means had he won the boy's heart? Even when Noel sprang to my side, he glanced back at Sharp.

"I'm so glad to see you, Dr. Halifax," he said. "Oh, I'm as well as I can possibly be—you ask Joe about me. Joe *is* clever; he's teaching me all sorts of things—I've got some carpenter's tools, and I'm making a ship. Joe knows the names of all the different sails. Then he's teaching me to imitate the birds—he says my throat is the right sort. I can do the robin and the thrush and the blackbird now, and next week I shall have a try for the lark's notes. You stay quiet, Dr. Halifax, and listen. Now, what bird am I imitating?"

He stepped back, screwed up his little mouth, and whistled some beautiful notes.

I made a correct guess.

"That's the sweetest thrush's song I've heard all the year," I said.

He clapped his hands with delight.

At dinner I observed that Marsden's place was empty. I inquired for him.

When I did so, Mrs. Marsden's cheeks became suffused with pink.

"I meant to tell you," she answered. "My husband has left us for a time."

"Left you?" I asked. "Where has he gone to?"

"To America—sudden business has called him to South America—he will in all probability be absent for the winter."

I guessed now why Mrs. Marsden's manner had so altered for the better. Marsden was away—she could do exactly as she pleased, therefore, about the boy. The boy was of course perfectly safe with her, and I might, therefore, cast all anxiety with regard to him from my mind.

Shortly afterwards I took my leave.

There was no necessity for me to see little Noel again for some time, and when I received a sudden telegram about him, he had to a certain extent passed into the back part of my memory.

The telegram was from my friend, Dr. Hart, in whose medical care I had placed the boy. It contained the following words: Sir Noel Temple ill—heart attack—wish to consult you."

I wired back to say that I would go to Bournemouth by the evening train. I did so, and reached Dr. Hart's house about ten o'clock.

"I'm heartily glad that you are able to come, Halifax," he said, as he led me into his smoking-room. "I have just come from the child—I don't like his condition."

"When I heard about him last, he was in perfect health," I replied.

"That is the case—he remained well until last Monday— I was suddenly sent for then, and found him in a state almost approaching syncope. I gave him the usual medicines, and he quickly revived. But since then his condition has been the reverse of satisfactory, and he was so weak to-day, and the medicine had so completely failed to produce the expected results, that I thought it best for you to see him."

"I am glad you sent for me," I replied. "The child has from time to time suffered from functional derangement of the heart. He had a nasty attack just before he was taken to Bournemouth, but on examination I could not trace the slightest organic disease."

"I have also examined the heart carefully," replied Hart, "and cannot trace any cardiac disorder. The state of the little patient, however, puzzles me considerably—there is nothing to account for the complete depression of the whole system."

"Well," I replied, "I will go with you at once to see the child."

It was nearly eleven o'clock when we arrived at the Marsden's House. Mrs. Marsden was up; she was evidently expecting us. When we rang the hall-door bell, she opened the door herself.

"Come in," she said. "Oh, Dr. Halifax, I'm so glad you are here. I think Noel is a shade better. The boy has spoken about you several times to-day—he has repeatedly said that he wanted to see you. He suffers greatly from restlessness and low spirits—that is, when Joe is not in the room with him. He is more attached to Joe than ever, but of course he can't be with him during the day, as Dr. Biggs requires all his time. Joe is with the child now—he sleeps in his room—they are quite cheerful together—I even heard Noel laugh as I came downstairs."

Mrs. Marsden's face looked much worn, and her eyes were red as if she had been crying. No one could doubt the genuineness of her trouble about the child. She hurried us into one of the sitting-rooms, and said she would go upstairs to prepare little Noel for our visit.

A moment or two later, Hart and I went upstairs to visit the little patient. The room in which he was lying was large and lofty. He was half sitting up in bed supported by pillows—his breath was coming quickly—there was a bright spot on one cheek, but the rest of the face wore a suspiciously blue tint.

I spoke to him cheerfully; he gave me one of his usual bright, affectionate glances, and put his hand into mine.

"Stoop down," he said, in a whisper.

I bent over him immediately.

"It takes my breath away to talk, but I'm awfully glad you've come," he said, with emphasis.

"I'm delighted to see you again, dear boy," I replied. "Now the thing is to get you better as quickly as possible. I will just listen to that troublesome little heart of yours, and see if I can't do something to set it right again."

"It's like a watch gone wrong," said Noel. "I wish it would tick properly."

"So it shall, by-and-bye," I answered.

I took out my stethoscope and made the usual examination. The action of the heart was feeble—the pulse intermittent; but I quickly came to the conclusion that the disorder was functional. There was no organic mischief to be detected in any of the sounds.

"What are you giving him?" I said to Dr. Hart.

Sharp, who had been standing by the head of the boy's bed now came hastily forward.

"Perhaps you want to see the prescription?" he said, stammering as he spoke. "I am very sorry—I left it at the chemist's. I took it there in a great hurry this evening, and brought away the medicine without waiting for it. Shall I run and fetch it?"

"No," replied Hart, "that is not necessary—I can tell you exactly what I prescribed, Halifax—digitalis, bromide of potassium, and a little of the alcoholic extract of aconite."

"I will talk the matter over with you downstairs," I said.

We left the room together.

After some consultation, I suggested the addition of ether to the medicine. I then proceeded to say :—

"The condition of the heart is not alarming in itself—there is no murmur, but there seems to be a slight dilatation of the left ventricle. You did quite right to order the extract of aconite—there is, in my opinion, no more useful medicine for such a condition. The boy will require rest and great care. The probabilities are that, with this, he will return to his normal condition within a few days. But I should like to have a trained nurse sent for immediately."

"I agree with you," said Hart. "I don't care for that fellow Sharp."

"The child seems attached to him," I replied ; "but in any case he can't be with him all the time. The boy will do much better with a nurse. I happen to have a nurse belonging to my own staff who will be just the person to undertake the case. I will telegraph to her to come here the first thing in the morning."

I saw Mrs. Marsden, and spoke on the subject of the nurse.

"I shall be delighted to have a proper nurse," she replied. "I thought of engaging one before you came, but the child clings so to Joseph Sharp, that I didn't dare to propose that anyone else should take his place."

"He must have a nurse," I answered ; "he can see Sharp now and then in her presence. The mere fact of his taking so much interest in the man's society is too much for him in his weak state."

I asked Mrs. Marsden if she could give me a bed, and spent the night in the house with my little patient. Towards morning I rose and went into his room. Sharp was lying on a stretcher bed in another part of the room. He didn't hear me when I came in. He was lying on his back with his mouth open. I thought his face repulsive, and wondered why the boy took to him as he did. I felt my little patient's pulse without awakening him. It was soft and regular ; there was a faint moisture on the skin. He had already taken two doses of the altered medicine. I was satisfied with the result of the new ingredient which I had introduced, and was about to leave the room when Joe's voice, sharp and sudden, smote on my ears.

"You might make it five thousand pounds, Mr. Marsden," he said.

He turned over on his side as he uttered the words, and fell off into profound slumber. I was too busy and preoccupied to give the queer sentence a second thought, but I was destined to remember it later on. I went off now to telegraph for Nurse Jenkins, a nurse I knew and could depend on. She arrived in the course of the morning, and I established her by little Noel's bedside before I returned to town. Hart and I had a further consultation about the boy. The nurse promised to write to me daily, and I went back to London under the conviction that the child would speedily recover from his present attack.

I received a bulletin every evening from the nurse. On the third day, her letter ran as follows :—

"I don't like my little patient's symptoms. I give him his medicine regularly, but I often feel inclined to leave it off altogether. Almost immediately after taking it, he complains of a feeling of sickness—he has even vomited once or twice. The vomiting is followed by a state of collapse more or less severe ; the pulse is very intermittent. Dr. Hart is ill, and has not seen the child for a couple of days ; his assistant promised to write to you about the medicine."

I expected a letter by the next post, but none came. I felt uneasy, and resolved to go to Bournemouth.

I arrived late in the afternoon and went straight to the Marsdens' house. Just as I reached the door, it was suddenly opened and Sharp came out. He evidently didn't expect me, for he started violently and his ugly white face assumed a green tint—his small eyes almost started from his head.

"Oh, the boy is just the same," he said. "He's weak—I don't believe he'll do—glad you've come—didn't know you were expected."

"I have come," I replied, briefly, "in consequence of a letter from Nurse Jenkins. I am sorry the boy is not so well."

"He doesn't gain strength," said Sharp. "Are you going up to see him now ?"

"Yes," I replied—I passed him as I spoke.

I ran quickly upstairs. No one knew I was in the house. I opened the door of the sick room. Mrs. Marsden was sitting by the little fellow's bed. He was lying flat on his back, his head was raised, he was breathing faintly, his eyes were shut. The nurse was arranging some bottles and medicine glasses in a distant part of the room. She turned on hearing my footsteps, put one finger to her lips, then beckoned to me to follow her into the ante-room.

"Oh, Dr. Halifax," she said, "I'm so relieved you've come. The child is, I fear, sinking fast."

"I hope not," I answered.

"But he is—he grows worse each moment. I am dissatisfied about the medicine. Dr. Hart is very ill—his assistant knows nothing about the case. It is a great relief to see you here."

"You ought to have telegraphed for me," I said. "Now don't keep me—I will ascertain the child's condition myself."

I returned to the sick room and took the boy's little wrist between my finger and thumb. The pulse was scarcely perceptible.

"He has been very sick again," said Nurse Jenkins; "he is sick every time he takes the medicine. I had almost decided not to give him another dose when you arrived."

"Bring me some brandy at once," I said.

The nurse did so. Mrs Marsden, who had started to her feet when I approached the bedside, gazed at me with eyes dilated with terror.

"Keep quiet," I said to her; "the boy is too weak to stand the slightest noise—he will be better when he takes this."

I mixed a strong dose, and put a little between the child's lips. After some difficulty he swallowed it—his beautiful eyes were glazed—he looked at me without recognition.

"That's right," I said, when I became certain that he had really swallowed the brandy; "the heart's action will soon be better."

As I spoke I took out my hypodermic syringe and injected a little ether under the skin. The effect was instantaneous—the child's breathing became easier, and a little colour came into his ears.

During the next half-hour I administed small doses of brandy at short intervals, and tried every means in my power to induce heat. After a time success attended my efforts—the boy sighed—moved a little, and opened his eyes wide—the state of collapse had passed. His cheeks now burned with fever, and the pulse galloped hard and fast in his little wrist.

I motioned to Mrs. Marsden to take my place by the bedside, and then asked Nurse Jenkins to accompany me into the next room.

"Show me the prescription," I said.

"I am very sorry," she replied; "I have just given it to Mr. Sharp."

It suddenly flashed through my memory that on the last occasion when I wanted to see Hart's prescription, I could not do so because Sharp had left it at the chemist's. The nurse went on apologizing.

"We were out of the medicine—I wanted to have some more made up. Mrs. Marsden's own chemist lives some way from here, and Mr. Sharp suggested that if I gave him the prescription he would get it made up by a chemist close by."

"How long is it since Sharp was here?" I asked.

"Just before you came—he rushed into the room making quite a noise. The child was very weak at the time. He came close up to the bed, and looked at the little fellow for two or three minutes. To tell the truth, Dr. Halifax, I never liked the man, but he must have been much attached to the boy. I seldom saw such a look of agony on any face. I can really describe his expression by no other word."

"Are you quite sure, nurse, that Sharp has not been alone with little Noel since you had the charge of him?"

"Quite; I have actually lived in the room. Mr. Sharp has been to see Noel once or twice every day. The little fellow delighted in his visits. Mr. Sharp used to imitate the birds— little Noel generally fell asleep while he was whistling."

I thought hard for a moment.

"What is the name of the chemist who usually makes up the medicine?" I asked.

"Howell and Jones—the shop is close to the sea at the bottom of the hill. Howell and Jones are the chemists Mrs. Marsden used to employ when she lived in her old house. She thought that Noel's medicine might as well be made up at her own chemist's."

"Have you any of the medicine left?" I asked.

"No, the last dose is finished—the bottle was forgotten to

be sent to the chemist's this morning—that is why Mr. Sharp rushed off with the prescription in a hurry. The hour is past now when the child ought to have his medicine."

"I should like to see the empty bottle."

Nurse Jenkins went to look for it. She came back in a few moments.

"I left it on the wash-hand stand in that room," she said. "It is not there—I wonder if Mr. Sharp put it in his pocket?"

"It doesn't matter whether he did or not," I replied.

My suspicions were fully aroused. There was more than anger in my heart at that moment.

"Do not say a word of what I suspect, nurse," I said, "but my impression is that there is foul play somewhere. The medicine which Dr. Hart and I prescribed could by no possibility have the effects which you describe. I am going immediately to see Howell and Jones. Give the boy a dose of brandy if there is the least return of faintness, and don't allow Sharp near the room on any terms."

I left the house, hailed the first cab I saw, and drove to the chemist's shop. I entered quickly; a tall, serious-looking man was standing behind the counter. I asked him if he was a member of the firm.

"I am Mr. Howell," he replied.

I took out my card and gave it to him.

"You have been making up medicines for a patient of mine," I said, "a little boy of the name of Sir Noel Temple. He is living with one of your customers, Mrs. Marsden. You have made up medicine for the child several times."

"I have, Dr. Halifax."

"I want to look at your copy of the last prescription"

The man turned to fetch his book.

"May I ask, doctor," he said, as he handed it to me, "if the child is better?"

"No; he is suffering from serious collapse and weakness."

"That seems scarcely to be wondered at," remarked the man. "There is a special ingredient in your prescription which surprised me—niconitin seems quite a new drug to order in cases of heart failure."

"Niconitin?" I exclaimed, horror in my tones. "What can you possibly mean? There was no niconitin in the prescription. Such a drug would act as direct poison in a case like the child's."

"Nevertheless, it is one of the principal ingredients in the prescription, doctor. Look at my copy—here—you see, the proportion is large—I have made up this medicine three or four times."

As the man spoke he turned his book towards me and laid his finger on the copy of Hart's prescription and mine. With a glance my eye took in the names of the different ingredients. The chemist was right—a large proportion of niconitin was one of them. This drug, as is well known, is the active property of tobacco. Its effect upon the heart would account for all the symptoms from which the child was suffering. Taken in quantities here prescribed, it would cause vomiting, collapse, and feeble action of the pulse. In short, its effect on the irritable heart of my little patient would be that of direct poison.

"Do you mean to tell me," I said in anger, "that you, an experienced chemist, would dispense a prescription so manifestly contradictory without referring to the doctor who wrote it?"

"I spoke to Mr. Sharp about it," replied the man. "I even pointed out the inconsistency. He replied that the case was peculiar, and that niconitin was necessary as a sedative. Had it not been for Mr. Sharp, whom we know so well ——"

"That will do," I interrupted, "I have no more time to waste over words. I shall probably want to see this book again. Meanwhile, give me a piece of paper, I must order another medicine."

I hastily wrote out a prescription for a strong restorative. The medicine was supplied to me, and I went back as fast as possible to the Marsdens' house.

Mrs. Marsden came downstairs to meet me.

"How is the child?" I said to her.

"Better; he is in a natural sleep."

I took the bottle of fresh medicine out of my pocket.

"Give this to nurse," I said. "The child is to have a tea-spoonful every quarter of an hour. By the way, at what hour does your boarder, Mr. Sharp, come home?"

"Not until evening, as a rule, but it so happens that he is in the house at the present moment."

"Where?"

"In his bedroom—he ran upstairs ten minutes ago. He asked if you were in. Do you want to see him?"

"Yes, I do. Which is his room?"

"I will send for him."

"No; tell me which is his room, and I will go to him."

My manner surprised her. She gave me a brief direction. I rushed upstairs and entered Sharp's room without knocking.

The fellow was standing near a small portmanteau which he was hastily packing. When he heard my step he turned—his face became ashy pale—he looked almost as if he would faint.

"Now, look here," I said, closing the door and walking straight up to the man, "I have discovered the whole of this villainous plot. If you don't confess everything immediately, you will find yourself in the hands of the police in a few moments' time. In short, neither you nor I leave this room until you have told me everything."

The fellow went on his knees in his terror—he covered his face with his shaking hands.

"Get up," I said, in disgust. "I can't speak to you nor listen to you in your present position."

He rose and tottered towards a chair—he was really too weak to stand.

"I'm glad you know," he said, with a sort of gasp; "yes, I am—I'm glad it's all known. I couldn't have gone on with it—I'd rather be hanged than go on with it for another hour."

"Tell me your story quickly," I said; "I have not a moment to listen to your sentimentalities—the child's life hangs at this moment in the balance."

"Is there a chance for him, doctor?" said the man, looking full up at me.

"Yes, yes, if you'll only be quick and pull yourself together."

"Then I will—my God, I will—I don't care about anything now in the world except the little fellow's life. Half an hour ago I stood by his death-bed. My God, it was torture to stand there and look at my own work!"

"Speak," I said; "if you don't tell me what you know at once, I will send for the police."

Sharp gave me another terrified look. I saw by the expression in his eyes that, whatever his sins, he at least repented now.

"It was this way," he began: "I was Marsden's tool. I

don't want to blame him over much, but I was his tool from the first. He wished the boy to die, and he wanted to get off himself scot-free. As soon as ever he heard who the child was, he began to plot this fiendish thing. He dragged me into it—I struggled against him, but he was strong, and I had no power. He knew one or two things against me, and he held them over my head. I agreed to help him. I wasn't a week with the boy before I began to get fond of him."

"You can leave that part out," I interrupted, with heat.

Sharp paused as if someone had dealt him a blow.

"Marsden went to America," he continued. "He promised to give me £4,500 on the day he entered into possession of the child's estates. I was always studying drugs, and he suggested that I should give the boy something to bring on an attack of the heart, and then that I should tamper with the doctor's prescription. I had been studying the effects of tobacco taken in excess, and it occurred to me that niconitin would do the deadly work. That's all. The boy has been taking large doses of niconitin disguised in your medicine for the last fortnight."

"Where's Marsden now?" I said, when the fellow paused.

"I can't quite tell you—somewhere in America—for God's sake, don't give me up to him—he'd murder me."

"Your future is nothing to me," I said, "but I shall take the precaution to lock you up in this room until I know if your little victim is to live or die. If he lives, you can go ; if not——" I did not finish my sentence, but, turning the key in the door, ran quickly downstairs. Mrs. Marsden was waiting for me in one of the passages.

"What is the matter? Why were you so long with Mr. Sharp?" she said.

"Come in here—I have something to tell you," I answered.

I opened a door which stood near—we entered a sitting-room—I closed the door behind me.

"I can't conceal the truth from you, Mrs. Marsden," I said. "I have made an awful discovery—that poor little fellow has been the victim of a fiendish plot."

She interrupted me with a cry.

"No, no," she began, "no, don't say it—it's impossible—he's far away—he is bad, but not so bad as that."

"I pity you from my heart," I answered, "but your husband is bad enough for anything—he left his tool behind him—

Sharp was his tool. I am only just in time to save the boy."

I then briefly told Mrs. Marsden of the discovery which I had made at the chemist's.

Her horror and agitation were excessive; she, at least, poor woman, was fully innocent.

"I must take the boy away from here," I said. "I am sorry—I know you have had nothing to do with it, but because you are that scoundrel's wife—I must take the child away from you as soon as ever he is fit to be moved."

"I submit," she answered. "The fact is, I would not have him now on any terms. Oh, what a miserable woman I am—why did I ever listen to my husband? Why did I ever consent to receive the child? Oh, he is a fiend—why have I the misfortune to be his wife?"

I had no reply to make to this—it was time for me to hurry back to my little patient's bedside. He was very ill. For the next few days his life really hung in the balance. The case was such a peculiar one that I resolved not to leave him. Nurse Jenkins and I watched by him day and night. After two days, the extreme weakness became less marked, and gradually and slowly the heart recovered tone and strength. After a very slow convalescence, little Sir Noel became much better. I brought him back to Harley Street—he is still with me. I mean to keep him until his mother returns to England. As to Sharp, I gave him his liberty when I saw that the boy was likely to live. I have not heard of him since.

A DOCTOR'S DILEMMA

A DOCTOR'S DILEMMA

I HAD taken an interest in Feveral since he was a lad, and had watched his early medical career with pleasure. His brains were decidedly above the average, and he was in all respects a first-rate sort of fellow. As a medical student, he was fond of coming to me for advice, which I always gave frankly. By-and-by he secured the post of house-physician at Guy's Hospital. His short career there was marked by much promise, and, when the death of a relative enabled him to buy a share in a good country practice, I told him that I regarded his future as secure. He married soon afterwards, and, at his special request, I was present at the wedding. After this event I saw much less of him, but his letters, which reached me once or twice a year, assured me that he was doing well and happily in every sense of the word.

I had not seen Feveral for nearly three years, when one day, towards the end of the winter of '93, he called at my house. I was out when he arrived, but when I opened my door with my latchkey, he came into the hall to greet me.

"Hullo!" I exclaimed, when I saw him. "How are you? What has brought you to town? I hope you are well. How are the wife and child?"

"My wife is well," replied Feveral; "the baby died a month ago—oh, the usual thing—influenza."

He paused, and looked me full in the face. I glanced at him, and almost uttered a shocked exclamation.

"We have had an awful visitation of the plague," he continued; "it is my belief that it has been worse at West-field than in any other part of the country."

"You don't look too fit. Have you had an attack your-self?" I said.

"Yes, and I am overdone in every way. The fact is I rushed up to town on purpose to consult you."

I gave him another quick glance. When last I saw him he was a handsome, well-set-up fellow, full of muscle and vigour, with the Englishman's indomitable pluck written all over him; now he looked like a man who had undergone a sort of collapse. He had contracted a slight stoop between his shoulders, his abundant black hair was slightly streaked with grey, his eyes were sunken and suspiciously bright, there were heavy, black lines under them, and his cheeks were hollow.

"I shall be all right presently," he said, with a laugh. "Will you have the goodness to overhaul me, Halifax, and put me into the way of getting back my old tone? Can I speak to you? Can you devote a little of your time to me?"

"All the time you require," I answered heartily. "You have arrived just at a convenient moment. I have come back to dinner, and don't mean to see any more patients before nine or ten o'clock to-night. I have several hours, therefore, at your disposal: but, before we touch upon medical subjects, you must have some dinner."

As I spoke, I ushered Feveral into my dining-room, and, ringing a bell, ordered Harris to lay places for two. Dinner was served almost immediately, but I noticed, to my dismay, that my guest only played with his food. He drank off several glasses of good wine, however, and the fact was soon discernible in his increased animation.

"Come into the study and have a smoke," I said, when the meal had come to an end.

He rose at once, and followed me. We drew up our chairs in front of a cheerful fire, and for a time smoked our pipes in silence. It needed but a brief glance to tell me that Feveral was completely broken down. I should never have recognised him for the bright, energetic fellow whose happy wedding I had attended three years back. I waited now for him to begin his confidence. He did not say a word until he had finished his first pipe. Then he sprang to his feet, and stood facing me.

"I can't attempt to describe what a time we have had," he said abruptly; "that awful influenza has raged all over the place. The more I see of that insidious, treacherous complaint, the more I dread it. It is my firm conviction that influenza has caused more deaths, and wrecked more lives, than the cholera ever did. You have seen Russell, my partner? Well, he and I have been completely worked off our feet. I can't tell you what domestic tragedies we have been through."

"Well, you have not come up to town simply to tell me about them?" I interrupted abruptly.

"Of course not; I daresay you can record just as dismal a tale."

"Worse, if possible. But, now, to turn to yourself; you say you have been attacked by the enemy?"

"Yes, worse luck; it was after the child's death. She was a bright, happy little soul, eighteen months old. Perhaps you don't know what a first child is in a house, Halifax? My wife and I simply lived for the little one. Well, she succumbed to the malady in a day or two. Poor Ingrid broke down completely. She did not have influenza, but her strength gave way. She lost appetite and sleep. Nothing roused her but my unexpected illness. I suppose one does feel surprised when a doctor knocks up. Yes, I was down with the complaint, and had a short, sharp attack. I was up and about again in no time. I thought myself all right, but——"

"You acted very unwisely in going about so soon," I interrupted; "you are not fit for work yet."

"Is it as bad as that? Do I show that things are amiss so plainly?"

"Any doctor can see that you are not the thing. You are broken down—your nerve has gone; you want rest. Go home to-night, or, better still, wait until the morning, and then take the first train to Westfield. See Russell, and tell him plainly that you must have a month off work. I can send him down a substitute, if you commission me to do so. Get away, my dear fellow, without delay. Take your wife with you; the change will do her as much good as it will you. Go somewhere on the Continent. Have complete rest in fresh surroundings, and you will be a different man when you return."

"God knows, I need to be different!" said Feveral. "At the present moment I don't recognise myself."

Here he hesitated, paused, and looked away.

"The fact is," he continued suddenly, "I have not yet told you the true reason which brought me to consult you."

"Well, out with it, old man," I said, encouragingly.

He tried to give me a steady glance, but his eyes quickly fell.

"The fact is this," he said abruptly, and rising as he spoke, "the influenza has left an extraordinary sequel behind. I have an inexpressible dread over me. By no means in my power can I drive it away."

"Sit down and keep calm," I said; "tell me your fears as fully as possible."

Feveral sat down at my bidding. After a pause, he began to speak.

"You know," he said, "what an up-hill thing an ordinary doctor's career is. I thought I had done a very good thing when I bought a share of Russell's practice. But I found that it was nothing like as large as I had been given to suppose. I have done all that man could to increase it. I have been popular as a doctor, and fresh patients now come daily to consult me. In short, I am likely to do well, and, if only I can keep my health, to make a fair provision for my wife."

"Why should you not keep your health?" I asked.

"That is just the point," he replied. "At the present moment, for practical, useful purposes, my health is gone— my nerve has deserted me."

"You must be more explicit," I said. "What is up?"

"I dread making a fearful professional mistake, and so ruining my prospects as a medical man."

"What do you mean?"

"I will try and explain myself. Since I have had influenza I have been subject to brief but extraordinary lapses of memory. You know we dispense our own medicines. Well, this is the sort of thing that happens almost daily: I see a patient: I diagnose his case with my usual care. I then go to the dispensary to prepare the right medicine for him. I take up a bottle, as likely as not of some strong poison, and find that the whole case has vanished from my mind; I do not in the least know what I am holding the bottle for, nor why I am in the dispensary; my patient and his case, the diagnosis I have made, the medicine I want to make up, become a complete blank to me. After a lapse of several minutes my memory returns; but this state of things comes on oftener and oftener, and the fear of it has made me thoroughly nervous and unfit for work. You see yourself,

Halifax, that grave consequences may arise from such a peculiar state of nerves as mine. I may, during a lapse of memory, put something into the medicine which may kill my patient. My terror on this point at times almost reaches mania—I am nearly beside myself."

"Does your memory desert you at any other time?" I asked.

"Yes, but the curious thing is that it only fails me in connection with my profession. When I am alone with my wife I feel at comparative ease, and almost like my usual self; but when I am driving to see patients, I often completely forget my most important visits. I neglect the patients whose lives are in danger, and visit those who have comparatively little the matter with them. Of late I have given my coachman a list of all the patients whom I wish to see. He takes me to the right houses, but when I see the patient I forget the complaint under which he is labouring. Only yesterday I encountered the rage of a man, who was suffering from an acute attack of double pneumonia, by asking him if his rheumatic pains were better. Of course, this state of things can't go on. Don't tell me that all my fears are fanciful. I have studied diseases of the brain, and know that my case is a serious one."

"It is serious, but temporary," I answered. "You have just been down with the complaint which leaves the most extraordinary sequelæ behind—a complaint which none of us, with all our study, have yet fully gauged. You are tired out, mind and body; you want rest. You must not attempt to make up your own medicines at present. I can't hide the truth from you; if you do, the consequences may be serious. You must get away at once, Feveral. I told you a moment ago that I can get a good man to take your work for a month, or even two months, if necessary. If you like, I will write to Russell on the subject to-night. He will, of course, see the necessity of your leaving home."

Feveral did not reply at all for a minute. After a pause, he said—

"I suffer from other symptoms of a distressing character. I am possessed by that very ordinary delusion of the insane— that I am followed. I walked to this house to-night, and, in spite of all my efforts to assure myself to the contrary, I could not resist the suspicion that someone tracked me from the station to this house. The only thing that comforts me is that we have no insanity in our family. I cling to that fact as a drowning man does to a spar."

"You are not insane," I replied, "but you will be if you don't take rest. All your present most distressing symptoms will disappear if you take my advice. You had better not return to Staffordshire. You are welcome to make my house your headquarters until you have arranged matters with Russell. Meanwhile, telegraph to your wife to join you here — get away to the Continent before the end of the week. I promise you that long before the summer you will have returned to work like a giant refreshed."

Feveral heaved a heavy sigh. After a time he rose from his chair and leant against the mantelpiece.

"I suppose there is nothing for it but to take your advice," he said.

"You will not repent it," I answered. "Shall I write to Russell for you to-night?"

"Better wait until the morning," he replied. "I will sleep over all you have said, and give you my final decision then."

"Well, I must leave you now," I said. "I have promised to look in on one or two patients this evening; we shall meet at breakfast."

The next morning I was down early, and entered my breakfast-room before eight o'clock. I noticed that a place was only laid for one. "How is this, Harris?" I said to my servant. "Have you forgotten that Dr. Feveral is in the house?"

"Dr. Feveral left this morning, sir," replied Harris. "He came downstairs very early, and told me to tell you that you would find a note from him in your study. I inquired if he would like breakfast, but he said that he did not wish for anything. He was out of the house before half-past six, sir."

I hurried off to my study in some alarm. Feveral's note was on the mantelpiece. I tore it open; it ran as follows:

"My dear Halifax,—I regret to say that I find it impossible to remain in your house another hour. I spoke to you last night about what I believed at the time to be a delusion, namely, that I was followed wherever I went. I now perceive that this is not a delusion, but a grim reality. Even in your house I am not safe. Last night two men entered my room —they watched me from behind the curtains, and did not leave until daylight. I have risen early, and am leaving London without delay. My fear is that I have already made some extraordinary mistake in my dispensary, and have, perhaps, during my queer lapses of memory, given medicine which has deprived a fellow-creature of life. In this way I have undoubtedly laid myself open to the punishment of the law. The men who came into my room were policemen. You will understand that I can't stay longer in London.

"Yours,   ARTHUR FEVERAL."

The moment I read this extraordinary letter I put my hat on and went out of the house. I went to the nearest telegraph office, and sent the following message to Mrs. Feveral :

"Your husband called on me last night—not well ; left suddenly this morning, giving no address. If you have no clue to his whereabouts, come and see me at once."

To my surprise, no reply came to this telegram for several hours. In the evening I found a yellow envelope lying on the slab in my hall. It was from Mrs. Feveral—it ran as follows :

"Thank you for telegram—no cause for uneasiness. Arthur returned this morning, better and cheerful. He is busy in dispensary now—I have not shown him telegram.—INGRID FEVERAL."

"This is not the last of what may turn out a bad business," I could not help saying to myself.

The next event in my friend's queer story scarcely surprised me. Within forty-eight hours after his sudden departure, Mrs. Feveral called to see me. I was just going out when she drove up to my door in a hansom cab. I had last seen her as a bride—she was now in deep mourning. She was a remarkably handsome young woman, with an extraordinary fairness of complexion which one seldom sees in an English girl. It suddenly flashed through my memory that Feveral had married a young girl of Norwegian origin. This fact accounted for the whiteness of her skin, her bright blue eyes, and golden hair. She stepped lightly out of the hansom, and, seeing me, ran up the steps to meet me.

"Thank God, you are here," she exclaimed. "I am in great trouble. Can I see you immediately?"

"Certainly," I answered, leading the way to my study as I spoke. "How is your husband, Mrs. Feveral? I hope you are not bringing me bad news of him?"

"I am," she replied. She pressed her hand suddenly to her heart. "I am not going to break down," she continued, giving me an eager sort of pathetic glance which showed me a glimpse into her brave spirit. "I mean to rescue him if a man can be rescued," she continued. "No one can help me if you can't. Will you help me? You have always been my husband's greatest friend. He has thought more of your opinion than that of any other man living. Will you show yourself friendly at this juncture?"

"Need you ask?" I replied. "Here is a chair—sit down and tell me everything."

She did what I told her. When she began to speak she clasped her hands tightly together. I saw by her attitude that she was making a strong effort to control herself.

"I asked my husband to visit you a few days ago," she began. "He had spoken of some of his symptoms to me, and I begged of him to put his case into your hands. I hoped great things from your advice. Your telegram a couple of days ago naturally frightened me a good deal, but almost in the moment of reading it I received another from my husband, in which he asked me to expect him by an early train, and told me he was better. He arrived; he looked cheerful and well. He said that he believed his grave symptoms had suddenly left him. Several patients were waiting to consult him; he went off at once to the dispensary. I felt quite happy about him, and telegraphed you to that effect. In the evening he was wonderfully cheerful, and said he did not think it necessary to go to the expense of a change. He slept well that night, and in the morning told me that he felt quite well. He went out early to visit some patients, and came home to breakfast; afterwards he spent some hours, as usual, in his dispensary. I had been very unhappy and depressed since the death of my child, but that morning I felt almost glad—it was so good to see Arthur like his usual self. I was upstairs in my room—it was a little after twelve o'clock — when someone opened the door in great excitement. I looked up and saw Arthur — he almost staggered into the room—his hair was pushed wildly back from his forehead—he went as far as the mantelpiece, and leant against it.

"'What has happened?' I asked.

"He pulled at his collar as if it would choke him before he replied.

"'I have just committed murder,' he said—then he stared straight past me as if he did not see me.

"'Oh, nonsense,' I answered; you can't possibly know what you are saying.'

"'It is true—I have taken a man's life,' he repeated. 'I am ruined; it is all up with me. There is blood on my head.'

"'Sit down, dear, and try to tell me everything,' I said.

"I went up to him, but he pushed me aside.

"'Don't,' he said; 'my hands are stained with blood. I am not fit even to touch you.'

"'Well, at least tell me what has happened,' I implored.

"After a time he grew calm, and I got him to speak more rationally.

"'You know those awful lapses of memory,' he began. 'A young man—a stranger—came to consult me this morning. I diagnosed his case with my usual care, and then went to prepare some medicine for him. I went into the dispensary as usual. I felt quite well, and my intellect seemed to me to be particularly keen. I remember distinctly putting some ammonia and some salicin into a glass—then followed an awful blank. I found myself standing with a bottle in one hand, and a glass containing medicine in another—I did something with the bottle, but I can't remember what. After another period, in which everything was once again a blank, I came to myself. I found myself then in the act of giving a bottle made up in paper, and sealed in the usual way, to my patient.

"'"By the way," I said, "would you not like to take a dose at once? If so, I will fetch you a glass—even one dose of this medicine will remove your troublesome symptoms almost immediately."

"'The man to whom I was speaking was a fine-looking young fellow of about three or four-and-twenty. He hesitated when I suggested that he should take a dose of medicine directly. After a pause, he said that he would prefer to take the medicine when he returned to his hotel. I shook hands with him, he paid me his fee, and then left the house. A moment later I returned to the dispensary. I there made the following awful discovery. In a moment of oblivion I had put strychnine instead of valerian into the medicine. The quantity of strychnine which I had used would kill anyone. I rushed from the house like a distracted person, hoping to be in time to follow my patient. I made inquiries about him, but could not catch sight of him anywhere. Even one dose of that medicine will kill him. He will die of convulsions after the first dose—in all probability he is dead now. Oh, what a madman I was to return to Staffordshire !'

" I tried to comfort my husband, Dr. Halifax, but I soon found that my words had not the slightest effect upon him. I saw that he was not even listening to me—he crossed the room as I was speaking and, going to one of the windows, flung it open and leant half out. He began to look up and down the street, in the vain hope of seeing his unfortunate patient amongst the crowd.

" 'I shall never see him again—he is a dead man,' he repeated. 'He is dead—his blood is on my head—we are ruined.'

" 'We must try and find him immediately,' I said.

" 'Nonsense, we shall never find him," replied Arthur.

" As he said these words, he left the room. I paused to consider for a moment, then I went to consult Dr. Russell. My husband's partner is, as you know, an old man. He was terribly disturbed when I told him what had happened, and said that immediate steps should be taken to find the poor fellow who had been given the wrong medicine. He went out himself to inquire at the different hotels in the town. Meanwhile, I began to search for Arthur. I could not find him in the house. I asked the servants if they had seen him. No one knew anything about him—he had not gone out in his carriage. Dr. Russell presently returned to say that he could get no trace of the stranger. Almost at the same time a telegram was brought to me. I tore it open—it was from Arthur.

" 'Don't attempt to follow me,' he wired; 'it is best that we should never meet again. If I can I will provide for your future. We must never meet again.'

" There was no signature.

"That is the whole story," said Mrs. Feveral, standing up as she spoke. "After receiving my husband's telegram, I went to the bank and found, to my astonishment, that he had drawn nearly all the money we possess. He took a thousand pounds away with him in notes and gold. That fact seems to point to the conclusion that he had no intention of committing suicide; but where has he gone—why did he want so much money? What did he mean by saying that he would provide for me? I know that he is not responsible for his actions—it is very unsafe for him to be alone. I thought the whole thing over, during last evening and the long hours of the night, and resolved to come to you this morning. I must find my husband again, Dr. Halifax, and I want to know now if you will help me to search for him?"

"I certainly will," I replied; "the story you have just told me is most disastrous. I warned Feveral the other day that he was in no fit state to dispense medicines at present. He did very wrong not to take my advice. Of course, I ought not to blame him, poor fellow, for he is not responsible for his own actions. Two duties now lie before us, Mrs. Feveral."

"Yes?" she replied, eagerly.

"We must first discover whether your husband has really caused the death of this man or not. After all, he may only have imagined that he put strychnine into the medicine."

"No, no," she interrupted; "there is no hope of getting out of the terrible dilemma in that way. My husband used two glasses to mix his medicines—they were found in the dispensary unwashed. Dr. Russell, on examining one, found some drops of strychnine adhering to the bottom of the glass."

"Then that hope is over," I answered. "Well, we must only trust that something prevented your husband's victim from taking the medicine. Our first duty is to find that young man immediately; our second, to follow Feveral. Will you rest here for a few moments while I think over this strange case?"

I left the room, ordered Harris to bring the poor young wife some refreshment, and went off to my consulting-room to think over matters. I was busy, it is true, but I resolved to cast everything to the winds in the cause of my unhappy friend. I had known Feveral since he was a boy. I was not going to desert him now. I came back presently and told Mrs. Feveral that I had made arrangements which would enable me to devote my time, for the present, to her service.

"That is just what I should have expected," she replied. "I won't thank you in words—you know what I feel."

"I know that you are brave, and will help me instead of hindering me," I rejoined. "Will you accept my hospitality for to-night? My servants can, I think, make you comfortable. I mean to go to Staffordshire by the next train."

"Why so?"

"I must set inquiries on foot with regard to your husband's patient—I must find out his name and all possible particulars about him. I hope to be back in town with news for you early in the morning. In the meantime will you hold yourself in readiness to accompany me the moment I get a clue as to Feveral's present whereabouts?"

"I will do exactly what you wish," she answered.

I saw that her lips quavered while she spoke, but I also perceived to my relief that she had no intention of breaking down. A few moments later, I found myself in a hansom driving as fast as I could to Paddington Station. I took the next train down to Staffordshire, and arrived at Westfield, the small country town where Feveral had his practice, about nine o'clock in the evening. I drove straight to Dr. Russell's house. He was in, and I was admitted immediately into his presence. The old doctor knew me slightly. When I appeared he came eagerly forward.

"I can guess what you have come about," he said: "that unhappy business in connection with poor Feveral. His wife told me that she was going to town to consult you. Of course, I am glad to see you, but I don't know that you can do anything."

"I mean to find the man if he is still alive," I rejoined.

"The whole case points to suicide, does it not?" replied Russell. "But sit down, won't you? Let us talk it over."

I removed my overcoat and sat down on the chair which Russell indicated.

"I don't believe in the suicide idea," I began. "If Feveral meant to commit suicide, he would not have drawn a thousand pounds out of his bank. He is undoubtedly at the present moment suffering from a degree of mania, but it does not point in that direction. I want, if possible, to get a clue to his whereabouts ; and, what is even far more important, to find out if the strychnine which, in a moment of oblivion, he put into his patient's medicine has really led to a fatal result."

"That I can't tell," replied Russell. "The young man who came to consult Feveral yesterday morning appears to be a stranger in Westfield. Just after Mrs. Feveral left for town, I succeeded in tracing him to a commercial hotel of the name of Perry's, in a back part of the town. He must have walked straight to the hotel after leaving my partner's consulting-room. The waiter there tells me that he looked ill when he entered the house—he observed also that he carried a bottle of medicine wrapped up in paper in his hand. The bottle was unopened when the waiter observed him—he asked for his bill, which he paid, and in ten minutes' time had left the hotel. Yesterday was market day at Westfield, and there were a good many strangers in the town. This young man evidently attracted no special attention—the waiter did not even know his name. He arrived early in the morning, asked for a room, had a wash and change ; had breakfast, of which he ate very little ; went out, evidently to consult my partner ; returned, paid his bill, and vanished. Where he is now, Heaven knows."

"The case must be put into a detective's hands immediately," I said. "Have you a good man in the town, or shall I wire to Scotland Yard?"

"There is, I believe, a private detective in Short Street," answered Russell ; "but may I ask what is your object in following up this man's history? If he really dies of the medicine, we are likely to know all about the affair soon enough."

"There is just one chance in a hundred that he has not taken the medicine," I replied, "and on that chance we should act promptly."

"I can't follow you," replied the old man, impatiently. "If this young fellow never takes the medicine, why move at all in the matter? If the thing is known, it will be disastrous to us in every way. It is hard enough, Heaven knows, in these times of keen competition, to keep one's connection, and if it were bruited about that we had a mad doctor on the premises, who administered poison instead of cure, we should lose all our patients in a month's time."

"Don't you see my point?" I answered. "In order to prevent your having a mad doctor on the premises, I insist on having this thing cleared up. If by a lucky chance the young man who called at your dispensary this morning is still alive and well, Feveral will in all probability recover from the mania which now threatens to overbalance his reason. From the nature of the medicine given, the patient was most likely only suffering from some simple disturbance. He refused to take the medicine while in Feveral's consulting-room—it is evident that he left the hotel with the bottle still unopened—it is not wrong, therefore, to infer that he was better. Being better, it is also on the cards, although I know it is scarcely likely, that he never touched the medicine at all. If this is the case and the fact is known, Feveral's reason may be saved."

"Oh, poor fellow, I doubt if he is in the land of the living," interrupted Dr. Russell.

"I am certain he is alive," I replied; "but the fact is this, doctor: he will be insane to the end of his days if he has really killed that young man. If his supposed victim is alive and unhurt, Feveral will in all probability soon be restored to his normal state of health."

"Perhaps you are right," said Dr. Russell, "and if so, you had better come with me at once to consult Hudson. He is a shrewd fellow, and will in all probability soon be able to trace the man to whom the strychnine was given. But how do you propose to find Feveral?"

"We will tackle Hudson first," I said. "I want to set him to work without a moment's delay."

Dr. Russell rose, put on his hat and great-coat, and we soon found ourselves in Short Street. Hudson, the private detective, happened to be in—we had an interview with him. I put the case as briefly as possible in his hands; he promised to take it up; assured us that it was a very easy and promising investigation, and told us that in all probability we should know whether Feveral's victim was alive or dead by the following morning.

As we were returning to Russell's house, a young man came up and spoke abruptly to the old doctor.

"How do you do?" he said. "Will you take a message from me to Feveral?"

"Feveral is from home at present," replied Dr. Russell.

"What a pity. The fact is, I heard from my brother this morning. He particularly begged of me to see Feveral, or by some means to convey his thanks to him."

"I hope your brother is better, North," said Dr. Russell, in a kindly tone.

"Thanks, he is getting as fit as possible—he thought Dr. Feveral would be glad to know about him—he is now at Monte Carlo, having a right good time—in short, his nerves are completely restored, and he proposes to return to work within the next fortnight or so."

Dr. Russell said a few more words, assured North that he would give Feveral his message when he saw him, and we continued our walk.

"What is that about Feveral sending a patient to Monte Carlo?" I asked, suddenly.

"I knew nothing about it until North mentioned it," said Dr. Russell. "Both the Norths have been down with influenza — the younger suffered considerably; he went through just the sort of nerve storm which seems, in a different degree, to have affected poor Feveral himself. I did not know that Feveral had recommended him change —I am surprised that he sent him to a place like Monte Carlo."

"Why so?" I asked.

"On account of the gaming-tables. There never was a man who had such a horror of gambling as Feveral. His father was bitten with the craze years ago, and, as a boy, he learnt something of the tremendous evils which spring from indulgence in such a vice. That he should recommend a patient to put himself in the way of temptation astonishes me a good deal."

I thought deeply for a moment or two.

"Do you happen to know," I asked then, "when the Norths had influenza?"

"Why do you ask?"

"I have a reason for wishing to know. In short, if Feveral gave this advice *since* his own attack, it may give me a clue to his present whereabouts."

"I can't see your meaning," said Dr. Russell, with impatience. "As a fact, the youngest North was down with the malady immediately after Feveral had made his own quick recovery—he had a short, sharp attack, followed by great depression—Feveral spoke about him to me one day. I said, casually, that he should have change—I did not know until to-night that my advice was acted upon.

"Thanks," I answered; "your information is of great importance. Now, if I can obtain North's address at Monte Carlo, I think my business here will be over, and I should like, if possible, to catch the midnight train to town."

"What in the world do you mean?"

"I am scarcely in a position to explain myself at the present moment," I answered. "Will you oblige me by sending a note round to North at once, asking his brother's address?"

"Why, yes; I will do that, certainly. Here we are, at home—you can have an answer to my note while we are at supper."

Russell was as good as his word; he sent a messenger to North's house asking him for the name of his brother's hotel at Monte Carlo. The answer came back quickly, and with it in my pocket I returned to London.

As I hurried back to town in the express train, the thought which had suddenly darted through my mind on hearing that Feveral had ordered North to seek change at Monte Carlo gathered strength and substance. The advice which he gave this young man was exactly the reverse of what he would have given had his mind been in its normal healthy state. If in a hasty moment he had ordered North to seek change of scene in the very place where he would be most exposed to temptation, was there not a possibility that he might himself seek the same relief? The fact of his having a horror of gambling in his sane moments would make it all the more probable that he would turn to it in his insane hours. In short, the idea grew stronger and stronger the more I thought it over, that North was the man to help me to find Feveral. In the early hours of the morning I reached town, and, driving straight to an office which was open all night, wired to North to his Monte Carlo address. I worded the telegram in the following manner:

"Dr. Feveral is ill, and has disappeared from home—look out for him at Monte Carlo. If he arrives, telegraph to me without delay."

Having sent off this message, there was nothing whatever to do but to wait. Until I heard either from Hudson, the detective, or from North, I could take no further steps.

On the evening of that day I received a telegram from the detective—it was unsatisfactory, and contained the simple words :

" No news ; writing."

The following morning I received his letter.

"DEAR SIR,"—it ran—"I am completely foiled in my efforts to trace Dr. Feveral's unknown patient ; beyond the fact that a young man in some respects answering to his description was noticed by a porter at the railway station, entering a third-class carriage for London, I have no tidings to give you. I will continue to make investigations, and will let you know immediately anything turns up.

"Yours respectfully,
"JAMES HUDSON."

I had scarcely read this letter before Mrs. Feveral, who had moved to a hotel close by, called to see me. I showed her the letter. She read it with impatience.

"Can nothing be done?" she cried. "Have you no plan to propose, Dr. Halifax?"

"I have the ghost of a hope," I answered, "but it is really so slight that I have not dared to tell it to you."

"Oh, do not deprive me of the slightest shadow of hope," she answered ; "you don't know what my despair is and what my fears are."

At that moment Harris entered the room, bearing a telegram on a salver.

"Wait one moment while I attend to this," I said to Mrs, Feveral.

I opened the envelope and saw, with a sudden leap at my heart, that my conjecture with regard to Feveral had been correct.

"There is no answer, Harris," I said to the man.

He withdrew. I glanced again at the words of the telegram, then placed it in Mrs. Feveral's hands.

"There," I said, "this will explain itself."

She almost snatched it from me, devouring the words with her eyes. They were as follows :

"Feveral arrived here last night—he is at the Hotel des Anglais—does not recognise me—visited the tables after dinner —lost heavily."

"Thank Heaven he is found !" exclaimed Mrs. Feveral.

Tears streamed from her eyes—she let the little pink sheet of thin paper flutter to the floor.

"He is safe—he is alive," she gasped. "How—how did you guess that he might be at Monte Carlo?"

I repeated in a few words my reasons for telegraphing to North—her tears ceased to flow as she listened to me—her eyes grew bright—a look of determination and courage filled her beautiful face.

"And now, what do you mean to do?" she asked, as soon as I paused.

"Go to him at once," I answered.

"I will come with you, if I may."

"You certainly may. There is still time to catch the eleven o'clock boat train from Victoria; we shall arrive in Paris this evening, and, if we are lucky, may catch the Mediterranean Express. Can you have your things packed and be back at this house in a quarter of an hour?"

"I can and will," she answered.

She left me immediately. I gave hasty directions to my servants, saw the doctor who was to take charge of my patients in my absence, and was ready when Mrs. Feveral returned. We drove to Victoria, caught the boat train by a minute or two, and soon found ourselves rushing away to Dover. We arrived in Paris without any adventure, and were fortunate enough to catch the Mediterranean Express at the *Gare de Lyon*. I wired to North to tell him of our proposed visit, begged of him to meet me at the railway station, asked him to watch Feveral, and to say nothing of the fact that his wife and I hoped to reach Monte Carlo the following day.

Mrs. Feveral and I reached Marseilles at eleven o'clock on the following morning. There we left the train for breakfast. During breakfast I said, suddenly:

"It would be well for us to arrange our plan of action."

She looked up at me in some surprise.

"Is there anything special?" she began.

"I want you to promise me one thing," I said.

"Yes, of course, anything," she answered, with a heavy sigh.

"I want you to be guided by me—I want you to obey me explicitly."

"Yes, I will, of course; but surely there is but one thing for me to do?"

"You think you must go straight to your husband?" I said.

"Certainly; that is why I am visiting Monte Carlo."

"It seems hard to say 'no' to such a natural desire," I said, "but I am anxious that you should not see Feveral on our arrival. All his future depends upon our acting with circumspection in the present crisis. I firmly believe that your husband's insanity is only of a temporary character, but one injudicious move would confirm his delusion and make him insane for the rest of his life. He has rushed from home now, under the impression that he has taken the life of a fellow-creature."

"There is little doubt that such is the case," replied Mrs. Feveral.

"I am by no means sure on that point. I have asked Hudson, the detective, to telegraph to me at the Hotel Métropole at Monte Carlo. I may find news on my arrival there. All depends on the nature of this news. When we reach our destination to-day, will you allow me to take you straight to a hotel, and will you stay there quietly until the moment comes for you to make your presence known to your husband?"

"It is hard for me to obey, but I will," answered the poor wife, with a heavy sigh.

We soon afterwards took our places in the train, and between three and four that afternoon arrived at Monte Carlo. Young North was waiting on the platform to receive us. He shook his head when I introduced myself to him. By a gesture, I warned him not to say anything in Mrs. Feveral's presence. She was completely worn out by her journey, and fortunately did not notice the expressive action by which he gave me to understand that he had bad news. I took her to a large hotel not far from the Casino, saw that she was accommodated with a comfortable room, and promised to return to see her after a few hours. I then went out with North. He walked with me to my hotel.

"Well, I am glad you've come," said the young fellow. "I have had an awful time ever since Feveral's arrival. He is as mad as a man can be—spends every moment of his time at the tables, eats nothing, drinks a good deal—either does not recognise me or won't. He is losing money at a frightful rate, but, from the manner of his play, seems to be absolutely reckless as to whether he loses or wins."

"And where is he staying?" I asked.

"At the Hotel des Anglais. He has rooms on the first floor, and evidently denies himself nothing."

I knew that Feveral was not rich. A little more of this reckless sort of thing, and he and his young wife would be beggars.

"The poor fellow is not responsible for his actions at the present moment," I said.

"No, he is as mad as a March hare," said North, with vehemence.

"Well, I trust his madness will not continue," I replied. "He is suffering at the present moment from a sort of double shock. The death of his child, followed immediately by an attack of influenza, produced the first bad effect upon his nerves—the second shock was worse than the first, but for that, he would not be losing money as fast as man can at the present moment."

"What do you mean?" said North.

I then told him what had occurred a few days ago at Westfield.

"The unfortunate thing is this," I said: "we cannot find the patient to whom Feveral gave the strychnine. I have put the best detective in Westfield on his track, but there are no tidings whatever of his whereabouts. I had hoped to have a telegram from the detective, Hudson, on my arrival. I desired it to be sent to this hotel, but none has yet arrived."

"Hudson is a very sharp fellow," said North. "If anyone can help to solve a mystery, he is the man. I am glad you put the case into his hands. My father, who is supposed to be the best solicitor at Westfield, often employs Hudson, and thinks most highly of him."

"Well," I said, "there is nothing to do at the present moment, but simply to wait. One false step now would confirm Feveral's insanity."

"Will you not let him know that his wife has arrived?" interrupted North.

"Not at present; I must be guided altogether by circumstances. It will be your business and mine, North, not to lose sight of him. If by any chance he leaves Monte Carlo, he must be immediately followed."

Shortly afterwards North left me, and I went to seek an interview with Mrs. Feveral. Poor girl, she was worn out in every sense of the word. I begged of her to take some rest, assured her that I would send for her the moment her presence was likely to be of use, and went away.

On the afternoon of the next day, I was walking in the gardens just outside the Casino, when I suddenly saw Feveral coming to meet me. The weather resembled that which we have in June in England. The tender blue of the sky was intensified in the deep blue of the Mediterranean. I was standing near a large bed of mignonette when Feveral walked by. He was dressed with care, and looked like what he was, a remarkably handsome and well-set-up fellow; he was evidently going to the Casino. He passed within arm's length of me, stared me full in the face, showed no gleam of recognition, and was about to pass me, when I could not help speaking to him.

"How do you do?" I said.

He stopped when I said this and looked at me fixedly. A curious change came over his face; his eyes, which had appeared quite frank and untroubled when first he saw me, assumed a secretive and almost sly expression.

"I know who you are quite well," he said. "Will you oblige me by walking down this path with me?"

He pointed to a shady avenue of eucalyptus as he spoke. I yielded immediately to his humour. We walked together for a few paces, then he turned abruptly and faced me.

"You are a detective officer from the London police force," he said. "I know you quite well, and what you have come about. The whole thing is perfectly fair, and I have not a word to say. It is my last intention to defeat the ends of justice in any way. I have committed murder—I am stained with blood. The law must, of course, have its course —all I beg of you is to give me time. Before I am arrested, I am anxious to win a sum of money to place my wife above want. I came to Monte Carlo for this purpose. Hitherto, I have been strangely unlucky, but I have a presentiment that my luck is about to turn. I shall win largely either this afternoon or this evening. After the gaming-tables are closed to-night, I am at your service, Inspector——"

He paused, but I did not supply any name.

"I will wait on you this evening at the gaming-tables," I said, suddenly.

"As you please," he replied, "but don't come until late—I

am certain to win largely. You know yourself how important it is for a man in my position to provide for his wife."

I nodded, and he left me. I sat down on a bench and watched his retreating figure. He went slowly up the steps into the Casino and vanished from view. The beautiful scenery which surrounded me—and, perhaps, there is no more beautiful scenery in the world than is to be found at Monte Carlo — no longer gave me pleasure. I thought very badly of Feveral. His malady had progressed even farther than I had anticipated. If he had indeed killed his man, all hope of his recovering his senses was completely at an end. I went back to my hotel and spent some anxious hours there, during which I could settle to nothing. I had asked North to dine with me, and he came at the appointed time. I told him of my interview with Feveral—he shook his head as he listened.

"He took me for one of the gardeners here," he answered, "and asked me how I acquired my very excellent English. His brain is quite gone, poor fellow. I must say that I am rather surprised, Dr. Halifax, that you don't——"

"Don't do what?" I asked.

"Don't use your authority, and take the poor fellow back to England. He surely is not in a condition to be at large."

"Any forcible step of that kind would make the case hopeless," I answered. "I am inclined to use the most cautious measures until we really know the fate of his unlucky patient."

"And do you intend to follow him to the Casino to-night?" said North.

"Yes, I promised to be there—I shall keep my word."

"May I accompany you?"

"Certainly; I should like you to do so."

"What about Mrs. Feveral?"

"Poor soul, I must have an interview with her before I go," I answered.

My brief interview with the poor young wife was full of pain. I told her that I intended to follow her husband to the tables, and would bring her word of the result before midnight. She replied to this with a ghastly smile. As I was leaving the room she called after me.

"You are expecting a telegram at the Hotel Métropole from Mr. Hudson?" she said.

"I asked him to wire there if he had any news," I answered.

"Suppose his message comes while you are at the Casino?"

"In that case it must wait until I return," I replied.

"Will you commission me to bring it to you, if it does come?" she asked.

"I would rather you did not come to the Casino," I replied; "it is not a fit place for you to visit alone."

She made no answer, but I noticed a queer, determined look creeping into her face.

The hour was growing late now, and North and I hastened to the Casino. We followed the crowd into the vast building, obtained the usual cards of admittance, and soon found ourselves walking slowly through the suite of rooms which contain the celebrated gaming-tables. The hour had approached ten o'clock, and the numerous visitors from the different hotels were crowding in for their evening's amusement. Both ladies and gentlemen were in full evening dress, and the scene which met my eyes was a very brilliant and animated one. Each of the long tables was surrounded by groups of players seated on chairs close together; outside these groups, three or four rows deep, were crowds of spectators, some merely watching the play, others playing themselves over the heads of their more fortunate neighbours, others again waiting for their turns to find seats at the tables. The *roulette* tables, which were eight in number, were all crowded; but as we walked through the rooms, North whispered to me that Feveral despised *roulette*, and only played for high stakes at the *trente et quarante* tables. We passed the first of these, and eagerly scanned the faces of the men and women who surrounded it. Feveral was not amongst them. We stood for a moment or two to watch the play. A woman, splendidly dressed, was drawing attention to herself by the reckless manner in which she was flinging one-hundred-franc pieces on different divisions of the table. She lost and lost, but still went on playing. Her play was reckless in the extreme, and some people who stood near begged of her to desist. The terrible passion for gambling in its worst form was written all over her excited face. I turned away with a sense of disgust, and followed North to the other *trente et quarante* table. Here I found the object of my search. Feveral was in irreproachable evening dress; his face was calm and pale, there was no apparent excitement either in his manner or appearance. He sat rather near one of the *croupiers*, and, to all appearance, was playing with extreme caution. From thirty to forty hundred-franc pieces were piled up at his left hand. He was making careful notes on a card which was placed in front of him, and was evidently playing with intelligence. At each deal of the cards he placed his gold on certain divisions, and, as we stood at a little distance and watched, I noticed that he won at every deal. His pile of gold grew larger, but his cautious and steady manner never deserted him. By degrees some people who were standing near began to remark on his invariable luck. Hearing a remark close by in the English tongue, he raised his eyes, and for an instant encountered mine.

"I told you I should win to-night," he said; "but you have come a little early, inspector. It is all right—quite right; but you must give me time."

As his success went on he began to double and quadruple his stakes—never once did he lose. A man who was standing near me said—

"That Englishman has been here for the last three nights, and he has not had a moment's success until now. He evidently means to carry all before him to-night. If only he has sense to stop playing before his luck turns, he may retrieve his losses, which must have been very considerable."

"He plays with caution," I answered.

"He does to-night," was the reply, "but last night and the night before his play was reckless beyond words."

Some people in the crowd of spectators moved away at this moment, and North and I stepped into the space which they had vacated. By doing so we stood at Feveral's left hand, and could look over his shoulder. In the midst of his play he glanced at me once or twice. My presence did not irritate him in the least. He supposed me to be a detective come to take him into custody—his impression was that his time was short to accomplish the task he had set himself to do—he went on doubling and doubling his stakes—still without any apparent recklessness—never once did he lose.

The moments flew by, and the time for closing was not far off. Feveral was already a rich man.

"Stop him now, if you can," said North. "Let him take away his enormous winnings, and whatever happens, his wife is provided for. Stop him, for God's sake, doctor, before his luck turns."

Before I could reply, a noise at my left caused me to turn my head—there was a slight commotion—a little pressure in the crowd, and I heard a woman's clear voice say—

"Pardon me if I ask you to allow me to pass. That gentleman sitting there is my husband—I have something I wish to say to him."

The gentle, high-bred tone had an effect. I turned quickly, and saw, to my astonishment and horror, that Mrs. Feveral had come into the room. Unlike the other women present, she was in the quietest morning dress. Her fair face looked all the fairer because of the deep mourning which she wore.

"Your telegram has come at last, Dr. Halifax," she said to me. "I have taken the liberty to bring it to you—don't keep me, please—I must speak to my husband."

Before I could prevent her she had reached his side, her arms were round his neck, her cheek was touching his. The crowded room, the gaze of the many spectators, were nothing to her—she only saw her husband.

"Come away, darling," she said; "come away at once."

He started up when she touched him, and stared at her more in impatience than surprise.

"Don't interrupt me, Ingrid," he said, "I will come presently. Leave me now; I am busy."

He tried to resume his seat, but she clung to him, holding one of his hands in both of hers with a sort of desperation.

"No; you must come now," she said. "You don't know where you are——"

"I don't know where I am!" he repeated, speaking fast and thick, his face scarlet with intense excitement. "Yes, by Heaven! I do. I am here because my hands are red with blood. I conceal nothing. All the world may know the truth. I am in this place to-night because I have taken a man's life. I am about to pay the forfeit of my crime. This detective," here he pointed at me, "will arrest me in a moment or two. Before I go, I wish to provide for you—don't touch me—I am a murderer. Hands off, I say."

He pushed her from him. His eyes were wild. The people in the immediate neighbourhood heard his words—they began to move away from him with looks of horror, even the *croupiers* turned their heads for a moment.

"Go home, Ingrid," said her husband. "Don't touch me. I have made a bargain with that man," again he pointed at me; "he is a detective from Scotland Yard. My bargain is that I am not to be arrested until I have won enough money to provide for your future. I am going to double my winnings. There is blood on my head—don't touch me."

His last words were uttered with a shout. Mrs. Feveral turned ghastly pale. Feveral sat down again by the table. At this moment I remembered the telegram, which was still unopen in my hand. I tore the seal open and read the contents. These were the words which almost took my breath away with relief and delight :—

"*Found Dr. Feveral's patient yesterday—he is a young man of the name of Norris. He lives at Colehill, in Warwickshire. He took the doctor's medicine to the last drop, and says that it restored him to perfect health. On hearing this, I went straight to Dr. Russell, who examined the bottle from which the strychnine was supposed to have been taken, and found it quite full. If Dr. Feveral took strychnine from the bottle by mistake, he must have poured it back again. It is evident that Norris had none in his medicine.*"

"Read this," I said to Mrs. Feveral; "read it quickly—tell your husband the truth—he may be saved even yet."

Her quick eyes seemed to flash over the words—she took in the meaning in a couple of seconds.

"You have committed no murder," she said to her husband. "Don't go on with that horrid play—it is unnecessary. You are not what you think yourself—you are innocent of any crime. The man you gave the medicine to is alive and well. Read this—read this."

She thrust the telegram before his eyes. He read it—staggered to his feet, turned first red, then pale.

"Is this true?" he said, turning and fixing his eyes on his wife.

"Yes, it is perfectly true; it has just come. The man you gave the medicine to is well, quite well. Your medicine cured him instead of killing him; you shall see him again when you return to England."

Feveral put his hand to his forehead—a bewildered look crossed his face.

"Then what, in the name of Heaven, am I doing here?" he cried.

He turned and looked with bewilderment around him.

The piles of gold which he had won lay close to him, but he did not touch them.

"What am I doing here?" he repeated. "How did I get into this place? They play for money here; I don't approve of it—I never play. Come, Ingrid, come home."

He grasped his wife's hand, and led her quickly out of the Casino. I followed the pair, but North stayed behind to gather up Feveral's winnings.

The next day, when I visited him, I found my friend quite sane. He received me with a look of surprise.

"I can't imagine how I came to this place," he said; "I have not the least remembrance of how I got here—in fact, I recall nothing since the evening I interviewed you, Halifax, in Harley Street."

"Well, you are here now, and a very good thing too," I interrupted.

"Yes," he replied; "and now that I am out of England, I think I shall stay away for a little, for although I feel ever so much better, I am not yet quite fit for work."

"Take a good, long change, while you are about it," I answered.

I saw, with a sense of relief, that Feveral had completely lost all knowledge of that terrible episode, during which he believed himself to be guilty of having taken the life of a fellow-creature. The winnings, which North had carefully secured, counterbalanced the large sums which he had lost during his first two evenings' reckless play at the Casino.

By my advice, Mrs. Feveral persuaded her husband to leave Monte Carlo that afternoon. They spent the next six months visiting different parts of Europe; and when he returned to his work in the following summer, he was completely restored to his normal state of health. I saw him shortly after his return, but he did not allude to the Monte Carlo incident—he is never likely to remember anything about it.

ON A CHARGE OF FORGERY

ON A CHARGE OF FORGERY

THE study of the human character in its many complex forms has always been of deep interest to the doctor. From long practice, he becomes to a great extent able to read his many patients, and some characters appear to him as if they were the pages of an open book. The hopes, fears, aims, and motives which influence the human soul are laid bare before him, even in the moment when the patient imagines that he is only giving him a dry statement of some bodily ailment. The physician believes fully in the action of mind on body, and can do little good for any patient until he becomes acquainted with his dominant thought, and the real motive which influences his life.

For the purpose of carrying on what has become such an absorbing study of my own life, I have often visited places not at all connected with my profession, in the hope of getting fresh insight into the complex workings of the human mind.

Not long ago, having a day off duty, I visited the Old Bailey while a celebrated trial was going on. The special case which was engaging the attention of judge, learned counsel, and twelve intelligent members of the British jury, was one which aroused my professional acumen from the first. The man who stood in the prisoner's dock was a gentleman by birth and appearance. He was young and good-looking—his face was of the keenly-intelligent order—his eyes were frank in their expression—his mouth firm, and his jaw of the bulldog order as regards obstinacy and tenacity of purpose. I judged him to be about twenty-eight years of age, although the anxiety incident to his cruel position had already slightly sprinkled the hair which grew round his temples with grey.

His name was Edward Bayard. The crime he was being tried for was forgery. He was accused of having forged a cheque for £5,000, and I saw from the first that the circumstantial evidence against him was of the strongest. I listened to his able counsel's view of the case, watching the demeanour of the prisoner as I did so. He leant the whole time with his arms over the rail of the dock, looking straight before him without a vestige of either shame or confusion on his fine face. I observed that his intellect was keenly at work; that he was following the arguments of his counsel with intense interest. I also noticed that once or twice his lips moved, and on one occasion, when a very difficult point was carried, there came the glimmer of a smile of satisfaction round his firmly-set lips.

The counsel for the prosecution then stood up and pulled the counsel's argument for the defendant to pieces. The case seemed black against the prisoner—still he never moved from his one position, and stood perfectly calm and self-possessed. The case was not finished that day. I went away so deeply interested that I resolved at all hazards to return to the Old Bailey on the following afternoon. I did so—the case of Edward Bayard occupied another couple of hours—in the end, the jury brought in a verdict of "Guilty," and the prisoner was sentenced to five years' penal servitude. I watched him when the sentence was pronounced, and noticed a certain droop of his shoulders as he followed his gaoler out of the dock. My own firm conviction was that the man was innocent. There was nothing for me to do, however, in the matter. A jury of his countrymen had pronounced Edward Bayard guilty. He had been employed in the diplomatic service, and hitherto his career had been irreproachable; it was now cut short. He had metaphorically stepped down, gone out, vanished. His old place in the world would know him no more. He might survive his sentence, and even live to be an old man, but practically, for all intents and purposes, his life was over.

I am not given to sentimentalize, but I felt a strange sensation of discontent during the remainder of that day; I almost wished that I had taken up the law instead of medicine, in order that the chance might be mine to clear Bayard.

That evening at my club a man I knew well began to talk over the case.

"It is a queer story altogether," he said; "it is well known that Levesen, the man who prosecuted, is in love with the girl to whom Bayard was engaged."

"Indeed!" I answered. "I know nothing whatever of Bayard's private history."

"Until this occurred," continued Teesdel, "I would have trusted Bayard, whom I have known for years, with untold gold. But the evidence against him has been so over-whelming that, of course, he had not the ghost of a chance of acquittal; still, I must repeat, he is the last man I should ever have expected to do that sort of thing."

"I was present at the trial," I answered, "and followed the story to a certain extent; but I should like to hear it now in brief, if I may"

"I will present it in a nutshell," said Teesdel, in his brisk way. "Levesen, the prosecutor, is a tolerably rich man—he has a house in Piccadilly, where he lives with his sister. Levesen is guardian to a very beautiful girl, a ward in Chancery—her name is Lady Kathleen Church. She has lived with Levesen and his sister for the last couple of years. Lady Kathleen is only nineteen, and it was whispered a short time ago in Levesen's circle of friends that he intended to make the fair heiress his wife. She is a very lovely girl, and, as she will inherit a large fortune when she attains her majority, is of course attractive in every way. Lady Kathleen met Bayard at a friend's house—the young people fell in love with each other, and became engaged. Bayard was rising in his profession—he was far from rich, but was likely to do well eventually. There was no reasonable objection to the engage-ment, and Francis Levesen did not attempt to make any. Levesen took Bayard up—the two men were constantly seen together—the engagement was formally announced, although the wedding was not to take place until Lady Kathleen's majority. One fine morning it was discovered that Bayard's banking account was augmented to the tune of £5,000, that Levesen's account was short of precisely that sum, that a cheque had been presented by Bayard at Levesen's bank, with Levesen's signature, for exactly that sum of money. The cheque was, of course, a forgery. Bayard was arrested, prose-cuted, and found guilty. His version of the story you have, doubtless, followed in court. Levesen is in Parliament, and has a secretary; Bayard was in money difficulties. He asked Levesen to help him, and declares that the cheque was handed to him by Mr. Franks, Levesen's secretary. There is no evidence whatever to support this story, and Bayard has, as you know, now to expiate his crime in penal servitude. Well, I can only repeat that he is the last man in existence I should ever have expected to do that sort of thing."

"We none of us know what we may do until we are tried," said a man who stood near.

"The story is undoubtedly a strange one," I said. "I have listened carefully to the evidence on both sides, and although the verdict is evidently the only one which could be expected under the circumstances, my strong feeling is that Bayard did not commit that forgery."

"Then how do you account for the thing?"

"I wish I could account for it—there is something hidden which we know nothing about. I am convinced of Bayard's innocence, but my reason for this conviction is nothing more than a certain knowledge of character which from long experience I possess. Bayard is not the sort of man who, under any circumstances, would debase himself to the extent of committing a crime. The whole thing is contrary to his character: men don't do things contrary to their characters. I believe him to be innocent."

My words evidently startled Teesdel; he gazed at me attentively.

"It is queer that you, of all men, should make such a remark, Halifax," he said. "You must know that character goes for nothing in moments of strong temptation. It was clearly proved that Bayard wanted the money. Franks, the secretary, could not have had any possible motive for swearing to a lie. In short, I can't agree with you. I am sorry for the poor fellow, but I am afraid my verdict is on the side of the jury."

"What about Lady Kathleen?" I asked, after a pause.

"Of course the engagement is broken off—people say the girl is broken-hearted—she was devoted to Bayard; I believe Miss Levesen has taken her out of town."

I said nothing further. It was more than a year before I heard Bayard's name mentioned again. Walking down Piccadilly one day I ran up against Teesdel; he stopped to speak to me for a minute, and as we were parting turned back to say:

"By the way, your face reminds me of something—yes, now I know. The last time I saw you, you had just come from poor Bayard's trial—well, the latest news is, that Lady Kathleen Church is engaged to Francis Levesen—the engagement is formally announced—they are to be married within a month—the wedding is to be one of the big affairs of the season."

"Poor Bayard!" was my sole exclamation.

I parted with Teesdel after another word or two, and hurried off to attend to my duties. A week later two ladies were ushered into my consulting-room. One was elderly, with a thin, somewhat masculine, type of face, shrewd, closely set dark eyes, and a compressed mouth. She was dressed in the height of the reigning fashion, and wore a spotted veil drawn down over her face. Her manner was stiff and conventional. She bowed and took the chair I offered without speaking.

I turned from her to glance at her companion—my other visitor was a girl—a girl who would have been beautiful had she been in health. Her figure was very slight and willowy—she had well-open brown eyes, and one of those high-bred faces which one associates with the best order of English girl. In health, she probably had a bright complexion, but she was now ghastly pale—her face was much emaciated, and there were large black shadows under her eyes. Looking at her more closely, I came to the quick conclusion that the state of her bodily health was caused by some mental worry. The melancholy in her beautiful eyes was almost overpowering. I drew a chair forward for her, and she dropped into it without a word.

"My name is Levesen," said the elder lady. "I have brought my ward, Lady Kathleen Church, to consult you, Dr. Halifax."

I repeated the name under my breath—in a moment I knew who this girl was. She had been engaged to Bayard, and was now going to marry Francis Levesen. Was this the explanation of the highly nervous condition from which she was evidently suffering?

"What are Lady Kathleen's symptoms?" I asked, after a pause.

"She neither eats nor sleeps—she spends her time irrationally—she does everything that girl can do to undermine her health," said the elder lady, in an abrupt tone—"in fact, she is childish to the last degree, and so silly and nervous that the sooner a doctor takes her in hand, the better."

"What do you complain of yourself?" I said, turning to the patient.

"I am sick of life, said the girl. "I am glad that I am ill —I don't wish to be made well."

"It is all a case of nerves," said Miss Levesen. "Until a year ago there could not have been a healthier girl than Lady Kathleen—she enjoyed splendid health—her spirits were excellent—from that date she began to droop. She had, I know, a slight disappointment, but one from which any sensible girl would quickly have recovered. I took her into the country and did what I could for her; she became better, and is now engaged to my brother, who is deeply attached to her. They are to be married in a month. If ever a girl ought to enjoy life, and the prospect before her, she ought."

"Ill-health prevents one enjoying anything," I answered, in an enigmatical voice. "Will you tell me something more about your symptoms?" I said, turning again to my patient.

"I can't sleep," she replied. "I do not care to eat—I am very unhappy—I take no interest in anything—in short, I wish to die."

"Your manner of speaking is most reckless and wrong, Kathleen," said the elder lady, in a tone of marked disapproval.

"Forgive me, but I should like to question Lady Kathleen without interruption," I said, turning to Miss Levesen.

Her face flushed.

"Oh, certainly," she answered. "I know that I ought not to speak—I sincerely hope that you will get to the bottom of this extraordinary state of things, Dr. Halifax, and induce my ward to return to common-sense."

"May I speak to you alone?" suddenly asked the young lady, raising her eyes, and fixing them on my face.

"If you wish it," I replied. "It may be best, Miss Levesen, to allow me to see Lady Kathleen for a few moments by herself," I continued, in a low voice. "In a case like the present, the patient is always much more confidential when quite alone with the doctor."

"As you please," she replied; "only, for heaven's sake, don't humour her in her fads."

I rang the bell, and desired Harris to take Miss Levesen to the waiting-room. The moment we were alone, Lady Kathleen's manner completely changed; her listlessness left her—she became animated, and even excited.

"I am glad she has gone," she said; "I did not think she would. Now I will confess the truth to you, Dr. Halifax. I asked Miss Levesen to bring me to see you under the pretence that you might cure my bodily ailments. But my real reason for wishing to have an interview with you was something quite apart from anything to do with bodily illness."

"What do you mean?" I asked, in astonishment.

"What I say," she answered. "I think I can soon explain myself. You know Mr. Teesdel, don't you?"

"Teesdel," I replied; "he is one of my special friends."

"He called at our house last week: I was alone with him for a moment. He saw that I was unhappy, that—that a great sorrow is killing me—he was kind and sympathetic. He spoke about you—I just knew your name, but no more. He told me something about you, however, which has filled my mind with the thought of you day and night ever since."

"You must explain yourself," I said, when she paused.

"You said"— she paused, and seemed to swallow something in her throat—"you said that you believed in the innocence of Edward Bayard."

"My dear young lady, I do," I replied, with emphasis.

"God bless you for those words; you will see now what a link there is between you and me, for you and I, in all the world, are the only people who believe in him."

I did not reply. Lady Kathleen's eyes filled with tears; she took out her handkerchief, and wiped them hastily away.

"You will understand at once," she continued, "how I have longed to see you and talk with you. I felt that you could sympathize with me. It is true that I am ill, but I am only ill because my mind reacts on my body—I have no rest of mind day nor night—I am in the most horrible position. I am engaged to a man whom I cordially hate, and I love another man passionately, deeply, distractedly."

"And that man is now enduring penal servitude?" I interrupted.

"Yes, yes. Did Mr. Teesdel tell you that I was once engaged to Edward Bayard?"

"He did," I answered.

"It is true," she continued; "we loved each other devotedly—we were as happy as two people could be—then came the first cloud—Edward in a weak moment signed his name to a bill for a friend—the friend failed, and Edward was called upon to pay the money. He said that he would ask my guardian, Francis Levesen, to help him. He did so in my presence, and Francis refused. 'Edward said that it did not matter, and was confident that he could get the money in some other way. Immediately afterwards came the horrible blow of his supposed forgery—he was arrested—he and I were together when this happened. All the sun seemed to go out of my sky at once—hope was over. Then came the trial—the verdict, the terrible result. But none of these things, Dr. Halifax, could quench my love. It is still there—it consumes me—it is killing me by inches—my heart is broken: that is why I am really dying."

"If you feel as you describe, why do you consent to marrying another man?" I asked.

"No wonder you ask that question. I will try and answer it. I consent because I am weak. Constant, ceaseless worrying and persuasion have worked upon my nerves to such an extent that, for very peace, I have said 'Yes.' Miss Levesen would like the marriage; she is a good woman, but she is without a particle of sentiment or romance. She believes in Edward's guilt, and cannot understand how it is possible for me to love him under existing circumstances. She would like me to marry her brother because I have money, and because my money will be of use to him. She honestly thinks that he will make me a good husband, and that after my marriage I shall be happy. I respect her, but I shrink from him as I would from a snake in the grass—I don't believe in him. I am certain that he and his secretary, Mr. Franks, concocted some awful plot to ruin Edward Bayard. This certainty haunts me unceasingly day and night. I am a victim, however, and have no strength to resist the claim which Mr. Levesen makes upon me. When Mr. Teesdel called, however, and told me that you believed in Edward, a faint glimmer of light seemed to come into my wretchedness; I resolved to come and see you. I told Miss Levesen that I should like to see a doctor, and spoke of you. She knew your name, and was delighted to bring me to you—now you know my story. Can you do anything for me?"

"I can only urge you on no account to marry Mr. Levesen."

"It is easy for you to say that, and for me to promise you that I will be true to my real lover, while I am sitting in your consulting-room ; but when I return to my guardian's house in Piccadilly I shall be a totally different girl. Every scrap of moral strength will have left me ; I shall only be capable of allowing matters to drift. They will drift on to my wedding-day. I shall go to church on that day, and endure the misery of a marriage ceremony between Francis Levesen and myself—and then I only sincerely trust that I shall not long survive the agony of such a union. Oh, sometimes I do not believe my mind will stand the strain. Dr. Halifax, is there anything you can do to help me ? "

The poor girl was trembling violently—her lips quivered —her face wore a ghastly expression.

"The first thing you must do is to try and control yourself," I said.

I poured out a glass of water, and gave it to her. She took a sip or two, and then placed it on the table—her excessive emotion calmed down a little.

"I will certainly do what I can to help you," I said, "but you must promise on your part to exercise self-control. Your nerves are in a very weak state, and you make them weaker by this excessive emotion. I can scarcely believe that you have not sufficient strength to resist the iniquity of being forced into a marriage which you abhor. You have doubtless come to me with some idea in your mind. What is it you wish me to do ? "

"I have come with a motive," she said. "I know it is a daring thing to ask. You can help me if you will—you can make matters a little easier."

"Pray explain yourself," I said.

"I want you to do this, not because you are a doctor, but because you are a man. I want you to go and see Edward Bayard—he is working out his sentence at Hartmoor. Please don't refuse me until I have told you what is exactly in my mind. I have read all the books I can find with regard to prisons and prisoners, and I know that at intervals prisoners are allowed to see visitors. I want you to try and see him, and then tell him about me. Tell him that my love is unalter-able—tell him that when I marry Mr. Levesen I shall only have succumbed to circumstances, but my heart, all that is worth having in me, is still his, and his only—tell him, too, that I shall always believe in his innocence."

"You make a strange request," I said, when she had finished speaking. "In the first place, you ask me to do something outside my province—in the next, it is very doubtful, even if I do go to Hartmoor, that I shall be allowed to see the prisoner and deliver your message. It is true that at stated intervals prisoners are allowed to see friends from the outside world, but never alone—a warder has always to be present. Then why disturb Bayard with news of your marriage? Such news can only cause him infinite distress, and where he is now he is not likely to hear anything about it."

"On the other hand, he may hear of it any day or any hour. Prisoners do get news from the outside world. Newspapers are always being smuggled into prisons—I have read several books on the subject. Oh, yes, he must get my message; he must know that I am loyal to him in heart at least, or I shall go quite mad."

Here the impetuous girl walked to one of the windows, drew aside the blind, and looked out. I saw that she did so to hide her intense emotion.

"I can make no definite promise to you," I said, after a pause; "but I will certainly try if it is in my power to help you. I happen to know the present Governor of Hartmoor, and perhaps indirectly I may be able to communicate with Bayard."

"You will do more than that—you will go to Hartmoor—yes, I am sure you will. Don't call this mission outside your province. You are a doctor. Your object in life is to relieve illness—to soothe and mitigate distress. I am ill, mentally, and this is the only medicine which can alleviate my sufferings."

"If possible, I will accede to your request," I said. "I'm afraid I cannot say more at present."

"Thank you; thank you. I know that you will make the thing possible."

"I can at least visit the Governor, Captain Standish; but remember, even if I do this, I may fail utterly in my object. I must not write to you on the subject—just rest assured that I will do my utmost for you."

She gave me her hand, turned aside her head to hide her tears, and hurried from the room. I thought a good deal over her sad story, and although I was doubtful of being able to communicate her message to Bayard, I resolved to visit Hartmoor, and trust to Providence to give me the opportunity I sought.

Some anxious cases, however, kept me in town for nearly ten days, and it was not until a certain Monday less than a week before the day appointed for the wedding that I was able to leave London. I went to Plymouth by the night mail, and arrived at the great, gloomy-looking prison about eleven o'clock on the following morning. I received a warm welcome from the Governor and his charming wife. He had breakfast ready for me on my arrival, and when the meal was over told me that he would take me round the prison, show me the gangs of men at their various works of stone-quarrying, turf-cutting, trenching, etc., and, in short, give me all the information about the prisoners which lay in his power.

He was as good as his word, and took me first through the prison, and afterwards to see the gangs of men at work. I was much interested in all I saw, but had not yet an opportunity of saying a special word about Bayard. After dinner that evening Captain Standish suddenly asked me the object of my visit.

"Well," he said, "has your day satisfied you?"

"I have been much interested," I replied.

"Yes, yes; but you must have had some special object in taking this journey—a busy man like you will not come so far from town, particularly at this time of the year, without a motive—even granted," he added, with a smile, "that we are old friends."

I looked fixedly at him for a moment, then I spoke.

"I have come here for a special object," I said.

"Ah, I thought as much. Do you feel inclined to confide in me?"

"I certainly must confide in you. I have come to Hartmoor to see a man of the name of Bayard—Edward Bayard; he was sentenced to five years' penal servitude about a year ago—I was present at the trial—I have brought him a message —I want, if possible, to deliver it."

While I was speaking, Captain Standish's face wore an extraordinary expression.

"You want to see Bayard?" he repeated.

"Yes."

"And you have brought him a message which you think you can deliver?"

"Yes. Is that an impossibility?"

"I fear it is."

He remained silent for a minute, thinking deeply—then he spoke.

"One of the strictest of prison rules is, that prisoners are not allowed to be pointed out to visitors for identification. It is true that at stated times the convicts are allowed to see their own relations or intimate friends, always, of course, in the presence of a warder. Bayard has not had anyone to see him since his arrival. Are you personally acquainted with him?"

"I never spoke to him in my life."

"Then how can you expect —— ?"

I broke in abruptly.

"The message I am charged with is in a certain sense one of 'life or death,' I said; "it affects the reason, perhaps the life, of an innocent person. Is there no possibility of your rule being stretched in my favour?"

"None whatever in the ordinary sense, but what do you say"—here Captain Standish sprang to his feet—"what do you say to seeing Bayard in your capacity as physician?"

"What do you mean?"

"Simply this. I should be glad if you would see him in consultation with our prison doctor. I know Bruce would be thankful to have your views of his case."

"Then he is ill?" I said.

"Yes, he is ill—at the present moment the prisoner whom you have come to see is in a state of complete catalepsy—stay, I will send for Bruce and ask him to tell you about him."

Captain Standish rose and rang the bell. When the servant appeared, he asked him to take a message to Dr. Bruce, begging him to call at the Governor's house immediately.

"While we are waiting for Bruce," said Standish, "I will tell you one or two things about Bayard. By the way, we call him Number Sixty here. He came to us from Pentonville with a good character, which he has certainly maintained during the few months of his residence at Hartmoor. He is an intelligent man, and a glance is sufficient to show the class of society from which he has sprung. You know we have a system of marks here, and prisoners are able to shorten their sentences by the number of marks they can earn for good conduct. Bayard has had his full complement from the first —he has obeyed all the rules, and been perfectly civil and ready to oblige.

"It so happened that three months ago a circumstance occurred which placed the prisoner in as comfortable a position as can be accorded to any convict. One morning there was a row in one of the yards—a convict attacked a warder in a most unmerciful manner—he would have killed him if Sixty had not interfered. Bayard is a slightly-built fellow, and no one would give him credit for much muscular strength. The doctor placed him in the tailoring establishment when he came, declaring him unfit to join the gangs for quarrying and for outside work. Well, when the scuffle occurred, about which I am telling you, Sixty sprang upon the madman, and, at personal risk, saved Simkins's life. The infuriated convict, however, did not let Bayard off scot-free; he gave him such a violent blow in the ribs that one was broken—it slightly pierced the lung, and, in short, he had to go to hospital, where he remained for nearly a fortnight. At the end of that time he was apparently well again, and we hoped that no ill-consequences would arise from his heroic conduct. After a consultation with Bruce, I took him from the tailoring and gave him book-keeping, and the lightest and most intelligent employment the place can afford. He has a perfect genius for wood-carving, and only this morning was employed in my house, directing some carpenters in putting together a very intricate cabinet. He is, I consider, an exceptional man in every way."

"But what about these special seizures?" I asked.

"I am coming to them. Ah, here is Bruce. Bruce will put the facts before you from a medical point of view. Bruce, let me introduce my friend, Dr. Halifax. We have just been talking about your patient, Number Sixty. What do you say to consulting Halifax about him?"

"I shall be delighted," answered Bruce.

"I think I understood you to say, Standish, that Bayard is ill now?" I asked.

"That is so. Pray describe the case, Bruce."

"Your visit is most opportune," said Dr. Bruce. "Sixty had a bad attack this morning. He was employed in this very house directing some carpenters, when he fell in a state of unconsciousness to the floor. He was moved at once into a room adjoining the workshop—he is there now."

"What are his general symptoms?" I asked.

"Complete insensibility—in short, catalepsy in its worst form. His attacks began after the slight inflammation of the lungs which followed his injury. Captain Standish has probably told you about that."

"I have," said Standish.

"He may have received a greater shock than we had any idea of at the time of the accident," continued Dr. Bruce, "otherwise, I can't in the least account for the fact of catalepsy following an injury to the lungs. The man was in perfect health before this illness, since then he has had attacks of catalepsy once and sometimes twice in one week. As a rule, he recovers consciousness after a few hours; but to-day his insensibility is more marked than usual."

"You don't think it by any possibility a case of malingering?" I inquired. "One does hear of such things in connection with prisoners."

The prison doctor shook his head.

"No," he said, "the malady is all too real. I have tested the man in every possible way. I have used the electric battery, and have even run needles into him. I am persuaded there is no imposture. At the present moment he looks like death; but come, you shall judge for yourself."

As Dr. Bruce spoke, he led the way to the door; Captain Standish and I accompanied him. We walked down a stone passage, entered a large workshop with high guarded windows, and passed on to a small room beyond. The one window in this room was also high, and protected with thick bars. On a trundle bed in the centre lay the prisoner.

For a moment I scarcely recognised the man. When I had last seen Bayard, he had been in ordinary gentleman's dress; he was now in the hideous garb of the prison—his hair was cut within a quarter of an inch of his head—his face was thin and worn, it looked old, years older than the face I had last seen behind the dock of the Old Bailey. There were deep hollows, as if of intense mental suffering, under the eyes —the lips were firmly shut, and resembled a straight line. The bulldog obstinacy of the chin, which I had noticed in the court of the Old Bailey, was now more discernable than of old.

"If ever a man could malinger, this man could," I muttered to myself; "he has both the necessary courage and obstinacy. But what could be his motive?"

I bent down, and carefully examined the patient. He was lying flat on his back. His skin was cold—there was not a vestige of colour about the face or lips. Taking the wrist between my fingers and thumb, I felt for the pulse, which was very slow, and barely perceptible—the man's whole frame felt like ice—there was a slight rigidity about the limbs.

"This is a queer case," I said, aloud.

"It is real," interrupted Bruce; "the man is absolutely unconscious."

When he spoke, I suddenly lifted one of the patient's eyelids, and looked into the eye—the pupil was contracted—the eye was glazed, and apparently unconscious. I looked fixedly into it for the space of several seconds—not by the faintest flicker did it show the least approach to sensibility. I pressed my finger on the cornea—there was not a flinch. I dropped the lid again. After some further careful examination, I stood up.

"This catalepsy certainly seems real," I said—"the man is, to all appearance, absolutely unconscious. I am sorry, as I hoped to have persuaded you, Captain Standish, to allow me to have an interview with him. I came to Hartmoor to-day for that express purpose. I have been intrusted with a message of grave importance, from someone he used to know well in the outer world—I should have liked to have given him the message—but in his present state, this is, of course, impossible."

"What treatment do you propose?" asked Bruce, who showed some impatience at my carefully-worded speech.

"I will talk to you about that outside," I answered—I was watching the patient intently all the time I was speaking.

Standish and Bruce turned to leave the room, and I went with them. When I reached the door, however, I glanced suddenly back at the sick man. Was it fancy, or had he looked at me for a brief second? I certainly detected the faintest quiver about the eyelids. Instantly the truth flashed through my brain—Bayard was a malingerer. He had feigned catalepsy so cleverly, that he had even imposed upon the far-seeing prison doctor. He would have imposed upon me, but for that lightning quiver of the deathlike face. I had spoken

on purpose about that message from the outside world. Mine
was truly an arrow shot at a venture, but the arrow had gone
home. When I left the room, I knew the man's secret. I
resolved, however, not to reveal it.

Bruce consulted me over the case. I gave some brief
suggestions, and advised the prison doctor not to leave the
man alone, but to see that a warder sat up with him during
the night. Standish and I then returned to the drawing-room.
We spent a pleasant evening together, and it was past one
o'clock when we both retired to rest. As we were going to
our rooms, a sudden idea flashed through my mind.

"Have you any objection," I said, turning suddenly to
Standish, "to my seeing Number Sixty again?"

"Of course not, Halifax; it is good of you to be so interested
in the poor chap. I will ask Bruce to take you to his room
to-morrow morning."

"I want to see him now," I said.

"Now?"

"Yes, now, if you will allow me."

"Certainly, if you really wish it ; but I don't suppose there
is the least change, and the man is receiving every care—
a warder is sitting up with him."

"I should like to see him now," I repeated.

"All right," answered Standish.

We turned, and went downstairs ; we entered the cold stone
passage, passed through the workshop, and paused at the door
of the little room where the sick man was lying. Standish
opened the door, holding a candle in his hand as he did so.
We both looked towards the bed ; for a moment we could see
nothing, for the candle threw a deep shadow, then the condition
of things became clear. The warder, who had charge of
Bayard, lay in an unconscious heap on the floor—the prisoner
himself had vanished.

"Good God! The man was malingering, after all, and has
escaped," cried the Governor.

I bent down over the warder; he had been deprived of
his outer garments, and lay in his shirt on the floor. I
turned him on his back, examined his head, and asked
Standish to fetch some brandy; a moment or two later the
man revived.

He opened his eyes and looked at me in a dazed way.

"Where am I?" he said. "What, in the name of wonder,

has happened? Oh, now I remember—that scoundrel—let me get up, there is not a moment to lose."

"You must not stir for a minute or two," I said. "You have had a bad blow, and must lie still. But you are coming to yourself very fast. Stay quiet for a moment, and then you can tell your story."

"Meanwhile, I will go and give the alarm," said Standish, who had been watching us anxiously.

He left the room. The warder had evidently been only badly stunned—he was soon almost himself again.

"I remember everything now, sir," he said. "I beg your pardon, sir, I don't know your face."

"I am a friend of the Governor," I answered, "a doctor from London. Now tell your story, and be quick about it."

"We all had a good word for Sixty," replied the man; "'e was a bit of a favourite, even though 'e wor a convict. To-night he laid like one dead, and I thought, pore chap, 'e might never survive this yere attack; all of a sudden I seed his eyes wide open, and fixed on me.

"'Simpkins,' he said, 'don't speak—you are a dead man if you speak, Simpkins, and I saved your life once.'

"'True for you, Sixty,' I answered him.

"'Well,' he says, 'it's your turn now to save mine. You 'and me over your hat, and jacket, and trousers,' says 'e. 'Be quick about it. If you say "no," I'll stun you—I can—I've hid a weapon under the mattress.'

"'Oh, don't you go and break prison, Sixty,' I answered; 'you'll get a heap added to your sentence if you do that.'

"'I must,' he said, his eyes wild-like. 'I saw it in the papers, and I must go—there is one I must save, Simpkins, from a fate worse than death. Now, is it "yes" or "no"?'

"It's "no,"' I answered, as I makes for him.

"I'd scarcely said the words," continued the man, "before he was on me—he leapt out of bed, and caught me by the throat. I remember a blow and his eyes looking wild—and then I was unconscious. The next thing I knew was you pouring brandy down my throat, sir."

"You are better now," I replied; "you had better go at once, and tell your story to the authorities."

The man left the room, and I hastened to find Standish. There was hurry and confusion and a general alarm. There was not the least doubt that Bayard had walked calmly out of

Hartmoor prison in Warder Simpkin's clothes. One of the porters testified to this effect. A general alarm was given, and telegrams immediately sent to the different railway and police stations. Standish said that the man would assuredly be brought back the following morning. Even if by any chance he managed to get as far as London, he would, in his peculiar clothes, be arrested there immediately.

I remained at Hartmoor for a good part of the following day, but Standish's expectations were not realized. Although telegrams were sent to the different police-stations, there was no news with regard to Edward Bayard. It was presently ascertained that Simpkins had money in the pocket of his jacket—he had just received his week's wages, and had altogether about £3 on his person. When this fact became known the success of Bayard's escape was considered probable. As there was nothing more for me to do, I returned to London on the evening of the following day, and reached my own house in time for breakfast.

I was anxious to see Lady Kathleen, but was puzzled to know how I could communicate with her. My doubts on this point, however, were set to rest in a very unexpected manner. When I returned home after seeing my patients that afternoon, Harris surprised me with the information that Miss Levesen was waiting to see me. I went to her at once. She came forward to greet me with a look of excitement in her face.

"You remember your patient, Lady Kathleen Church?" she asked.

"Perfectly," I replied. "I hope she is better."

"Far from that, she is worse—I consider her very ill. Her wedding is to take place in a few days, but unless something is done to relieve her terrible tension of mind, we are more likely to have a funeral than a wedding on that day."

"What are her special symptoms?" I asked.

"She has been going from bad to worse since you saw her, Dr. Halifax. This morning she went out by herself for a short time, and returned in a very strange state of excitement. Her own impression was that she was losing her senses. She begged and implored that I would send for you. And I resolved to come to fetch you myself. Can you come to see her?"

"Certainly," I replied; "at what hour?"

"Now, if you will; there is no time to be lost. Will you return with me? Your patient is very ill, and ought to have attention without a moment's delay."

"My carriage is at the door; shall we go back to your house in it?" I asked

"Certainly," replied Miss Levesen.

She rose from her chair at once—she was evidently impatient to be off. As we were driving to Piccadilly, she turned and spoke to me.

"While we have an opportunity, I wish to say something," she said.

"What is that?" I asked.

"I should naturally be glad if Lady Kathleen married my brother, but I wish you clearly to understand that I am not one to force the marriage. I fear the poor girl has not got over another most unfortunate attachment. Under present circumstances, I have made up my mind to cease to urge the wedding which we had hoped would so soon take place. I can't get my brother, however, to view matters in the same light; he is determined at any risk to keep Lady Kathleen to her promise."

"He cannot force her," I said.

"By moral suasion, yes—you do not know the man, Dr. Halifax."

I said nothing further—we had drawn up at the magnificent mansion in Piccadilly, and a few moments later I found myself in the presence of my patient. Miss Levesen brought me as far as the door, then she withdrew.

"Go in alone," she said, "that will be best. I don't want my brother to think that I'm in any way plotting against his interests."

She said these last words in an almost frightened whisper, and vanished before I had time to reply. I knocked at the door—a man's voice called me to enter, and I found myself in a pretty boudoir.

The young girl whom I had come to see was lying on a sofa—her eyes were shut—a handkerchief, wrung out of some eau de Cologne and water, was placed over her brow. A man was seated by her side—he was evidently nursing her with extreme care, and there was a look of solicitude on his face. I guessed at once that this man was Levesen. A hasty glance showed me that he was in the prime of life. He was dressed irreproachably, and looked not only gentlemanly, but aristocratic. He rose as I entered, and bowed to me rather stiffly. I hastened to tell him my name and errand. Without a word he offered me his seat near the patient. Lady Kathleen had opened her eyes when I came in — she roused herself from the sort of death-like stupor into which she had sunk, and gave me one or two glances of interest and relief. I put some questions to her, but I quickly saw that in Levesen's presence she was constrained and uncomfortable.

"Do you object to my seeing the patient for a few moments alone?" I asked of him.

His answer surprised me.

"I do," he said; "there is nothing you can say to Lady Kathleen that I have not a right to listen to. She is suffering from nervousness—nervousness bordering on hysteria—she needs sleep—a sedative will supply her with sleep. Will you have the goodness to write a prescription for one?—you will find paper, pen, and ink on this table."

He spoke in a quiet voice, the rudeness underneath being covered by a very suave manner. I was just turning to put some more questions to Lady Kathleen, when she surprised me by sitting up on the sofa and speaking with startling emphasis and force.

"You won't go away?" she said to Levesen.

"I will not," he replied.

"Then I will speak before you. No, you cannot cow me—not while Dr. Halifax is here. You shall hear the truth now, Francis, unless you change your mind and leave the room."

"I prefer to remain," he answered, with a sneer. "I shall be glad to know what is really in your mind."

"I will tell you. I only marry you because I am afraid to refuse you. The only influence you have over me is one of terror. At the present moment I feel strong enough to defy you. That is because Dr. Halifax is here. He is a strong man, and he gives me courage. I don't love you—I hate you—I hate you with all my heart and strength. You don't love me—you only want to marry me for my money."

While Lady Kathleen was speaking, Levesen rose.

"You see how ill your patient is, doctor," he said, "you perceive how necessary a sedative is. My dear child," he added, "you are quite unaccountable for your words. Pray don't talk any more while you are so feverish and excited."

"But I have something more to say," she answered. "Perhaps you will think I am mad—perhaps I am mad—still, mad or sane, I will now say what is in my mind. I hate you, and I love Edward Bayard. I saw Edward in the park this morning. He was standing close to Stanhope Gate. I passed him. I wanted to turn and speak to him, but before I could do so, he had vanished. Yes, I saw him. It was that sight which completely upset me—it took my last remnant of strength away. When I returned home I thought I should die—the shock was terrible—perhaps I did not really see him—perhaps I am mad, and it was a case of illusion. Oh, Francis, don't ask me to marry you—don't exercise your strength over me—give me back my freedom. Don't make a girl who hates you as I do, your wife."

"Come," said Leveson, "this is serious. Stay quiet, Kathleen; you are really not in a condition to excite yourself. I did not know, doctor," he added, turning to me, "that the case was so bad. Of course, Lady Kathleen is suffering from illusion, seeing that Bayard is at present working out the sentence he so richly deserves at Hartmoor."

"He is an innocent man, and you know it," said Lady Kathleen.

"Poor girl, her malady has grown much worse than I had any idea of," continued Levesen.

I interrupted.

"That does not follow," I replied. "Lady Kathleen is very ill, but she is not suffering from illusion. It is very probable that she did see Bayard this morning, seeing that he escaped from Hartmoor two nights ago."

"What?" said Lady Kathleen.

My words seemed to electrify her. She sprang from the sofa, and clasped one of my hands in hers.

"Edward has escaped from prison?" she said, with a sort of gasp.

Levesen said nothing, but his face assumed an ugly, greenish tint.

"It is true——" I began.

My words were interrupted. A sudden noise was heard in the drawing-room which communicated with the boudoir. Quick footsteps approached, the door of the boudoir was burst open, and a man whom I had never seen before rushed in, and clasped Levesen by one of his hands.

"What in the world is the matter, Franks?" said Levesen, in a tone of displeasure.

"Matter!—it is all up," said Franks, in a choking, trembling voice, "that—that poor fellow has escaped—he is in the house. Oh, I know he has come for me—he—he'll murder me—he'll shoot us both, Levesen. I saw him in the hall, and he carried a revolver. He'll kill us, Levesen, I say—he will—there is murder in his eyes—he is a madman—oh, what shall we do?"

"For God's sake restrain yourself," said Levesen; "it is you who have taken leave of your senses."

"No, it isn't," said another voice; "he has reason enough for his fears."

The door had been opened a second time, and Bayard, the man I had seen last in prison garb, looking like death upon his trundle bed, stood before us; he carried a revolver, but did not use it. Franks, who had been almost beside himself, rushed now towards Bayard, and flung himself on his knees at his feet.

"Spare my life," he said; "don't take my life. I have repented for months. Spare me—don't murder me—I'm afraid of you. Let me go, I say."

The wretched man raised his voice almost to a shriek.

"Don't kneel to me," said Bayard. "I won't take your wretched life—I don't want it. Tell the truth, you coward. You gave me that cheque?"

"I did, Bayard, I did. I've been in misery ever since. I was tempted and I fell. It is true. Don't take my life."

"I don't want your life," said Bayard. "I would not soil my hands with you—I would not pollute myself with your blood. But you have got to answer me one or two questions. You gave me the cheque for £5,000.

"Yes, yes."

"Levesen gave it to you for the purpose?"

"He did."

"Franks, you don't know what you are saying," interrupted Levesen; "terror has turned your head."

"No, it hasn't, Levesen," replied Franks. "You did give me the cheque to give to Bayard. I can't help telling the truth. I would do a great deal for you, but I prefer ruin and disgrace to the mental anguish our crime has caused me. This fellow will shoot me if I don't tell the truth now, and by heavens, I'm not going to lose my life for you, Levesen."

"As far as I am concerned, you are safe," said Bayard, laying his pistol on the table. "You have admitted the truth; that is all I want. As to you, Levesen, the game is up. You never guessed that I should break prison to confront you. You and Franks, between you, invented the most malicious conspiracy which was ever contrived to ruin an innocent man : you got me false imprisonment, but it is your turn now. You sha'n't escape, either of you. This gentleman here, I think I know him—I saw him two days ago at Hartmoor—will be my witness. Your game is up; I, too, can plot and contrive. I feigned serious illness in order to lull suspicion, and so got out of prison. I did this because you, Levesen, goaded me to madness—you took away my liberty—my character—you ruined my entire life; but when, added to these iniquities, you determined to force the girl whom I love, and who loves me, to be your wife, I felt that matters had come to an extremity. By a mere accident, I saw the notice of your engagement to Lady Kathleen in a paper which another convict lent me. I was in hospital at the time. From that moment I played a desperate game. I escaped from prison with the intention of shooting you, if necessary, you black-hearted scoundrel, rather than allow you to become the husband of the girl I love."

"The girl who loves you, Edward," said Lady Kathleen.

She flew to his side, and threw her soft, white arms round his neck. He gave her a quick, passionate glance, but did not speak.

"You must make a statement in writing," he said to Franks. "As to you, Levesen——No, you don't leave the room"—for Levesen had softly approached the door—"I have a pistol here, and I'm a desperate man. You will know best if it is worth exciting my rage or not. You will witness Franks's confession. Now, then, Franks, get your deposition down. I see paper, pen, and ink on that table. Now write, and be quick about it."

"You write at your peril, Franks," said Levesen. "Are you mad to give yourself away as you are doing? What is this fellow here, but an escaped convict? Don't put anything on paper, Franks."

"Yes, but I will," said Franks, suddenly. "It is not only

that I am frightened, Levesen—upon my word, I am almost glad of the relief of confession. You don't know what I've been through—perfect torture—yes, no more and no less. Bayard was no enemy of mine. I know you gave me money, and I have not much moral courage, and I fell; but the fact is, I'd rather serve my own time at Hartmoor than go through the mental misery which I have been enduring of late."

"Put your confession on paper without a moment's delay,' said Bayard, in a stern voice.

His words rang out with force. Notwithstanding his dress, his shaven head, his worn and suffering face—he had the manner of the man who conquers at that moment. The spell of fear which he had exercised over Franks he so far communicated to Levesen that he ceased to expostulate, and stood with folded arms, sullen face, and lowered eyes, not far from the door. I saw that he would escape if he could, but Bayard took care of that.

"Write, and be quick about it," he said to Franks.

The wretched Franks bent over his paper. He was a short, thickly-set man, of middle age. His face was red and mottled. Large beads of perspiration stood on his brow. His iron-grey head was slightly bald. The hand with which he wrote shook. All the time he was writing there was absolute silence in the room. Lady Kathleen continued to stand by Bayard's side. She had lost her nervousness and hysteria. Her cheeks were full of beautiful colour, her eyes were bright—she had undergone a transformation.

At last Franks laid down his pen. He took his handkerchief from his pocket and wiped the moisture from his brow.

"Give me the paper," said Bayard.

Franks did so.

"Will you, sir, read this aloud?" said the ex-prisoner, turning suddenly to me.

"Certainly," I answered.

The queer group stood silent around me, while I read the following words :—

"On the 4th of May, 189—, Francis Levesen, whose secretary I have been for several years, brought me a cheque for the sum of £5,000, which he had made payable to Edward Bayard. He told me to give the cheque to Bayard, remarking, as he did so :—

"'The fellow is in difficulties, and will find this useful.'

"Bayard at the time was engaged to Lady Kathleen Church, Francis Levesen's ward. I replied that I did not know Mr. Bayard was in money difficulties.

"'He is,' said Levesen; 'he has been fool enough to put his name to a bill for a friend, and has to meet a claim for £3,000 within the next ten days. He asked me to lend him that sum to meet the difficulty in Lady Kathleen's presence yesterday. I refused to grant his request at the time, and he seemed in distress about it.'

"'And yet you are now giving him £5,000,' I said. 'That seems strange, seeing that he only requires a loan of £3,000.'

"'Never mind,' said Levesen, 'a little ready cash will be acceptable under the circumstances. Get him to take the cheque. The fact is, there is more in this matter than meets the eye. I want you to help me in a small conspiracy, and will make it worth your while. You are to give this cheque to Bayard when no one is present. See that he presents it at my bank. If you can act quietly and expeditiously in this matter, I will give you that thousand pounds in cash you want so badly.'

"'What do you mean?' I asked, looking at him in fear and astonishment.

"'You know you want that money,' he replied.

"'God knows I do,' I answered.

"'To meet that bill of sale on your furniture,' continued Levesen. 'Your wife is just going to have a baby, and if the furniture is sold over her head, you fear the shock will kill her. Is not that so? Oh, yes, I know all about you—a thousand pounds will put all straight, will it not?'

"'Yes, yes; but the deuce is in this matter,' I replied. 'What are you up to, Levesen—what is your game?'

"Levesen's face became ashen in hue.

"'My game is this,' he hissed into my ear: 'I mean to do for that wretched, smooth-tongued sneak, Bayard.'

"'I thought he was your friend,' I answered.

"'Friend!' said Levesen. 'If there is a man I hate, it is he. He has come between me and the girl I intend to marry. I have made up my mind to ruin him. In short, he shan't have Lady Kathleen—I shall lock him up. Now, if you will help me, the deed can be done, and you shall have your £1,000.'

"I was as wax in his hands, for the state of my own affairs was desperate. I asked what I was to do.

"'I mean to have Bayard arrested,' said Levesen. 'I mean to have him arrested on a charge of forgery. When the moment comes, you are to help me. I mean to prove that Bayard forged the signature to the cheque which you now hold in your hand. He will declare that you gave it to him—you are to deny the fact—in fact, you and I will have to go through a good deal of false swearing. If we stick together and make our plans, I am convinced that the thing can be carried through. My ward can't marry a man who is going through penal servitude, and, by Heaven, Bayard shall have a long term.'

"I said I couldn't do it, but Levesen said: 'Sleep over it.' I went home. The devil fought with me all night, and before the morning he had conquered me. That thousand pounds and the thought of saving the home were what did for me. We carried out our scheme. I am prepared to swear to the truth of this statement before a magistrate.

"JOHN FRANKS."

"It would be well to have witnesses to this," I said, when I had done reading. "Lady Kathleen, will you put your name here?"

She came forward at once, writing her full name in a bold, firm hand. I put mine under hers.

"And now, Bayard," I said, "this is not a moment for showing mercy; a foul deed has been committed, and only the stern arm of justice can set matters right. Will you have the goodness to go at once for the police? Levesen and Franks must be taken into custody to-night on the charge of malicious conspiracy against you, for causing you to be falsely imprisoned, and for perjury."

"One moment before you go, Bayard," said Levesen— moving a step forward and speaking with the studied calm which all through this strange scene had never deserted him. "There is another side to Franks' story, and when I have said my say to-morrow morning before the magistrate, I can easily prove that the statement made on that piece of paper is worth no more than the paper on which it is written. There is not a magistrate on the Bench who is likely to give even a moment's serious consideration to such a trumped-up tale told under pressure, and at the instigation of an escaped convict. You can do your worst. I am so conscious of my own innocence that I have no wish to escape."

" Have you done speaking ? " asked Bayard.

" I have. You will repent of this."

Bayard left the room. In less than half an hour, Levesen and Franks had been carried off to the nearest police-station, and Bayard was left alone with Lady Kathleen. I went then to find Miss Levesen. I had a painful task in telling the poor lady the shameful truth. She was a hard woman, but she at least had been no partner in Levesen's horrible conspiracy.

The events which followed can be told in a few words. The next morning, early, I took Bayard to see my own solicitor, who instructed him to return to Hartmoor, and to give himself up; in the meantime, a petition would be immediately presented to the Queen for his free pardon.

That pardon was obtained in less than a week—although Bayard had to go through a short nominal punishment for his assault on the warder and his escape from Hartmoor.

One of the sensational trials at the autumn assizes was that of Levesen and Franks. The intelligent jury who listened to the trial were not long in making up their minds with regard to the verdict. I do not know that I am a specially hard man, but I could not help rejoicing when the judge's sentence was known. Levesen and Franks are now serving their time at Hartmoor—their sentence was seven years' imprisonment.

As to Lady Kathleen, she has completely recovered her health, and the long postponed wedding took place before the Christmas of that year.

THE STRANGE CASE OF
CAPTAIN GASCOIGNE

THE STRANGE CASE OF
CAPTAIN GASCOIGNE

IT has for some time seemed to me that in the treatment of many diseases the immediate future holds a great secret in its hands. This secret is becoming more, day by day, an open one. I allude to the marvellous success which has already attended the treatment of disease by the elaboration and discovery of new forms of inoculation of serotheropic virus. The following story may serve as a proof of this theory of mine. One evening at my club I came across an old college chum; his name was Walter Lumsden. He had also entered the medical profession, and had a large country practice in Derbyshire. We were mutually glad to see each other, and after a few ordinary remarks Lumsden said, abruptly:—

"I was in a fume at missing my train this evening; but, now that I have met you, I cease to regret the circumstance. The fact is, I believe your advice will be valuable to me in connection with a case in which I am much interested."

"Come home with me, Lumsden," I replied to this; "I can easily put you up for the night, and we can talk over medical matters better by my fireside than here."

Lumsden stood still for a moment to think. He then decided to accept my offer, and half-an-hour later we had drawn up our chairs in front of the cheerful fire in my study, and were enjoying our pipes after some port. The night was a chilly one, in the latter end of November. The wind was roaring lustily outside. It is under such circumstances that the comforts of one's own home are fully appreciated.

"You have done a good thing with your life," said Lumsden, abruptly. "I often wish I had not married, and had settled in London—oh, yes, I have a large practice; but the whole thing is somewhat of a grind, and then one never comes across the foremost men of one's calling—in short, one always feels a little out of it. I used to be keen for recent discoveries, and all that sort of thing in my youth; now I have got somewhat into a jog-trot—the same old medicines—the same old treatments are resorted to, year in, year out; but there, I have not come to talk of myself."

"You want to give me particulars with regard to a case?" I said.

"Yes; an anxious case, too—it puzzles me not a little."

"Have another pipe before you begin," I said.

"No, thanks; I don't want to smoke any more. Now, then, this is the story."

Lumsden had been leaning back in his chair, taking things easy; he now bent forward, fixed me with two anxious eyes, and began to speak forcibly.

"The case, to put it briefly, is as follows," he said. "One of my best patients and staunchest friends in the parish of Wolverton is Sir Robert Gascoigne. He is a rich man; his people made their money in iron during the latter end of the last century. His great grandfather bought a fine estate, which goes by the name of 'The Priory.' The old man strictly entailed the property, leaving it in every case to the eldest son of the house, and failing direct succession to a distant branch of the family. The present baronet—Sir Robert (the title was accorded a couple of generations ago)— is between fifty and sixty years of age. His wife is dead. There is only one son—a captain in an infantry regiment. Captain Gascoigne is now thirty years of age, as fine-looking a fellow as you ever met. For many years the great wish of Sir Robert's heart has been to see his son married. Captain Gascoigne came home two years ago on sick leave from India; he recovered his health pretty quickly in his native land, and proposed to a young lady of the name of Lynwood—a girl of particularly good family in the neighbourhood. Miss Helen Lynwood is a very handsome girl, and in every way worthy to be Captain Gascoigne's wife. His father and hers were equally pleased with the engagement, and the young couple were devoted to each other. Captain Gascoigne had to return to India to join his regiment, which was expected to be ordered home this year. It was arranged that he should leave the Army on his return, that the wedding was to take place immediately, and the young people were to live at 'The Priory.' All preparations for the wedding were made, and exactly a fortnight after the captain's return the marriage was to be solemnized. All the reception-rooms at 'The Priory' were newly furnished, and general rejoicing was the order of the hour. Let me see, what day is this?"

"The 24th of November," I answered. "Why do you pause?"

"I thought as much," said Dr. Lumsden—"this was to have been the wedding-day."

"Pray go on with your story," I said.

"It is nearly told. Gascoigne appeared on the scene looking well, but anxious. He had an interview with his father that night, and the next day went to London. He stayed away for a single night, came back the next day, and went straight to see Miss Lynwood, who lives with her father and mother at a place called Burnborough. Nobody knows what passed between the young couple, but the morning after a hurried message arrived for me to go up at once to see Sir Robert. I found the old baronet in a state of frightful agitation and excitement. He told me that the marriage was broken off; that his son absolutely refused to marry either Miss Lynwood or anyone else; that he would give no reasons for this determination, beyond the fact that he did not consider his life a healthy one; and that no earthly consideration would induce him to become the father of children. The whole thing is a frightful blow to the old man, and the mystery of it is, that nothing will induce Captain Gascoigne even to hint at what is the matter with him. There is no hereditary disease in the family, and he does not look out of health. By Sir Robert's desire, I ventured to sound him on the subject. It seemed impossible to associate illness with him in any way. I begged of him to confide in me, but he refused. All I could get him to say was:

"'An inexorable fate hangs over me—by no possible means can I avert it. All I have to do is to meet it as a man.'

"'Do you mean that your life is doomed?' I asked of him.

"'Sooner or later it is,' he replied; 'but that is not the immediate or vital question. Nothing will induce me to hand on what I suffer to posterity. My father and Miss Lynwood both know my resolve.'

" ' But not your reason for it,' I answered.

" ' I prefer not to tell them that,' he replied, setting his lips firmly.

" ' Have you seen a doctor? Are you positive of the truth of your own statement?' I ventured to inquire.

" ' I have seen one of the first doctors in London,' was the reply. 'Now, Lumsden,' he added, giving me a wintry sort of smile, 'even an old friend like you must not abuse your privileges. I refuse to answer another word.'

" He left me, and returned to 'The Priory.' This conversation took place yesterday morning. I saw Sir Robert later in the day. He is completely broken down, and looks like a very old man. It is not only his son's mysterious conduct which affects him so painfully, but every dream and ambition of his life have been bound up in the hope that he could hand on his name and property to his grandchildren. Captain Gascoigne's unaccountable attitude completely crushes that hope."

"Why do you tell me this story?" I asked, after a pause.

"Well, with the vain hope that you may, perhaps, help me to get a clue to the mystery Gascoigne refuses to fulfil his engagement on the ground that he is not in a fit state of health to marry. He refuses to tell his ailment. By what means can I get him to speak?"

"There is no way of forcing his confidence," I replied. "It seems to me that it is simply a matter of tact."

"Which valuable quality I don't possess a grain of," replied Lumsden. "I wish the case were yours, Halifax; you'd soon worm the captain's secret out of him."

"Not at all," I answered; "I never force any man's confidence."

"You possess a talisman, however, which enables you to effect your purpose without force. The fact is, this is a serious matter. Gascoigne looks miserable enough to cut his throat, the old man is broken down, and the girl, they tell me, is absolutely prostrated with grief."

"Do you think by any chance Gascoigne has confided the true state of the case to her?" I inquired.

"I asked him that," said Lumsden—"he emphatically said he had not, that his determination was to carry his secret to the grave."

I sat silent, thinking over this queer case.

"Are you frightfully busy just now?" asked Lumsden, abruptly.

"Well, I am not idle," I answered.

"You could not possibly take a day off, and come down to Derbyshire?"

"I cannot see your patients, Lumsden, unless they wish for my advice," I replied.

"Of course not, but I am on very friendly terms with Sir Robert. In fact, I dine at 'The Priory' every Sunday. Can you not come to Derbyshire with me to-morrow? As a matter of course, you would accompany me to 'The Priory.'"

"And act the detective?" I answered. "No, I fear it can't be done. If you can induce Captain Gascoigne to consult me I shall be very glad to give him my opinion. But I can't interfere in the case, except in the usual orthodox fashion."

Lumsden sighed somewhat impatiently, and did not pursue the subject any farther.

At an early hour the following morning he returned to Derbyshire, and I endeavoured to cast the subject of the Gascoignes from my mind. Captain Gascoigne's case interested me, however, and I could not help thinking of it at odd moments. The fact of the man refusing to marry did not surprise me, but his strange determination to keep his illness a secret, even from his medical man, puzzled me a good deal.

As I was not Gascoigne's doctor, however, there was nothing for it but to try and cast the matter from my mind. I did not know then that it was my fate to be mixed up in the affair to a remarkable degree.

On the following evening a telegram was put into my hand. I opened it and gave a start of surprise. It ran as follows :—

"*Sir Robert Gascoigne suffering from apoplexy. Wish to consult you. Come to 'The Priory' by the first possible train.— Lumsden.*"

Harris waited in the room while I read the telegram.

"The messenger is waiting, sir," he said.

I thought for a few moments, then took up my *A. B. C.*, found a suitable train, and wrote a hasty reply.

"*With you by nine to-morrow morning.*"

The messenger departed, and I went to my room to pack a few things. I took the night train into Derbyshire, and arrived at Wolverton Station a little after eight o'clock the next morning. A carriage from "The Priory" was waiting for me, and I drove there at once. Lumsden met me just outside the house.

"Here you are," he said, coming up to me almost cheerily. "I can't say what a relief it is to see you."

"What about the patient?" I interrupted.

"I am glad to say he is no worse; on the contrary, there are one or two symptoms of returning consciousness."

"Why did you send for me?" I asked, abruptly.

"Well, you know, I wanted you here for more reasons than one. Yesterday Sir Robert's case seemed almost hopeless— Captain Gascoigne wished for further advice—I suggested your name—he knows you by repute, and asked for me to send for you without delay."

"That is all right," I answered. "Shall I go with you now to see the patient?"

Dr. Lumsden turned at once, and I followed him into the house. The entrance-hall was very large and lofty, reaching up to the vaulted roof. A gallery ran round three sides of it, into which the principal bedrooms opened. The fourth side was occupied by a spacious and very beautiful marble staircase. This staircase of white marble was, I learned afterwards, one of the most remarkable features of the house. Sir Robert had gone to great expense in having it put up, and it was invariably pointed out with pride to visitors. The splendid staircase was carpeted with the thickest Axminster, and my feet sank into the heavy pile as I followed Lumsden upstairs. We entered a spacious bedroom. A fourpost bedstead had been pulled almost into the middle of the room—the curtains had been drawn back for more air; in the centre of the bed lay the old man in a state of complete unconsciousness— he was lying on his back breathing stertorously. I hastened to the bedside and bent over him. Before I began my examination, Lumsden touched me on the arm. I raised my eyes and encountered the fixed gaze of a tall man, who looked about five-and-thirty years of age. He had the unmistakable air and bearing of a soldier as he came forward to meet me. This, of course, was Captain Gascoigne.

"I am glad you have been able to come," he said. "I shall anxiously await your verdict after you have consulted with Lumsden."

He held out his hand as he spoke. I shook it. I saw him wince as if in sudden pain, but quick as lightning he controlled himself, and slowly left the room. The nurse now came forward to assist us in our examination. My patient's face was pallid, his eyes shut—his breath came fast and with effort. After a very careful examination I agreed with Lumsden that this attack, severe and dangerous as it was, was not to be fatal, and that in all probability before very long the old baronet would make the usual partial recovery in mild cases of hemiplegia. I made some suggestions with regard to the treatment, and left the room with Lumsden. We consulted together for a few minutes, and then went downstairs. Captain Gascoigne was waiting for us in the breakfast-room, a splendid apartment lined from ceiling to floor with finely carved oak.

"Well?" when we entered the room. There was unmistakable solicitude in his tones.

"I take a favourable view of your father's condition," I replied, cheerily. "The attack is a somewhat severe one, but sensation is not completely lost, and he has some power in the paralyzed side. I am convinced from the present state of the case that there is no progressive hemorrhage going on. In short, in all probability Sir Robert will regain consciousness in the course of the day."

"Then the danger is past?" said the captain, with a quick, short sigh of relief.

"If our prognosis is correct," I replied, "the danger is past for the time being."

"What do you mean by 'the time being'?"

"Why, this," I replied, abruptly, and looking full at him. "In a case like the present, the blood centres are peculiarly susceptible to dilatation. Being diseased, they are soon affected by any change in the circulation—a slight shock of any kind may lead to more hemorrhage, which means a second attack of apoplexy. It will, therefore, be necessary to do everything in the future to keep Sir Robert Gascoigne's mind and body in a state of quietude."

"Yes, yes, that goes without saying," answered the son, with enforced calm. "Now, come to breakfast, doctor; you must want something badly."

As he spoke, he approached a well-filled board, and began to offer us hospitality in a very hearty manner. My account of his father had evidently relieved him a good deal, and his spirits rose as he ate and talked.

At Lumsden's earnest request I decided not to return to London that day, and Captain Gascoigne asked me to drive with him. I accepted with pleasure; my interest in the fine, soldierly fellow increased each moment. He went off to order the trap, and Lumsden turned eagerly to me.

"I look upon your arrival as a godsend," he exclaimed. "The opportunity which I have sought for has arrived. It has come about in the most natural manner possible. I am sincerely attached to my old patient, Sir Robert Gascoigne, and still more so, if possible, to his son, whom I have known for many years. Of course, it goes without saying what is the primary cause of the old baronet's attack. Perhaps you can see your way to induce Captain Gascoigne to confide in you. If so, don't lose the opportunity, I beg of you."

"I am extremely unlikely to have such an opportunity," I replied. "You must not build up false hopes, Lumsden. If Captain Gascoigne likes to speak to me of his own free will, I shall be only too glad to listen to him, but in my present position I cannot possibly lead the way to a medical conference."

Lumsden sighed impatiently.

"Well, well," he said, "it seems a pity. The chance has most unexpectedly arrived, and you might find yourself in a position to solve a secret which worries me day and night, and has almost sent Sir Robert Gascoigne to his grave. I can, of course, say nothing farther, but before I hurry away to my patients, just tell me what you think of the captain."

"As fine a man as I ever met," I replied, with enthusiasm.

"Bless you, I don't mean his character; what do you think of his health?"

"I do not see much amiss with him, except——"

"Why do you make an exception?" interrupted Lumsden. "I have, metaphorically speaking, used magnifying glasses to search into his complaint, and can't get the most remote trace of it."

"I notice that his right hand is swollen," I answered; "I further observe that he winces when it is touched."

"Well, I never saw it," answered Lumsden. "What sharp eyes you have. The swollen state of the hand probably points to rheumatism."

"Possibly," I replied.

At that moment Captain Gascoigne returned to us. His dog-cart was at the door; we mounted, and were soon spinning over the ground at a fine rate. The mare the captain drove was a little too fresh, however; as we were going down hill, she became decidedly difficult to handle. We were driving under a railway-bridge, when a train suddenly went overhead, rushing past us with a crashing roar. The mare, already nervous, lost her head at this juncture, and with a quick plunge, first to one side and then forward, bolted. I noticed at that moment that Gascoigne was losing his nerve—he turned to me and spoke abruptly.

"For goodness sake, take the reins," he said.

I did so, and being an old hand, for in my youth it had been one of my favourite amusements to break-in horses, soon reduced the restive animal to order, I turned then to glance at the captain—his face was as white as a sheet—he took out his handkerchief, and wiped some moisture from his forehead.

"It is this confounded hand," he said. "Thank you, doctor, for coming to my aid—the brute knew that I could not control her—it is wonderful what a system of telegraphy exists between a horse and its driver; she completely lost her head."

"I notice that your hand is swollen," I answered, "Does it hurt you? Do you suffer from rheumatism?"

"This hand looks like rheumatism or gout, or something of that sort, does it not?" he retorted. "Yes, I have had some sharp twinges—never mind now—it is all right again. I will take the reins once more, if you have no objection."

"If your hand hurts you, shall I not drive?"

"No, no, my hand is all right now."

He took the reins, and we drove forward without further parley.

The country through which we went was beautiful, and, winter as it was, the exhilarating air and the grand shape of the land made the drive extremely pleasant.

"It is your honest conviction that my father will recover from his present attack?" said Captain Gascoigne, suddenly.

"It is," I replied.

"That is a relief. I could not leave the old man in danger, and yet it is necessary for me soon to join my regiment."

"Your father will probably be himself in the course of a few weeks," I replied. "It is essential to avoid all shocks in the future. I need not tell you that an attack of apoplexy is a very grave matter—that a man once affected by it is extremely subject to a recurrence; that such a recurrence is fraught with danger to life."

"You think, in short," continued Captain Gascoigne, "that a further shock would kill Sir Robert?"

"Yes, he must on no account be subjected to worry or any mental disquietude."

I looked at the man at my side as I spoke. He was sitting well upright, driving with vigour. His face expressed no more emotion than if it were cast in iron. Something, however, made him pull up abruptly, and I saw a dark flush mount swiftly to his cheek. A girl was coming down the road to meet us; she was accompanied by a couple of fox-terriers. When she saw us she came eagerly forward.

"Take the reins, will you, doctor?" said Captain Gascoigne.

He sprang from the cart, and went to meet the young lady. I guessed at once that she must be Miss Lynwood. She was a very slight, tall girl, with a quick, eager expression of face. Her eyes were dark and brilliant; the expression of her mouth was sweet, but firm; her bearing was somewhat proud. I was too far away to hear what she said. Captain Gascoigne's interview with her was extremely brief. She turned to walk in the opposite direction; he remounted the dog-cart, and suggested that we should go home. During our drive back he hardly spoke. When we reached "The Priory" I went at once to visit my patient, and did not see much of the captain for the remainder of the day. The sick man was making favourable progress, but I thought it well not to leave him until the following morning. Towards evening, as I was standing by the bedside, I was surprised to see Sir Robert suddenly open his eyes and fix them upon my face. Lumsden and Captain Gascoigne were both in the room. The old man looked quickly from me to them. When he saw his son, a queer mixture of anxiety and satisfaction crept into his face.

"Dick, come here," he said, in a feeble voice.

Captain Gascoigne went immediately to the bedside, and bent over his father.

"What's up, Dick? Who is that?" He glanced in my direction.

"I have come here to help to make you better," I said, taking the initiative at once. "I am a doctor, and your old friend Lumsden wished to consult me about you. I am glad to say you are on the mend, but you must stay very quiet, and not excite yourself in any way."

"No, no. I understand," said Sir Robert. "I have been very bad, I suppose? You have done it, Dick, you know you have."

"Pray rest, father, now," said the son; "don't think of any worries at present."

"Tut, boy, I can't rest — I'm a disappointed man, Dick — I'm a failure — this is a fine place, and it will go to the dogs — it is all your fault, Dick, and you know it. If you want to help me, you will do what I wish — get Helen here, and have the marriage solemnized as quickly as possible. Oh, I know what I am saying, and I won't be silenced—there needn't be a fuss—everything is ready—the rooms furnished—the place in order. You can be married by special license—you know you can, Dick. I shan't rest in my grave until this thing is set right. You get Helen here, and have the wedding by special license, yes, yes. There'll be no rest for me, Dick, until I know that you and Helen are —yes—that you and Helen are man and wife."

"Stay quiet, sir; stay quiet, I beg of you," said Captain Gascoigne, in a voice of distress.

"I can't while you are so obstinate—do you mean to do what I wish?"

The old man's tone was very testy.

"I will talk the matter over with you presently," was the reply; "not now—presently, when you are stronger."

There was something in the captain's voice which was the reverse of soothing. An irritable frown came between the patient's eyes, and a swift wave of suspicious red dyed his forehead.

"I must ask you to leave the room," I whispered to the younger man.

He did so, his shoulders somewhat bent, and a look of pain on his face.

"Has Dick gone for the license?" said Sir Robert, looking at Lumsden, and evidently beginning to wander in his mind.

Lumsden bent suddenly forward. "Everything shall be done as you wish, Sir Robert," he said. "Only remember that we can have no wedding until you are well—now go to sleep."

I motioned to the nurse to administer a soothing draught, and sat down by the bed to watch the effect. After a time the patient sank into troubled sleep. His excitement and partial delirium, however, were the reverse of reassuring, and I felt much more anxiety about him than I cared to show when I presently went downstairs to dinner.

"There is no immediate danger," I said to Captain Gascoigne, "but your father has evidently set his heart on something. He has a fixed idea—so fixed and persistent that his mind will turn to nothing else. Is it not possible," I continued, abruptly, "to give him relief?"

"To do as he wishes?" said Captain Gascoigne. "No, that is impossible. The subject can't even be talked over," he continued. "Now, gentlemen," he added, looking from Dr. Lumsden to me, "I think dinner is ready."

We went into the dining-room, and seated ourselves at the table. A huge log fire burned in the grate. The massively-furnished room looked the picture of winter comfort; nevertheless, I don't think any of us had much appetite—there was a sense of tragedy even in the very air. After dinner, as we were sitting over wine, Dr. Lumsden's conversation and mine turned upon medical matters; Captain Gascoigne, who had been silent and depressed during the meal, took up a copy of the *Times*, and began to read. Dr. Lumsden asked me one or two questions with regard to recent discoveries in preventive medicines. We touched lightly on many subjects of interest to medical men like ourselves, and I did not suppose for a moment that Captain Gascoigne listened to a word of our conversation. He rose presently, and told us that he was going to find out how his father was now. When he returned to the room, I was telling Lumsden of one or two interesting cases which I had lately come across in my hospital practice.

"I am certain," I said, "that inoculation with attenuated virus is to be the future treatment of many of our worst diseases."

Captain Gascoigne had come half across the room. When I said these words, he stood as motionless as if something had turned him into stone. I raised my head, and our eyes suddenly met. I observed a startled, interested expression on his face. Quick as lightning an idea came to me. I turned my eyes away and continued, with vigour—

"Such inoculation is, without doubt, the future treatment for consumption. Even granted that Dr. Koch's theory has failed, there is every reason to hope that in that direction the real cure lies. The new anti-toxin treatment for diphtheria proves the same thing; even now there are not unknown cases where certain forms of cancer have been completely eradicated—the poison absolutely eliminated from the body by means of inoculation."

"We medical men accept such theories very slowly," said Dr. Lumsden. "It will be many years before we can confidently employ them."

"Why not, if by so doing you can cure disease?" said Captain Gascoigne, abruptly.

We both looked at him when he spoke.

"Why not, if you can cure disease?" he repeated.

"Why not?" repeated Dr. Lumsden; "because we doctors dare not run risks. Why, sir, we should be responsible for the deaths of our patients if we attempted to use means of cure which were not proven—established, in fact, by long precedent."

"Well, gentlemen," he said, "I can't attempt to argue with you. It is my firm belief, however, that the general run of medical practitioners are over-cautious. I allude, of course, to cases which are supposed under the ordinary treatment to be hopeless. Surely if the patient wishes to try the chance of a comparatively immature discovery, it is allowable for him to do so?"

"Such a case is uncommon," I replied; "as a rule, the sick man prefers to go upon the beaten track—in other words, does not trouble himself about the treatment of his disease, leaving it entirely to his doctor."

"How have you found the patient, Captain?" interrupted Dr. Lumsden.

"Asleep, but restless; the nurse thinks there is an increase of fever."

"I will go and see for myself," I said, rising.

My conversation with Lumsden was broken, and was not again resumed. We both spent an anxious night with the patient, whose case was the reverse of satisfactory. As the hours flew on, the restless wanderings of mind seemed to increase rather than diminish. The fixed idea of an immediate marriage for his son was again and again alluded to by the sick man. He was restless when Captain Gascoigne went out of the room. When he was present he was even more restless, calling him to his side many times, and asking him in strained, irritable tones if the special license had been applied for, and if Helen—as he called her—was in the house.

Towards morning the delirious and excited state of the patient became so alarming that I felt certain that if nothing were done to relieve him, fresh hemorrhage of the brain would set in. I went out of the room, motioning Captain Gascoigne to follow me.

"I fear," I said, "that the evident anxiety from which your father is suffering is acting prejudicially. Unless something can be done to relieve him, I must modify the favourable opinion which I have already given you of his case. Unless his mind is immediately relieved, he may have another attack before many hours have gone by. Such an attack will be, in all probability, fatal."

I looked hard at the captain as I spoke. He had folded his arms, and stood very erect facing me.

"What do you propose?" he said, abruptly.

"You have evidently given him distress," I said. "Can you not reconsider the position?"

He gave a short, irritable laugh. "Good heavens, doctor," he exclaimed, "don't you suppose I am man enough to accede to my father's wish, if it were possible? Can you not see for yourself that the present state of affairs is agony to me?"

"I am certain of it," I replied. "I must not urge you further. The fact is, Lumsden has told me something of your story. Only a very grave cause would make you refuse to fulfil your engagement with Miss Lynwood."

"You are right; the cause is very grave."

"You can't tell me what it is? It is possible that I might be able to counsel you."

"Thanks; but I am past counsel—the end is inevitable—unless, indeed—but, no—I must not bring myself to entertain hope. The person now to be considered is my father. You say, doctor, that if his wish in this matter is not gratified, he will die?"

"It seems extremely like it," I said. "He has evidently set his heart on your marriage—in his present diseased state the longing to see you married has become a mania."

"There is nothing whatever for me to do, then," he said, "but to lie to him."

"I would scarcely do that," I exclaimed.

"Yes you would, if you were me. I must pledge myself; he must be saved. Not another word—my mind is made up."

He left me before I could expostulate further, and returned to the sick room. The old man's arms were flung out over the bed-clothes; he was muttering to himself, and pulling feebly at the sheets.

Captain Gascoigne went and sat down by the bed; he laid one of his hands on his father's, holding it firmly down.

"Listen to me," he said, in a low voice. "I have reconsidered everything. I alter my determination not to marry. I swear now, before Heaven, that if I live I will marry Helen Lynwood."

"Do you mean it, Dick?" said Sir Robert.

"On my honour, yes, father; I have spoken."

"Good boy—good boy; this is a relief. That queer scruple about your health is laid to rest, then?"

"Quite, father. If I live, Helen shall be my wife."

"You never told me a lie yet, Dick; you are speaking the truth now?"

"On my honour," said the soldier.

He looked his father full in the eyes. The sick man gave a pleased smile, and patted his son's hand.

"I believe you, Dick," he said; "I am quite satisfied—when can the marriage take place?"

"We need not fix a date to-night, need we?"

"No, no; I trust you, Dick."

"Perhaps, sir, you will try to sleep now—your mind being at rest."

"Yes, my mind is quite at rest," said the baronet—"Dick never told me a lie in his life—thank the Almighty for His goodness, I shall live to see my grandchildren about the old place—yes, I am sleepy—I don't want a composing draught—keep at my side, Dick, until I drop off. We'll have Helen here early in the morning—how happy she will be, poor little girl—I should like to see Helen as soon as I awake."

The patient kept on mumbling in a contented, soothed voice—all trace of irritation had left his voice and manner. In less than half an hour he was sound asleep. He slept well during the night, and in the morning was decidedly better —the anxious symptoms had abated, and I had every hope of his making a quick recovery.

One of his first inquiries was for Miss Lynwood.

"I am going to fetch her," said the captain.

I saw him drive off in the dog-cart. In about an hour and a half he returned with the young lady. I was standing by the patient's side when she came in. She was dressed in furs, and wore a small fur cap over her bright hair. The drive had brought a fresh colour to her cheeks—her eyes sparkled. She entered the room in the alert way which I had observed about her when I saw her for a moment on the previous day. She went straight up to the sick man and knelt down by his side.

"Well, dad," she said, "you see, it is all right."

I marvelled at her tone—it was brisk and full of joy. Had Captain Gascoigne told her the truth? Or had he, by any chance, tried to deceive this beautiful girl, in order more effectually to aid his father's recovery? Watching her more closely, however, I saw that she was brave enough to play a difficult part.

"Yes, Helen, it is all right," said the baronet. "Dick is well, and has come to his senses. That illness of his turned out to be a false alarm—he had an attack of nerves— nothing more. We'll have a gay wedding in a few days, little girl."

"You must get well," she answered, patting his cheek. "Remember, nothing can be done until you are well."

"Bless you, child, I shall be well fast enough. Your face and Dick's would make any man well. Where is that nurse? Why doesn't she bring me food—I declare I'm as hungry as a hawk. Ah, doctor, you there?" continued the baronet, raising his eyes, and fixing them on my face. "Remember, you didn't cure me. It was Dick's doing, not yours. Dick, bless him, has set the old man right."

I left the room abruptly. Captain Gascoigne met me on the landing.

"You play your part well," I said; "but what about the *dénoûment?*"

"I have considered everything," said the captain. "I shall keep my word. If I live, I will marry."

I looked at him in astonishment. A glance showed me that he did not mean to confide further in me then, and I soon afterwards returned to town. Lumsden promised to write to report the patient's progress; and, much puzzled as to the ultimate issue of this queer story, I resumed my town work. I arrived in London early in the afternoon, and went immediately to visit some patients. When I returned to my own house it was dinner-time. The first person I met in the hall was Captain Gascoigne.

"Have you bad news?" I cried, in astonishment. "Is there a change for the worse?"

"No, no, nothing of the sort," was the reply. "My father mends rapidly. The fact is, I have come to see you on my own account. I have made up my mind to consult you."

"I am right glad to hear it," I answered, heartily. "You must join me at dinner now, and afterwards we will go carefully into your case."

"I am anxious to catch the night mail back to Wolverton," said the captain; "but, doubtless, you can spare an hour to me after dinner, and that, I am sure, will be quite sufficient."

During the meal which followed, Captain Gascoigne was silent and *distrait.* I did not interrupt him with many remarks, but as soon as it was over we went straight to the point.

"Now," he said, "I will tell you what is up. I had made up my mind to carry my secret to the grave. The strange state of affairs at 'The Priory,' however, has induced me to break this resolve. I have a double reason for confiding in you, Dr. Halifax. First, because of what occurred last night— second, in consequence of some words which you let drop in conversation with Dr. Lumsden. These words seemed very strange to me at the time, but the more I think over them, the more anxious I am to talk further with you on the subject. They have inspired me with the ghost of a hope."

"What is the matter with you?" I said, abruptly. "What is your malady?"

The captain had been seated—he now stood up.

"Help me off with this coat, doctor, if you will," he said.

I removed it carefully, but notwithstanding all my precautions I saw him wince as I touched his right arm.

"You notice this hand," he said, holding out his right hand as he spoke; "you noticed it the other day when I was driving?"

"Yes," I replied; "it is much swollen."

"It is. That could be set down to gout or rheumatism, could it not?"

"It could," I answered; "it has, doubtless, another cause."

"It has, Dr. Halifax. You shall examine my terrible disease for yourself—but first let me tell you what ails me."

He leant against the mantelpiece as he spoke—his face was very white. One or two beads of perspiration stood prominently out on his forehead. When he began to speak he looked straight at me with a frown between his eyes.

"God knows I never meant to whine about this to anyone," he said; "I meant to take it as a man—it was the state of the old governor and Helen's grief and her wonderful bravery that upset me. Well, here's the case. You must know that my mother died of cancer—the thing was hushed up, but the fact remains—she suffered horribly. I recollect her last days even now. I was a small boy at the time. The dread of cancer—of having inherited such a fearful disease—has haunted me more or less all my life. Two or three years ago in India I had a bad fall from my horse. I came down with great weight on my right shoulder. The stiffness and soreness remained for some time, and then they passed away. A year later the stiffness and soreness began to return—my shoulder-bone began to thicken—I could only move it with difficulty. I consulted some doctors, who set down the whole affection to rheumatism, and gave me ordinary liniments. The pain did not abate, but grew worse, The shoulder began to swell and soon afterwards the arm, right down, as you see, to my finger-tips. These painful symptoms set in about six months ago. I was expected home, and all the arrangements for my wedding were complete. I was seized, however, with forebodings. As soon as ever I landed in England, I went to see the well-known specialist for tumours, Sir John Parkes. He was not long in giving his verdict. It was concise and conclusive. He said I was suffering from osteosarcoma of the shoulder—that the disease was advanced, that the removal of the entire arm and shoulder bone might save my life, but the disease was in such a position, involving the bones of the shoulder girdle, and having already invaded the glands, that the probabilities were almost certain that it would return. I had a bad quarter of an hour with the surgeon. I went away, spent the night in town, and quickly made up my mind how to act. I would break off my engagement and go from home to die. I shrank inexpressibly from my father or Miss Lynwood knowing the exact nature of my sufferings. It would be necessary to tell them that the state of my health forbade matrimony, but I firmly resolved that they should never know by what horrible disease I was to die. That is the case in brief, doctor."

"May I look at your shoulder?" I said.

I carefully removed the shirt and looked at the swollen and glazed arm and shoulder.

There was little doubt of the accuracy of the great Sir John Parkes's diagnosis.

"Sit down," I said; "from my heart I am sorry for you. Do you suffer much?"

"At times a good deal—the effort to keep back even the expression of pain is sometimes difficult; for instance, in driving the other day—but, ah, you noticed?"

"I did—I saw that you winced—little wonder. Upon my word, Captain Gascoigne, you are a hero."

"Not that," he answered. "In some ways I am a coward. This thing humiliates me as well as tortures me. I have had the instincts of the animal ever since I knew the worst ; my wish has been to creep away and die alone. After what occurred last night, however, matters have changed."

"What do you mean?" I said.

"Can you not see for yourself what I mean? In a moment of extremity, I promised my father that I would marry Helen Lynwood, *if I lived.* You see for yourself that nothing will save me from the consequences of that promise except death."

"Still, I don't understand you," I answered.

"I can soon make myself plain. Do you remember what you said to Lumsden about an immature discovery—a discovery which has been known to cure diseases such as mine?

You both spoke of this discovery as in its infancy—never mind, I want you to try it on me."

"My dear fellow, you must be mad."

"Not at all; this is my last chance. It is due both to Helen and my father that I should take advantage of it. In a case like mine a man will submit to anything. I have quite made up my mind. Whatever the risk, I am willing to run it. The treatment may kill me; if so, I am willing to die. On the other hand, there is an off chance that it may cure me—then I can marry Helen. There is not an hour to lose, doctor. When can you operate?"

"You astonish me more than I can say," I answered. "I almost wish you had never overheard my remarks to Lumsden. I only talked over the new treatment with him as one medical man would mention a possible discovery to another."

"But you believe in it?"

"I do believe in its ultimate success."

"It has been tried, has it not?"

"In France, yes."

"And with success?"

"I am given to understand that there has been success."

"That is all right—you will try it on me?"

"My dear fellow, I am inclined to say that you ask the impossible."

"Don't say that—in my extreme case, nothing is impossible; think the matter over, Dr. Halifax. Try and picture the horrible dilemma I am in. I am suffering from an incurable complaint—I have the prospect before me, at no very distant date, of a terrible and painful death. I am my father's only son—the property goes from the direct line if I die. In order to save my father's life I promised him to marry if I lived. There is, therefore, no thought for me of a prolonged life of ill-health. I must either get well quickly or I must die. Surely a desperate man may risk anything. The treatment which I beg of you to adopt is kill or cure, is it not? Then kill or cure me."

"The treatment which you beg me to adopt," I repeated, quoting his words, "is undoubtedly death from blood poisoning, if it does not effect its end of killing your disease, not you."

"I am willing to take the risk—anything is better than the present awful state of suspense."

"Does Miss Lynwood know of this?"

"She does—God bless her! I shrank from telling her the truth—I did not know what mettle she was made of. This morning, in my despair, I confided everything to her. You don't know what stuff she has in her. She bore the whole awful truth without wincing. She said she was with me in the whole matter—it is as much at her instigation as my own desire that I now consult you. We have both resolved to be true to my father, and to keep the promise wrung from me last night by his desperate state. If I live we will marry. You see for yourself that it must be a case of kill or cure, for I cannot run the risk of bringing children into the world in my present terrible state of health. You see the situation, do you not? My father is recovering, because his mind is relieved. Everything now depends on you. Will you, or will you not, help me?"

"I ought to say 'No,'" I answered. "I ought to tell you frankly that this is not a case for me. I ought, perhaps, to counsel you to put yourself into the hands of one of those French doctors who have already made this matter a special study, but ——"

"But you won't," said Captain Gascoigne—"I see by your manner that you will give me the advantage of your skill and knowledge—your kindness and sympathy. On the next few weeks the whole future of three people depends. The thing will be easier both for Helen and myself, if you will be our friend in the matter."

"Can you come again in the morning?" I said. "I must think this over—I must make up my mind how to act."

"You will give me a definite answer in the morning?"

"I will."

Captain Gascoigne rose slowly—I helped him into his coat, and he left the room.

As soon as he was gone, I went to see a very able surgeon, who was a special friend of mine. I described the whole case to him—gave him in brief Sir John Parkes's verdict, and then asked his opinion with regard to the other treatment.

"It is a case of life or death," I said. "Under ordinary circumstances, nothing could save Captain Gascoigne's life—he is anxious to run the risk."

"As I see it, there is no risk," replied my friend.

"What do you mean?"

"The man will die if it is not tried."

"That is true."

"Then my opinion is—give him a chance."

"I agree with you," I said, rising to my feet. "I know you have studied these matters more carefully than I have. I will go to Paris to-morrow, and make all necessary inquiries."

In the morning, when Captain Gascoigne arrived, I told him the result of my interview with Courtland.

"I am prepared to treat you by this new method, provided my investigations in Paris turn out satisfactory," I said. "I shall go to Paris by the night mail, returning again the following night. Let me see—this is Thursday morning. Be here by ten o'clock on Saturday morning, and I shall have further news for you."

"I have no words to thank you," he said. "I am going back to Derbyshire now to see Helen, and to tell her what you have done."

"You must not build absolute hopes on anything until after I have seen the doctors in Paris."

"I will not."

He smiled as he spoke. Poor fellow, I saw hope already returning to his eyes.

I went to Paris—my investigations turned out satisfactory. I saw one of the leading doctors of the new school, and talked over the anti-toxin system in all its bearings. His remarks were full of encouragement—he considered *sérotherapie* as undoubtedly the future treatment for cancer—three cases of remarkable cure were already on record. He furnished me with some of the attenuated virus, and begged of me to lose no time in operating on my patient. Having obtained the necessary instructions and the attenuated virus, I returned to London, and prepared to carry out this new and most interesting cure. Captain Gascoigne arrived punctually to the moment on Saturday morning. I told him what I had done, and asked him to secure comfortable lodgings in Harley Street, as near my house as possible. He did so, and came back that evening to tell me of the result.

"To-morrow will be Sunday," I said. "I propose to begin the new treatment to-morrow morning. I shall inoculate you with the virus three times a day."

"How long will it be before the result is known?" he asked.

" I shall very soon be able to tell whether the new treatment acts as direct blood poison or not," I answered. "Your business now is to keep cheerful—to hope for the best—and to turn your thoughts away from yourself as much as possible. By the way, how is Sir Robert?"

"Getting on famously—he thinks that I have come up to town to make preparations for my wedding."

"Let him think so—I begin to hope that we shall have that wedding yet. And how is Miss Lynwood?"

"Well, and full of cheer—she has great faith—she believes in you and also in the new remedy."

"Well, Captain Gascoigne, if this succeeds, you will not only have saved your own life and that of your father, but will have added a valuable and important contribution to modern science."

He smiled when I said this, and shortly afterwards left me.

I began a series of inoculations the following morning. I introduced the attenuated virus into the shoulder—inoculating small doses three times a day. The patient required most careful watching, and I secured the attendance of my most trustworthy nurses for him. His temperature had to be taken at short intervals, and his general health closely attended to. The first day there was no reaction—on the second, the temperature rose slowly—the pulse quickened—the patient was undoubtedly feverish. I inoculated smaller doses of the virus, and these unfavourable symptoms quickly subsided.

In a week's time the treatment began to tell upon the arm —the pain and swelling became less, the arm could be moved with greater freedom, the hand became comparatively well. Captain Gascoigne appeared in every other respect to be in his usual health—he ate well, slept well, and was full of hope. I began to introduce larger doses, which he now bore without serious reaction of any kind. I had begged of Courtland to help me in the case, and he and I made interesting and important notes evening after evening.

From what I had learned from the French doctors, I expected the cure, if successful, to take about forty days. On the twentieth day the patient suffered from great depression— he suddenly lost hope, becoming nervous and irritable. He apprehended the worst—watched his own symptoms far too closely, and lost both appetite and sleep. His conviction at that time was that the cure would not avail, and that death must be the result.

"This inaction kills me," he said; "I would gladly face the cannon's mouth, but I cannot endure the slow torture of this suspense. I told you that in some respects I am a coward— I am proving myself one."

During these anxious few days all my arguments proved unavailing—Captain Gascoigne lost such hope that for a time he almost refused to allow the treatment to be continued. I watched over him, and thought of him day and night. I almost wondered if it might be best to send for Miss Lynwood, and one day suggested this expedient to the patient.

He started in irritation to his feet.

"Do you think I would allow the girl I love to see me in this condition?" he said. "No, no, I will fight it out alone. You said it would be kill or cure. I hope, doctor, that I shall face the worst as a soldier should."

"But the worst is not here," I answered. "If you would but pluck up heart, you would do splendidly. The cure is going well; there is every reason to hope that within three weeks' time you will be as well as ever you were in your life."

"Do you mean it?" he said, his face changing.

"I do—if you will but conquer your own apprehensions."

He looked at me. The colour dyed his forehead. He abruptly left the room.

My words, however, had turned the tide. In the evening he was more hopeful, and from that time his spirits rose daily.

"The chance of cure is excellent," I said to him one morning.

"The wedding can soon take place," was my remark a week later.

At last a day came when there was no tumour to treat. The arm and shoulder were once more quite well; nothing appeared of the disease but a comparatively harmless induration. I injected large doses now of the virus without the slightest reaction of any sort.

One morning Captain Gascoigne came early to see me.

"I saw a look on your face last night which told me something," he said.

"What?" I asked.

"That I am cured!"

"You are," I said.

"Quite, doctor?" he asked. "Is the poison quite eliminated from my system?"

"Wonderful as it is to relate, I believe that this is the case," I replied.

"Then I may safely marry?"

"You may."

"My children, if I have any, have no chance of inheriting the horrors which I have gone through?"

"It is my belief that the hereditary taint is completely eliminated," I answered.

"Good," he replied.

He walked abruptly to the window, and looked out. Suddenly he turned and faced me.

"My father is an old man," he said. "The illness through which he has passed will probably leave its sting as long as he lives."

"Probably," I answered.

"Then I have made up my mind. He must never know the storm through which I have passed. I promised him, when he was apparently dying, that I would marry Helen if I lived. Helen tells me that my mysterious absence from home during the last six weeks has puzzled and irritated him much. He has even threatened to come to town to look for me. I mean to put this suspense at an end in the quickest possible manner. I shall immediately get a special license—Helen will come to town if I telegraph to her. We can be married to-morrow morning. Will you attend us through the ceremony, doctor, and so see the thing out? We can then return to 'The Priory' and set the old man's fears at rest for ever. Will you come, doctor? You owe it to us, I think."

I promised—and kept my word.

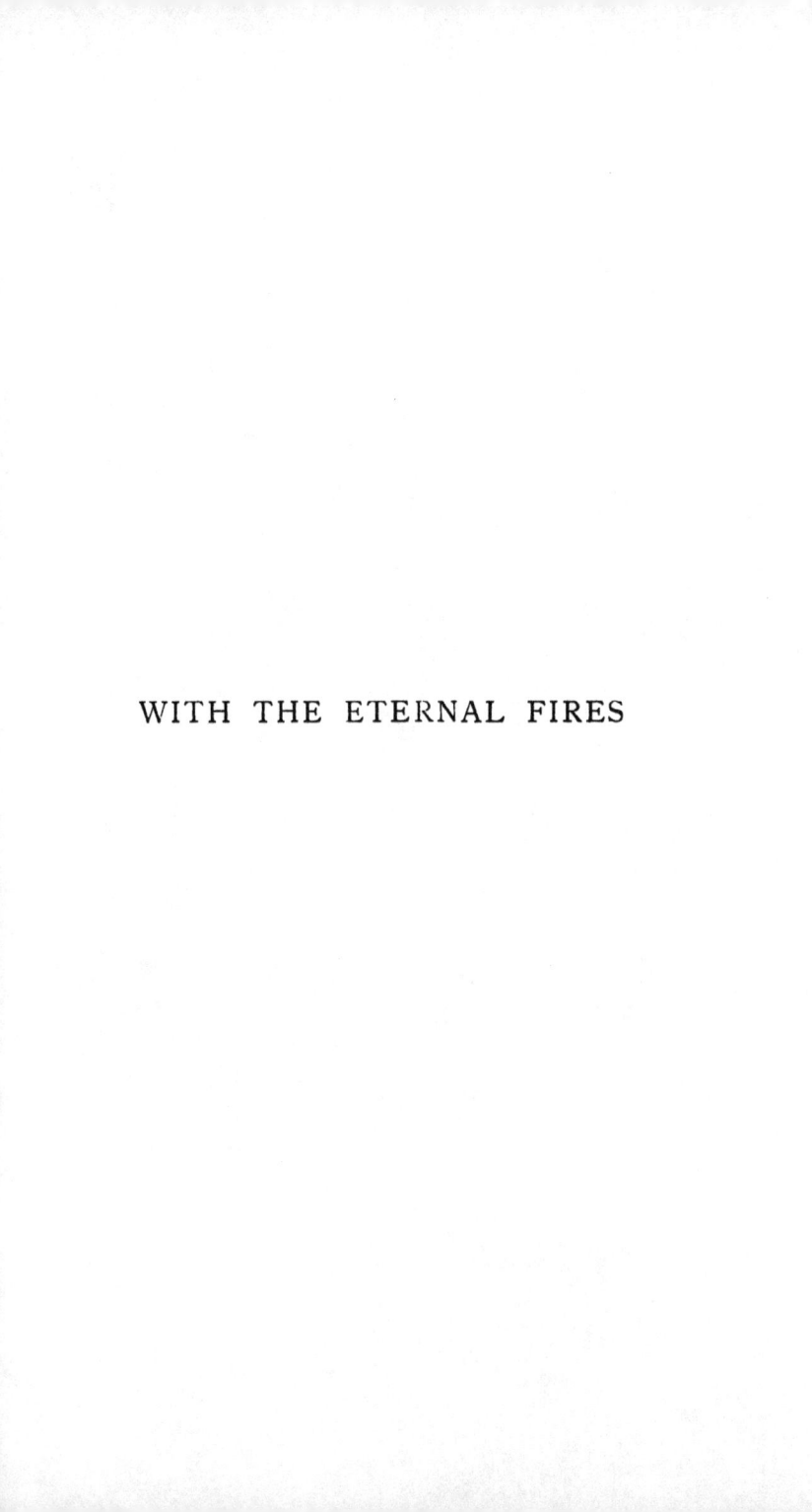

WITH THE ETERNAL FIRES

WITH THE ETERNAL FIRES

I WAS sent for one day towards the end of a certain very hot June to see a boy who was ill, at a large preparatory school in the neighbourhood of London. The school was in the country, about an hour's drive from town. My message was urgent, and I did not lose any time in attending to it. I had but a very few minutes to catch my train, an express, and had, at the last moment, to make a rush, first for my ticket, and then for a seat in the railway compartment. I opened the door of a first-class carriage just as the train was moving, and found that I was to take my brief journey to Wickham in the company of a single fellow-passenger. He was a man inclining to the elderly side of life, and when I got into the carriage his head was buried in a large sheet of the *Times*. He just glanced up when I appeared, and then, quickly looking down, resumed his reading. I did not interrupt him, but sat leaning back in my own seat lost in anxious thought. I had several bad cases on my visiting list just then, and was in no mood even to read. Presently I observed that my fellow-traveller had folded up his paper, and sitting so that I could get a view of his profile, was looking steadily out at the landscape. Hitherto, I had regarded him with the most scanty measure of attention, but now, something in the expression of his face aroused my keen and immediate interest.

He was a handsome man, tall and well-developed—the outline of his face was delicate and finely carved. The nose was slightly aquiline—a snow-white beard hid the lower part of the features, but the forehead, nose, and finely-shaped head were magnificently proportioned. It gives me pleasure to look at perfection in any form, and this man's whole appearance very nearly approached my ideal. He must suddenly have observed that I was paying him marked attention, for he turned swiftly and glanced at me. His eyes, of a bright hazel, seemed to lift and lighten for a moment, then they filled with a most impenetrable gloom, which was so marked as to be almost like despair. He opened his lips as if to speak, but evidently changed his mind, and once more confined his gaze to the landscape, not a feature of which I am sure by his expression did he see.

Soon afterwards we arrived at Wickham, a small country town, after which the school was named. I saw that my travelling companion was also getting out here. We found ourselves the only passengers on the platform, and the next moment I heard the stranger inquiring, in somewhat testy tones, for a conveyance to take him immediately to Wickham House. The doctor's brougham was waiting for me, and as Wickham House was also my destination, I stepped up at once to my fellow-traveller, and offered him a seat.

He stared at me as if he had only seen me then for the first time.

"I am extremely obliged to you, sir," he said, recovering himself with a start; "the fact is, I am anxious to reach the school in order to catch an early train back to town. I will accept your offer with pleasure."

"Step in, won't you," I said.

We both entered the brougham, and were soon bowling away in the direction of the school. As we were driving through the antiquated little town, my companion roused himself to be animated and talkative, but when we got into the more country parts, he lapsed into silence, and the stupor of dull despair once more spread itself over his features. I endeavoured to keep the conversation going, touching lightly on many topics of general interest, but he scarcely responded.

As we approached the house, driving up to it through a winding avenue, he heaved a profound sigh, and cast a glance up at the many windows. The building was a fine old gabled mansion of the Elizabethan period—the main part of the house was completely covered with ivy.

"Wickham House looks quite imposing," I said, with a smile; "this is my first visit—can you tell me if there are many boys here?"

"A couple of hundred, I believe," he replied. "It is a fine building, and the situation is exceptionally good. You would suppose that a lad would be safe here, would you not?"

"It seems to me that boys are safe nowhere," I replied. "I am a doctor, and am coming here to-day to see a little chap who has fallen on his head and hurt himself badly."

"Ah!" he answered, "I did not allude to that sort of ordinary danger. Sir, there is something in your face which makes me willing to confide in you. I am the father of an only boy—if he is alive now he is fourteen years of age—as fine a lad as ever stepped, strong and hearty, with all the athletic propensities of the best order of young Britain. I sent him here, to prepare for Eton; he would have gone there at the end of the summer holidays. Two months ago he vanished—yes, that is the only word. Ah! here we are."

We drew up at the front door. My companion got out first, and I followed. I was met on the threshold of the house by the local doctor—a man of the name of Hudson; he was waiting for me anxiously, and took me off at once to see my patient. I had no time, therefore, to observe my fellow-traveller any further.

The boy whom I had come to see was very ill—in fact, in great danger; and my attention was completely taken up by his case until late in the evening. In the interest aroused by this acute illness, I had forgotten all about my strange companion, but just as I was leaving, Dr. Hudson, who was taking me through the hall of the great house on my way to the carriage, spoke abruptly.

"By the way, Halifax, I saw that you gave Mr. Cavendish a seat to the school. He has spent the day here, and is returning to London now. You have no objection, have you, to his sharing your conveyance back to the station?"

"None whatever," I replied. "He is a fine-looking man— I did not know his name until you mentioned it. There is something about him which interests me. By the way, he told me a queer story—he said that he once had a son here, but that the boy vanished about two months ago."

"That is perfectly true. The case is a terrible one; in fact, quite a tragedy. The boy was, without the least doubt, the victim of a horrible plot. The circumstances of his disappearance were as follows: One day, Dr. Hughes, our head master, received a letter purporting to be written by the boy's father. It was to all appearance in his handwriting; the paper was headed with his crest and his private address in

Essex. The letter was a very brief one, and requested Dr.
Hughes to send Malcolm up to Paddington the following day,
in order to see an aunt whom the boy had not met since he
was an infant.

"'Either his aunt or I will meet him at the bookstall on
the arrival platform,' wrote Mr. Cavendish. 'In case, by any
chance, I am not present, let him wear a red tie—Lady
Seymour will recognise him by that. Send up one of the
masters with him, and do not fail to let him be there—he
shall return to school the following day.'

"Naturally, after the receipt of such a letter, there was
nothing for Dr. Hughes to do but to comply. He sent the boy
to town accompanied by one of the junior masters, Mr. Price.
They went as directed, and stood near one of the bookstalls.
Presently a well-dressed, middle-aged lady came up—she
embraced the boy tenderly, and told him that she was his
aunt, Lady Seymour, and took him away with her in a
hansom. Price, quite satisfied that all was right with the
boy, returned here, and it was not until the following day,
when Malcolm failed to appear, that the first idea of anything
being wrong entered Dr. Hughes's mind. He telegraphed to
Mr. Cavendish at his place in Essex, but received no reply.
He became possessed with a sense of uneasiness which he
could scarcely account for, and went himself to Essex that
night. On his arrival at 'The Howe,' Mr. Cavendish's place,
you can imagine his consternation when he heard that the
house was shut up, that Lady Seymour was still in India with
her husband, and that Mr. Cavendish was somewhere on the
Continent, address not known. What followed can be better
imagined than described. The letter was, of course, a forgery ;
the woman who took the boy off had left no address behind
her, nor has Malcolm Cavendish from that hour to now been
heard of. Such is the pitiable story. There was a short
delay in getting Mr. Cavendish's address ; but as soon as
possible the distracted father returned to England, and not
a stone has been left unturned to try to obtain a trace
of the missing lad. Up to the present all our efforts have
been unsuccessful. The boy is an only son, the heir to a
fine estate ; the poor father's agony of mind I leave you to
conjecture. Unless something happens soon to relieve the
tension of anxiety and despair, his mind may be seriously
over-balanced."

"It is a terrible story," I said. "What an awful villain that woman must be. Who is she?"

"Nobody knows. When questioned, Mr. Cavendish always shirks the subject. Even the detectives can get nothing out of him. If he does know anything about her, he refuses to tell."

"Well," I said, "your story quite accounts for the expression on his face. I wish with all my heart that something could be done to relieve him."

"Get him to confide in you if you can, doctor, on your way to town; you will be doing a good work, I assure you; one of the saddest features of the case, as far as the old man is concerned, is that he keeps his grief so completely to himself. If you can manage to break the ice, you will be doing him a service."

"I will do what I can," I answered.

Soon afterwards I had left Wickham House, and in Mr. Cavendish's company returned to London. Our compartment was full, and if I had wished to draw my companion out, I should not have had the opportunity. During our short run to town, he sat nursing his grief, staring straight before him, apathy if not despair in his eyes—he was evidently at present in no mood to confide in anyone. We reached Paddington in good time, and I turned to bid him "good-bye." He looked at me with a queer expression on his face.

"They spoke of you at the school to-day," he said; "they told me one or two things about you—you do not quite fulfil the *rôle* of the ordinary physician—I wonder if it is possible for you to administer to a mind diseased?"

"That is the priest's mission, as a rule," I said; then I added, suddenly, "but try me—come home with me now, if you like."

"There is no time like the present," he answered.

My carriage was waiting—I conducted him to it, and in a short time we found ourselves at my house in Harley Street. I took him at once into my study, offered him refreshment, and then waited for him to speak.

"Do you make brain disease your special study?" he said, abruptly.

"Not my special study," I replied; but I have given a good deal of attention to mental disease."

"Then what do you say to this? I told you this morning

that I once had a boy at Wickham House—a fine lad, well-proportioned, sound, brave, and good in body and mind. Owing to the strangest and most diabolical stratagem, he was entrapped away from school—a forged letter was used, and the name of my sister, Lady Seymour, brought into requisition. It is two months now since the fatal day when the boy was taken to London—since then, not the slightest clue has been obtained of his whereabouts; as far as he is concerned, the earth might have opened and swallowed him up."

"The story is most tragic," I replied.

"Ah, you may well call it that. Such a tragedy happening to a man in connection with his only son is enough to—eh, doctor—enough to turn his brain, is it not?"

As Mr. Cavendish said these last words, his face suddenly altered—the look of despair gave place to a curious expression of stealthiness mingled with fear. He rose to his feet and gazed at me steadily.

"I should like the truth from you," he said, coming a step nearer. "Is it true that I ever had a son? For the last few weeks I have seriously considered every circumstance of this most strange case, and have almost come to the conclusion that I am suffering from a very queer state of illusion. More and more, as the days go by, I incline to the belief that I never had a son. It is true that I carry the photograph of a boy in my pocket—I often take it out and look at it—I gaze at it sometimes for nearly an hour at a time, and say to myself, over and over, 'I have watched your face since you were an infant. Yes, I have certainly seen you—I have held you in these arms. I have seen the look of intelligence growing in your eyes. I have observed your progress from childhood to boyhood. But, no, perhaps you are only a dream-child—perhaps I never possessed you. Here is a photograph, but may it not represent another man's son?' My mind is in this state of torture, Dr. Halifax; always vacillating from belief to unbelief, until I scarcely know what I am doing. Can you not see my point for yourself? How is it possible for me seriously to believe that a lad of fourteen could vanish from the face of the earth leaving no clue behind him?"

"The case is most mysterious," I replied; "but with regard to its truth, I can absolutely and completely relieve your mind.

You are not suffering from an illusion—you have really had a son—nay, I firmly believe him to be still alive. It so happens that Hudson, the doctor who attends the boys at Wickham House, told me your story to-day. Your boy was certainly at school there—he certainly did exist. Your mind is slightly unbalanced by the terrible grief and anxiety you have undergone. Your duty now is to turn your thoughts resolutely from the idea that you are suffering from a case of delusion."

"The story of the disappearance is too unaccountable to believe," said Cavendish.

"Have you a photograph of your boy about you?" I asked.

"I certainly have a photograph in my pocket, but whether it is a photograph of a stranger or of my son, I am unable to tell you."

As he spoke he produced a thin morocco case, touched a spring, opened it, and placed it in my hands. It contained the photograph of as frank and handsome a lad as any man could desire to possess—the eyes, the face, the smiling lips, the open, courageous expression of the brow, all showed that there was no duplicity or anything mean in the boy himself. One glance at his face, as it was reflected in the photograph, was quite sufficient to dispel any doubt as to his having connived at his own disappearance. What had happened to the boy? Whose victim was he? How and by what means had he been kidnapped so effectually as not to leave the ghost of a trace behind?

While I was looking at the picture of the lad, the father's eyes were fixed on me. I looked up suddenly and encountered his gaze.

"This is a splendid boy," I said, "and," I continued emphatically, "he is your son."

"Why do you say that?" he asked.

"For the simple reason that he is like you—he has got your eyes, and the expression you must have worn when you were happy."

"I never thought of that," he answered.

He took the photograph into his hand and studied it carefully.

"I suppose he must be my son," he said. "I see what you mean. I used to have those particularly bright hazel eyes when I was young."

"You have them still," I said; "you have transmitted them to your boy."

"Well, be it so. It is a relief to hear you speak, for you speak with confidence; but when I am alone the intolerable delusion invariably returns that I never had a son—all the same, I am as tortured as if I really possessed and lost a boy like that."

"The thing to cure you is simple enough," I said.

"What is that?"

"We must find your boy and bring him back to you."

"Ah, Dr. Halifax—ah, if you could!"

"Sit down," I said, "let us talk the matter out carefully."

"I have talked it out carefully so often," he said, pressing his hand to his brow in a bewildered manner. "At first I was all on fire—I was nearly distracted—I spent money wildly, here, there, and everywhere—I was full of hope. Although I was nearly mad, my hope of finally discovering the lad never deserted me. But of late the queer feeling that the whole thing is a delusion comes to me whenever I attempt to take any steps to find the boy. Granted that you have cured me for the time being, I shall go back to my rooms at the Albany to-night, and assure myself once again that it is useless to fret, for I never had a son."

"We will not encourage that delusion by talking of it," I said. "Rest assured that you had a son, that in all probability you still have one, and that it is your bounden duty to search the earth until you recover him."

"Do you say so, indeed? With what energy you speak."

"It is necessary to speak with energy," I replied; "the case is pressing, you must move Heaven and earth to get back that boy. It is impossible for you to tell what fate may now be his."

"I cannot do more than I have done, doctor—at the present moment there are two detectives working day and night in my service. From the moment Price, the junior master at Wickham House, saw the boy step into a hansom with a woman who pretended to be his aunt, he has vanished as completely and utterly as if he had never existed."

"The boy has been very cleverly kidnapped," I said. "The woman who pretended to be his aunt is, of course, at the bottom of the whole affair. There is no reason to suppose that money has had anything to do with this strange case; the boy was also much too old to be trained as an acrobat. The case plainly points to revenge."

"Revenge," said Cavendish, fixing his eyes on me, and giving me a startled and astonished glance—"Who could possibly hate a boy like that?"

"Not likely," I replied; "but someone could hate you. Have you an enemy?"

"If you ask me if I *have* an enemy, I think I can honestly reply 'No,'" he answered, after a little pause.

"You speak with doubt," I said. "I will slightly change my question. Had you an enemy in the past?"

"Oh, the past," he repeated, thoughtfully. "You are half a detective, doctor."

"Only so far a detective," I replied, "that I have made human nature the one study of my life."

"Doubtless such a study gives you clues to men's secrets," was the answer. "Well, I can give you an unpleasant history, but before I speak of it, I will just tell you one or two things with regard to my present. I married late in life. Shortly after the birth of the boy my wife died. Almost immediately after her death I came in for a fine property—an estate in Essex worth some thousands a year. The place is called 'The Howe,' and my boy and I have spent some happy Christmases there. The boy was the brightest creature—I could never be dull in his society—I was glad to feel that he would inherit my acres some day. When with him my past ceased to worry me."

"I am sorry to have to ask you to rake up unpleasant memories," I interrupted.

"Yes, yes, I will tell you all. The fact is this:—

"I was once obliged, owing to strange circumstances, to act in a very unpleasant, and what appeared to be almost a vindictive, way towards a woman. She was a Creole, a passionate and strikingly handsome creature. She had made the acquaintance of a young fellow, who was at the time one of my greatest friends—she induced him to promise her marriage. I doubted and distrusted her from the first, and moved Heaven and earth to keep my friend from committing himself to such a disastrous step as a marriage with her. All my expostulations were in vain—he was madly in love; and this woman, Thora, had a most unbounded influence over him. Unexpectedly, it was given to me to put a spoke in her

wheel. Even at the altar I was just in time to save my friend
—I discovered that Thora had a husband already, and
brought him to the church at the critical moment. All was
up for her, then, of course; but I shall never forget the look
on her face. My poor friend died of yellow fever two months
afterwards, and Thora's husband himself fell a victim to the
fell disease. But I had made an enemy of this woman, and
during the remainder of my stay in Jamaica she was a thorn
in my side. One day she forced her way into my presence,
and asked me if I would give her compensation for the injury
I had inflicted on her. I asked her what she meant. She
suggested that I should marry her myself. I refused, with
horror. She bestowed upon me a glance of the most
unutterable hate, and told me that I should rue the day
when I had ever interfered with her.

"Shortly afterwards I went home, and sincerely hoped that
I should never see her or be troubled by her again. Judge,
therefore, of my feelings when, on the eve of my marriage, I
received a most intemperate letter from her. She again
repeated the words which she had uttered when parting from
me: 'You will rue the day you interfered with me.' She
wrote to me from Jamaica, and, being so far away, I did not
think it possible that she could carry out her threat, although,
from what I knew of her character, I believed her to be quite
capable of any mode of revenge. I married, and was happy.
Some years afterwards I received a newspaper with a marked
passage; it contained an account of this woman's marriage to
a Swede. Since then I have heard nothing about her. Let
us forget her, Dr. Halifax; she could not possibly have had
anything to do with the disappearance of my son, and the
subject is most distasteful to me."

"Nevertheless, from what you have told me, it is more
than evident that, if this woman is still living, you have
an enemy."

"I had an enemy at the time, no doubt; but I scarcely
think that even Thora would keep up her evil feelings for
fourteen or fifteen years, and then suddenly rise up, as if from
the grave, to do me a fearful injury. The greatest dare-devil
that ever lived would surely not allow her revenge to slumber
so long."

"That may or may not be," I said. "I consider what you
have told me a most important clue to the recovery of your

boy. Not a moment should be lost in finding out where this woman now is."

Mr. Cavendish shrugged his shoulders.

"If she is really at the bottom of it," he said, after a pause, "we shall never find her. She was quite the cleverest woman I have known; she was capable, in the old days, of outwitting twenty detectives. I have no reason to suppose that her talents have rusted with years. If she is at the bottom of this affair, the boy is hopelessly lost."

"You have no right to say so," I answered, with some indignation. "However bad and unscrupulous a woman may be, it is possible, surely, to outwit her. You will forgive me for saying that this story should have been confided to your detectives some time ago."

Mr. Cavendish looked at me fixedly.

"If you think so, I will tell them," he said. "It did not occur to me to connect her with the affair. My belief is that she is in all probability dead; she comes of a short-lived race. Yes, I think you are mistaken; but, as you say, no stone should be left unturned, and I will have a talk with one of the detectives this evening."

Mr. Cavendish left me soon afterwards. I felt that our interview had at least done this much good, it had shaken the terrible delusion which made him doubt that he had ever been the father of a son. I was glad at least of this, and wondered if it would be my fate to hear anything more of this strange story.

The next day, to my surprise, Mr. Cavendish called again upon me.

"Well," I said, "I am glad to see you. What does your detective say? How is the affair progressing? What steps are being taken to find the woman Thora?"

He gave me a queer and somewhat unsteady glance.

"The fact is this," he said, "I have said nothing whatever about that woman to the detectives employed in my service."

I could not help feeling regret, and showing it.

"Are you not aware," I said, "that there is not a day to be lost if you are ever to get possession of your boy again?"

"Ah! there's the rub," he said, slowly. "*Had I a boy?*"

He folded his hands tightly together, and looked straight out of the window. Then he turned suddenly round, and looked me full in the face.

"It is useless for you to argue the point," he said. "When I left you last night that thing occurred which I told you would happen. I went to my rooms in the Albany, ordered dinner, and telegraphed to the detective MacPherson to call upon me. I had no sooner done so than I laughed at myself for my pains. I felt the delusion, or whatever you like to call it, coming upon me in full force. How could MacPherson recover for me what had never existed? How could I who never had a son embrace one? I sat down to dinner, ate with appetite, refused to believe that I was suffering under any grief whatever, and, when the detective arrived, apologized for having troubled him, told him that I had nothing fresh to talk over, and dismissed him. No sooner had he gone than I regretted my own action; I perceived that my mind was verging to the other end of the pendulum. I spent a night of agony, bewailing the boy whom I then believed in, cursing myself for having dismissed the detective; but now again the belief that I have no son is with me. You see for yourself what a state is mine; I am incapable of taking any efficient steps in this matter."

"You are," I said abruptly. "May I not take up the case for you?"

"You?" he said, opening his eyes. "Good heavens! what has a doctor to do with it?"

"I undertake it for you because you are ill," I said, "because the story is peculiar, and because I am deeply interested."

"You are good," he said. "Yes, act as you think well."

"Give me your detective's address," I said. "I will have an interview with him this evening; and as you know that a woman called Thora certainly did exist in the past, give me what particulars you can with regard to her appearance."

"She was dark and handsome," he answered; "a tall woman with flashing eyes. That was the description of her in the old days. If she is still alive she is probably past recognition — her hair would in all probability be snow-white. I am an old man, and she is older. Oh, she is dead, doctor! Do not let us waste our time in thinking of her further."

I made no reply to this, but took down in my note-book several particulars which I almost forced Cavendish to give me. He left me after a time, and in the course of the day

I saw the detective, MacPherson. The man was a shrewd fellow, and I thought it best to take him completely into my confidence. He believed the fresh clue which I was able to furnish him with of the utmost importance—said that the name Thora was in itself so uncommon as to be a valuable guide, and promised to let me hear from him in a few days.

A week passed by without anything fresh occurring. Cavendish was beginning to haunt my house; he came each morning and evening; his mind was still in a terrible state of unbalance, verging one moment to the extreme limits of despair at the thought of the lad he had lost, half-an-hour afterwards doubting not only that he ever possessed a lad, but even that he himself really existed. I waited anxiously for news from the detective, but day after day passed without any clue whatever being forthcoming.

One morning, early, I received a telegram which upset my own arrangements considerably—the telegram was from a very wealthy patient who was travelling in Russia, and who had been taken seriously ill. He believed himself to be dying in an out-of-the-way place called Bakou. He begged of me to come to him without a moment's delay. Expense was of no moment; he urged me not to delay an hour in setting out on my long journey. The sick man was not only a patient of some years' standing, but was also a very old friend of mine. I could scarcely desert him in such stress, and, after a brief reflection, decided to go to him. I wired to him to expect me as soon as train and steamer could bring me to his side, and then went to Cook's office to get particulars with regard to my unlooked-for journey. Bakou is a small town on a tongue of land jutting into the Caspian Sea; it is on the west coast. I found, to my dismay, that it would not be possible for me to reach this remote corner of the world under ten days' hard travelling. I might slightly shorten my journey by going from London to Vienna, and then on to Odessa by train; but, travel day and night as fast as I could, it would be impossible for me to reach my poor friend under nine to ten days. I telegraphed to him again to this effect, but his reply, which reached me in the course of the evening, implored me to set off without an hour's delay.

"I am alone in this horrible place," he telegraphed; "no English doctor within reach. My last chance of life depends on your coming."

I had scarcely read the words of this long foreign telegram, before the detective, Mac Pherson, was ushered into my presence.

"Well, sir," he said, doffing his hat as he spoke, "I am sorry to have kept you and the other gentleman waiting so long, but I do think I have got a bit of a clue at last."

"Pray be seated," I said, "and tell me all about it."

MacPherson seated himself on the edge of a chair, holding his round, soft hat between his knees.

"It is a queer business altogether," he said, "but the fact is, I have traced the boy to Vienna."

"Vienna !" I said, startled. "What do you mean ?"

"What I say, sir. After very careful inquiries, I have found out that a lad, exactly answering to the description of Master Cavendish, went in the company of two women— one young, one middle-aged, *via* Calais and Dover, to Vienna about ten weeks ago. Let me see, this is the 5th of July; the day the boy went to London was the 26th of April. A fair and a dark lady, accompanied by a lad in all points answering to the photograph, a copy of which I hold in my pocket, started for Vienna on that day. From there they went straight on to Odessa. I can't trace them any farther. One of the women would answer to the description Mr. Cavendish gave you of the Creole whom he used to know in his early youth. She is a handsome, tall woman, with a slender, well-preserved figure— flashing, dark eyes, and hair which is only slightly sprinkled with grey—she evidently had an accomplice with her, for a fair-haired woman, much younger, accompanied her and the boy. Now, sir, I propose to start for Odessa to-night, in order to follow up this clue. In a case of this kind, and in such a remote part of the world, only personal investigation can do anything."

"You are right," I answered. "Now, I have something strange to tell you. I am also starting for Odessa this evening."

The man gaped at me in astonishment.

"Yes," I replied, "I am going to Odessa *en route* to a place on the Caspian Sea of the name of Bakou. After what you have just informed me, I shall endeavour to persuade Mr. Cavendish to go with me."

The detective rubbed his hands slowly together.

"Nothing can be better for my purpose," he answered, after

a pause—"only Mr. Cavendish must be quite certain to keep himself dark; for if this woman Thora really kidnapped the boy, she will be able, in a Russian town like Odessa, effectually to hide him or even to take his life, if her object is revenge and she knows that his father has arrived."

"What can have induced the boy to go with her?" I said. "A lad of fourteen has surely a will of his own."

"Oh, she made up something, sir; the matter seems to me plausible enough. The lad was sent for to town on the pretext of meeting his aunt. This woman would tell the unsuspecting boy that his father, who was then on the Continent, had desired her to bring him out to him. Of course, the lad would follow her then to the world's end, and be only too pleased to do so. Well, doctor, I will leave you now, and prepare for my long journey."

I bade the man "good-bye," and sent a wire to Mr. Cavendish, to ask him to call on me at once. He was at home, and arrived at my house between six and seven o'clock.

"I have news for you," I said, the moment he appeared.

I then told him of the sudden journey which I was obliged to make, briefly related the interview which I had just had with the detective, and then proposed that he should accompany me to Odessa.

"I feel full of hope," I said. "Your presence on the spot may be necessary in order to identify your son. How soon can you be ready to join me?"

He had been looking depressed and full of despair when he entered the room, but the news which I had for him acted like champagne. His eyes brightened, he clenched his hands in a thoroughly healthy manner, used some strong words with regard to Thora, and then said that he would accompany me.

"Go back to the Albany at once," I said; "pack what is necessary for your journey, get some money, and meet me at Victoria at a quarter to eight. We can talk as much as we like *en route*, but now there is not a moment to lose."

"You are right," he said. "I am a new man; the terrible delusion seems to have left me completely. I will be at Victoria at the hour you name."

He had drawn himself up to his full height; already he looked ten years younger. He left my house, and, punctually to the moment, I met him on the departure platform at

Victoria Station. We took our seats in the train, and were soon steaming away at a rapid pace towards Dover. I need not describe the early part of our journey; it was absolutely uneventful. Travelling right through, we reached Vienna in about thirty hours from the date of our departure from London. At Vienna I got my first glimpse of the detective, Mac Pherson, who was travelling in the same train, but second-class. He was dressed in a rough tweed suit, which completely metamorphosed his appearance.

We reached Odessa at night, and I found, almost to my relief, for I was completely tired out, that there were no means of continuing my journey until the following morning. On making inquiries, I found that I must now take steamer and cross the Black Sea to a place called Batoum. The journey by steamer would take some days, as the only boats available would coast a good deal. My duty, of course, lay straight and clear before me. I was on my way to my sick friend, but I found rather to my dismay that Cavendish, left alone, would be almost incapable of guiding himself. His mind was, without any doubt, in a weak state. Full of hope as he was during the greater part of that long journey, the painful delusion that he was following a vain quest, a will-o'-the-wisp, the dictation of a dream, came over him from time to time. Left alone at Odessa, he would in all probability spoil MacPherson's game.

"You had better come with me," I said; "you will do no good here. MacPherson is as sharp a fellow as I ever met. As soon as he gets a real clue, he can telegraph to you, and you can return. Your best plan now will be to come with me, and give him a clear coast."

"I see no good in that," he replied; "it seems that a boy, answering to my son's description, has undoubtedly reached this place. I should know that woman among a thousand— I should know the boy—whether he is a dream-boy, or my own son, God alone can tell; but I should know his face again. Why should I leave the place?"

"You must please yourself, of course," I answered; "my own course is plain. I must take steamer for Batoum at nine o'clock to-morrow morning. If you like, you can accompany me, and I shall be glad to have you; but if not, I trust you will telegraph to me as soon as anything transpires."

"I will do so assuredly," he answered.

Almost immediately afterwards we both retired for the night. In the early morning I received a note from Cavendish.

"I have made up my mind to remain at Odessa for a week, at least," he wrote.

I tore up the note, and prepared for my own journey—I was to be on board the steamer at nine o'clock. When I went down to the quay, I saw MacPherson standing there, looking about him with all an Englishman's curiosity. In his rough suit, he looked like the typical traveller; he touched his hat, and came up to me.

"Mr. Cavendish stays behind," I said to him, briefly; "you will look after him, will you not?"

"Yes, sir; but it is best for me not to appear to know him."

"Have you made any plans for yourself?" I asked.

"I believe I have got a clue, Dr. Halifax, but I am not quite certain yet. I know a little of many languages—even a few words of Russian. At a café last night I met a Russian who knows the part of the world where you are going. There is a great colony of Swedes there—that woman married a Swede."

I nodded.

"Well, there are Swedes at Bakou—in fact, the most important part of the population consists of that nationality—the great firm of Nobel Brothers have their kerosene works there—theirs are much the largest kerosene refining works in the world. My Russian friend knows all about them. He informed me that there is a woman there who speaks English—the wife of one of the overseers. The point for us to find out now is: Who is this English-speaking woman? Can she be the one whom we are seeking? I shall not leave Odessa until the next steamer starts, in order to search this place thoroughly, but it is more than probable you will see me some day, before long, at Bakou."

"If you come, you had better bring Mr. Cavendish with you," I said.

"I must be guided by circumstances," he answered.

It was now time for me to go on board the steamer, which almost immediately afterwards got under way.

I shall not soon forget the tedium, and yet the wonderful beauty, of that voyage—the steamer coasted almost the entire way, and, in consequence, our progress was slow; but in process of time we reached the large town of Batoum. From there I took train to Tiflis, and in course of time found myself at Bakou. My journey had, as I anticipated, quite covered ten days. A more desolate-looking town than Bakou it would be difficult to find. The place at one time belonged to the Persians, but is now owned by Russia—it is built on a sand hill, and overlooks the Caspian Sea. High winds, and clouds of sand, scour the little town from morning to night. Of trees, or green of any sort, there is none. I drove straight to the Hôtel Métropole—the best in the place, where my friend, General Morgan, had rooms. The hotel was built, as is usual on the Continent, round a courtyard, and the sick man, of course, occupied the best rooms. I found him very ill, and my hope that I might be able immediately to bring him home was frustrated—he was suffering from a sharp attack of typhoid fever, and although the worst symptoms had now abated, there was little chance of his being moved for many weeks to come. When I entered his bedroom, I was surprised to see a woman, dressed as an English nurse, seated by his bedside. She rose when I entered, and stood respectfully—when I spoke she answered me in English—the patient's state had evidently filled her with alarm, and she was much relieved at seeing me. General Morgan was too ill to enter into any conversation, and, after a short time, I left the room, beckoning to the nurse to follow me.

"I am glad that you are here," I said; "my patient is fortunate to have obtained the services of an English nurse."

"Oh, I live here," she replied, speaking with a slightly foreign accent; "my home is here: I am the wife of a Swede of the name of Nehber. I happened to hear that an Englishman was very ill at the Métropole, and came a week ago to offer my services. I have been well trained as a nurse, and was glad of the chance of earning a little money on my own account. My patient told me that he had telegraphed to his English doctor to come out to him, so we have been expecting you, sir, and I took the liberty to engage a room in advance. May I show it to you now?"

She led the way, as she spoke, along a gallery, opened the door of a spacious, but not uncomfortable bedroom, and left me. When she had done so, I went straight to the window, and looked out. The sight of this woman had aroused my keenest interest—her appearance on the scene was absolutely unexpected—she had doubtless saved my patient's life; but, thankful as I was to her for that, it was not on General Morgan's account that my pulse beat faster than usual at the present moment. Was this, by any strange chance, the woman whom Cavendish had known long ago? She spoke English well, she was extremely well preserved, but several signs showed me that she was no longer young—her figure was upright, she was well made—in her youth she was doubtless handsome. I felt disturbed, and at first regretted that neither the detective nor Cavendish had accompanied me. But, on second thoughts, I began to believe that I might manage this matter best by myself. Fru Nehber, as she was called, had no reason to suspect me. I was, in very truth, a *bonâ-fide* English doctor, who had come, at great inconvenience, to visit my patient. I might be able to draw her out—it might be my mission to rescue the boy. My heart beat high at the thought.

After refreshing myself with a bath, I went into the town to collect my thoughts. The foreign and peculiar aspect of the place would, at any other moment, have filled me with interest. Almost every Eastern nationality seemed to be represented in the streets. Turks in green and rose colour, Persians with long yellow silk coats, Tartars in their white tunics, small caps, and yellow boots—the place was alive with colour and vivacity. The cries of all sorts of nations—a regular confusion of tongues—resounded through the streets. I entered one of the bazaars, and tried to make myself understood, but found it impossible, as the only languages spoken were Russian or Persian, with an occasional mixture of Swedish. I came back to the Métropole, and entering my patient's room, sat down by his side. The nurse—dressed quietly, as an English nurse should be—stood now by one of the windows; the casement was open to let in some air. My patient had awakened, after a long sleep; he turned his eyes, and fixed them on my face.

"You are good to come, Halifax," he said. "I am more grateful to you than I can say. I feel now that, what with Fru Nehber's care and yours, I have every chance of recovery."

"Yes, you are very fortunate in securing the attendance of an English nurse," I said.

"I should have been dead long ago, but for her," he

replied, speaking in a thin, weak voice. "I owe my life to her."

He gave the nurse a grateful glance, which she did not return—her hands were tightly locked together, her black eyes seemed to be watching the crowd, ever changing, but always present, who wrangled and chattered in the courtyard. A cart rattled in, making a loud noise—it was slightly built, with very high and slender wheels—some travellers alighted, and entered the hotel—Fru Nehber left her position by the window, and came into the centre of the room.

"Have you noticed our peculiar and interesting streets, doctor?" she said, speaking with a low, rather strange, intonation, as if she weighed each word before she uttered it.

"I have been in the streets," I replied. "I have never visited an Eastern town like this before—it is full of strange wonder to me; but, of course, being unacquainted with any language spoken here, I am rather at a loss how to proceed."

"You will permit me to be your interpreter," she said again —"I shall have pleasure in helping you in any way in my power."

"That will be kind of you," I answered.

"The patient will sleep after he has had his composing draught," she continued. "Will you come with me and see the place by moonlight?"

I responded in the affirmative. I went downstairs presently to supper, and by-and-by Fru Nehber, who now wore a long grey cloak, and a neat little nurse's bonnet, also grey, joined me.

She took me out with her, and explained much of the strange scene.

"This is a queer place to live in," she said suddenly, clasping her hands; "it is death in life; you can imagine, can you not, how I hate it?"

"I suppose you have a good reason for staying here," I said. "This is certainly the last place in the world in which I should expect to see a trained nurse and an Englishwoman."

"An Englishwoman never knows where she may go," was the reply; "and then, have I not told you that I am married? I am married to an overseer of the great kerosene works."

"By the way, where are they?" I asked. "I have heard a good deal of them from different travellers on my journey, and would much like to see them."

She was silent for a moment, and seemed to hesitate.

"You shall see them," she said then; "but first tell me if it is your purpose to remain here long."

"I shall probably stay for two or three days," I answered. "Of course, it is impossible for me to remain long out of London; but now that I have come so far, I must see my patient right through the crisis."

"It is past, I assure you, doctor; your friend will live."

"You seem to know a good deal about illness," I answered, giving her a keen glance.

"There are few things I do not know," she replied; "I have travelled much; I understand life. Sorrow, regret, bitterness, have been my portion, but through these things we learn. You are doubtless a great doctor, and a clever man, but you do not understand our Eastern illnesses. Your friend would have died but for me—now he will live, have no fear for him."

"Well, I shall stay here for a day or two," I answered. "I will then return home, and send out a friend of mine, also a medical man, who can bring General Morgan by easy stages to England when he is fit to travel."

"That will be a good plan," she replied. "That will relieve me."

"Then you do not nurse as a profession?" I said.

"Not now. But I was glad to nurse the Englishman, for he will pay me well."

"Is not your husband well off?"

"Oh, yes, and I have plenty to do at home—still, the news that an Englishman was sick unto death drew me to his side."

"Have you children?" I asked.

She looked hard at me; her black, piercing eyes seemed to read me through.

"No," she said; then abruptly turned aside.

"It is very kind of you to trouble to show me this place," I continued, after a pause.

"I am pleased to help you," she answered; "you seem good and strong. I don't care for goodness, but I have a great respect for strength."

T

I made no answer to this, and soon afterwards we returned to the hotel. I noticed that she said nothing more with regard to my request to see the kerosene works, but the next day when I alluded to the subject I found that she had not forgotten my wish.

"I have arranged everything," she said; "your patient is better—you need not fear to leave him. You can spend an interesting day. It is impossible, of course, for me to accompany you; but I have a friend—a young girl—who lives with me in my home. My home is not here, but five miles distant, just on the borders of the great kerosene works. I have asked my friend to meet you there. She speaks very little English, but she is a good French scholar—you understand French, do you not?"

"I can speak French, of course," I answered.

"Oh, then, that is excellent. There is a Swede here who speaks French. He will drive you straight to the works of the Brothers Nobel. Doubtless, after you have seen them, you would like to go on to the great feature of this place."

"What is that?" I asked.

"The Eternal Fires—they are wonderful! No one ought to come as far as Bakou without seeing them. Now go—your patient is in my charge—have a pleasant day."

She waved her hand to me in a somewhat theatrical style, and I left her.

Half an hour afterwards, I was driving in one of the queer native carriages in the direction of the great refining works of Nobel Brothers. My driver, who was also to act as my interpreter, understood a few words of the French language. The country over which we went was extremely desolate. After driving about five miles, I saw in the distance a hill, crowned with many tall, black, pyramid-shaped objects, looking something like a pine forest. As we came nearer I quickly discovered what they really were—numberless chimneys, out of which the liquid naphtha was rising, sometimes to the height of two or three hundred feet into the air. Fru Nehber was evidently inclined to be kind to me, and had left no stone unturned to provide for my comfort. When I arrived at the works, I was met by her husband—an elderly man, with a great white beard and heavy moustache.

He took me all over the kerosene works, gave me a carefully-prepared meal, and showed me every attention. It was late in the afternoon—almost evening—when I parted from him.

"By the way," I said, suddenly, "your wife told me that I should meet a young French lady here."

"Oh," he answered, with a start; "she alludes, of course, to Felicia La Touche, a girl who has been staying with us for some time; she is away to-day; important business called her suddenly from home."

I noticed as he spoke that, simple as his words were, a look of irritation and annoyance crossed his face.

"My wife is a peculiar woman," he said, slowly; "she takes whims, Monsieur le Docteur, and sometimes those who are with her suffer, but Felicia means well. I presume, sir," he added, breaking off abruptly, "that you are now about to visit the old Temple of the Fire Worshippers?"

"That is my intention," I replied. "It is surely worth seeing?"

"It is. The fires at night make a weird and fantastic spectacle. I will now say farewell."

He shook hands with me as he spoke, and a few moments later I was continuing my drive. The distance from the kerosene works to the Fire Worshippers' Temple was a matter of about twelve miles. The sun was now sinking beneath the horizon, and a night of great darkness was ushered in.

The road was of the roughest, and I quickly perceived the advisability of using the queer carriages built of withies, with their very high and slender wheels—the wheels could sink deep into the sand, and their height kept the travellers at a respectful distance from the choking dust. We had gone some distance when I suddenly saw on the horizon what looked like long, low, white walls; in short, what seemed to be the inclosure of an Eastern city. I asked my guide what these walls were, and he informed me with a nod that they were the white walls which surrounded the old Hindoo Temple of the Fire Worshippers.

As we came nearer, little tongues of fire shot out of the ground at short intervals—they rose from a foot to two feet high, spouting up suddenly, and then dying away. Our horse, a very strong animal, was evidently accustomed to this subterranean burning, and was not in the least alarmed, moving quietly aside when the fire sprang up directly in his path. My guide and charioteer drove with care—he was now absolutely silent—I also sat quiet, musing on the strangeness of my present situation, wondering if an adventure were before me, and if it was really to be my happy lot to rescue Mr. Cavendish's long-lost son.

By-and-by we reached the white walls—my guide jumped down from his driver's seat, and pulled a bell. The custodian of the deserted temple—for the fire-worshipping had long ago been given up—now appeared. He held a lantern in his hand, which lit up his weird and wrinkled face. He was dressed in the garb of a Russian soldier, and took care quickly to inform me, my driver acting as interpreter, that he was one hundred and nine years of age.*

We soon found ourselves in a large courtyard, surrounded by very broad and fairly high walls. Piercing these walls at regular intervals were small doorways, which I discovered led into low, dark rooms. In these rooms the monks used to live. The centre of the court was occupied by a building raised on thick pillars. This was doubtless the ancient temple. On one side of the surrounding walls rose a heavy, square building, surmounted by two low towers. Out of each of these ascended now high columns of flame, lighting up the entire place, and giving it a most strange and weird appearance. The flames rose to several hundreds of feet, and shot up clear and steady into the night air. My guide, having tied up the horse outside, quickly joined us, and began to interpret, as well as he could, the old custodian's remarks, but his knowledge of any language but his own was extremely slight, and the scene spoke for itself. I soon left the guide and custodian, and, walking across the court, began to make investigations on my own account. The men stood together, talking in low tones just where the light fell fully upon them, but behind the temple, in the middle of the court, there was deep shadow. I had just approached this shadow, when I was startled by the touch of a light hand on my arm—I turned quickly, and saw a girl standing by my side.

"I have been expecting you," she said; "I have been hoping you would come—you are the English doctor, are you not?"

"I am a doctor," I replied; "and who are you?"

"Felicia La Touche—oh, I know Fru Nehber will kill me, but I don't care—I have waited for you here all day.

* A fact.

When I heard you were coming, I brought the boy. Oh, he is ill, very ill—he will die if something is not soon done. My God, I can't stand it any longer—his cries, and the way he wails for his father! I think his mind must be wandering a little—he thinks that his father is coming to him—he has been thinking so all day. Oh, can you do anything—can you save him?"

"One moment first," I said. "What is the boy's name?"

She clasped her hands together with some violence—her agitation was extreme.

"He is an English boy," she said; "Malcolm Cavendish. I helped to kidnap him a couple of months ago. Oh! how wretched I have been ever since! But this is not the time for me to talk of my own feelings. Come, come at once. Oh, you may save him yet!"

As she spoke she pulled me forward—she was a young girl, and very pretty, but her fair face was now absolutely distorted with misery and terror. She opened a door in one of the walls, and the next moment I found myself in a tiny room in which I could scarcely stand upright.

"Here I am, Malcolm," said the girl; "I have brought a good doctor to see you."

"I don't want any light, Felicia," was the strange reply. "When my eyes are shut I can see father—I know he is coming to me. Don't bring a light; I shall see the horrible faces, and all the queer things, if you do—let me be; I am quite happy in the dark."

"You must bear the light; you will be better soon," she replied.

She struck a match, held it to a candle in a swing lantern, and motioned me to come forward. A boy was lying stretched out flat on the ground at one end of the Fire Worshippers' cell; a rough sackcloth covered him—a bundle of the same was placed under his head—his face was very white and thin —his big, dark eyes, which were looking up eagerly, had an unmistakable pathos in them which stabbed me to the very heart.

"Who are you?" he said, half sitting up, and gazing at me in a kind of terror. "Are you—is it true—*are* you father?"

"No, my boy," I replied, "but I know your father, and I have come to take you to him. Fear nothing now that I have come."

"Oh, take him, take him away," said Felicia, "take him at once. I don't care if I die afterwards, if only his life is saved. He is so sweet—such a dear boy—he has been so brave—he has kept up his courage through so much. I don't mind giving up my life for him. Take him away."

The boy lay back exhausted on his rough pillow. The relief of seeing me and of hearing my voice was evidently great, but he was too weak for the least exertion. The atmosphere of the wretched little cell was terribly oppressive, and I thought that he might revive in the open air.

I lifted him in my arms and took him outside.

"You are very brave," I said, looking down at the French girl. "This boy's father will thank you for what you have done some day."

"No," she answered; "I shall die—she will kill me—you don't know what her powers of revenge are; but, never mind —never mind; take him and go."

"I will take him," I said; "there is a carriage outside, and he shall return with me to Bakou to-night, but I cannot leave you in extreme peril. Can I do anything for you?"

"It does not matter about me—take him away, go."

She was evidently beside herself with terror and anxiety.

"Why are you delaying?" she said, stamping one of her feet. "Herr Nehber is a good man; but, listen—he is *afraid of his wife*. If he knew what I am doing, he would frustrate me; take the boy and go—go before it is known. I have been waiting for you here all day long. I feared beyond words that you would be prevented coming. The man who drove you here is a friend of mine; he will take you safely back to Bakou. Stay, I will speak to him."

She left me and ran quickly across the court—the boy lay in my arms half-fainting—weighted with such a burden, I was obliged to follow her slowly.

"It is all right," she said, when I came up; "my friend will take you safely to Bakou. He is glad—I think we are all glad—to know that the English boy has a chance of escape. Don't fret about me—old Ivan will take care of me, and there are hiding-places here. Good-bye, Malcolm; get well, be happy, and don't forget Felicia."

She flung her arms round the boy's neck, pressed a quick kiss on his forehead, and the next moment had vanished into the great shadow and was lost to view.

It was past midnight when I found myself back again at the Hôtel Métropole. I had thought much during that drive, and resolved by a bold stroke to take the lad right into the enemy's camp. In such an extremity as mine, only great daring could win the day. I resolved for the sake of the boy to brave much. I would meet this terrible Fru Nehber on her own grounds. I felt, however, that the odds were against me. As far as I could tell, I was the only Englishman in the place. I was mistaken. The first person I saw, when I entered the courtyard, was a tall traveller bearing the un- mistakable air and dress of my own country.

"You speak English?" I said, the moment my eye met his.

"Yes," he replied, coming forward; "can I do anything for you?"

"Have you taken a room here?"

"Yes."

"This boy is ill—he is an English boy. I have just rescued him from a most terrible situation. May I take him straight to your room? I can't explain anything now, but the case is critical."

"I will help you, of course," he said; "my room is at your service."

"May I rely on you to watch the boy, and not to leave him a moment by himself until I go to him?"

"I will do all in my power."

I placed the lad in his arms and ran upstairs at once. Almost to my relief, for I was anxious to get the crisis over, I saw Fru Nehber waiting for me in the long gallery which led direct from my room to that occupied by General Morgan.

"I hope you have had a pleasant day, Dr. Halifax," she said, coming forward, and speaking in that low, rather monotonous, voice, which was one of her peculiarities.

"I have had an exciting one," I replied. "Can I speak to you for a moment?"

I saw her brow darken, and a peculiar expression fill her dark eyes—she swept on before me with the bearing of a queen, entered the salon which led into General Morgan's bedroom, and then turned and faced me.

"Will you eat first?" she said—"I have had supper pre- pared for you here—or will you tell me your adventures?"

"I will tell you my adventures," I answered, "I visited the Fire Worshippers to-night."

"Ah !" she said. "The effect of the fire rising straight up out of the earth is fine at midnight, is it not ?"

"It is weird," I replied, "weird and terrible—the place is the sort of place where a crime might be committed."

"My God, yes," she said, slightly moistening her lips.

"I was just in time to prevent one," I said, giving her a steady glance.

She did not reply—her arms fell to her sides ; she advanced a step to meet me, and flung back her head.

"Yes," she said, after a very long pause, "you prevented a crime ! That is interesting ; of what nature was the crime ?"

"You will know all that you need know," I replied, "when I tell you that Malcolm Cavendish is at present in this house, under the care of an English gentleman, who will effectually guard him, and prevent your kidnapping him again. I know all, Fru Nehber. I know who you are, and what you have done. Had I not gone to the Fire Worshippers to-night, you would have had that boy's blood on your head ; as it is, I believe he can be saved. You are aware, of course, what a grave crime you have committed ; even in Russia such a crime would not be tolerated. You have failed in your object, for the boy will live, and it will be my happy task to restore him to his father."

"You can have him," she said, suddenly. "I do not wish you to lodge a complaint against me with the authorities."

"I will certainly do so, if you do not leave this hotel immediately."

"I will go," she said. "When I saw you yesterday, I had a premonition that you would defeat me."

"You thought that I suspected you ?"

"I had a premonition. Do you know Mr. Cavendish ?"

"Yes."

She was silent again, and walked to the window.

"I have lived so long in this world," she said, suddenly, "that the unexpected never astonishes me. I have tasted some of the sweets of revenge, but you have thwarted me, and for the time being I acknowledge that I am powerless. Take the boy back to his father; but take also a message from me. Tell Mr. Cavendish that I bide my time, and that I *never forget.*"

With these last words she abruptly left the room. I never saw her again,

The boy had a bad illness, and my stay at Bakou had to be indefinitely prolonged, but when Cavendish and MacPherson arrived, matters became far easier for me, and in the end I had the satisfaction of bringing back two convalescents to England. The boy is now quite well, and his father has long recovered his mental equilibrium, but I do not know anything about the fate of Felicia.

THE SMALL HOUSE ON STEVEN'S
HEATH

THE SMALL HOUSE ON STEVEN'S HEATH

AMONGST my numerous acquaintances was an old friend who lived on a somewhat remote part of a common situated between fourteen and sixteen miles out of London. For the purpose of this strange story I shall call it Steven's Heath, although its real name is another. The common stretches for many miles in several directions, and although within a very short distance of the Metropolis, is as lonely as if it belonged to one of the Yorkshire moors. My friend was a retired officer in the Army—he had a great fancy for lonely places, and chose the neighbourhood of Steven's Heath with a due regard to its solitude when he arranged to build a house upon its borders. He was an old man of between sixty and seventy—his children had long ago left him, and he and his wife lived a very happy Darby and Joan existence in their pretty new house and extensive grounds. The air was of the purest and freshest, and I always enjoyed paying my friend a visit. It so happened that an illness of a trifling character called me to Clover Lodge towards the end of a certain October. Colonel Mathison would never consult any medical man but myself, and I found him nervous and excited when I went to visit him. After a careful examination I was able to reassure him with regard to his physical condition. My verdict instantly put him into the highest spirits, and he insisted on my remaining to dine with him and his wife. Mrs. Mathison took me for a walk round the grounds just before dinner.

"Your verdict about Edward has made him very happy," she said.

"If he follows my advice he will be all right within a week," was my reply.

"Yes, yes," she answered.. Then she added, with a sigh, "You admire this place very much, don't you, Dr. Halifax?"

"You have the finest air in the country," I said; "no one would imagine that you are so close to London."

"Ah, that is just it," she answered; "but for my part, fine as the air is, I should much prefer wintering in town—the fact is, I am fond of seeing my fellow-creatures, and except for the society of one or two old cronies, the Colonel would rather spend his days in solitude. The fact of my being lonely is, however, a small reason, and it is not on that account that I am particularly anxious to go to a more civilized part of the country for the winter."

"What do you mean?" I asked.

"Well," she said, after a moment's hesitation, "I don't like the people I meet on this common."

"I daresay you do come across strange characters," I replied; "but surely they have nothing whatever to do with you?"

"Oh, I don't mean gipsies," she said. "I am not the least afraid of the ordinary gipsy; but of late, when out walking, I have met two very savage-looking men. It was only a fortnight ago that one of them, a man with dark eyes, a heavy moustache, and very tawny complexion, suddenly started up in front of my path, and asked me, quite politely, what the hour was. Some sort of instinct told me not to take out my watch. I replied by guess-work, and the man did not say anything further. Now, his tone was quite gentlemanly, and his dress was that of a country squire—nevertheless, his manner, and the look on his face, terrified me so much that I returned to the Lodge trembling in every limb. The Colonel asked me what was the matter, and I told him. He naturally laughed at my fears, and, of course, I could not get him to see the affair at all in a serious light. In short, it needed to come face to face with that man to see anything serious in such a trivial incident—but the Colonel is an old man, doctor, and of a very fiery, irascible disposition, and if there were any danger——"

"Which of course there is not," I interrupted, with a smile.

I looked hard at the little old lady as I spoke—she had evidently got a shock. I thought it was scarcely well for her to wander about this desolate common by herself.

"After all, it would be a very good thing for you to go

to town for the winter," I said. "I will speak to Colonel
Mathison on the subject after dinner. There is nothing
serious the matter with him, but if he were close at hand I
could look him up at intervals, and perhaps put him on a
treatment which might prevent the recurrence of the attack
which alarmed you both.

"I wish you would speak to him," she said eagerly.

Soon afterwards we returned to the house. After dinner I
broached the subject, but found the Colonel quite obdurate.

"Nonsense, nonsense," he said ; "no towns for me. If
Mary is nervous, and finds the place lonely at night, we can
get in another man-servant, or the gardener can sleep in the
house. As to my health, that is folly ; I should die in a
fortnight in your stuffy London ; and when I am ill, and need
your services, I know you won't refuse them to me, Halifax."

"That I won't," I replied heartily.

There was nothing further to say, and soon afterwards I
rose, remarking that it was time for me to catch my train.

"I will ring the bell for the trap to be brought round," said
Colonel Mathison.

The servant answered the summons, and an order for the
trap was given. In a moment the man re-appeared with a
long face—the mare had suddenly gone lame, and was unable
to travel. Colonel Mathison was greatly upset, jumped from
his chair, and began to excite himself in a very unnecessary
manner. I went to the window and looked out. There was
a moon, which would set within about an hour and a half—
it would give me plenty of light to walk to the station. The
nearest way thither lay straight across the common, about the
distance of from three to four miles. I felt that I should
enjoy the exercise.

"You must not give the matter a second thought," I said
to my old friend. "I shall start at once, and walk to
Haverling Station. The fact is, I shall like it, and there is
plenty of moon to show me over the ground."

"But the common is so lonely," said Mrs. Mathison.

"All the better for me," I replied. "I like to be alone
with Dame Nature now and then. But I have no time to
spare. I will wish you both good evening."

I left the house, holding my umbrella in one hand, and
a bag which contained a few surgical instruments and a
Burroughs and Wellcome medicine case in the other, and

started on my long walk. The clock in the hall just struck eleven as I left—my train would arrive at Haverling at ten minutes to twelve. I should therefore do the walk comfortably in the time. The night was a perfect one, and the moon flooded the entire place with a soft silver radiance. The trees which were dispersed at intervals across the common cast huge shadows, but my path lay where the moonbeams fell in an uninterrupted line.

The air was crisp and bracing, with just a touch of frost in it. I was in particularly good spirits, and could not help feeling that Colonel Mathison was right in refusing to exchange this fragrant and perfect air for the close atmosphere of town. But I had also a certain sympathy for the wife, who had not the passion for the country which her husband possessed, and was evidently easily frightened. As to her meeting a rough - looking man with a fierce aspect on a common like this, nothing was more natural, and I did not give the matter a serious thought. I walked quickly forward, little guessing what horror was lying directly in my own path.

I have, in my long and varied experiences, turned some sharp corners and gone through more than one moment of peril, but the adventure which I am now about to describe I shall always look back upon as the high-water mark of my own personal suffering and deadly peril. The situation, in the very midst of our civilized England, the close vicinity to London, the apparently trivial beginning of the incident—only heightened the horror when it did occur; but I must hasten to tell my story.

I had gone about half-way across the common, and the moon was rapidly approaching the horizon—in a short time she would set, leaving the entire place in complete darkness. I hurried my footsteps, therefore, wishing to gain the high road before this took place. I must by this time have reached almost the centre of Steven's Heath — miles of undulating, broken land stretched to right and left of me.

A sensation of loneliness suddenly struck at my heart. I am not a coward, and was surprised at the sensation. The next moment, with a sigh of relief, I saw that I was not alone. A tall man, dressed in the garb of a country gentleman, was walking slowly in advance of me. He was evidently keeping to the same path over which I was travelling—a clump of trees must have hidden him from my sight until now; but now, owing to the peculiar position of the moon, I saw him with great distinctness. There was nothing remarkable in this sight, and I should soon have passed my fellow-traveller without a thought, had not my attention been arrested by his peculiar gait and manner. He walked slowly and with some pauses; he stooped a good bit, and stopped from time to time to cough. His cough was wafted back to me on the evening breeze—it had a sound of great distress about it, and seemed to indicate that the man was in severe pain. When he coughed I further noticed that he took a handkerchief out of his pocket and pressed it to his lips. At once I felt an interest in him, and, hastening my footsteps, came up to his side.

"Forgive me," I said, abruptly, "you seem ill and in pain."

He had not heard me as I approached over the soft, springy grass, and started violently when I suddenly addressed him. He wore a soft felt hat, which was pushed rather far over his eyes, and now, from under his bent brows, two haggard, suffering, and very dark eyes peered restlessly at me.

"I am not well, I thank you, sir," he said, speaking with a cultivated accent; "but I am not far from home, and when I get there, I have not the least doubt that a little rest will restore me."

His words were uttered in jerks, and he had scarcely come to the end of his sentence before he coughed again, and immediately a quantity of blood poured out of his mouth.

"You are seriously ill," I said. "I am a doctor on my way to London. Can I do anything to assist you?"

"A doctor!" he exclaimed.

He pushed his hat away from his forehead, and gazed at me earnestly.

"This seems like a Providence!" he muttered. "Do I understand you to say that you are a London doctor, sir?"

"I am," I replied.

He carried a stout stick, on which he suddenly leant heavily.

"The fact is," he said, abruptly, "I have met with a nasty accident; I am seriously hurt, and——"

He broke off to resume the painful coughing.

"Will you permit me to see you to your house?" I said.

"No," he replied; "that would not be wise. I am much obliged to you, but I would rather you did not see me home.

Perhaps it might be possible for you to give me a little advice here."

"Scarcely," I said. "You are either wounded or have broken a blood-vessel. You must lie down, and be properly examined before anything can be done for your relief."

He coughed again.

"I—I thank you, but I would rather go home alone," he repeated.

A fresh fit of coughing interrupted the words, and the red stream flowed from his lips.

"Come," I said, "you have met me unexpectedly; you must look upon it, as you have just remarked, as a Providence. You are not fit to go home alone. Accept my assistance, and regard yourself lucky to have met someone who can help you."

"There's my wife to consider," he said. "I—I can't speak much—my wife will feel it if anything happens to me. You can get away quickly after you have examined me—yes, perhaps it is best."

"It is the only thing to do," I said. "Take my arm, now, and pray speak as little as possible, or the bleeding will become worse. But just answer me one question first. What do you believe to be the nature of your injury?"

"A bullet wound," he said, speaking now in gasps. "The villain has shot me in the lung, I believe."

His words were unexpected, and they startled me, but I had not a moment to think of myself.

"Lean on me," I said, in an authoritative voice, "and indicate from time to time with your finger the direction we are to take."

He was too weak and ill to expostulate further. I drew his hand through my arm, and we turned abruptly to the left.

Our way led us away from the railway station. We soon reached a dingle, into which we descended. The man was now past speech, but at intervals he pointed out the direction which we were to take. We crossed the dingle, ascended a slight hill, found ourselves in a thicket of trees, and the next moment out again in the middle of a little clearing, in which a long, low, old-fashioned house stood. A faint light was shining out of the porch, which streamed direct on our path—the man gave a perceptible sigh of relief.

"Is that your house?" I asked.

He nodded. The next moment we were standing in the porch. A young woman, who evidently must have heard our footsteps, rushed out. She wore a white dress, and her hair fell in some disorder down her back.

"Ben!" she said, putting one arm round the man's neck, "how terrified I have been, and how late you are!"

She suddenly saw me, and started back with a stifled exclamation of alarm.

"Why have you brought this stranger home with you?" she asked of the injured man.

My patient was evidently making an effort to speak, which I saw in his present condition would be highly hazardous. I took the initiative, therefore, without delay.

"This gentleman is seriously hurt," I said. "Pray do not question him at present. I happened to meet him on the common, and, seeing the state of his sufferings, volunteered my assistance. I am a doctor, and it is possible that I may be able to relieve him. Let me help you to take him to a bedroom immediately. We must get him to bed at once. I shall then examine him, and render what assistance lies in my power."

The girl did not answer, but with a deft movement she flashed the full light of the lantern upon my face. From me she looked earnestly at the deathly pale face of my companion.

"Ben," she said, "did you knowingly bring this gentleman here?"

He nodded and frowned at her. The expression of his face seemed to convey some sort of warning. She took the initiative at once—her manner changed, her nervousness vanished, she became self-controlled and calm.

"It was kind of you to see my husband home," she said to me. "If you will give him your arm, we will take him to his bedroom at once."

She set down her lantern as she spoke. A paraffin lamp was burning in the hall. It had been turned low; she went to it and raised the light. Motioning me to follow her, she ascended some stairs, and in a moment or two we found ourselves in a good sized bedroom, which opened on to a small landing. It did not take me long to get the sick man on the bed and partly undressed. I unfastened his cravat, and opened his shirt. A glance at his chest showed me that the hemorrhage was caused by a wound. The nature of the wound made it evident that it was caused by a revolver; most probably the bullet was now embedded in the left lung.

It was impossible for me to discover the full nature of the injury, but it was all too evident that the man's life was in a precarious state, and if something were not quickly done to stop the excessive hæmorrhage, his life must be the forfeit. I quickly opened my medicine case, and without a moment's delay injected a dose of ergotine. I directed the young woman to prepare cold bandages to lay over the man's chest, and having plugged up the wound, I turned my patient on his side, and told him quite plainly that his chance of recovery depended entirely on his lying perfectly still. When I spoke he fixed his eyes on my face—there was an expression of dumb anguish about them which painfully upset the young woman, who was standing close to him. She leant against the bed, trembling in every limb, and for an instant I feared that her self-control would give way—but another glance showed me that she was made of sterner metal—she soon recovered herself, and, as at that moment hurried footsteps were heard in the hall beneath, she suddenly drew herself up, and a watchful, alert look crept into her face. The steps came quickly along the passage, they bounded up the stairs, the room door was flung noisily open, and a tall man with broad shoulders and much muscular strength entered.

I could not help giving a very perceptible start when I looked at him. I have seen evil faces in my day, but I do not think I ever before beheld one so sinister, so absolutely devoid of all trace of goodness. His eyes were small, of piercing blackness, and closely set—his features were aquiline, but his mouth was flabby and nerveless, and the under lip was so large and protruding that even the heavy moustache which he wore could not effectually hide it. He marched quickly up to the bed, and stood looking down at the wounded man without speaking; then his eyes caught sight of me, the angry colour flamed up all over his face, and a muttered oath dropped from his lips. The wounded man could not speak, but his eyes became painfully anxious in expression. The girl went up to the new arrival, and touched him on his shoulder.

"Leave the room, Hal," she said; "you see that Ben is very ill, and must not be disturbed. He has met with a bad accident—you doubtless know all about it; this gentleman met him on the road, and brought him home."

"I should have thought the gentleman would have known better than to interfere," muttered the man called Hal; "we don't care to have strangers about this place."

He bit his lower lip as soon as he had spoken. I was watching him narrowly. I saw that he was a man of violent passions, which he had very little power of keeping under control. The young woman touched him again on the arm, and drew him aside to a distant part of the room. He bent his ear to her, and she began to speak in an eager whisper.

My patient again fixed his eyes on my face; he motioned me nearer with his hand. I bent over him.

"Get out of this as fast as you can," he murmured.

His hoarse whisper nearly cost him his life. A fresh and violent flow of hæmorrhage set in. The wife, uttering a cry, rushed to her husband's side, and the other man left the room. I did all that I could to stop the fresh flow of blood, and after a time it ceased. The patient was now drowsy, and closed his eyes as if he wished to sleep.

When I saw that this was the case, I beckoned the wife to follow me on to the landing.

"Is there any hope of saving him?" she asked, the moment we were alone.

"He is in very great danger," I said, "but if we can keep him alive during the night, it may be possible to extract the bullet to-morrow. He has had a bad wound, and in all probability the bullet is embedded in the left lung. The danger is that he may die of hæmorrhage before anything can be done to extract the bullet. It is lucky that I happened to meet him."

"Lucky!" she repeated, gazing up at me, her eyes staring. "Heaven knows!"

She turned away, and, taking a handkerchief out of her pocket, wiped some moisture from her forehead.

"Can you really do him any good, sir?" she asked; "for if not ——" Her voice faltered; she was evidently putting a great constraint upon herself—"if not, sir, it may be best for you to go away at once."

"No," I said, "I will not do that. I have come here, and I will stay until the morning."

"Well, sir, if you will not go, let me take you downstairs and get you some refreshment."

She ran down a short flight of stairs, and I followed her. The flush of excitement had now mounted to her cheeks, replacing the extreme pallor which I had noticed ten minutes ago. She showed me into a well-furnished dining room, surprisingly large and solid for the appearance of the house. As soon as I entered I saw that the fierce-looking man, who had come into the bedroom, was standing on the hearth. He had changed his dress, which was in much disorder when I saw him last; his manner had also altered for the better. When he saw me he came forward, and moved a chair at right angles to the fire.

"Sit down," he said. "I am obliged to you for coming to our assistance. Is my brother badly hurt?"

"The wound is a very severe one," I replied.

"I thought so," he answered. "We were both together, and he must have slipped away from me in the dark. I have been all round the place waiting for him for nearly an hour. I guessed that he was hurt."

"I always knew that something bad of this kind would take place," cried the wife, with passion.

"Keep your tongue between your teeth," said the man, with an ugly oath. "The fact is, sir," he continued, fixing his bloodshot eyes with a peculiar glance on my face, "Rachel, here, is nervous; the place is lonely, and there is no woman near to keep her company. Ben and I are a rough lot, and nothing will keep Ben out of mischief when his blood is up. He had a row with some fellows at a public-house not two miles from here, and this is the consequence. We are all Colonials, and, as you may know, sir, rough and ready is the word still in most of the Colonies. We came to England two years ago, and took this cottage. We had a fancy to live a retired life. We heard that a chicken farm was a good speculation, and we started one; it gives us something to do, and the air of this common suits us. As to Rachel, she is always making the worst of things, but I suppose she does find the life somewhat tame."

"Tame!" cried the young woman, clasping her hands tightly together.

"Get the gentleman something to eat, Rachel, and then leave us," said Hal in a blustering tone.

"Thank you," I answered, "but I do not wish for any refreshment."

"Well, at least, you'll have some wine," said Hal. "I have got a bottle of port which I can recommend; I'll go and fetch it at once. Come, Rachel, you can hold a light for me to the cellar."

He left the room immediately, his sister-in-law accompanying him. They paused in the passage outside to exchange some words, but I could not hear anything they said. I went and stood by the hearth and looked around me. I considered the situation peculiar, but up to the present saw no cause for any special alarm as far as my own safety was concerned. The men were a lawless pair, and I did not believe the lame story offered to me about the revolver wound; but, having undertaken the case, I had no intention of deserting my patient, and felt certain that I should be able to defend myself should occasion arise.

The man and young woman were not long absent. They quickly returned to the room. The woman carried a tray, on which were some glasses and a box of biscuits. The man followed with a bottle of port. He drew the cork carefully, and put it on the tray.

"I'll go back to my husband now, sir," said the young woman, glancing at me.

"Do so," I replied, "and be sure you call me should my services be required. Pray remember, the main thing is to keep him perfectly quiet, and under no provocation to allow him to speak."

She nodded. She had nearly reached the door, when she turned and came quickly back.

"You will like to know our names," she said. "I am Mrs. Randall. My husband and this man are brothers. My husband is Ben; this man is called Hal. I am deeply grateful to you, sir, for the services you are rendering to me and mine."

Her eyes were very bright—so bright, that tears did not seem to be far away. She paused again, with her hand resting on the table.

"Is there any chance of Ben's life?" she asked suddenly.

I had in reality very little hope, for the hæmorrhage which had already taken place was of the most serious character, but I could not quench the longing in the young, eager eyes fixed on my face.

"Absolute quiet is the one and only chance of life," I said emphatically.

"I understand," she said, nodding; "your directions shall be carried out to the letter."

She left the room as she spoke.

When she had done this Randall flung himself on a large sofa at one side of the fire.

"Drink your wine, doctor; it will do you good," he said, with a sort of assumption of heartiness which sat ill upon him. "Upon my word," he added, "it was devilish good-natured of you to come out of your way to attend to a stranger."

"Not at all," I replied, "if I can save the stranger's life; but I must tell you that I have very little hope of doing so."

He cried in excitement, "Do you think that my brother will die of his wound?"

"It is not only possible, but highly probable," I answered.

He swore a great oath, jumped up from the sofa, sat down again, and ground the heel of one big foot into the carpet.

"This thing will upset Rachel," he said, after a pause; "she's awful spoons upon Ben—the fact is, he rescued her from some of the aborigines, years ago, in Australia; she grew up with us, and when she was old enough he married her."

"She appears to me little more than a child now," I said.

"Women marry young in Australia," was the brief reply. "Drink your wine, won't you?"

He had filled a glass with port wine before he sat down. I raised it now to my lips and sipped it. After doing so, I put the glass down quietly; I do not think a muscle of my face showed emotion, but I knew at once what had happened—the wine was heavily drugged. It was loaded with morphia. Randall's eager eyes were fixed greedily on my face. At that moment his sister-in-law called him. I jumped up, but he interrupted me.

"She wants me," he said. "I'll let you know if your services are required—finish your wine and help yourself to more."

He left the room, when I immediately walked to the window, flung it open, and dashed the contents of the wine-glass outside. I shut the window noiselessly again, and returned to my seat. I had scarcely done so when Randall re-appeared. I noticed that he glanced at my empty glass the moment he entered the room. A gleam of satisfaction lit up his swarthy face.

"It is all right," he said; "my brother is quiet — he is dozing off. Rachel is sitting with him. She wanted to ask me a question about the chickens—we send some to the London market almost daily."

"Do you make it pay?" I asked.

"I can't say that we do," he replied, "but why should I bother you with this? My brother and I have an income independent of the farm—we keep the chickens for the sake of occupation. The night is far advanced now, and I am dead-beat, if you are not. Shall I take you to a bedroom? If you are good-natured enough to spend the night here, you may as well have some rest until you are required."

I simulated a yawn with good effect, doing so with intention. I knew that if I had any chance of escape from the danger in which I undoubtedly was, I must quiet this man's suspicions. He must suppose that I had really swallowed the drugged wine.

"I am sleepy," I said, "and shall be glad to lie down; but don't take me to a bedroom. If you will permit me to have a stretch on that sofa, I shall do admirably."

"As you please," he said, with a careless nod. "The sofa is wide, and, as I can do nothing further, I will go to my room. You will find the wine on this table if you want any more. I will let Rachel know you are here, in case she may require you. Good night."

He left the room, slamming the door behind him, and I heard his footsteps noisily and clumsily ascending the stairs. I stretched myself on the sofa, fearing that he might unexpectedly return. There was no manner of doubt now that I was in a most grave situation, and that my life might be the forfeit of what had appeared to me to be an act of common humanity. Who were these people—what was their occupation? They were undoubtedly not what they seemed—the chicken farm was in all probability a blind to cover enterprise of a widely different character. The story of the revolver-wound was, on the face of it, false. Why had the girl looked so terrified? Why had the wounded man asked me to go? Why had Hal favoured me with glances of such diabolical hatred? Above all, why was the wine drugged? When the house was perfectly quiet, I slipped off the sofa and approached the window. It was a large one, and occupied the greater part of the wall at one end of the room.

I had opened it with ease when I had flung the wine away, and now again it yielded to my touch. I threw it up without making the least noise, and bending forward was just preparing to put out my head to judge of the possibility of escape, when I started back with a voiceless exclamation. The window was effectually barred from without, with a shutter composed of one solid piece of iron. I pressed my hand against it—it was firm as a rock. Half an hour ago this shutter had not been raised. By what noiseless method had it been slipped into its place? I closed the window again and went over to the door. I turned the handle—it turned, but did not yield. The door was locked. I was caught in a trap. What was to be done?

At that moment I heard a creak on the stairs, and the un-mistakable sound of heavy footsteps. I instantly returned to the sofa, lay down at full length, and assumed, as I well knew how, the appearance and the breathing of a man suffering from morphia poison. I made my breath stertorous and quick. I assumed the attitude of the deepest slumber. My hearing was now preternaturally acute, and the walls of this queer house were thin. I heard steps approaching the door. The lock was noiselessly turned, the handle was moved, and the door opened a very little. I knew all this by my sensations, for I did not dare to raise an eyelid. There was plenty of light in the room—the fire was blazing merrily, and a big paraffin lamp shone with a large globe of light on the centre table. Beside the lamp lay the tray which contained the glasses and the bottle of drugged wine. I seemed to see everything, although my eyelids were tightly shut, and I lay slightly forward on my face, breathing loudly.

"Aye," said Randall, coming up and bending over me, "he's all right—he's fast enough—as fast as a nail. Now, what's the matter?" he continued, evidently addressing Mrs. Randall, and speaking in a growling whisper. "You don't like this job, eh? There's no use in your snivelling, it has got to be done. He's fast, ain't he? Come over here and have a good look at him."

"I won't look at him; you are the cruellest man that ever lived—you are a ruffian. I must speak to you alone—come with me at once; if you don't, I'll say what I have to say out here.'

"You may shout as loud as you please, you won't wake him. I knew what I was about when I put the stuff into the wine; he's fast. What's up, girl? Now, none of your blarneying, and none of your passion, either. All our lives are in jeopardy, I tell you."

"Be that as it may, you have got to let that gentleman go, Hal."

"There are two words to that; but if you must interfere and give trouble, come out of this. He is fast, I am sure, but there is no saying what your muttering may do for him. He looks dead-beat, don't he? It seems a pity to disturb him."

The man uttered a low laugh, the horror of which almost curdled my blood.

"Come into the pantry," he said, re-addressing his companion; "he won't hear us in there."

They approached the door, walking on tip-toe; they closed it behind them, and I heard the key turn softly in the lock. If I had the faintest chance of escape, it was necessary for me to know if possible what fate was about to befall me. Where was the pantry? I opened my eyes now, and was immediately attracted by a gleam of light coming in a slanting direction through a window which I had not previously noticed. This window was high up in the wall, and was evidently used as a through light into another room. It had certainly not been illuminated when last I had examined the dining-room. Could it possibly belong to the pantry which Randall had alluded to? The sound of voices reached my ears. They were muffled, and I could not distinguish their tones, but at this instant I also perceived that the window in question was open at the bottom about two or three inches. If I could press my ear to the wall just below the open window, I might hear what the pair were saying. The risk was great, for if Randall came back and found me it would be a fight for life, and he, of course, would be armed, whereas I had not even a walking-stick. I thought the situation over carefully, and decided that it was better to die fighting than motionless. I further observed that there was a heavy poker in the fender. I seized it, mounted a chair, and pressing my ear just where I could not be seen, but also directly under the partly-open window, I found to my relief that I was able to hear perfectly well. The first sound that reached me was that of a woman's sob.

"You shan't do it," said Mrs. Randall. "I have borne with you too long. I know that Ben is bad, but I love him—he has always been kind to me—he is my husband—he never was an out-and-out bad 'un like you. You never had a heart. Now, listen; my mind is quite made up—you shall not take the life of the man who came here to succour my husband."

"Stop your snivelling," was the harsh reply. "I tell you he must go. Ben must have been out of his mind to bring him here. I have no enmity against the man himself, but he was a fool to put himself into the lion's den. He knows too much, and he must go. Don't you understand me, girl? Haven't you a grain of sense left? Well, I'll tell you something. *Ben killed his man to-night*, and he'll swing for it if we let that doctor escape. The thing was clumsily managed, and everything went wrong—the police came up just at the nick of time to ruin us, and Ben put a bullet into one—the whole thing will be in the papers to-morrow, and the doctor—curse him!—knows enough to swear away the life of that precious husband of yours. Now, for Heaven's sake, stop crying—control yourself."

"The doctor must be saved," said the young woman. "You are saying all this to frighten me, but I won't be frightened. Anyhow, come what may, I am not an out-and-out villain, and neither is Ben, and we can't allow the life of the man who has been good to us to be sacrificed. You want to murder him, Hal, but I won't let you. If you don't promise to let the gentleman go, you have got me to answer to, and I'll just tell you what I'll do. I have Ben's revolvers upstairs—oh, yes, I have hidden them, and you can't get at them, but I will take them down to the doctor before you can prevent me, and tell him to fight for his life. You are a bit of a coward when all is said and done, you know you are, Hal."

The man replied with an ugly oath. He must have taken the young woman by her shoulder as he spoke, for I heard her utter a faint scream.

"Don't," she said. "Let me go this minute; you are a coward to try to hurt a girl like me."

"I could kill you if it comes to that," was the reply. "I tell you I am desperate, and what is a man's life, or a girl's either, to me? My brother will swing if that doctor gets out of this. And, then, if I escape with penal servitude for life, I may consider myself lucky. I have no taste for penal servitude, so the doctor must go—and you, too, if you don't submit."

I heard Mrs. Randall laugh in reply.

"You think penal servitude is all you have to suffer," she answered; "but I know things that may bring you in a worse fate. How would you like to be hung up yourself? Perhaps you will, if I have the managing of things. Do you remember that old man on the common, last winter, and the purse of twenty sovereigns?—the purse had the man's initials inside— you never could find it. Do you remember the search you made, and how I pretended to help you? Well, I had the purse all the time. I thought I might as well keep it—it might prove handy some day. I have it upstairs now. You see, I can turn Queen's evidence any day and make it hot for you, and I will if you kill that doctor."

Her words were evidently unexpected — they had weight with the ruffian. I could hear him shuffling about, and I could even distinguish the young woman's quick, agitated breathing.

"I have got the key of the dining-room, too," she went on; "I slipped it out and put it in my pocket when you weren't looking, so I can do what I said. If you try to wrest the key from me, I'll rouse the house with my screams. You have drugged the doctor, but he is not dead yet."

"He'll never wake again, " said Hal, with a laugh; "you can't save him, girl, even if you tried—I tell you he is done for. I put enough morphia into that one glass of port to finish two or three men. He is sound—sound as a bell; fast as a nail— dead to all intents and purposes—they never wake when they breathe as he is doing."

"You are mistaken," was the reply. "I watched him, too, and at the present moment he could be roused, I am convinced. Do you remember the man you drugged in Australia? I saw him die; he was far worse than this doctor."

Hal swore another oath, and again tried to use personal violence on the girl. I knew this, because she evidently sprang away from him, and threw open the pantry door. A breath of fresh air which came in through the aperture in the window acquainted me with this fact.

"Now," she said, "you have got to choose. You have no weapons on you at the present moment; I am nearest the door; I can lock you in in a twinkling, and fetch Ben's revolvers. I will, if you don't do what I wish. Spare that man's life, and I'll stick to you through thick and thin; but kill him, and I'll give Queen's evidence. I don't believe Ben will recover, and I don't care that for you. I am so sick of this horrible life that, so far as I am concerned, the sooner it is over the better. Remember, I have got the purse, and I can tell a lot. Oh, I can make things look ugly for you, Hal, and, before Heaven, I will!"

"All right," said the man, assuming a soothing tone, "do stop canting—you always were a tigress; I've told Ben over and over that you would sell us, and I was in the right; but I suppose I must yield to you now. I'll go in and wake the doctor presently. I was only pretending that I had given him such a lot of morphia. He'll wake when I shake him up. I'll get him to take an oath that he'll never tell of what occurred here to-night. He'll do it fast enough when he sees his precious life in jeopardy; but, remember, I only do this on one condition—you hand me over that purse."

"Can I trust you?" she asked.

"Yes, I know you, you cat, and I don't want to feel the scratch of your claws. Fetch the purse, and I'll do what you want."

Again I heard her quick breathing—the next moment she had turned and rushed upstairs. I stepped suddenly down from my dangerous eminence, and hiding the poker just under my body—for I did not for a moment believe the man's words, and meant to lose my life hard if I lost it at all—resumed the stertorous breathing and the apparently profound slumber of the morphia victim. I heard the girl's footsteps returning through the silent house. Then she went upstairs to where the wounded man lay. His room was evidently over the dining-room, for I heard her steps moving about overhead. There was an awful silence of ten minutes. During that time, I think I lived through the worst moments of my life. Each nerve was stretched to the utmost—each faculty was keenly on the alert; I felt more and more certain that my chance of escape was of the smallest—against an armed ruffian I could do nothing. As long as I was alone in the room, I kept my eyes wide open, but a sudden and unexpected sound caused me to shut them quickly. I had seen a head protrude suddenly from out of the pantry window—it looked right down on me where I lay, and then softly and noiselessly withdrew.

A moment later the door of the dining-room was opened, and I heard Randall's heavy footsteps as he approached my sofa.

"No humbug," he shouted, in a loud voice. "If you are awake, open your eyes and say so. Wake up, I say, if you can. I had my suspicions of you just now—open your eyes."

I did not respond; my head was sunk low, my breathing was coming in longer and slower respirations than it had done when last the man bent over me. He put his hand roughly under my chin, raised my face and looked at me—then he removed his hand with an audible sigh of relief.

"He's all right," he said, aloud. "Lord, I got a fright just now—I fancied he looked at me when I thrust my head through that window, but I was mistaken—of course I was; he can't escape after that dose I gave him, and he drank the glass full—the glass was empty when I returned to the room. He's alive still, but not much more. I won't move him while he lives. If he dies like that fellow did in Australia it will be all over within an hour. Well, I have got the purse, and Rachel may do her worst now. I wonder what's keeping Jasper; I shall want him to help me move the body."

He began to pace up and down the room, not taking the least pains to keep quiet; he without doubt regarded me as practically dead.

"What a —— fool Ben was!" I heard him mutter, sitting down on the edge of the table; "but for me he'd have been in quod now; I told him not to fire that shot; he needn't have done it. What a fright the police got—it is as good as a play even to think of it. That big fellow went down like a ninepin. Ben shot him through the heart as clean as a whistle. How he had strength to give it back hot to Ben, is more than I can understand. But he is dead now, stone dead, and Ben will swing if I let this doctor go.

"If!" he exclaimed, bursting into another hoarse laugh; "why, he's quiet already; I do believe the chap is dead."

He again approached my side, pushed my head roughly round, and listened to my breathing. I had made it on purpose a little fainter, but it was still audible.

"He's going, just like the man did in the bush," muttered Randall. "Confound that Jasper, why ain't he in? I'll go to the door and listen for him—he ought to be back by now."

He left me—being so sure of his deadly work that he did

not even trouble to shut the dining-room door. I felt the cold air coming in through the open hall door, and suddenly stood up.

"I won't feign sleep any more," I said to myself; "if I am quick, I may be able to knock him senseless with this poker before he has time to fire at me."

I speculated whether I should follow the ruffian into the hall, but before I had time to act, my overstrained hearing had detected hurried sounds in the chamber overhead—footsteps fled across the room, they rushed downstairs, and the young wife burst into the dining-room. I came to meet her—she showed no surprise—she was evidently past surprise at that supreme moment; agony, terror, and despair were detected on her features.

"Oh, doctor, you are awake," she cried; "that is good—I knew he hadn't given you enough of that horrid drug to kill you; but come upstairs at once—he is bleeding his life away. Come, you may save him if you are quick. Oh, I love him madly—whether he is bad or good! I love him with all my heart. He is dying. Come, doctor, come."

I followed her upstairs. As I did so, I glanced back at the open hall door. I expected to see it blocked by the huge figure of the ruffian, Randall, but he must have gone to meet his pal, for the coast was clear. A fierce temptation shook me for a moment. From the wife's account, the man upstairs was evidently dying. If the wound were bleeding to the extent she described, no human help could save him. If I left the house now I might escape. The temptation came and went. Life was sweet, but my duty called me to the succour of one *in extremis*. I entered the sick room and approached the bed—the patient was alive, but little more. Over his features had already stolen the grey hue of death. One of his hands was extended outside the bed-clothes—from his lips continued to pour the flood of crimson life. I saw that the slightest attempt to move him, or even to administer remedies, would but accelerate the death which was waiting to claim him. I motioned to the wife to calm herself; she gave me a passionate glance of despair.

"Can't you do something?" she whispered.

"Nothing," I replied. "It would torture him to touch him —let him die in peace."

I took the patient's wrist between my thumb and finger—

the pulse was scarcely perceptible; it came in faint throbs at longer and longer intervals—the glazed eyes were partly open. The young wife flung herself on her knees by the side of the bed, and pressed feverish kisses on the man's extended hand.

"Oh, take me with you, Ben!" she panted.

Her words roused him—he made a feeble last effort to move—to speak—fresh blood poured from his lips—in that final struggle his spirit fled. I bent forward and pressed down the lids over the staring eyes. As I did so, Mrs. Randall sprang up and faced me.

"Is he dead?" she asked.

"Yes," I replied.

She pressed her hand to her forehead, as if she scarcely knew what she was doing.

"Try to keep calm," I said to her; "think of yourself—you are in danger."

"I know it," she said, "and so are you—listen, what is that?"

There was a noise downstairs. Heavy footsteps sounded through the little hall. I counted the steps—there were four.

"The man Jasper has returned," I said to the girl.

"Jasper," she said, in astonishment; "how do you know his name?"

"I heard your conversation with your brother-in-law. He has no intention of sparing my life, and went a moment or two ago to fetch a man called Jasper. I heard him mutter to himself that he would require Jasper to remove my dead body. He has been false to you: he is not going to keep his word."

Her face could scarcely turn any paler, but her breath came quickly. She gasped and suddenly clutched at the neck of her white dress, as if it were strangling her slender throat.

"I might have known," she said, in a hoarse voice, "but I was distracted, and I had no time to think. Hal is more fiend than man; his word signifies less than nothing—I might have known."

She tugged again at her dress, and pressed her hand to her forehead.

"Let me think," she said.

I did not interrupt her. I was listening to the footsteps

downstairs. For some reason they were quiet. The men had evidently not yet approached the dining-room. When they did so, and discovered my escape, all would undoubtedly be lost. They would make a sudden rush for the bedroom fully armed, and take no account of the man whom they supposed to be dying within the chamber.

During that moment's suspense, Mrs. Randall recovered her courage. She had been bending forward, something in the attitude of a broken reed; now she drew herself erect.

"I believe we shall manage them," she whispered; "anyhow, we'll try. My husband is dead, and I care nothing whatever for my life. You did what you could to save Ben, and I am your friend. Here is a case of revolvers."

As she spoke, she flew to the dressing-table, took up a case which lay upon it, and brought it forward.

"All the chambers are loaded," she said, handling the revolvers as she spoke; "take this and I will take the other. Now follow me: don't hesitate to fire if necessary."

"You had much better stay here," I said; "I believe I can fight my own way out with these fire-arms."

"You would not leave me to be butchered in cold blood?" she cried. "No, you can't manage them alone—there are two of them, and they are without scruple—I know them."

I said nothing further. My hearing, strained to the utmost, had detected the sound of the men's footsteps approaching the dining-room. I heard the door open and knew that they had entered the room. There was a full moment's pause, and then the bustling, eager, angry sound of incredulous and alarmed voices.

At that instant Mrs. Randall and I approached the head of the stairs. There was plenty of light in the hall, but where we stood was comparative shadow. Just as we reached the top of the last flight of stairs, the two ruffians, who had returned to the hall, looked up and caught sight of us. They both carried revolvers, but were evidently astonished to see us also furnished with deadly weapons.

"Fire at once, if necessary," whispered the young woman.

I saw her at the same moment cover Randall with her revolver.

"Hold!" he cried. "You've played me a dastardly trick, Rachel; you shall pay for this."

"Ben is dead, and my life is valueless," she replied. "Let

this man leave the house immediately, or I'll blow your brains out."

The ruffian turned his ugly eyes full on my face.

"So you think you have done me?" he said. As he spoke he backed a step into the hall. I covered him with my revolver. I saw him shrink, and his tone changed. "I see I must give you a chance," he cried. "You may go if you take an oath. As you hope to meet your God, swear that you will never tell what has happened here to-night! You can go, if you swear it; but if you don't, before Heaven I swear——"

"Folly," cried the high-strained girl's voice at my side; "of course the doctor won't swear. You know perfectly well you haven't a leg to stand on. If you or Jasper attempt to raise your revolvers, we'll both fire."

Hal swerved again, and looked uneasy—his full, loose lower lip shook, but the man Jasper was of tougher metal.

"We must do for 'em both," he said. "Why should our lives be sacrificed to the whim of a minx?"

"Jove!—you're right," cried Hal.

I saw him raise his revolver—he aimed it full at my forehead. But before he could touch the trigger, a sharp report sounded through the house—the revolver fell from the man's right hand—his arm dropped—he gave a howl of agony—Rachel had shot him clean through the shoulder. At the same moment, I covered Jasper with my revolver.

His courage oozed out of him at the sight of Hal. "For God's sake, don't fire, sir!" he called out.

"Put your revolver down, Jasper, or I'll shoot you," shouted Rachel. He instantly complied.

"Now, doctor, you must get out of this at once," cried the excited woman. "Make way, Jasper; Hal, get out of the way."

She pushed past me, running down the stairs, and before either of the men could prevent her, picked up their revolvers.

"Come," she said to me, "we are safe now; they have got no others."

The next moment we found ourselves in the open air. She had been as cool and alert as possible during the whole of this brief and terrible scene, but now she trembled so violently, I thought she would have fainted.

"Don't worry about me," she panted; "I'll be all right in a moment. I never fired at a man before, and I nearly took his life—well, I would, before I'd have allowed him to touch a hair of your head. He is badly wounded, and there'll be no more courage in him for a day or two. As to Jasper, he is wretch enough to follow us, only he has no fire-arms—stay, he might remember Ben's old gun. Well, that's not worth considering. I'll see you to the edge of the common, doctor; come, let us get off quickly."

"I can go alone," I said; "you are not fit to walk."

"I am; it will do me good," she said. "Come."

She plunged suddenly to her right—we found ourselves in a thicket of trees, and pursuing a winding path which I, alone, would never have discovered. We walked without articulating a single word for two to three miles. When we got to the edge of the common, Mrs. Randall paused abruptly.

"You are safe now," she said; "the railway station is not half a mile away, and that is the high road yonder."

"How am I to thank you?" I said.

"By not thanking me," she answered; "you did what you could for him. I tried to save you, but remember that my life is valueless."

"You have no right to say that—you are very young. Surely you can get yourself out of your present terrible predicament."

She shook her head.

"I don't know that I want to," she answered. Then she paused, and looked earnestly at me.

"You will, of course, give evidence against us?" she said.

I was not prepared to reply, and did not speak.

"Do not scruple to," she continued; "the life I lead is beyond endurance, and now that Ben is dead, I want to end it, one way or another."

"I think I can help you if you will let me," I said. "You will be in danger if you go back to the cottage. Let me try to get you into a place of safety."

"No," she said; "I am all right; I know how to manage them. I belong to them, and must take the rough with the smooth. Besides, my husband's body lies unburied, and I can kiss him again. Good-bye."

She turned as she spoke. The day was just beginning to break in the east, and I saw her white dress vanish amongst the furze-bushes and wild undergrowth of the common.

When I reached town, I sent a messenger to Scotland Yard

to ask an inspector to call upon me. I had a sort of hope that I might be in time to save Mrs. Randall, for, notwithstanding her brave words, I dreaded the fate that would be hers if she were left to the tender mercies of ruffians like her brother-in-law and Jasper. My interview with the police inspector resulted in his going down that very morning to the cottage on Steven's Heath. News of a daring burglary and of the murder of a policeman had already got into the papers, and my evidence was considered of the utmost value. In order to expedite matters, I accompanied the inspector to the scene of my last night's adventure.

The small house in which I had endured such long hours of agony looked calm and peaceful seen by the light of day. It was a rustic, pretty place; a few barn-door fowls strutted about; in a field near by were some downy chickens. Doubtless, the idea of the chicken farm was kept up as a sort of blind. On making inquiries, we found that the Randalls were known by their few neighbours as harmless, reserved sort of people, of the name of Austen; they had lived in the cottage for over two years; they had made no friends, and never until now had a breath of suspicion attached to them.

The cottage was two or three miles from any other dwelling, and beyond the fact that a young woman and two men lived there, the neighbours could give little information. The police and I passed now through the little porch and entered the hall, which was flooded with sunshine. The door stood wide open—a more peaceful spot could scarcely be imagined. It was almost impossible to connect so pretty a cottage with scenes of bloodshed and murder. I looked around me for any sign of Hal or Jasper, and still more anxiously for Mrs. Randall, but although we shouted and made a noise, no one appeared. Accompanied by the police I went upstairs. The dead man lay on the bed just where I had left him the night before—his eyes were closed, and someone had thrown a white sheet over him, but no sign of any human being was visible. The police and I searched the cottage from cellar to attic. Not a trace of Jasper or Hal could we discover—not a trace either of Mrs. Randall. A quantity of stolen goods, plate, and other valuables were found in one of the cellars, as well as some almost priceless wine, which was afterwards identified as the property of a gentleman who lived not far from my friends, the Mathisons.

For a long time large rewards were offered, and there was a hue and cry all over that part of the country for the three missing individuals—but from that day to now, no trace has been found of them. The dead man could tell no tales, and the living had vanished as completely as if they had never existed.

These things happened a few years ago, but even now, in the midst of my active life, I think at times of Mrs. Randall—of her youth, and of the horrible life which was hers. Is she still in the land of the living, or what has been her fate? I am not likely to be able to answer that question until the curtain is lifted.

"TO EVERY ONE HIS OWN FEAR"

"TO EVERY ONE HIS OWN FEAR"

A MONGST his friends Charlie Fane's name was always
spoken of as a synonym of good luck. I happened to
meet this gay and *débonnaire* youth during a short visit which
I paid to my friends, the Cullinghams, at their beautiful place
in Warwickshire. The time of year was towards Christmas,
and there was a merry house party at "The Chase." The old
house rang with mirth and festivity from morning to night.
The spirit of the time seemed to get into the rooms, and to
infect us all to a more or less degree. Even the elderly
amongst us yielded to the all-prevailing spirit of frolic, and
forgot for a time, in the most pleasurable manner in the
world, the graver side of life. There were several light-
hearted young fellows in the house, but amongst them all
Fane was the gayest. His spirits ran the highest, his wit was
the most appreciated, his songs were invariably encored, and
his society sought for wherever he turned. All alike petted
and fêted him—in short, his presence was looked upon as
sunshine, and his praise was on everyone's lips.

Cullingham, my host, was a grave, middle-aged man on the
shady side of fifty. Mrs. Cullingham was a charming hostess,
possessing, I think, only one failing, and that was an incessant
and almost tiresome habit of praising the hero of the hour—
Charlie Fane. It is tiresome to hear even the best person
always vaunted to the skies, but I must say of Charlie that he
took the good things which were said about him with so little
conceit or self-consciousness, that it was difficult to feel
annoyed when one heard him quoted as the best fellow of his
day. He was in high favour when I arrived at "The Chase,"
but before my brief visit terminated, he was more than ever
the cynosure of all eyes. Amongst the guests was a very
beautiful girl, of the name of Alice Lefroy. Charlie's susceptible heart was immediately smitten with her charms ; he

followed her about like a shadow, and it was more than evident to all present that Miss Lefroy was not unwilling to receive attentions from him. The happy youth made love in the most open and undisguised style, having little doubt that, according to his invariable good luck, he would obtain without much difficulty the object of his desire.

On the evening before I left "The Chase" to return to my London duties, I spent an hour or two with Cullingham in his smoking-room.

"By the way," I said, as I rose to say good-night, "you will let me know how affairs progress between Fane and Miss Lefroy. I am interested in them—in short, they look like a couple who have come straight from Eden, and have never had anything to do with the bad ways of this troublesome world."

Cullingham laughed in a rather strained manner when I spoke. He was silent for a moment, looking thoughtful.

"It isn't my affair, of course," he said, after a long pause; "but, nevertheless, I am not thoroughly happy about this business. Fane is one of the most attractive fellows I have ever come across."

"If he is attractive to Miss Lefroy, that is all right," I replied. "She evidently likes him—I do not think either of the young folks have taken much trouble to disguise their feelings."

"That is just it," said my host, "that is just what bothers me; Fane is in love with Alice, and I greatly fear that Alice is in love with him. Now it happens that she is engaged to another man."

"Impossible!" I said.

"It is only too true; she has been engaged for the last couple of years to a man considerably her senior, of the name of Pennington. Philip Pennington is sincerely attached to her, and until now I considered the engagement as a very happy one. When first she came, I regarded the little flirtation between her and Fane as nothing more than a joke, but now I begin to doubt whether I did wisely in not telling him of her engagement."

"I know Miss Lefroy very slightly," I said; "but the little I have seen of her makes me doubt whether it would be possible for so sweet and frank a girl to act with duplicity—she has doubtless mentioned her engagement to Fane. Well,

I am sorry. I did hope that couple would have made a match of it—they seemed so pre-eminently suited to each other."

"So they are, Halifax," said Cullingham. "I feel as sorry as you do at the present moment about the affair. I sincerely hope it is not serious, and will say something to Fane to-morrow."

Soon afterwards I bade my host "good night," and retired to my own room.

The hour was late, but I was not at all inclined for slumber. I sat down, therefore, by my cheerful fire, and taking up a book tried to engross myself in its contents. To. my surprise —for I am a voracious reader—I found I could not do so. Between me and the open page appeared, with tiresome reiteration, the face and figure of Fane. I saw with strange insistance the clear eyes, the straight, well-cut features, the broad, athletic figure, the muscular hands, the splendid physique. By his side I saw also the ethereal and exquisitely proportioned face and form of the fair young girl whom, after all, he might never hope to win.

"There comes a day when the luckiest man finds his luck forsake him—it is the course of life," I could not help muttering to myself. As this reflection came to me, I started suddenly to my feet: a sharp and somewhat imperative knock had come to my bedroom door.

I went quickly across the room and opened the door. Fane stood without.

"I hope you won't find me an awful nuisance," he said, "but I saw a light under your door—can you spare me five minutes of your time?"

It is my luck to find myself often appealed to in an emergency. This young man had never made a special friend of me up to this moment. One glance at his face, however, was sufficient to show that he meant to confide in me now. I was glad of it, for I had taken a great liking for him.

"Wait a moment," I said, "until I get into my coat; there is a fire in the smoking-room—we can go down there."

"Yes, we can have the smoking-room to ourselves," said Fane, "for every other soul in the house is in bed."

"Go down, then, and wait for me," I said. "I will join you in a moment."

I did so.

When I entered the smoking-room, Fane was standing with his back to the fire, which he had built up into a glowing and compact mass—he had also turned on the electric light, and the room looked cheerful.

"Now, what can I do for you?" I said, dropping into a chair as I spoke.

"Confound it!" he muttered.

He gnawed his moustache almost savagely, and looked down at me without adding to this exclamation. I waited for him to go on.

"It is awfully hard lines to worry you," he said; "but Alice and I——"

"Alice?" I interrupted.

"Oh, Miss Lefroy I mean—hang it all, you may as well know the truth—Miss Lefroy and I are engaged. Hear me out, please."

I was preparing to interrupt him, but sank back now in my chair and allowed him to finish his story.

"We are engaged," he said—his tone had a certain defiance in it—"it came about to-night, unexpectedly; I am coming to particulars in a moment or two. We are in trouble, I daresay you guess; but our engagement is hard and binding, thank Heaven! Alice thought we had best confide in you—it is a shame, of course, for you are not even a special friend—but she shrank from Cullingham or from Mrs. Cullingham knowing anything about it, and you are a doctor, and a good fellow, people say; may I go on?"

"You certainly may," I answered.

"Thanks. You see, Alice guessed all right about you— I won't tell you what she said—but I wish you could have seen her face——"

"Go on with your story now, my dear fellow," I interrupted.

"Alice is engaged to me—that is the main thing—it is to that rock I cling."

"But how can you be engaged to Miss Lefroy?" I said. "It is scarcely an hour ago since Cullingham informed me that she was the promised wife of a man of the name of Philip Pennington."

"Pennington is in the house," said Charlie, clenching his hand. "He arrived at Ashworth by the last train, and drove over in a fly—it was that hurried matters on. Alice wants to break with him, doctor—she never loved him—why, he is twenty years her senior. I vow before Heaven I won't give her up—now what is to be done?"

"It is an ugly business," I said. "I don't know that I ought to help you—you had no right to steal Pennington's promised bride from him."

"You mustn't blame Alice," he began, eagerly. "She told me of her engagement the first day I saw her, and showed me her ring; we played at love at first, and never knew that it was going to be reality until we found ourselves deep in the fire. Alice and I often sat and talked by the hour of Pennington; we saw no danger, and knew of none until to-night when she heard his voice in the hall—she and I were together in the conservatory. She turned like a sheet, and I, well, I broke down then; I had her in my arms in a minute, and, of course, after that, it was all up; but, hang it, Pennington thinks she is still engaged to *him*, and what is to be done? The thing must be broken off—it is a horrid business for her and for me, and for Pennington too, poor beggar! Now I think of it, I can almost pity him for having lost her."

"You want my advice?" I said, abruptly.

"Well, yes—that is, Alice thought—the fact is, we must consult someone, and you are in the house."

"I will tell you what I should do if I were you," I said.

"Yes?"

Fane remained standing—his good-humoured, happy face looked quite haggard—there were heavy lines round his mouth —he was as white as death.

"I should be man enough," I said, looking him full in the face as I spoke, "to leave this house by the first train in the morning, in order to give Miss Lefroy a fair chance of reconsidering the position."

Fane opened his lips to interrupt me, but I went on, doggedly.

"That is the right thing to do," I said; "go away at once. Give Miss Lefroy three months—you took her by surprise— let her know her own mind when you are not present to influence her. The fact is this, Fane, it is your plain duty to endeavour to look at things from Pennington's point of view—it is your duty to put yourself in his place. How would you feel if, during your absence, another man tried to alienate the affections of the girl you were engaged to? Remember, the fact of the engagement was never concealed from you."

"I know—I am a scoundrel," said Fane.

He turned his back abruptly, leant his elbow on the mantel-piece, and covered his face with his hands.

"You have done what many another hot-headed young fellow has done before you," I continued. "Up to the present your conduct has been excusable, but the test of your manhood will depend upon how you act now."

"I know," he said, turning fiercely round and looking at me; "but I can't do it, sir—before God, I can't!"

"Then I have nothing more to say," I remarked, rising as I spoke. "I am sorry for you and sorry for Pennington. Good-night."

I held out my hand as I spoke; he grasped it silently—his eyes would not meet mine. I left him and went back to my room.

I had to return to town by the first train in the morning, and did not think it likely that I should see Fane again. Cullingham saw me off. He informed me that Philip Pennington had arrived unexpectedly by the last train the night before.

I had scarcely any remark to make to this, for I could not betray young Fane's confidence, but I begged of Cullingham to let me know the issue of events.

"There 'll be the mischief to pay," he said, gloomily. "At the present moment neither Alice Lefroy nor Fane know of Pennington's arrival; of course, the fat will be in the fire now. Well, I will write to you, Halifax, when I have anything to say."

A moment later I was bowling away on the dog-cart which was to convey me to the station. My train left Ashworth at eight o'clock, and I had just ensconced myself comfortably in the corner of a first-class compartment, when a porter hastily opened the door and admitted a young lady. She threw up her veil the moment she saw me, and taking the seat opposite mine, bent forward impulsively.

"I thought you would be going to town by this train, and hoped I might have your company to London," she said. "You don't mind, do you?"

"I am surprised to see you, Miss Lefroy," I answered.

"But you are not angry with me?" she questioned. "Charlie told me of your interview with him last night. Under the circumstances, I could not meet Mr. Pennington, so I thought it best to leave 'The Chase'—Charlie will see him after breakfast and tell him everything."

She panted slightly as she spoke; she was a very fragile, beautiful girl. At the first glance one would suppose that she scarcely possessed the physique which would stand much shock; but as I observed her more closely I came to the conclusion that she was possessed of a considerable amount of tenacity of purpose, and might, on occasion, be obstinate, in a cause which she took to heart. It was not my place to find fault with her; I therefore saw that she had a foot-warmer, helped her to unfasten her rug from its strap, and, when the train was in motion, asked her how she contrived to get away without Cullingham's knowledge.

"Oh, I sneaked off," she said, with a little laugh; "my maid helped me. I left a note for Mrs. Cullingham, and we drove away by the back avenue. We saw your trap ahead of us most of the way. My maid is in a second-class compartment next to this. If you really wish it, I can join her at the next station."

"By no means," I answered; "I shall be glad to have your company up to town."

I unfolded a newspaper as I spoke, and for a short time engrossed myself in its contents. Looking up presently, I observed that Miss Lefroy was gazing fixedly out of the window, and that her pretty soft eyes were full of tears.

"Well," I said, laying down my paper, "I suppose you want to tell me your story?"

"Oh, no; I don't wish to say much," she answered, in a steady, grave voice—"there is not much to tell. My mind is absolutely made up. I shall marry Mr. Fane—if I do not marry him I will never marry anybody. It is quite true that for the last couple of years I have been engaged to Philip Pennington, but I never loved him. I am an orphan, and have no money, and Philip is rich—enormously rich; and my aunt, Mrs. Leslie—she lives in London—I am going to her now—urged and urged the marriage—so I consented to be engaged, but I did not love him. That fact did not matter perhaps, until the moment came when I learned to love another man. You must know for yourself that under existing circumstances it would be a sin for me to marry Philip Pennington."

"That is the case," I replied, after a pause. "I am

sincerely sorry for you. May I ask what you intend to do when you get to town?"

"I shall tell Aunt Fanny the truth, and will then immediately write to Philip—but he will have heard the story before then."

"Do you mind telling me what sort of a man he is?"

She looked distressed. "People think a good deal of him," she said, after a pause; "but I—I have never really trusted him. Oh, it seems a dreadful thing to say of the man you expected at one time to marry. Please don't ask me any more —it is wrong of me to have said even what I did."

She turned her head aside, and drawing down her veil sank back in her seat. At the next station some other passengers got into the compartment, and I had not an opportunity of making any further inquiries. At Paddington I saw Miss Lefroy into a cab, and as I said "Good-bye," told her that if at any time I could be of service to her she had but to command me. I then returned to Harley Street.

A week passed before I heard anything further of Fane or Miss Lefroy; then one morning a letter arrived from Cullingham—it was satisfactory as far as it went.

"You will be anxious to hear full particulars with regard to what I am pleased to call Fane's entanglement," said Cullingham, after he had prefaced his letter with remarks of general interest. "By the way, I believe that little goose Alice travelled up to London in the same train with you. Imagine her sneaking off in that fashion! However, now to particulars. I think I gave you to understand that I always had a high respect for Pennington, which I am sure you will share when I tell you how well he has behaved in this matter. On the morning you left, Fane had an interview with me. He spoke in a very manly way, poor lad, and told me everything. I saw that the case was a serious one, and that neither of the pair were really much to blame. Fane begged of me to break the news to Pennington, who was already, I could see, very much annoyed by Alice's unexpected departure. I had a bad quarter of an hour when I told my old friend how matters really stood. The tidings were scarcely pleasant ones, but there was no help for it—I could not mince matters. Pennington's *fiancée* had given her heart to another man. That being the case, I assured him that his own engagement could not possibly go on. I confess that he looked ugly for a time, and refused to see Fane at all.   But he recovered himself in the most surprising manner, and told me on the following morning that he withdrew from his position as Miss Lefroy's lover, and would do what he could for the young couple.   This was more than could have been expected of him, and I told him what I thought of his generosity.   He went up to town that day and saw Alice; her aunt, Mrs. Leslie, wrote to say no one could have behaved better than Pennington.   She said she felt very angry with Alice, who shrank from the poor fellow with ill-concealed dislike.   He took no notice of this, but spoke to her in the most affectionate way.

"'I see, child,' he said, 'that I cannot be your husband; but, as I am sincerely attached to you'—here his voice quite shook—'I am willing and anxious now to act the part of a father.   I will do all in my power for you and Fane, and you must both arrange to pay me, as soon as possible, a long visit at Birstdale Abbey, my place in Roxburgh.'

"This arrangement was made on the spot, although Miss Lefroy began by objecting to it very strongly.   Pennington and Mrs. Leslie, however, over-ruled all objections.   Pennington is to have a large house party in February, and Mrs. Leslie, Alice, and Fane are to be amongst the most favoured guests.   Fane is poor, and Alice has no fortune, so the young couple must not think of matrimony for some little time.

"Yours truly,
"JOHN CULLINGHAM."

I had scarcely read this letter before my servant threw open the door to admit a visitor.   I was sitting in my breakfast-room at the time; I raised my eyes to see who my guest was, and then rose up with a smile to see and congratulate Charlie Fane.

"I wonder if you have heard the news?" he said.

"I am just reading about it," I said, pointing to Cullingham's letter as I spoke.   "Sit down, won't you?   May I give you some breakfast?"

"No, thanks; I have had some at my club.   Well, I am the luckiest fellow in the world."

"You have my best wishes," I answered.   "You had a generous rival, Fane; few men, under the circumstances, would have acted as Pennington has done."

"So everyone says," replied Fane.

He sank down on a seat and, resting his elbow on his knee, pressed his hand to his head—his eyes sought the floor. He had just won the girl of his choice, but at this moment he scarcely looked like a rapturous or happy lover.

"What's up now?" I could not help muttering to myself.

The thought had scarcely rushed through my brain before Fane fixed his eyes on my face.

"You are surprised to find me in the blues," he said. "Of course, it goes without saying that I am the luckiest dog in Christendom. I am madly in love with Alice, and she with me, bless her. As to our engagement being a long one, we both of us are prepared to face that. Pennington has been good—well, to tell the truth, I wish he had been worse—it is horrible to take favours from a fellow whom you have just robbed of his dearest possession. The fact is, doctor, Alice and I hate beyond words the idea of going to Birstdale Abbey.

"That seems a trifle," I began.

"I know—I ought not to mention it. Pennington's kindness is almost overpowering; he has not only taken Alice completely under his wing, by regarding her now, as he says, in the light of a dearly-loved daughter, but he has done the same for me. He talks to me by the hour about my prospects, and assures me that he will not leave a stone unturned to further my interests. Nevertheless, ungrateful as it is of me to say the thing, I can't abide him. The thought of going to stay at his place is most repugnant to me—Alice shares my antipathy."

"I can quite understand your feelings," I replied; "were I in your place it is possible that I should be similarly affected; but may I ask why you go?"

"I cannot get out of it—nor can Alice. Pennington wrung a promise from her when he went to release her from her engagement to him. At such a moment she was not in a position to refuse him anything in reason that he asked. Mrs. Leslie, Alice's aunt, is also most anxious that we should keep on friendly terms with Pennington. She is to accompany us to the Abbey—we go on Monday. I assure you, sir, I by no means look forward with pleasure to the visit."

"Well, after all, it is not a serious matter," I said, rising as I spoke, "and as you yourself admit, you owe a great deal to Mr. Pennington for behaving so well."

"I should think I do. The fact is, I'm a brute for not worshipping him; he has done even more than I have told you. I am a good linguist, and he believes that he can give me substantial help in that direction. Pennington's brother is in the Embassy, and Pennington is trying to get me a post as his secretary. Of course, that would mean foreign service, and parting from Alice for a time, but would eventually lead to our marriage. Yes, the man has behaved like a brick; nevertheless, I hate the idea of staying at his place."

"I am afraid you must bear it," I said.

"Yes, of course."

Here Fane paused—he raised his eyes and looked full at me. "It is a sin to waste your time with this sort of grumble," he said. "You don't suppose I have come here this morning just to whine about such a small matter. The fact is, I want to consult you on something else. Will you please regard my visit as professional?"

"You are surely not in bad health?" I asked, looking in astonishment at the splendid, athletic-looking youth.

"Not really, but I sometimes fancy that I have something wrong with my heart. When a man contemplates marriage, he ought to be certain that he is sound in every point. Will you examine my heart, doctor?"

"Certainly, if you wish it."

I rose as I spoke, fetched my stethoscope, and soon had the satisfaction of telling Fane that he must not give way to nervous fancies, for his heart was perfectly sound in every particular. I thought my words would reassure him, but his face still looked pale, his eyes were full of gloom, and the haggard lines which I had noticed about his jovial, good-humoured face when he first told me of his engagement to Miss Lefroy again manifested themselves.

"I cannot get over it," he said. "I must confide in you. Do you know that once, as a boy, I was supposed to be dead?"

"You had an attack of catalepsy?" I asked.

"You would perhaps call it by that name—anyhow, it was a sort of trance. May I tell you the story?"

"Take a seat, Fane. I am much interested in this subject, and would be glad to listen to any information you can give me."

"You believe that death can sometimes be assumed?"

"I know it for a fact," I answered.

"I am relieved to hear you say so—I have asked that question of more than one doctor, and in almost every case have received a smile of derision."

"These assumed deaths are not so common as some nervous people imagine," I continued, "but I firmly believe that there are cases on record where persons have been buried alive. This would be more likely to occur in foreign countries, where interment, as a rule, takes place on the day of the death. There is only one remedy for such a state of things— but that, perhaps, is too professional to interest you."

"Not at all—I am morbidly interested in this subject, as you will know when I tell you my own experience."

"The law, as it at present stands, is not sufficiently strict with regard to the death certificate," I said. "No doctor ought to give a certificate of death, under any circumstances whatever, without having viewed the body. As the law now stands, if for any reason it is inconvenient for the doctor to be present after death, he has only to put in the words : ' As I am informed.' Apart from any danger of burial alive, which is, of course, very slight, the present arrangement leaves a loophole for crime. The law should be altered on this point without delay."

"I am heartily glad that those are your views," answered Fane. "I only wish that every doctor in the land could hear you. Now then, I will tell you my own story. My mother died when I was eighteen—she died suddenly of failure of the heart. I was her only son—we were passionately attached to each other. I left her quite well on a certain morning, and came back after a day's fishing to find her no more. The news came on me as a sudden and awful blow. I succumbed to it immediately, and became very ill. I don't remember how I felt, nor exactly from what I suffered, but I lay in bed, refusing food, and with a dull weight of indifference which possessed me more and more strongly day after day. My nurse and attendants were, I feel convinced, under the impression that I was quite unconscious, but the strange and terrible thing is, that this was never the case. I heard the faintest whisper which was breathed in the room in which I lay—I understood with almost preternatural clearness everything that went on. I knew when the doctor visited me, and when the nurse moved about by my bedside, and when my

mother's old servant bent over me and sobbed. There came
a day when I heard the doctor say :—

"'The case is hopeless—he is dying—nothing more can be
done for him. There is no use worrying him with medicines.
He will pass away quietly within the next hour or two. Let
me know when he dies ; I will send you down a certificate.'

"The doctor was an old man—he had attended my mother
for years. After pronouncing my death warrant, I heard him
leave the room. I lay motionless on my back with my eyes
tightly shut—the weight which pressed me down grew heavier
and heavier. The nurse lingered for a time in the room. I
knew she bent over me—I felt her breath on my cheek—
there was a slight warmth and an impression of added light,
and I think she was moving a candle before my eyes. I think
also that she placed a glass over my lips to see if there were
any breath ; after a time she left me. I was alone. I felt
myself incapable of moving an eyelid—I was bound tightly as
if in solid iron. After a long time—it seemed almost like
eternity to me—I heard the door open again, and a brisk
young step came over the threshold.

"'You say he died half an hour ago, Mrs. Manning?' said
a voice, which I recognised as belonging to another doctor of
the same firm.

"'Yes, sir, about half an hour ago,' was the reply.

"A stab of horror went through my heart. I made a frantic
effort to move, but could not stir. The invisible irons bound
me down more tightly than ever.

"'Well, as I am here, I will have a look at him,' said the
doctor.

"He approached the bedside, raised my eyelids—I could
see him, though I could not stir—and looked into my eyes. I
watched him through an awful film—he felt for my pulse, and
finally applied his stethoscope to my heart. There was a long
pause, and then I heard him say the following blessed
words :—

"'I don't believe he is dead—there are still sounds of the
heart's action, though faint.'

"How I blessed that doctor—his words lifted me from hell
to Heaven. He took one of my hands and suddenly raised
my arm into the air—it remained in the position where he had
placed it. He again pressed it down, and it fell.

"'This is a case of catalepsy,' he said. 'There can be no

certificate of death given at present.   Keep the room warm,
and at intervals introduce a little nourishment into the mouth
by means of a feather.   I will come and see the patient again
to-morrow.'

"I was told afterwards that I lay in this state for two or
three days, and was finally restored to animation by means of
electricity.   After this had been applied several times, I sat up
and opened my eyes.

"Now, sir," continued Fane, taking his handkerchief from
his pocket and wiping the moisture from his forehead as he
spoke, "but for the fact of the other doctor coming on the
chance to inquire how I was, I might—indeed, I may add,
I should—have been buried alive."

"Your story is full of interest," I said, "but it has upset you,
and the tale is, undoubtedly, a gruesome one.   I have listened
to it with attention, and find that it confirms my own theory to
the letter.   Now let us turn to more cheerful topics."

"I cannot do so, doctor.   I have told you this story with a
reason.   You may laugh at me or not, but you have got
to hear me out."

"I shall certainly not laugh at you.   Tell me all that is in
your mind."

"I was eighteen when I ran that narrow shave of being
buried alive," said Fane ; "I am now twenty-eight.   Ten years
have gone by since that terrible date.   When you first saw me
at 'The Chase,' what did you think of me ?"

"That you were the jolliest, most thoughtless, and happiest
youth of my acquaintance," I replied.

He smiled faintly.

"I always take people in," he said.   "Over and over, I
have been assured that I personate the happy boy to perfection.   Now listen.   I am not a boy, I am a man—a man,
haunted ever with a terrible and inexpressible dread."

"What is that ?" I asked.

"That I shall once again fall into a trance and be really
buried alive."

"Oh, come, you talk nonsense," I said, rising as I spoke.
"Your nerves are not as strong as they ought to be.   I
scarcely like to tell you that you ought to be ashamed of yourself, but seeing that you are in perfect health, and are young,
and just engaged to the girl you love, it seems to me to be
your manifest duty to cast off these dismal imaginings."

"It may be my duty, but, all the same, I cannot do it," he replied, doggedly. "Let me tell you something, sir. It was never your lot to lie as I did, in what seemed an iron cage, and to hear your death pronounced when the part of you that felt and suffered was alive and full of vigour. What my tortured spirit underwent during the few hours of that one day I have no words to express. God! I recal the horror now. Scarcely a night passes that the memory of it does not come back to me. There are times when the thought of it, and the inexpressible fear that it may return, almost drive me mad."

I saw that the poor fellow was shaking in uncontrollable agitation; his terrors were real; they were not to be gainsaid.

"To everyone his own fear," I murmured. Poor Fane's was in truth a ghastly one.

"I see," I answered, "that what you suffer from is very real. It has been your fate to go through a very terrible experience. Try nevertheless to take comfort in what I am about to tell you—a repetition of such a state of things is almost impossible."

He shook his head.

"I cannot reason about it, doctor," he said. "It seems to me that a repetition of such a state of things is all too probable. There are times when this horror affects me much less acutely than others. Just now I am in the full throes of the agony. There are moments when I feel completely overpowered with a premonition of a coming catastrophe—such is my feeling with regard to this visit to Birstdale Abbey. I am convinced that I shall have a cataleptic seizure while there. Now, I know, that from a common-sense point of view this is all nonsense; but the fact is, there is not a man living who can reason me out of my conviction. I know perfectly well that Pennington does not love me. Why should he?—I have ruined his life; I have taken Alice away from him. Although the man looks so cool and quiet, I am persuaded that he is still consumed by passion for her. Think of the matter yourself, doctor—why, of course he hates me. If, for any reason, I were to fall into a trance while at Birstdale, what more likely than that I should be quickly buried. Do you think it would be to Pennington's advantage to keep me above ground for a considerable time, on the off chance that I might not be dead? What would his local doctor know of the peculiar conditions of such a trance as mine? Yes,

I should be laid in my grave, and by-and-by Pennington would marry Alice. She would grieve for me, poor little girl, but Pennington is stronger than she, and by-and by he would compel her to become his wife. I don't trust him—I know he is good to me, but I hate the fellow."

"Listen to me, Fane," I said. "It is my duty to speak to you very seriously. The horror to which you allude has acted on your nerves to a dangerous degree. If you do not quickly overcome your overwrought feelings, they may assume the magnitude of a monomania, and then you will be the wretched victim of a peculiar form of insanity. It rests entirely with yourself to prevent this state of things."

"Not quite," he replied.

His hands shook—his troubled eyes sought the ground. Suddenly he looked up at me.

"I believe you pity me?" he said.

"From my heart I do."

"Then will you make me a promise?" he asked, with great eagerness.

"I will do anything in my power to reassure and comfort you."

"If at any time the news of my death should reach you, will you *personally* ascertain beyond doubt that death has actually occurred?"

"You may be far away from me when you die," I answered. "Remember you are many years my junior. I hope it will be your fate to follow, not precede me, into the Land of Shades.'

"If you die first, there is nothing more to be said," he replied; "but if you are alive, and if I am anywhere in the British Isles, will you make me a promise that I shall not be buried without your verifying my death?"

I looked him full in the eyes.

"I will," I answered.

He shivered, and tears of actual relief sprang to his eyes. I laid one of my hands on his broad shoulder.

"Listen to me, Fane. In a case of this kind two words are enough. You have my promise. Now rest happy and turn your thoughts to healthier subjects."

"I will do so—thank you—God bless you!"

He took up his hat, and a moment or two later he left me.

When he had gone, I went to my day-book and made certain notes. I then locked the book, and put it back into the drawer which it usually occupied. Fane was not the first man who had got me to promise that I would take measures to ascertain that his death was genuine, before he was buried and put out of sight. Fane's fear was shared by others, but I had never seen it in such an exaggerated form as in his case. He was a man doubtless with a morbid, nervous, hereditary strain, and was all the more likely to fall a victim to cataleptic seizures. I felt sure, however, that my promise had comforted him, and hoped that the visit which he dreaded would not lead to any disastrous results.

A fortnight afterwards he wrote to me. His letter was dated from Birstdale Abbey, and was quite cheerful in tone. He assured me that Pennington made a delightful host—that Alice and he were enjoying themselves to their hearts' content —that the weather was crisp and fine, and that his own health was much better.

"Pennington is a good fellow," he said, in conclusion. " I am almost certain to get that foreign post. If such is the case, our marriage need not be deferred more than a couple of years—Alice is only eighteen now, and she will not at all mind waiting. Pennington acts like a father to her, and she assures me that she is beginning quite to like him in that capacity. We are likely to stay here for another month. If you will allow me, I will call to see you when I return to London.—Yours sincerely, CHARLIE FANE."

There was a P.S. to the letter, which ran as follows :—

"I have not forgotten your promise, doctor—it lifts an enormous weight from my mind."

I received this letter at breakfast time, but had not time to read it until I was going my rounds in the afternoon. I was pleased to learn that things were going well with the young pair, and also that Fane was overcoming the morbid distress which if indulged in might destroy the peace of his life. It was on the evening of that same day that my servant brought in an evening paper, and laid it as usual on my writing-table. I took it up, and opening it at random, my eyes fell on the following words :—

"SAD ACCIDENT FROM DROWNING.—Mr. Charles Fane, a young man of about twenty-eight years of age, met his death in a tragic manner on Tuesday night on Loch Ardtry. The weather was exceptionally fine, and the young gentleman went out duck-shooting by moonlight. His boat evidently sprang a leak, and must have filled with water when in the middle of the lake. The unfortunate man started to swim for the shore, but the exertion and shock must have caused failure of the heart's action, for he was discovered early on Wednesday morning clinging to some water-weeds, with his head well out of water, but quite dead. The melancholy occurrence has caused the deepest grief at Birstdale Abbey, the country seat of Philip Pennington, Esq., where Mr. Fane was staying."

I read the paragraph with horror—the paper fell from my hands. In the room in which I now sat, Fane had talked to me less than three weeks ago, telling me of his premonition of a coming catastrophe. I had naturally thought nothing of his fears. Poor youth! as the sequel showed, he had reason for them. He was dead—he had died from drowning. Was he dead? I started up with impatience—I remembered my promise.

"I must see to this," I murmured to myself; "the lad trusted me. That death must be verified."

I stooped and lifted up the paper which lay on the floor, and carefully read the paragraph over again.

"Failure of the heart's action," I repeated. "When the body was found the head was well out of water."

When I examined Fane's heart a short time ago, it was in a perfectly healthy condition; he was a man of robust frame, in the prime of youth. Would his heart's action be likely to fail to the extent of causing death during a short swim? Then, on the other hand, his was the temperament most favourable to the cataleptic state. He had already suffered from trance. Certainly this death must be verified, and the duty lay with me. I rang the bell sharply—Harris appeared.

"Bring me the A B C at once," I said.

He left the room to fetch it, and then stood by while I looked up the various trains. I remembered having heard Fane say that Castleton was the nearest station to Birstdale Abbey. The train to Haworth stopped at Castleton. The next train would leave St. Pancras at 9.15 p.m.

"I am going north almost immediately, Harris," I said. "Put some things into my portmanteau, and have a hansom at the door in time for me to catch the 9.15 train at St. Pancras."

" Yes, sir," replied my servant. He quickly left the room.

I hurried to my consulting-room to arrange one or two matters, and to write a note to the doctor who looks after my most important cases during my absence. I had scarcely finished the note before Harris entered with a telegram.

" The messenger is waiting," he said.

I opened the little missive, and saw to my dismay that it was a request that I should immediately visit a patient about fifty miles out of London who was taken with an apoplectic seizure. I could not go north that night. I sent a reply to the telegram, naming the train by which I would arrive at Dorking, and then stretching out my hand prepared to fill in another form. I had a moment of anxious thought before doing this. After a little reflection I decided to address my second telegram to Miss Lefroy. It ran as follows :—

" Have just seen account of accident in *Westminster Gazette.* Defer funeral until my arrival.—HALIFAX."

Both my telegrams being dispatched, I soon afterwards went off to visit my patient in the country. I found him dangerously ill, and saw that there was no chance of my leaving him that night, nor probably during the following day. The case was one of life or death, and it was impossible for me to trust it to the hands of another. Nevertheless, my promise to poor young Fane kept always rising up before me. At any cost it must be fulfilled. Harris brought me down my letters on the following morning, and amongst them was a telegram from Miss Lefroy.

" Mr. Pennington does not wish to postpone funeral—I am distracted—come at once," she wired.

To this telegram I sent an instant reply—I addressed it now boldly to Pennington himself—it ran as follows :—

" I am under a promise to verify the death of Charles Fane, but am unfortunately detained here with an anxious case. Impossible for me to go north to-day. Get local doctor to verify death by opening vein.—CLIFFORD HALIFAX, Harley Street."

I sent off the telegram, but my uneasiness continued. As the hours of the day flew by, and the patient, for whom I was fighting death inch by inch, grew gradually worse and worse, I could not help thinking of the bright-looking, happy-faced young man who yet in some ways had such a sombre history. Again and again the question forced itself upon me—Is he really dead! May not this, after all, be a second condition of trance?

At three o'clock that afternoon my patient died. I returned to town by the next train, having made up my mind to go down to Birstdale Abbey that night. When I arrived at home, Harris told me that a gentleman had called to see me who expressed regret at my absence, but said he would look in again later—he gave no name. On my consulting-room table, amongst a pile of letters, lay one telegram. I opened it first —it was from Miss Lefroy.

"Why don't you come? Dr. Bland will not open vein. Coffin is to be screwed down to-night. I don't think he is dead.—ALICE LEFROY."

"Harris," I said, "wait one moment. I must write a telegram, which you are to send off immediately."

I wrote one quickly, addressing it to Miss Lefroy. It ran thus :—

"Am starting by the 9.15 from St. Pancras. Do not have lid of coffin screwed on.—HALIFAX."

I had scarcely written the words, and Harris was about to leave the room with the telegram, when there came a ring at my front door; he went to open it, and the next moment a tall, aristocratic-looking man of middle age was ushered into my presence. He came up to me with a certain eagerness, and yet with an undeniable self-repression of manner.

"I must introduce myself," he said; "my name is Philip Pennington."

I was startled at seeing him, but, concealing any evidence of emotion, asked him to seat himself.

"I am glad you have called," I answered, "and you are just in time—I am about to start for your part of the world."

"I thought that highly probable," he said, "and have come here now on purpose to save you the trouble. I received your telegram at the station to-day, just when I was leaving for London—I thought the best thing I could do would be to answer it in person: but in order to assure you that no stone has been left unturned, I sent a messenger on with it to our local doctor, Bland, who, superfluous as it is, has doubtless acceded to your strange request. The poor fellow is to be conveyed to his father's place in Somersetshire early to-morrow, and the coffin, by my orders, will be fastened down to-night."

"That cannot be," I replied; "I am under a promise to Fane to verify the death. I feared this morning that I could not do so in person, but the patient who was then detaining me has since died, and I am at liberty to start for the north. I shall have just time to catch the 9.15 train, and can examine the body early in the morning."

As I was speaking Pennington looked disturbed. He had the sort of face which can best be described as a wooden mask —the features were regular and even handsome—the eyes full and well-shaped—the man wore his years lightly, too, not looking to the casual observer anything like the age I believed him to be; but the absence of all expression—the extreme thinness of the lips, and a certain sinister cast of the eyes inclined me not to trust him from the first. As I looked at him I understood Fane's antipathy, and wondered how, under any circumstances, Alice Lefroy could have promised herself to this man. He sat calmly in his chair now—his mental depression only visible in a certain twitch of his lips, which a man less cognizant of the human physiognomy might never have observed. While I was reading him, he was evidently reading me—his eyes travelled to a little clock on the mantelpiece, which pointed to twenty minutes after eight—in a very few moments I must start for St. Pancras, if I would catch the 9.15 train.

"You will doubtless understand for yourself, doctor," he said, speaking slowly, and perhaps with the idea of killing time, "that I can have no possible dislike to your making any experiments you please on the body of poor young Fane. His death is most tragic, and has filled us all with the most lively sense of grief; but as he is dead—dead beyond recall—it seems to me unnecessary to excite false hopes and to waste the valuable time of a busy London doctor, on what must certainly prove a wild-goose chase."

"I understand," I answered, "but a promise is a promise, Mr. Pennington. I am obliged to you for calling, and would, perhaps, feel less inclined to go to Birstdale Abbey if my telegram of this morning had been attended to. Had your local doctor opened the vein and thus proved death beyond doubt, I should have felt that I had kept my promise to poor Fane to the best of my ability."

"Why do you assume that he has not done so?" asked Pennington.

I stretched out my hand, and taking Miss Lefroy's telegram from the table, gave it to him to read.

His thin lips twitched most visibly then, and I saw his eyelids jerk as if he had received a sort of shock.

"You understand," he said, abruptly, a contraction of pain coming between his brows, "that the man who is now dead has been in life my bitterest and cruellest rival. I love that girl to distraction. For her own sake, and because my love is unselfish, I gave her to another; but now that he is dead, there may be hope for me. Why should she be tortured with unnecessary and false hopes? The man is dead—dead as a nail—there is not a doctor in Europe who could give him back his life."

I stood up as he spoke. "I happen to know Fane's story," I said, with a certain significance. "He died from an accident —that is, if he is dead."

Pennington stood up also at these words, and his lips curled sarcastically.

"Really, doctor," he said, "for a man of the day—an up-to-date person, as I presume you call yourself—your faith is extraordinary."

I did not reply to this taunt.

"It so happens," I said, "that Fane suffered from a condition of trance ten years ago—he was found now with his head above water. I will not consent to the coffin being screwed down until the death is verified. You do it at your peril, Mr. Pennington."

"Then you insist on going north?"

' I do, and, pardon me, I have not a moment to lose—I have only just time to catch my train."

Pennington shrugged his shoulders.

"I can say nothing further," he answered. "I came up to town this morning to make some arrangements with regard to the funeral. As you are going to Birstdale Abbey, doctor, of course, you must come as my guest—I am also returning by the 9.15 train."

"Then will you share my hansom?" I asked.

"With pleasure," he replied.

A moment or two later we were bowling away as quickly as possible to St. Pancras Station. My companion's manner had now completely altered; he was the suave and agreeable man of the world. He kept up a continual strain of light conversation, touching, with much intelligence and force of observation, on many subjects of the day. He was a well-read man, and, I also perceived, a somewhat profound thinker. But all through the conversation, I could not fail to perceive that he was still evidently on guard, also that he was watching me. At St. Pancras he left me for a few minutes, and I presently saw him issue out of the telegraph office. He was doubtless sending a telegram to countermand my order with regard to the coffin. If it were screwed down before we arrived, all would be lost.

I am certainly not given to premonitions, but I had a premonition almost from the moment that I heard of poor Fane's accident that he was not really dead; there was an uncomfortable want of certainty about the whole thing which made me anxious for my own sake, as well as because I had given a promise to see this thing out myself. There is much talk at the present day of premature interment, and although far more than half the stories are utterly unworthy of credence, there is a substratum of truth in this horror, which ought to receive more serious attention than it has hitherto done. At rare intervals people in a state of trance have been committed to the grave. If Fane were only in a cataleptic state, and if a shock had produced it once, it surely might do so a second time—the fact of screwing down the coffin lid would make the assumed death in a few moments an actual one. Our train would start in three minutes. I looked full at Pennington when he came up to my side.

"You will forgive my asking you a blunt question?" I said.

"Ask what you please, Dr. Halifax," he replied, looking me straight in the eyes.

"Have you sent a telegram to the Abbey countermanding my order?"

"I have not," he said, without the smallest hesitation.

There was nothing further to be said, but I knew the man lied to me. The next moment we took our seats in the railway carriage, and were soon steaming out of London.

My feelings were the reverse of comfortable, but perceiving on reflection that I could now do absolutely nothing, and must wait as best I could the issue of events, I ensconced myself in a corner of the carriage and tried to court sleep. I had been up all the previous night and was naturally very weary, but the state of suspense is not conducive to slumber, and I soon found it hopeless to woo the fickle goddess. Pennington sat opposite to me. We had two fellow-passengers in the other corners of the carriage, but they were both in the land of dreams. Pennington, on the other hand, was as wide awake as I was. He had provided himself with a small reading lamp, which he now fastened to his side of the carriage, and taking out a copy of the *Times* pretended to absorb himself in its contents. The light fell full upon his face, and I was able to watch it without being myself observed. I saw that he was in reality not reading a word. I also perceived that, notwithstanding his outward calm of demeanour, he was in reality a highly nervous man. He must have felt my eyes upon him, for he suddenly threw down his paper, and bending forward began to speak to me.

"Yes," he said, "the whole thing was most tragic."

"Tell me how it occurred," I said. "Up to the present, remember, I have only seen the very bald newspaper report."

"I fancy the newspapers have got the exact truth," replied Pennington, in his driest voice. "On Tuesday Fane was in the best of health and the highest spirits. He was, as perhaps you know, an excellent sportsman, and, as the night was fine, he asked my permission to go out duck-shooting on Loch Ardtry. Part of this magnificent piece of water belongs to my property. He intended to be home soon after midnight, and when he did not appear at the given hour, we were none of us specially alarmed. I ordered the side entrance to be left on the latch, and we all went to bed, our natural supposition being that he had found excellent sport and was loth to return home as long as the moon was high in the heavens. I rose early on the following morning, and went out just when the dawn was breaking. I was under the supposition then that Fane was snug in his bed for some hours. I strolled down to the margin of the lake, and one of the first objects that met my horrified eyes was the body of the unfortunate fellow—his head above water—his hands clutching some water-weeds—his eyes shut and his face cold and pallid. I saw him simultaneously with two gardeners who were on their way to work. We brought him to the house and sent for the doctor. He pronounced life extinct, and said that Fane had probably been dead for some hours. As the body was found with the head above water, the death could not be attributed to drowning, and our doctor supposed it to be due to heart failure. The verdict was, naturally, death by accident and shock. I think that is the whole story."

"Not quite," I replied. "How did Fane happen to be on the middle of the lake in an unseaworthy boat?"

"Oh, that I can't say," replied Pennington; he turned the sheet of his paper as he spoke. "The boats had not been used for some little time, but I was under the impression that they were all water-tight."

"Then the boat he used, sank to the bottom of the lake?"

"Yes."

"Has it been raised?"

"Not yet; we have been too much disturbed to worry about such a trifle as the lost boat."

"Nevertheless, the boat is of great importance," I said. "With your permission, I should wish it to be raised immediately, in order that it may be examined."

"Really, doctor, you are very persistent," said Mr. Pennington, a shade of annoyance flitting for a moment round his thin lips, and as soon vanishing. "Of course, it can be done if you wish it," he added, in a few moments, "that is, when the funeral is over." Do you propose to make a long stay in the north?"

"I shall stay until I have got the business through about which I am coming down," I answered, somewhat shortly.

We relapsed into silence after this, which was broken in about half an hour's time by Pennington, who said, with a profound sigh :—

"Alice has behaved far better than I could have expected."

"She is doubtless sustained by hope," I said.

"What folly this is, doctor; you must know that there can be no possible hope—the man is as dead as a door-nail."

"Nevertheless, she does not think him dead," I replied; "but we will soon see."

An ugly smile crept round his face—he did not reply.

We reached Castleton about four in the morning. Pennington's carriage was waiting for us, and we drove straight to Birstdale Abbey. As we approached the house, I saw that it was well lit up, and even noticed figures flitting behind the blinds. When our carriage-wheels were heard crunching the gravel, the entrance door was flung open, a servant appeared, and the next instant a small, girlish figure ran down the steps.

"Alice, you ought to be in bed," said Pennington, in a tone of annoyance.

"Is Dr. Halifax with you?" she asked, pushing him aside.

"Yes, yes; but what does that matter to you? Have you been sitting up all night?"

"Of course I have — do you think I could rest? Dr. Halifax, please, come with me at once."

"Where is he?" I asked.

She took my hand, and began to draw me, to my surprise, away from the house.

"*I* will take you to view the body, doctor," said Pennington —his eyes shone with sudden fury. "Go to bed, Alice; I insist," he cried.

"I won't obey you," she answered, flinging out her words with great excitement and defiance. "I know now that I have always hated you—I hate you at this moment beyond words to describe. Why did you dare to send that last telegram? Why did you dare to countermand Dr. Halifax's orders? But the coffin is *not* screwed down—I would not allow it. Come, doctor, come at once to the church—his body was laid in the church yesterday. Oh, no, it isn't only his body—not yet, not yet—it is he—himself—he only wants you to awaken him—he is only asleep—I know he is only asleep—come and wake him at once—come, come!"

She clasped my hand with passionate insistance.

Pennington stood back with a startled and stricken look on his face. Miss Lefroy hurried me down a side walk which led to a small turnstile. Passing through the stile we found ourselves in the churchyard. It was a little old Norman church, which, I understood afterwards, had belonged to the Penningtons for hundreds of years. The church was situated in the very centre of the estate. Lights shone through the painted glass windows; the porch was open. The excited girl led me right into the sacred building. The interior was well lighted; the brightest light centring round that part where the coffin on trestles stood. It was a massive coffin; the shell was inclosed in lead, covered with oak; the heavy lid lay on the ground beneath. The coffin was placed in the centre of the chancel. A middle-aged servant, who looked as if she had been crying bitterly, was standing by. When she saw Alice enter, and observed that I was with her, she uttered an exclamation of thankfulness,

"Is this the good doctor you have been expecting, Miss Lefroy?" she asked.

"Yes, Merriman," replied the young lady, "this is Dr. Halifax. He has come in time, after all—my efforts were not in vain—oh, how thankful I am! Now my darling will awaken from his sleep."

"Poor young lady," said the old servant—she gave me a meaning glance as she spoke. "Poor Miss Alice, she has got the notion that Mr. Fane is only asleep; she has got it on the brain, sir, she really has."

"Please stand aside," I answered.

I went close to the coffin and looked earnestly down at the dead man's face.

"He is asleep—is he not?" repeated Alice, coming up to my side, laying her hand on my arm, and glancing first at me, and then at the dead face of her lover. "See for yourself—he only sleeps. How lifelike he looks. There is even colour in his lips. You will awaken him, won't you, doctor?"

"Poor thing, she has got it on the brain," mumbled the servant.

"Move a little away, please," I said to Miss Lefroy.

When she did so, I bent more closely over the coffin— I took the hand of the dead man in mine—it was cold and stiff—the face looked rigid—my heart sank. I could not bear to meet the agonized look in Alice Lefroy's beautiful eyes.

"After all, I greatly fear the poor fellow is dead," I said to myself. "Were it not that he already had a cataleptic fit— were it not—but stay—the rigidity in that hand is, after all, not quite the rigidity of the dead."

My heart beat with renewed hope. I dropped the cold hand. Miss Lefroy was looking at me with a face of such anguish that I felt certain she would faint if I did not quickly ask her to leave the church.

"He is alive—do say he is alive?" she questioned, in an almost voiceless whisper.

"I cannot say at present," I answered, "but if you will leave me I will tell you in a moment or two. I am now going to make an experiment, but cannot do so until you go. Take Miss Lefroy into the vestry for a few moments," I said, turning to the maid.

"No, I will stay," answered Alice.

"But I would prefer that you left me.   Go now, like a good girl."

She went without another word, her head drooping, her hand clasped by the faithful servant.   The dead man and I were alone in the church.   Was the man in his coffin really dead?   I should soon know.   If he were alive, he was simulating death as few had done—nevertheless, he must have the chance I had promised him.   I would open one of the veins.   I took a case of instruments out of my pocket.   As I did so, I heard the creaking noise of a door being softly shut. Pennington was coming up the aisle of the church on tip-toe. I waited for him to approach the coffin.   He did so, coming close to me and looking down with a smile on his face at the dead face below.

"You see now," he said, slowly, "how much of your valuable time you have wasted in coming all this way to look at a dead man—you see also how cruelly and wantonly you have awakened false hopes!"

"Not quite yet," I answered; "stand aside, will you?"

As I spoke I bared the arm of the dead, and taking out my lancet carefully opened a superficial vein in the forearm.   I heard Pennington laugh satirically—I had no time to notice his laughter then.   I waited with a beating heart for the result.   Would that imprisoned blood ever flow again?   Had the man been in full life and health it would have issued freely from the wound.   The first few seconds after the division of the vein were some of the longest I ever lived through; then my heart gave a leap of triumph—a drop of blood oozed through the opening, then another, then another. Slowly, sluggishly, faintly, the blood dropped and dropped on the white winding-sheet—after the first couple of minutes it began to flow in a languid stream.   I carefully raised the head.   The next moment, to Pennington's horror, the dead man sat up.

Three months afterwards I received a visit from Fane in Harley Street.   He was in perfect health, and his spirits were as high as I had ever seen them.

"You have not only saved my life," he said, after he had spoken to me for a few moments, "but you have done more —you have absolutely removed the awful horror under which I lived for the last ten years.   I do not expect that I shall be laid out for dead a third time before the event really takes place."

"With the passing of the horror, the tendency to catalepsy has doubtless vanished," I replied. "I am more glad than I can tell you. That was a lucky visit of mine to the north."

"Ah!" he replied, his bright face suddenly becoming grave; he came up to my side and spoke almost in a whisper. "Did you know that a hole, about the size of a pea, was found evidently drilled in the bottom of the boat?" he said.

I started, but did not reply.

"It is true," he continued. "I dare not ask myself what it means."

"Be satisfied to leave that mystery alone," I said, after a brief pause. "You are a happy man—you are going to have a happy future. God Himself took the matter into His hands when He rescued you as He did from the very jaws of death."